THE GLITCH FORCE BOOK #1

ATTACK OF THE KILLER BUNNIES

AN UNOFFICIAL GRAPHIC NOVEL FOR MINECRAFTERS

MEGAN MILLER

SKY PONY PRESS
New York

This book is not authorized or sponsored by Microsoft Corp., Mojang AB, Notch Development AB or Scholastic Inc., or any other person or entity owning or controlling rights in the Minecraft name, trademark, or copyrights.

Sky Pony Press books may be purchased in bulk at special discounts for sales promotion, corporate gifts, fund-raising, or educational purposes. Special editions can also be created to specifications. For details, contact the Special Sales Department, Sky Pony Press, 307 West 36th Street, 11th Floor, New York, NY 10018 or info@skyhorsepublishing.com.

Minecraft® is a registered trademark of Notch Development AB.

The Minecraft game is copyright © Mojang AB.

Visit our website at www.skyponypress.com.

10 9 8 7 6 5 4 3 2 1

Library of Congress Cataloging-in-Publication Data is available on file.

Cover design by Kai Texel

Cover and interior art by Megan Miller

Print ISBN: 978-1-5107-7249-6
Ebook ISBN: 978-1-5107-7356-1

Printed in China

INTRODUCTION

Imagine that your mother is a quantum electronics researcher with an experimental lab in your basement, and she leaves the key to the lab in a really obvious spot. You might want to sneak down to the lab at night and start playing around with the equipment. You might learn a massive amount about experimental electronics. You might even make a radical discovery while you are messing around with the programming code of your favorite game, VR technology, and some nifty quantum electro-tube gizmos. A radical discovery that lets you and your two best friends enter right into your favorite game. I don't have to imagine, because I'm Duncan and this is exactly what happened to me.

MEET THE GLITCH FORCE

DUNCAN

A genius redstoner who can't resist testing out the quantum electronic gizmos in his mother's research lab.

MIRANDA

A sharpshooter with encyclopedic knowledge of Minecraft.

ZED

An expert builder with a prankster heart.

Chapter 1: Anomaly

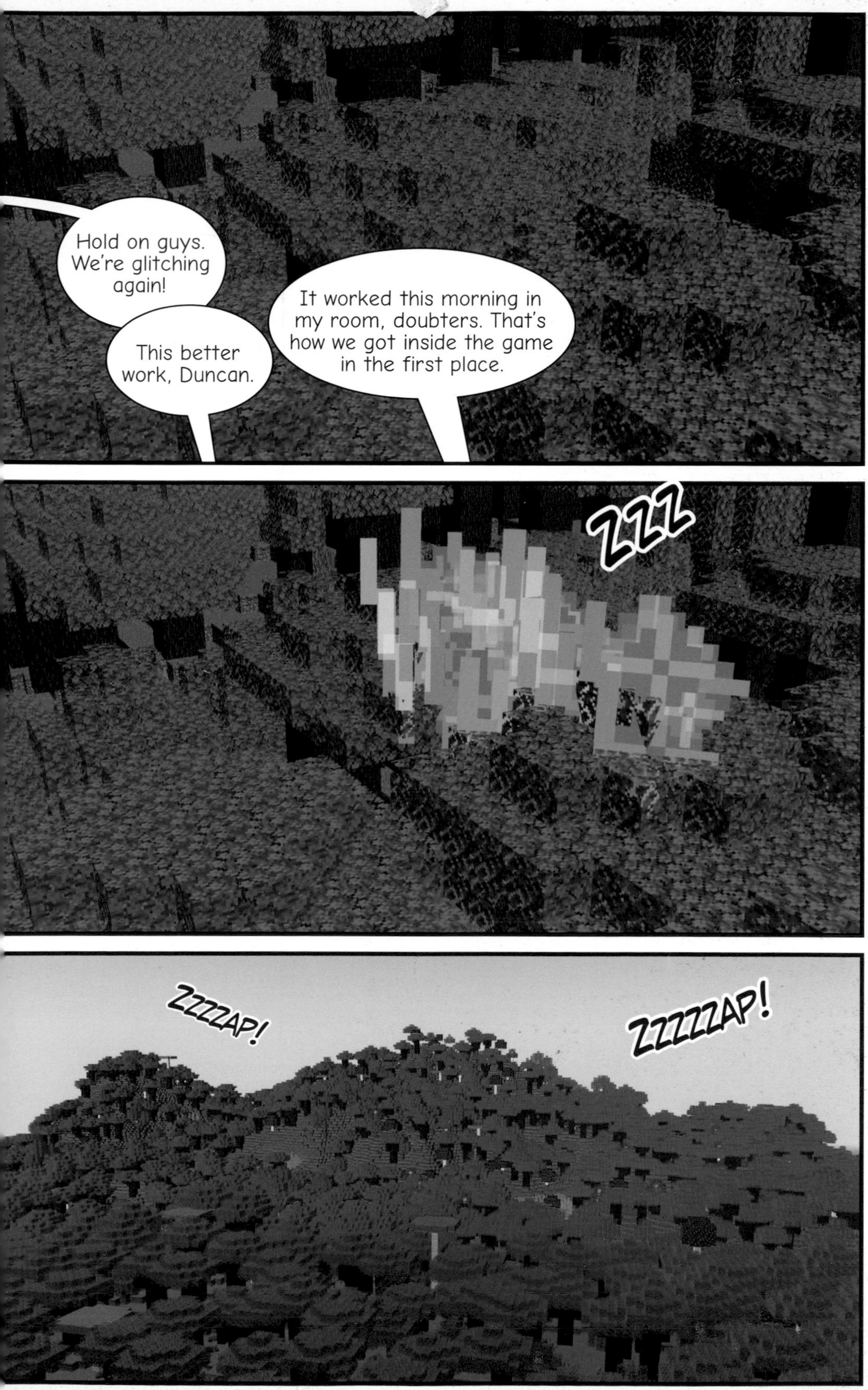
Hold on guys. We're glitching again!
This better work, Duncan.
It worked this morning in my room, doubters. That's how we got inside the game in the first place.
ZZZ
ZZZZAP!
ZZZZZAP!

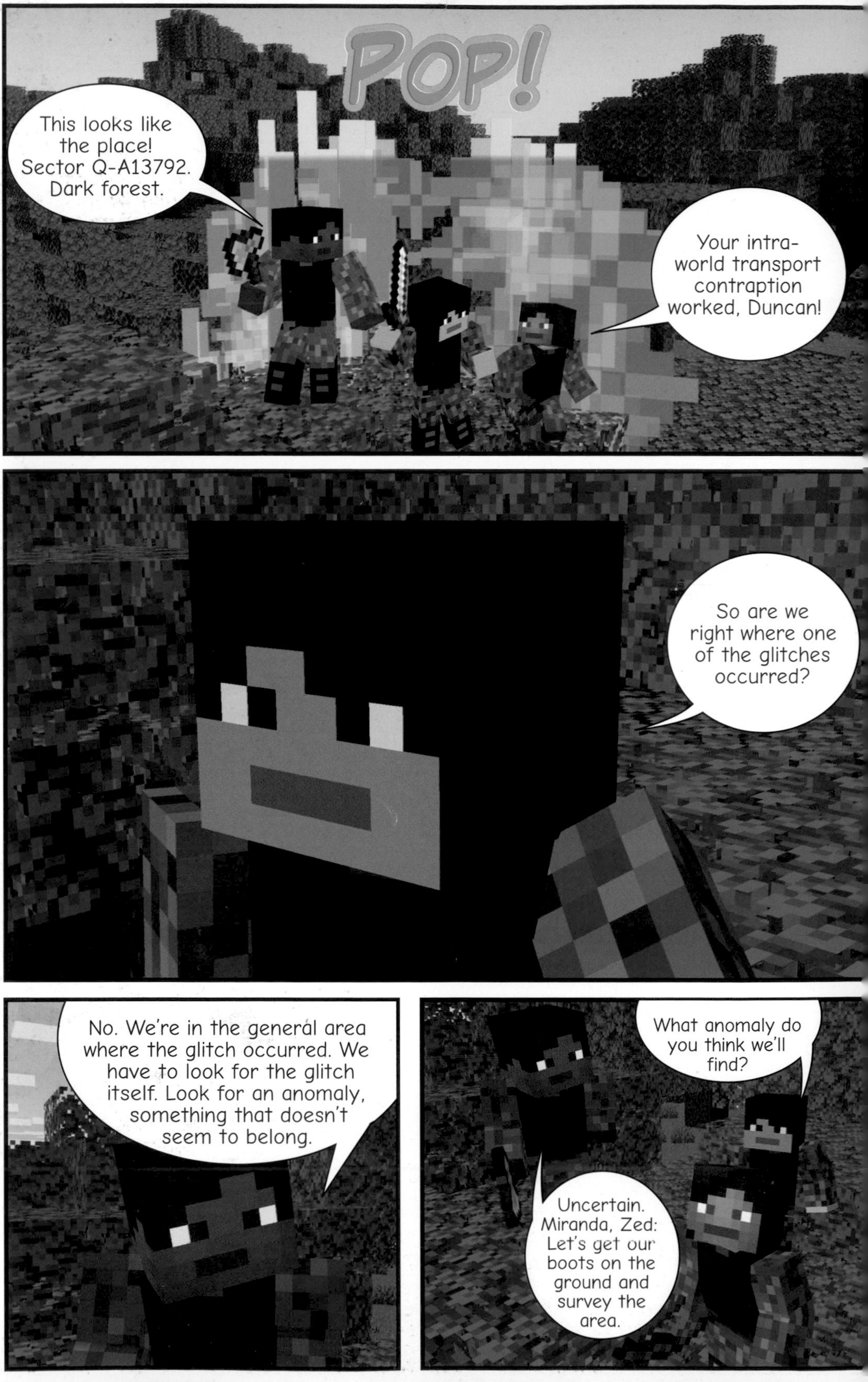
POP!
This looks like the place! Sector Q-A13792. Dark forest.
Your intra-world transport contraption worked, Duncan!
So are we right where one of the glitches occurred?
No. We're in the general area where the glitch occurred. We have to look for the glitch itself. Look for an anomaly, something that doesn't seem to belong.
What anomaly do you think we'll find?
Uncertain. Miranda, Zed: Let's get our boots on the ground and survey the area.

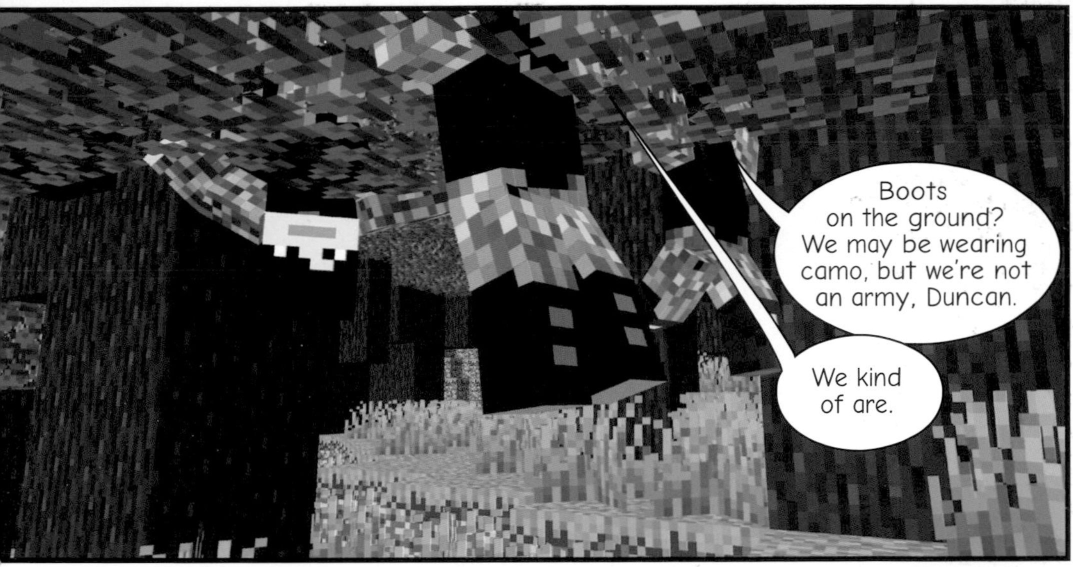
Boots on the ground? We may be wearing camo, but we're not an army, Duncan.
We kind of are.

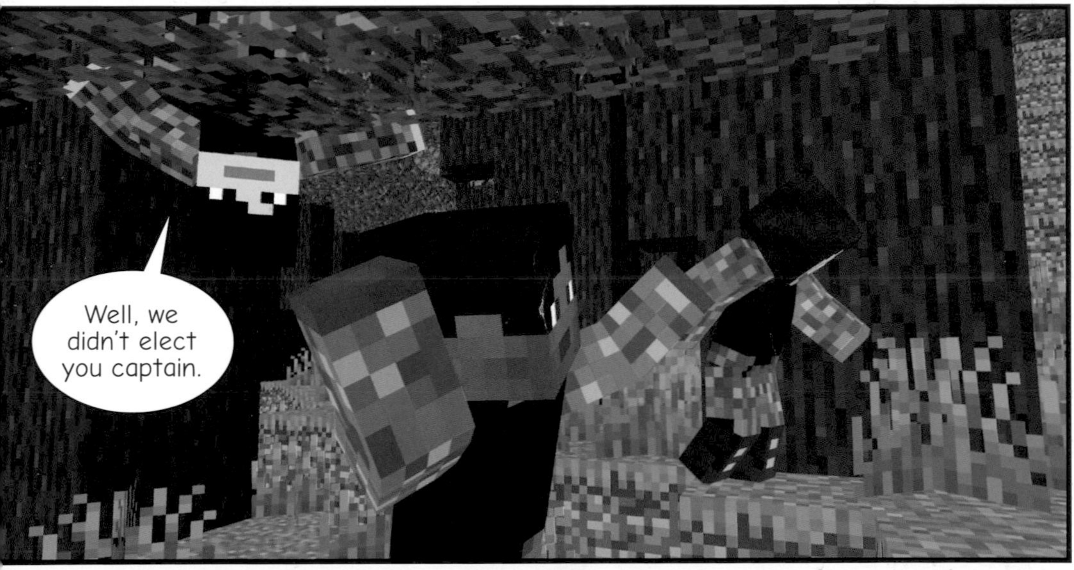
Well, we didn't elect you captain.

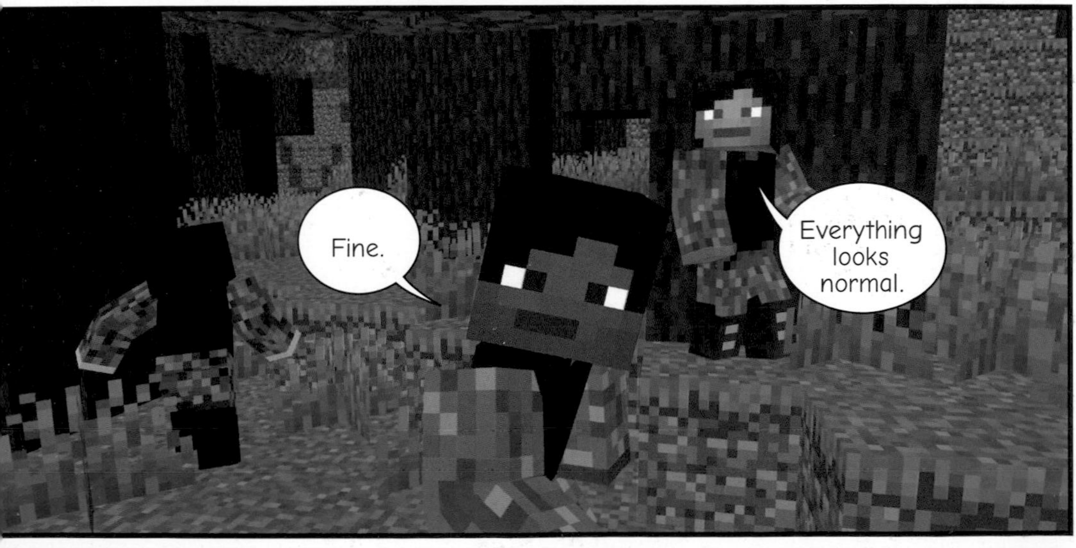
Fine.
Everything looks normal.

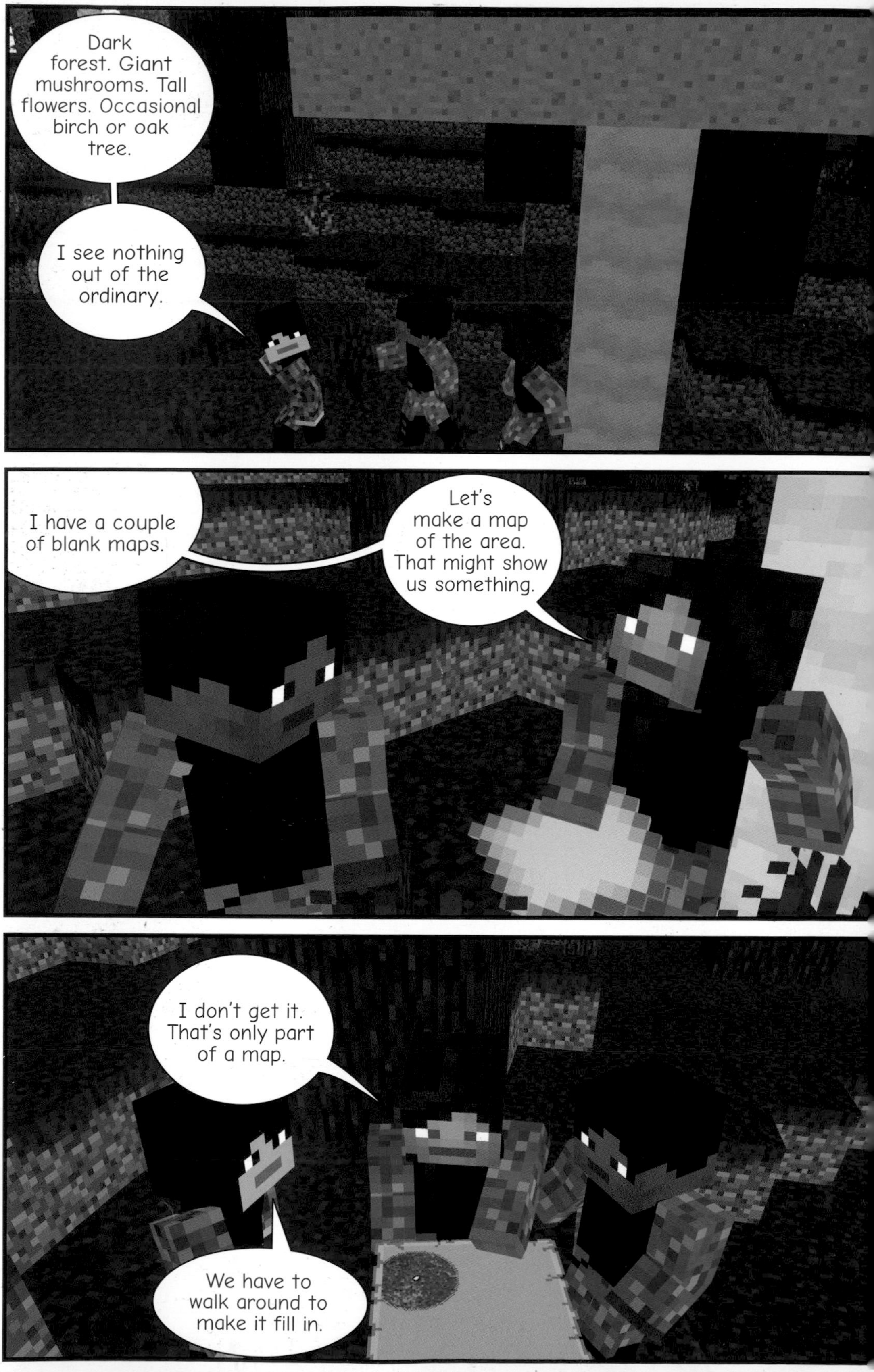
Dark forest. Giant mushrooms. Tall flowers. Occasional birch or oak tree.
I see nothing out of the ordinary.
I have a couple of blank maps.
Let's make a map of the area. That might show us something.
I don't get it. That's only part of a map.
We have to walk around to make it fill in.

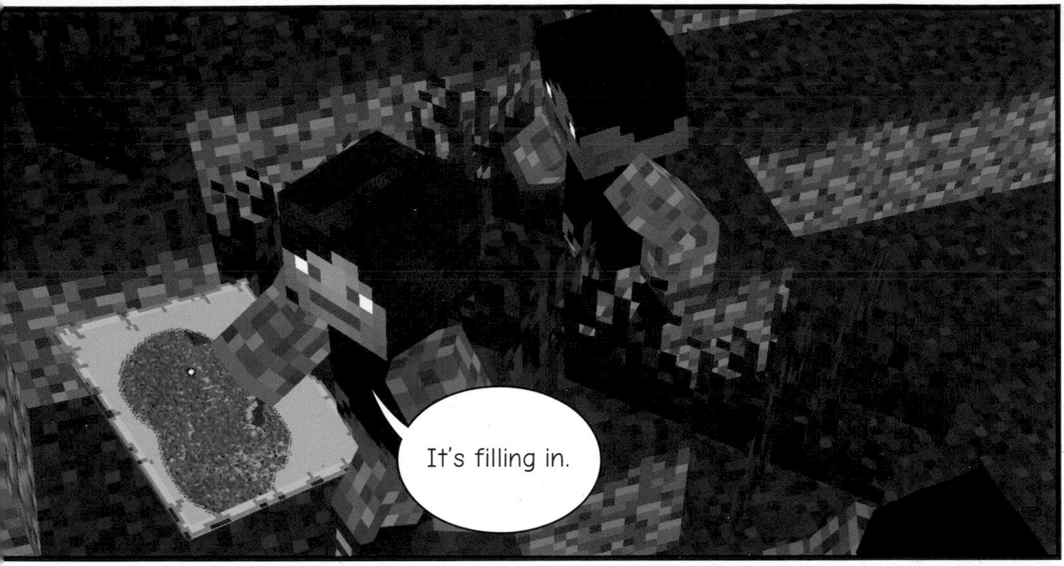
It's filling in.

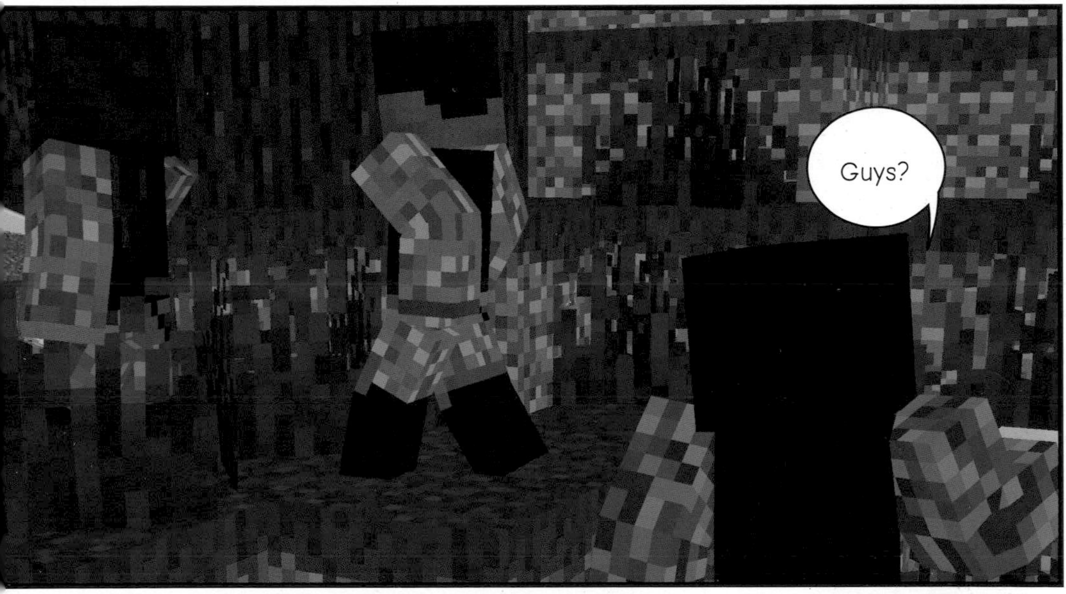
Guys?

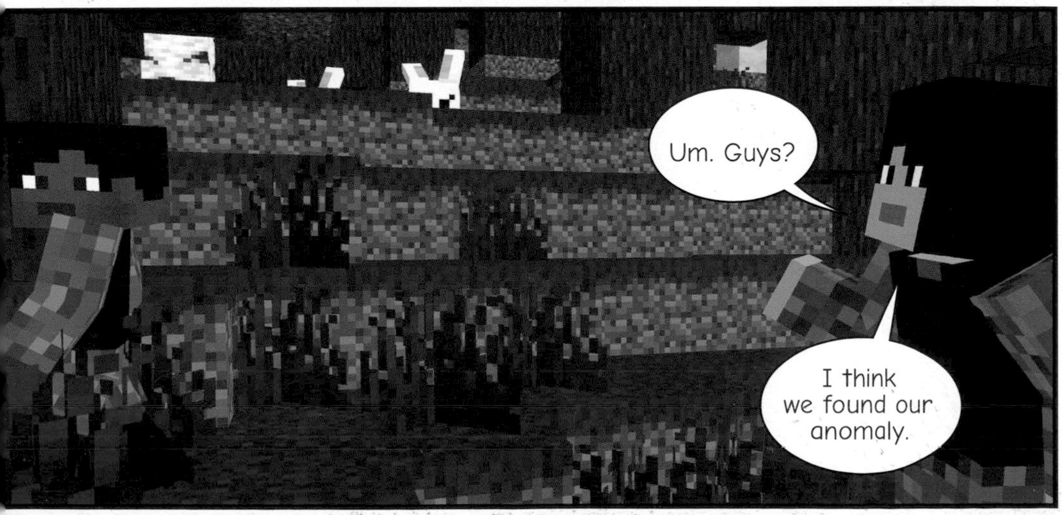
Um. Guys?
I think we found our anomaly.

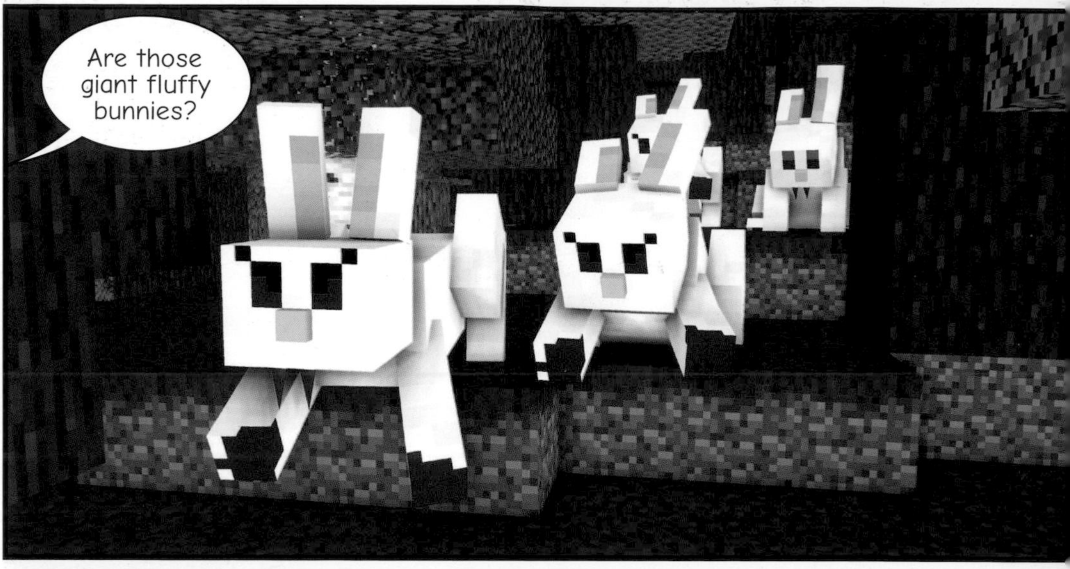
Are those giant fluffy bunnies?
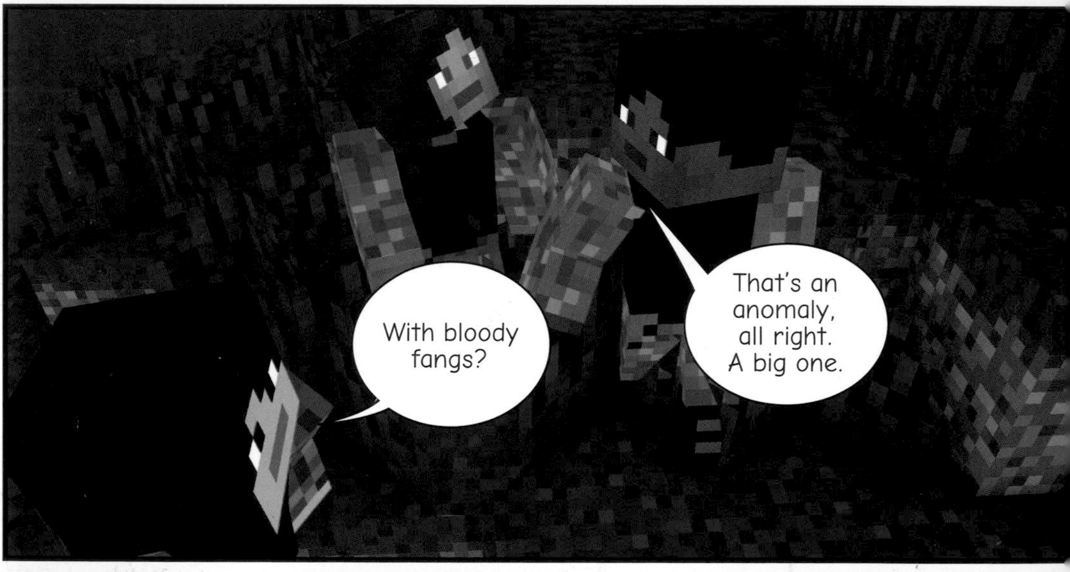
With bloody fangs?
That's an anomaly, all right. A big one.
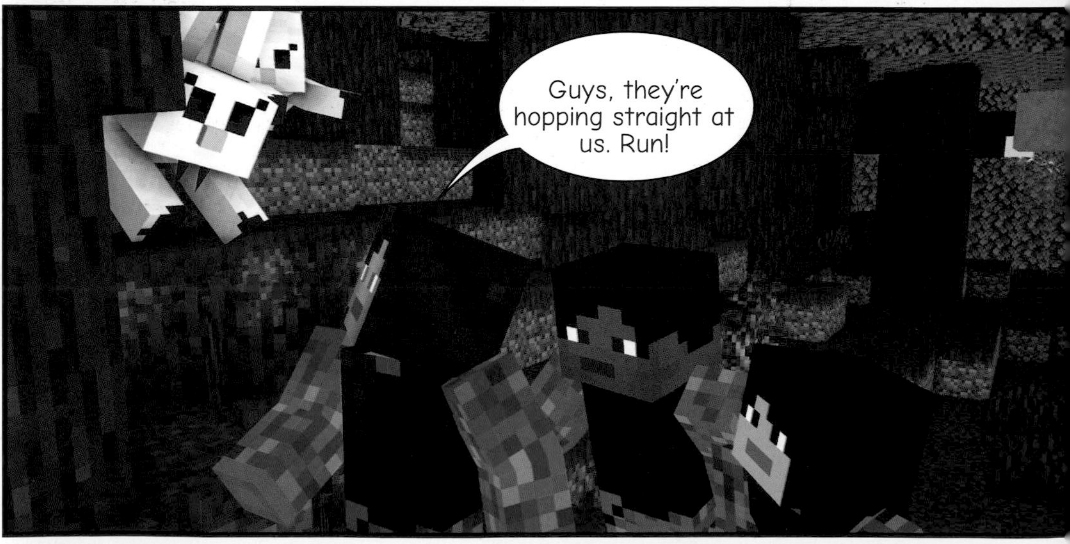
Guys, they're hopping straight at us. Run!

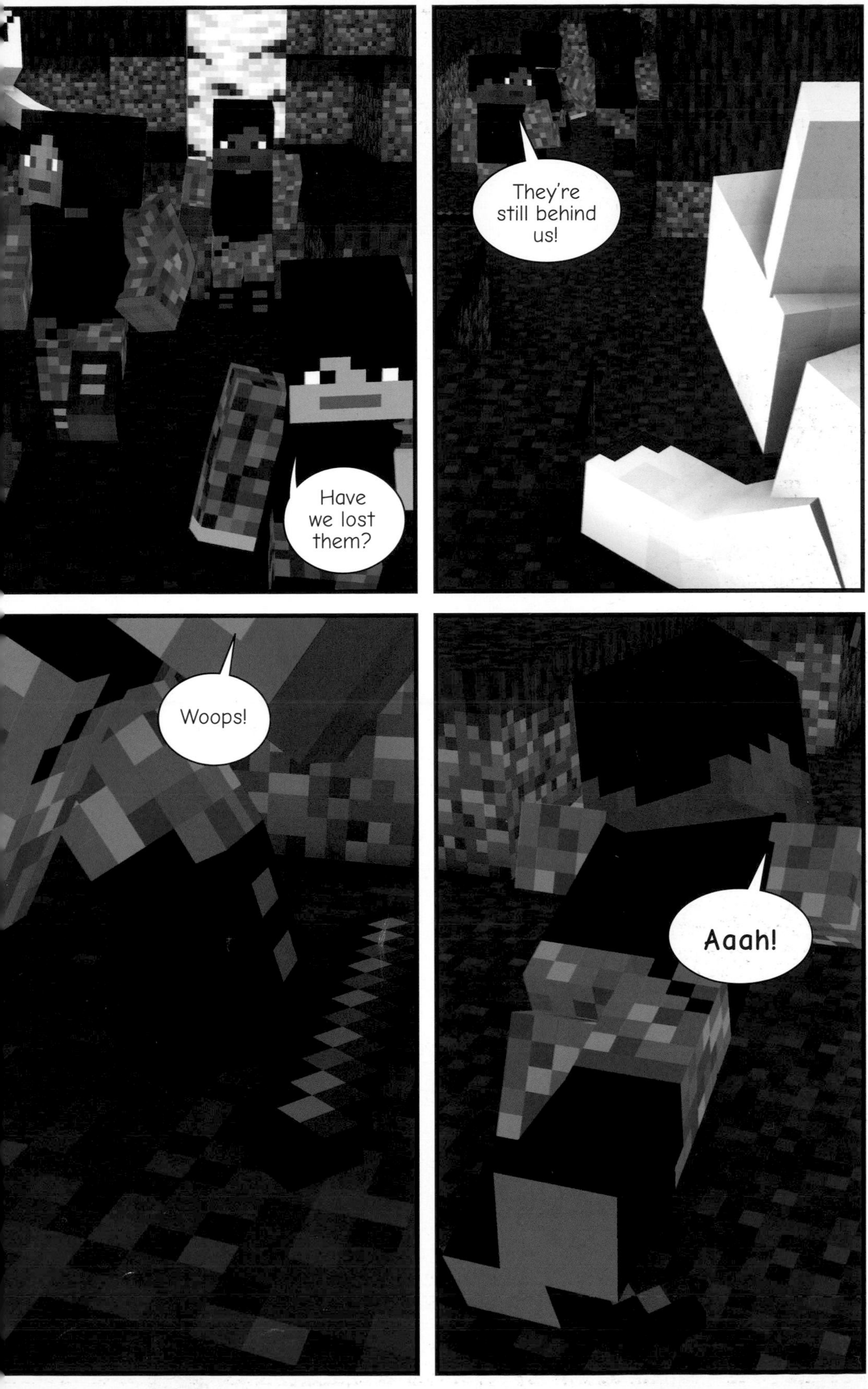
Have we lost them?
They're still behind us!
Woops!
Aaah!

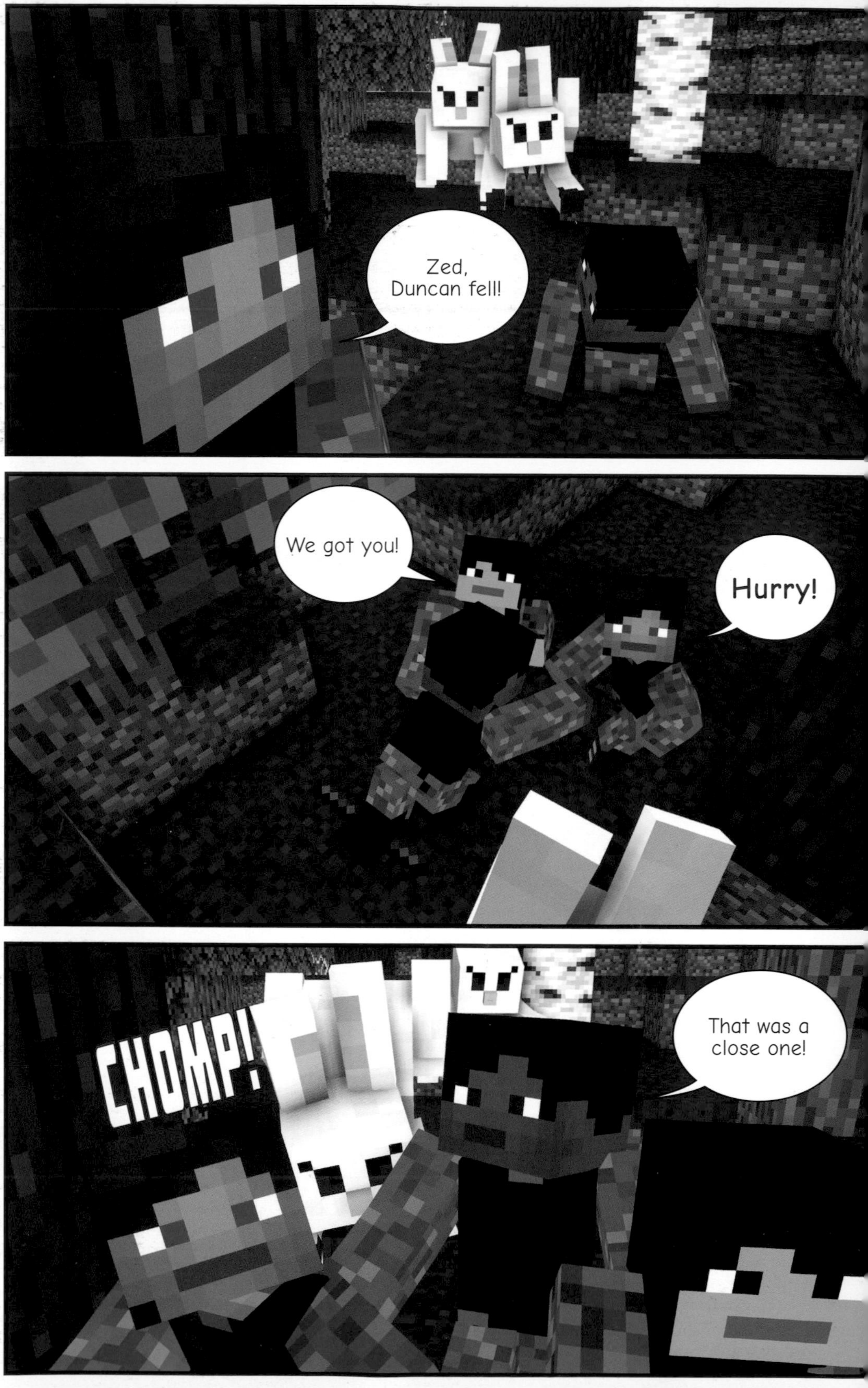
Zed,
Duncan fell!
We got you!
Hurry!
CHOMP!
That was a
close one!

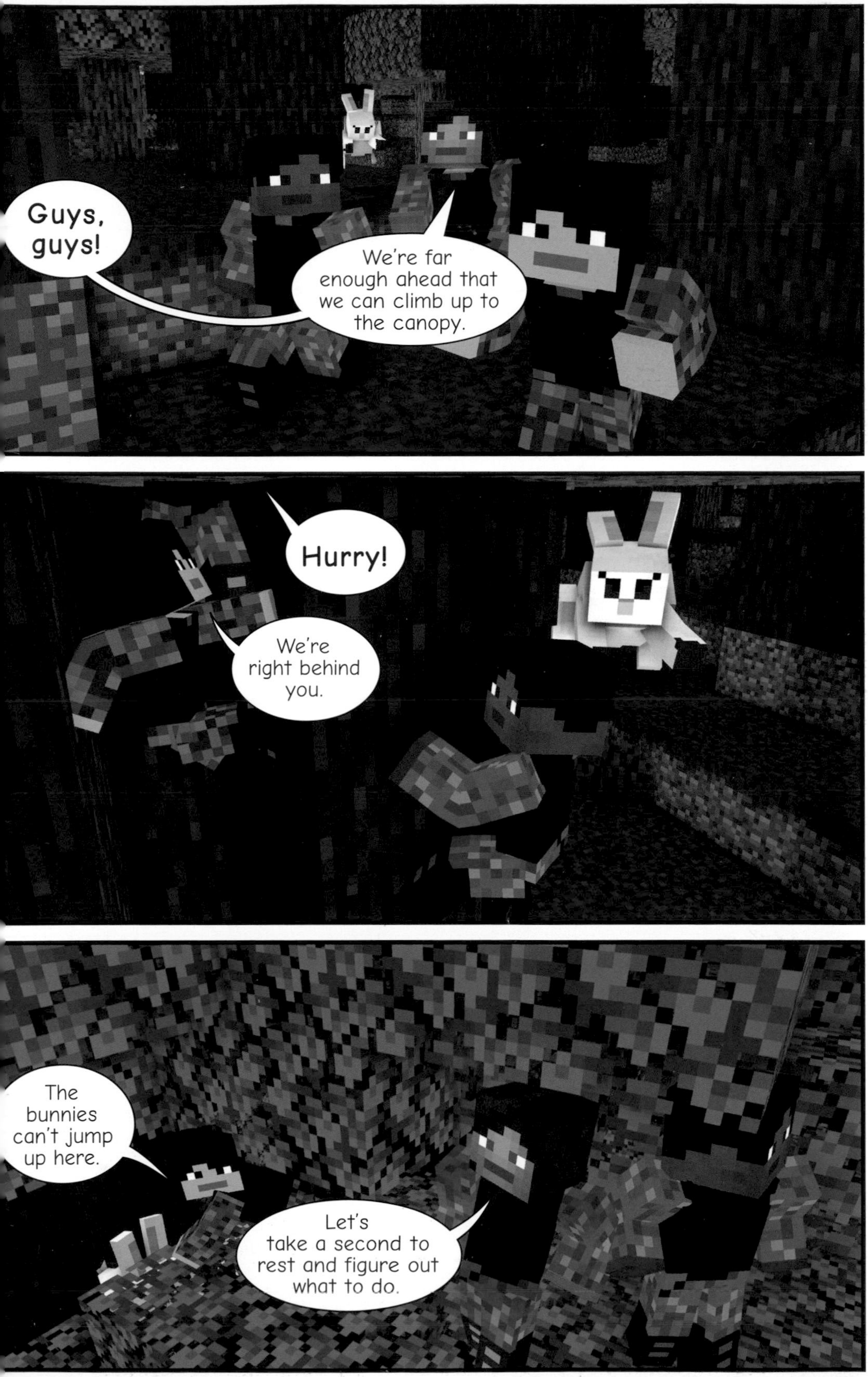
Guys, guys!
We're far enough ahead that we can climb up to the canopy.
Hurry!
We're right behind you.
The bunnies can't jump up here.
Let's take a second to rest and figure out what to do.

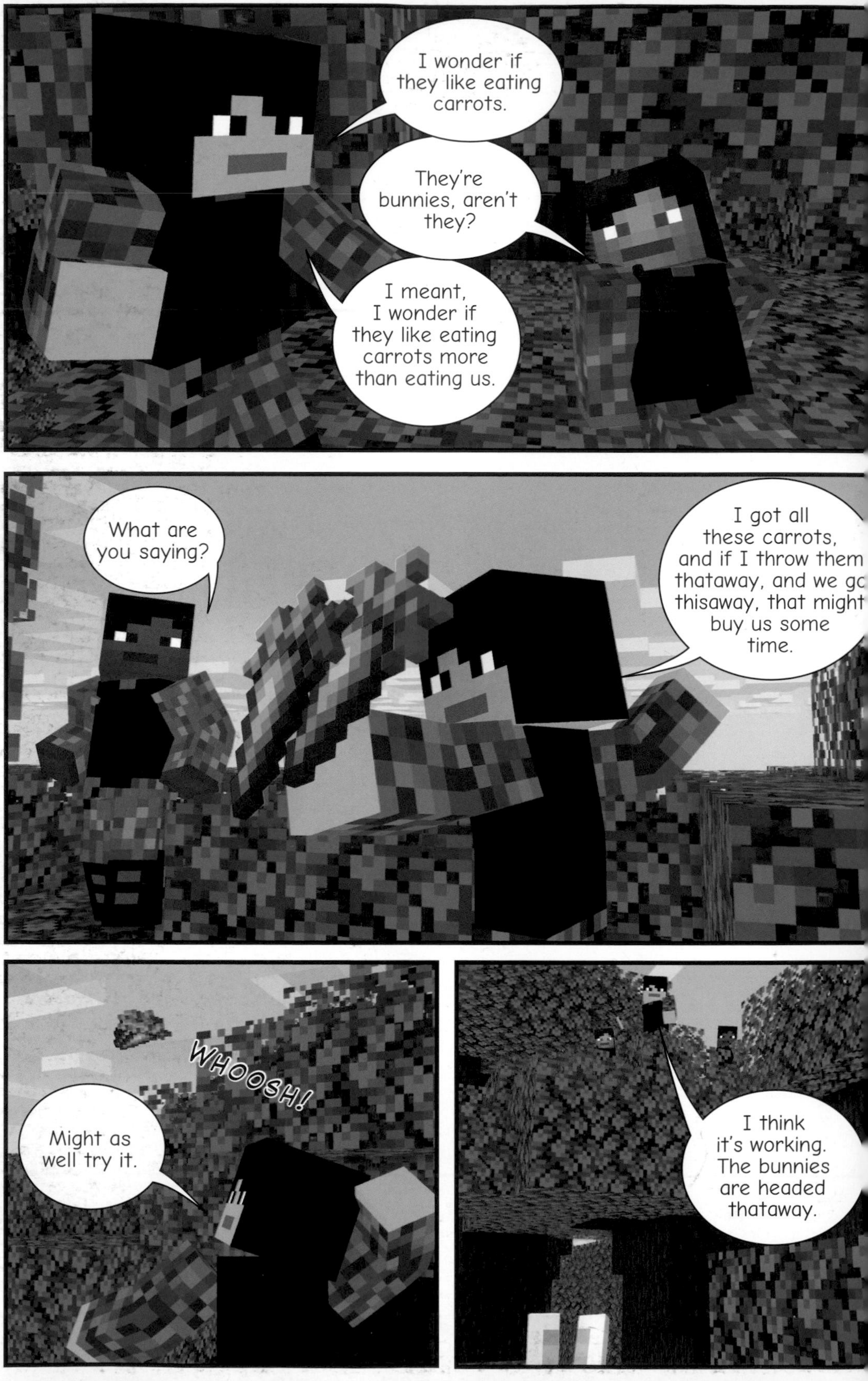
I wonder if they like eating carrots.
They're bunnies, aren't they?
I meant, I wonder if they like eating carrots more than eating us.
What are you saying?
I got all these carrots, and if I throw them thataway, and we go thisaway, that might buy us some time.
WHOOSH!
Might as well try it.
I think it's working. The bunnies are headed thataway.

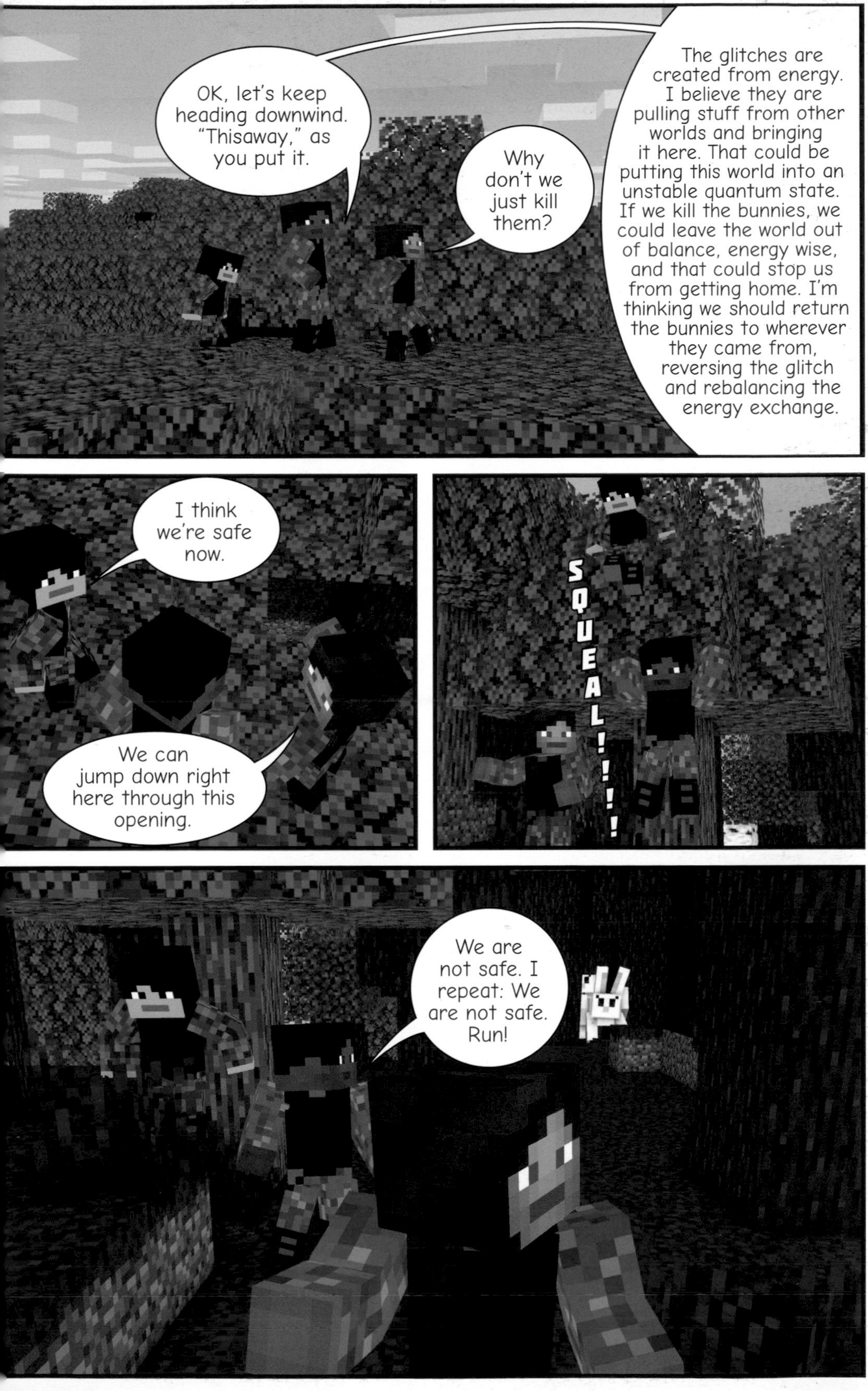
OK, let's keep heading downwind. "Thisaway," as you put it.
The glitches are created from energy. I believe they are pulling stuff from other worlds and bringing it here. That could be putting this world into an unstable quantum state. If we kill the bunnies, we could leave the world out of balance, energy wise, and that could stop us from getting home. I'm thinking we should return the bunnies to wherever they came from, reversing the glitch and rebalancing the energy exchange.
Why don't we just kill them?
I think we're safe now.
We can jump down right here through this opening.
SQUEAL!!!!
We are not safe. I repeat: We are not safe. Run!

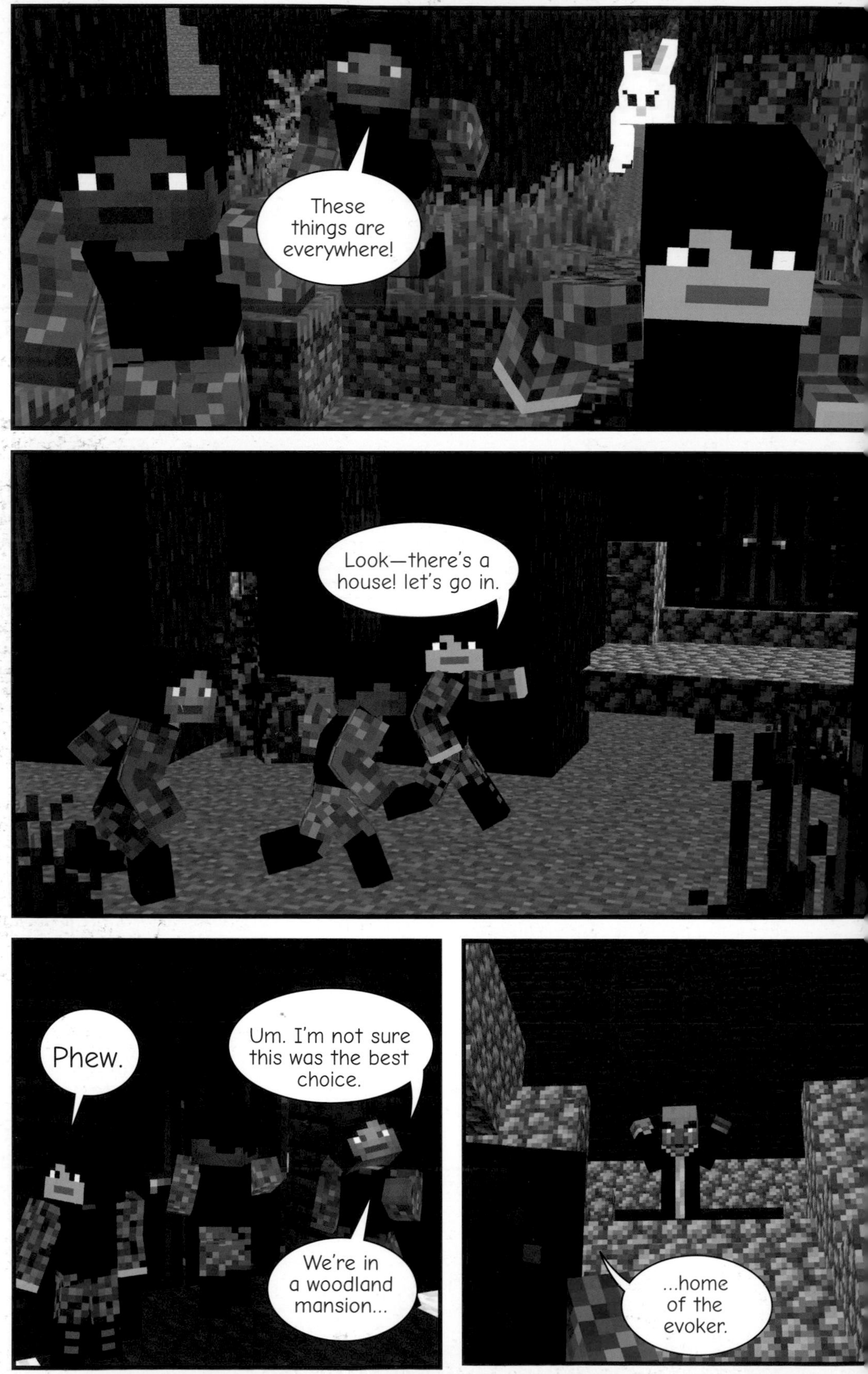
These things are everywhere!
Look—there's a house! let's go in.
Phew.
Um. I'm not sure this was the best choice.
We're in a woodland mansion...
...home of the evoker.

Chapter 2: Evoker

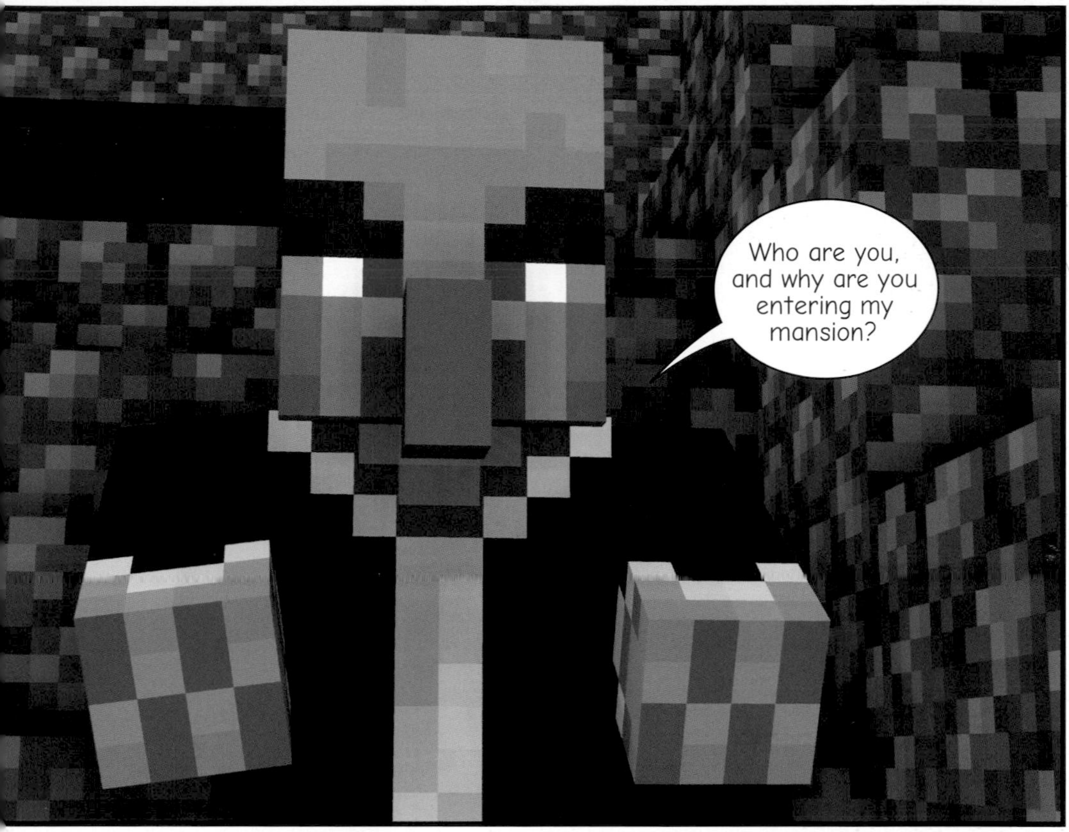
Who are you, and why are you entering my mansion?

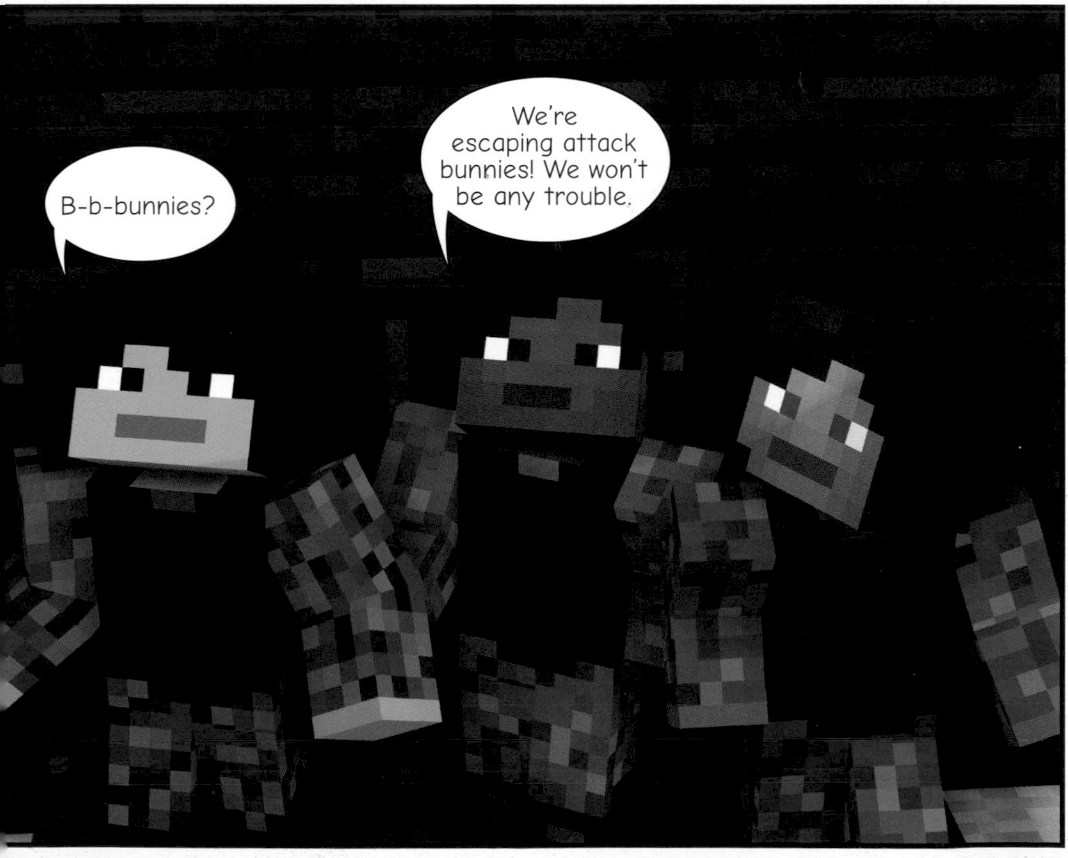
B-b-bunnies?
We're escaping attack bunnies! We won't be any trouble.

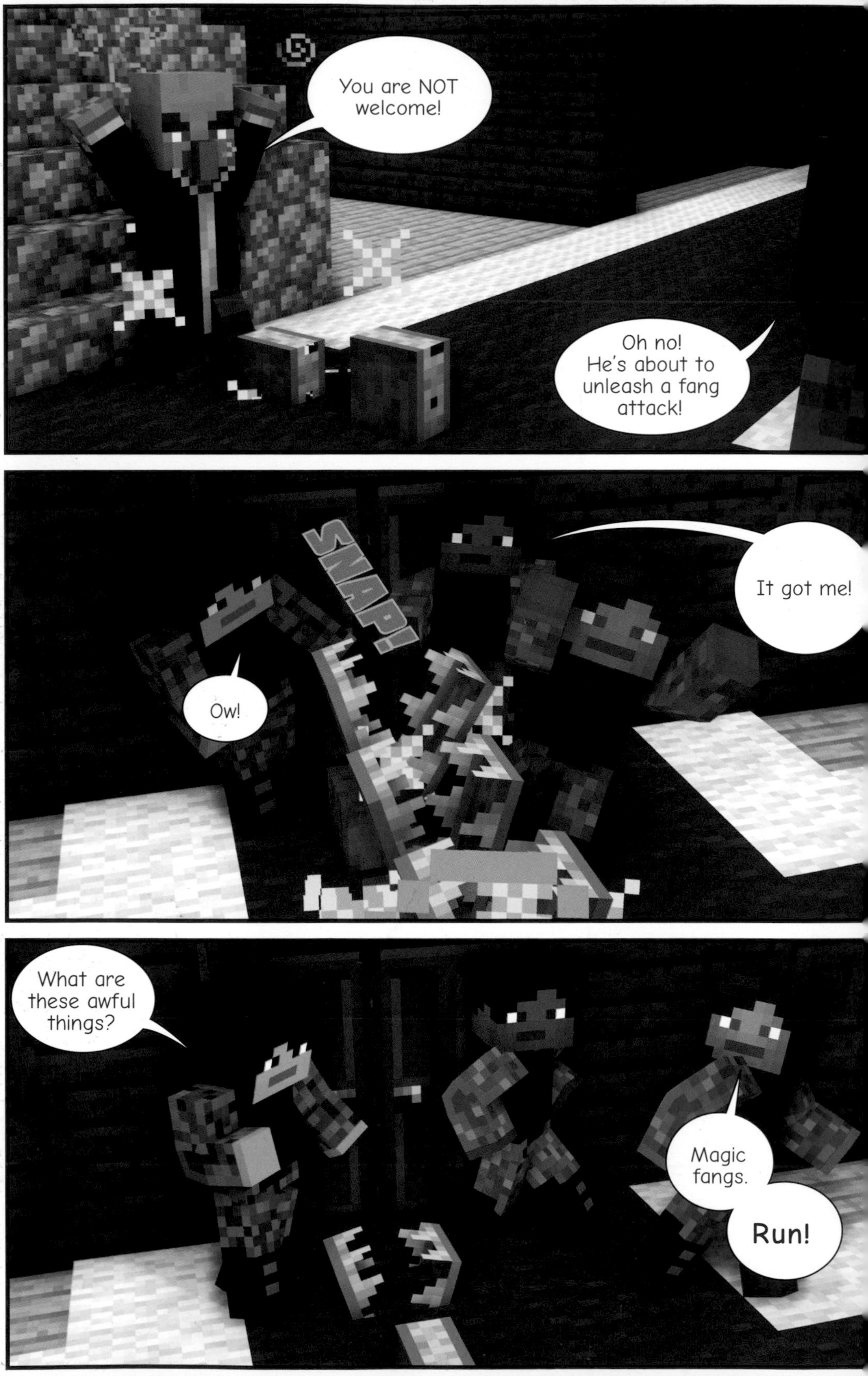
You are NOT welcome!
Oh no! He's about to unleash a fang attack!
SNAP!
It got me!
Ow!
What are these awful things?
Magic fangs.
Run!

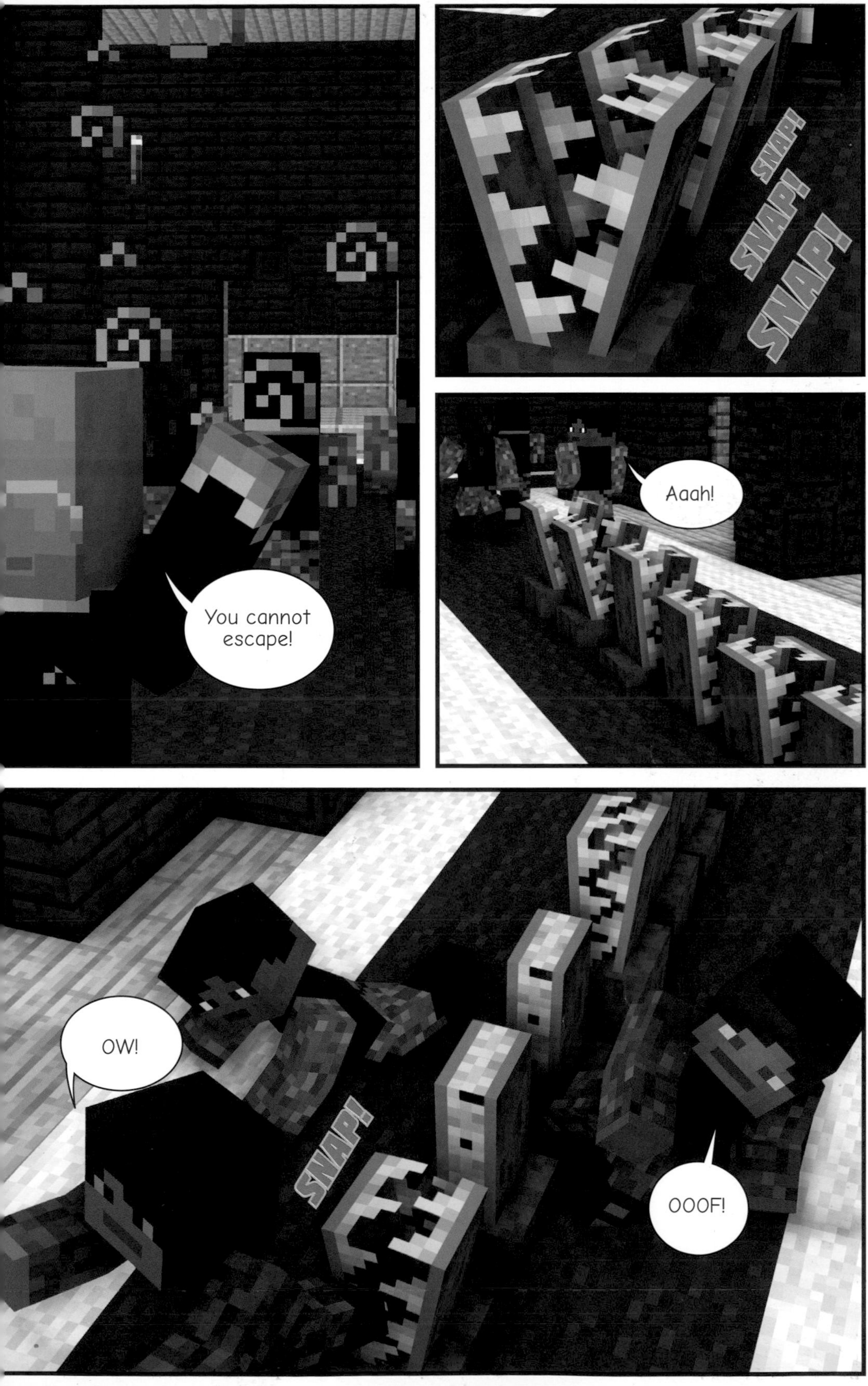
You cannot escape!
SNAP!
SNAP!
SNAP!
Aaah!
OW!
SNAP!
OOOF!

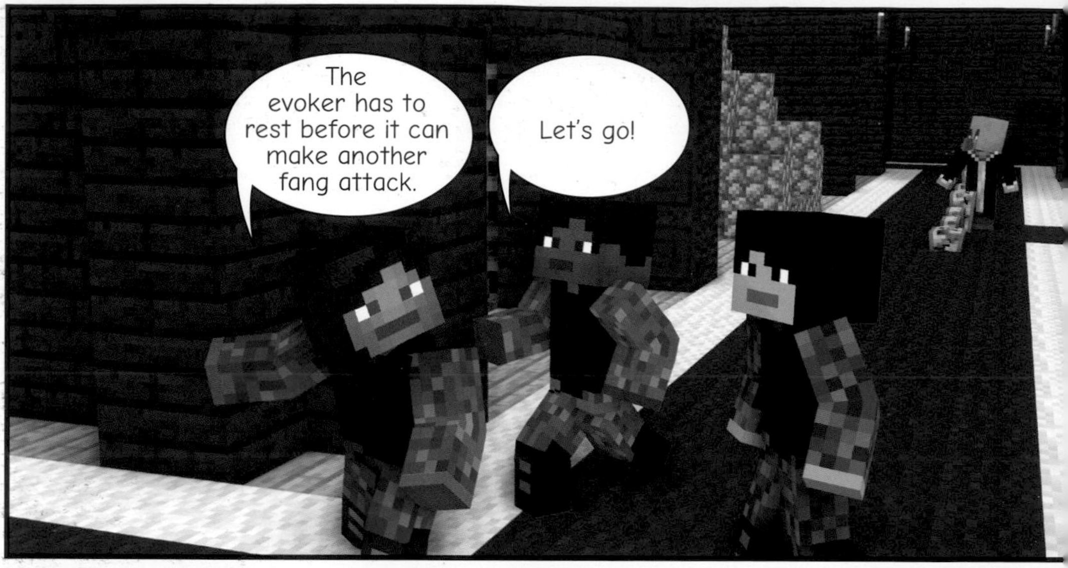
The evoker has to rest before it can make another fang attack.
Let's go!
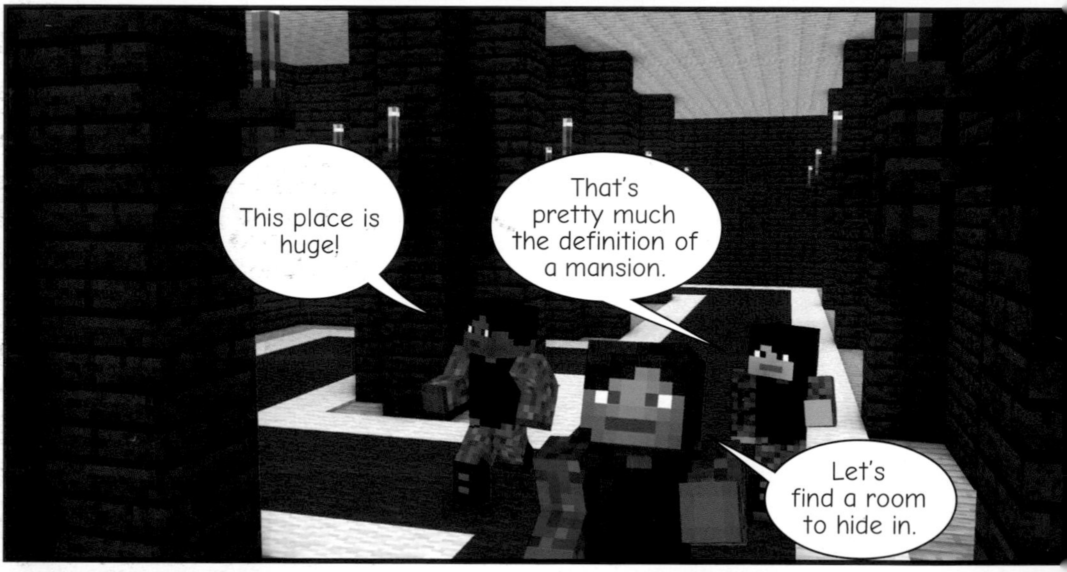
This place is huge!
That's pretty much the definition of a mansion.
Let's find a room to hide in.
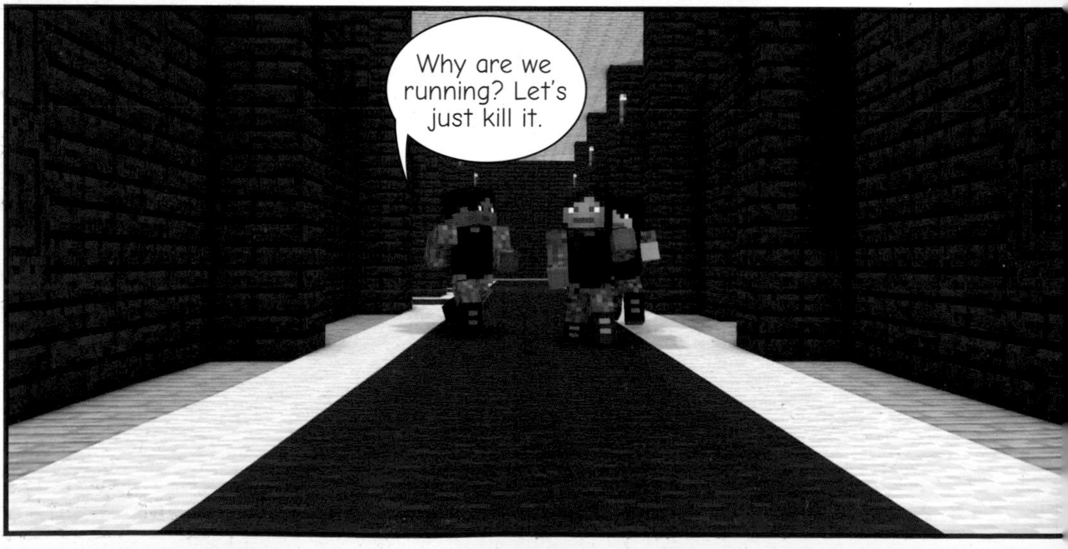
Why are we running? Let's just kill it.

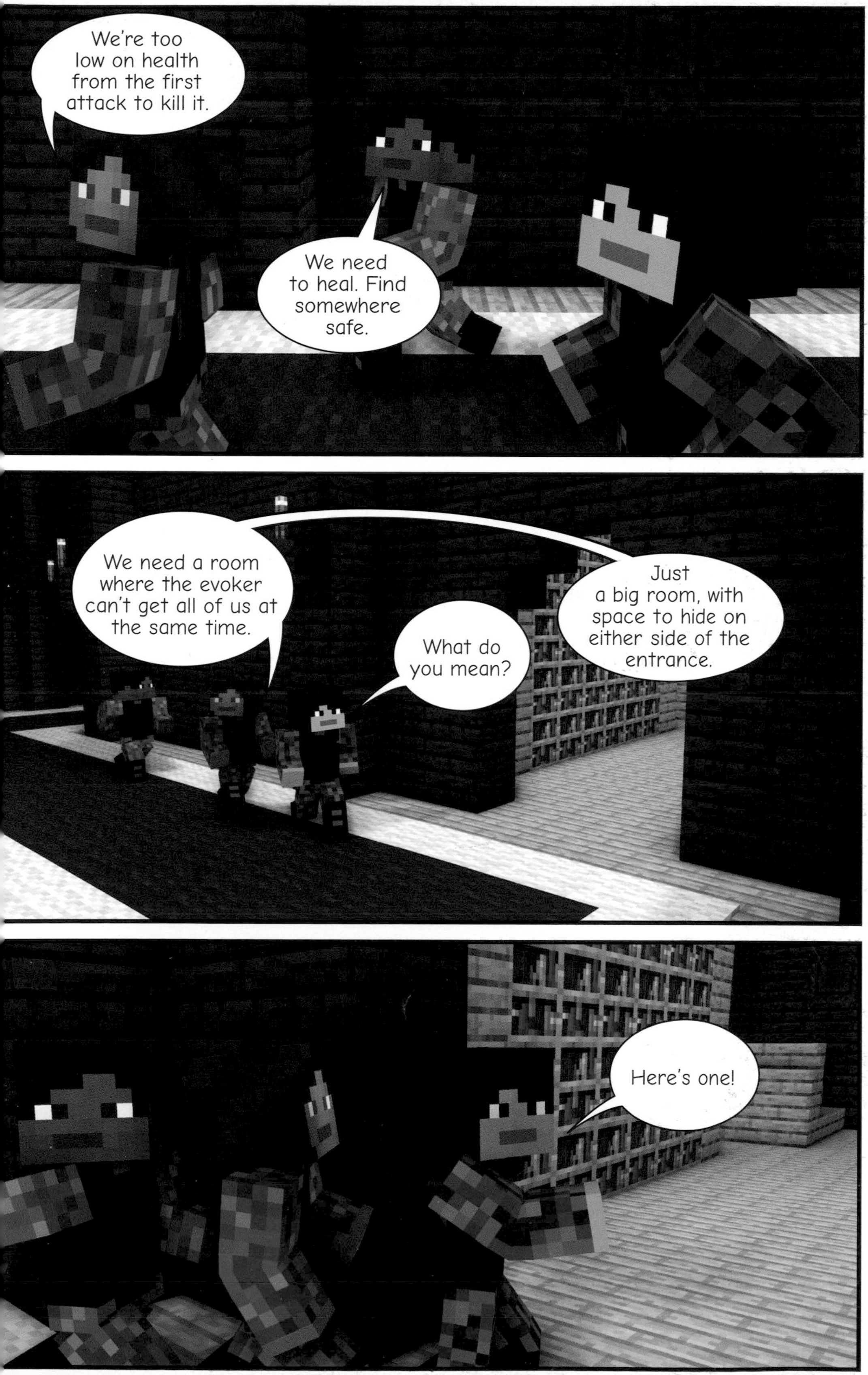
We're too low on health from the first attack to kill it.
We need to heal. Find somewhere safe.
We need a room where the evoker can't get all of us at the same time.
What do you mean?
Just a big room, with space to hide on either side of the entrance.
Here's one!

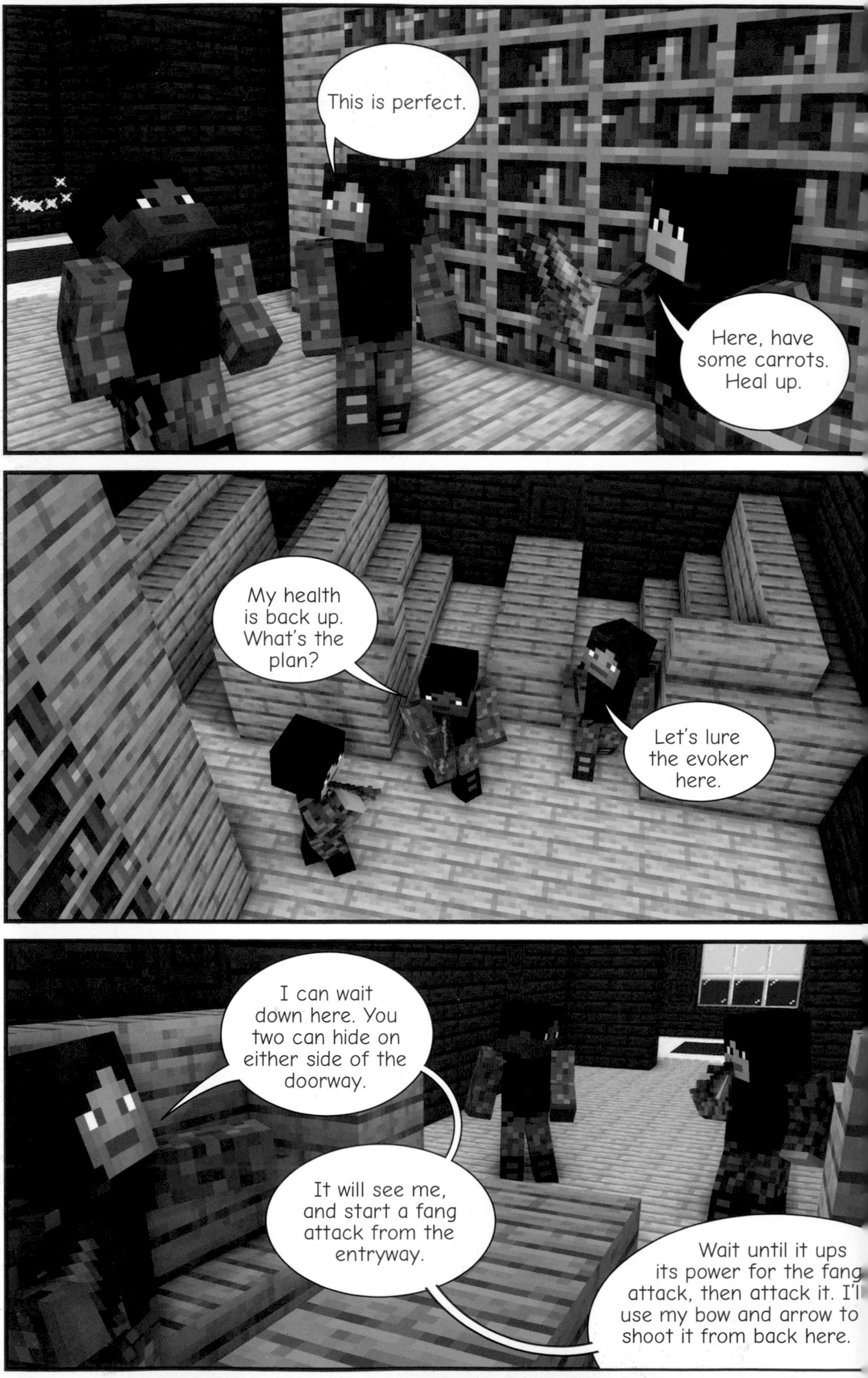
This is perfect.
Here, have some carrots. Heal up.
My health is back up. What's the plan?
Let's lure the evoker here.
I can wait down here. You two can hide on either side of the doorway.
It will see me, and start a fang attack from the entryway.
Wait until it ups its power for the fang attack, then attack it. I'll use my bow and arrow to shoot it from back here.

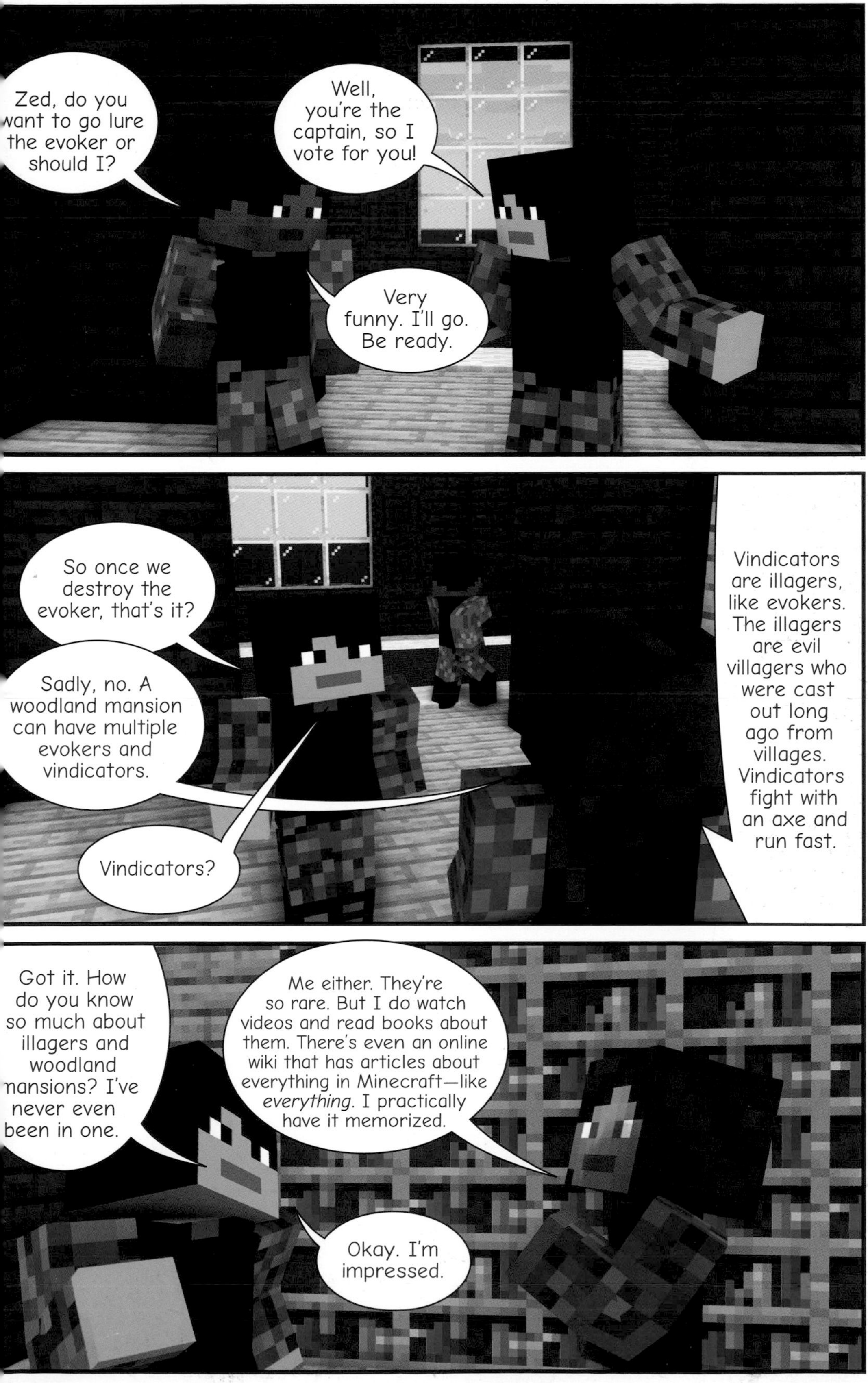
Zed, do you want to go lure the evoker or should I?
Well, you're the captain, so I vote for you!
Very funny. I'll go. Be ready.
So once we destroy the evoker, that's it?
Sadly, no. A woodland mansion can have multiple evokers and vindicators.
Vindicators?
Vindicators are illagers, like evokers. The illagers are evil villagers who were cast out long ago from villages. Vindicators fight with an axe and run fast.
Got it. How do you know so much about illagers and woodland mansions? I've never even been in one.
Me either. They're so rare. But I do watch videos and read books about them. There's even an online wiki that has articles about everything in Minecraft—like *everything*. I practically have it memorized.
Okay. I'm impressed.

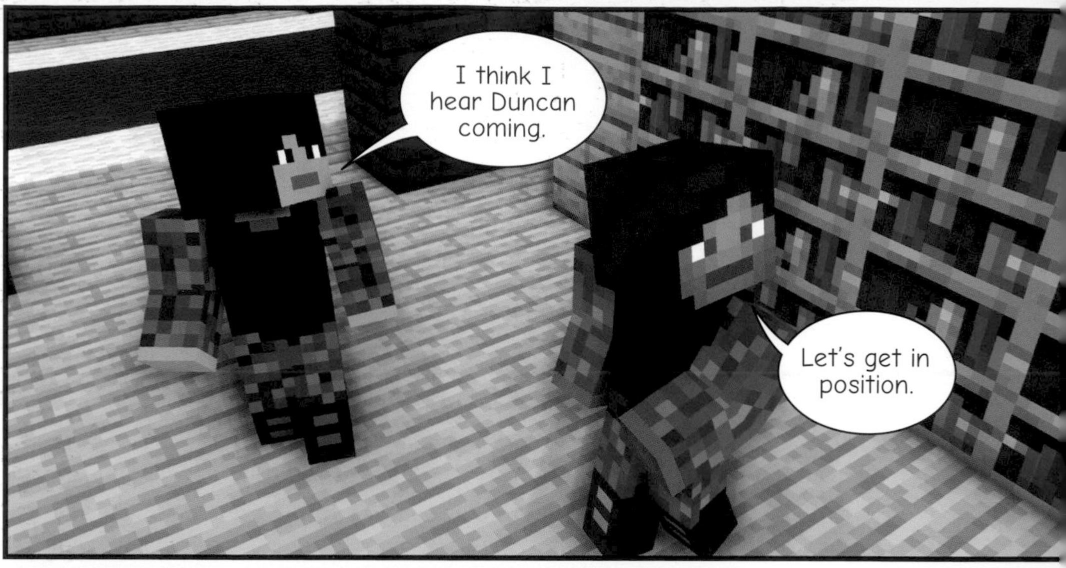
I think I hear Duncan coming.
Let's get in position.
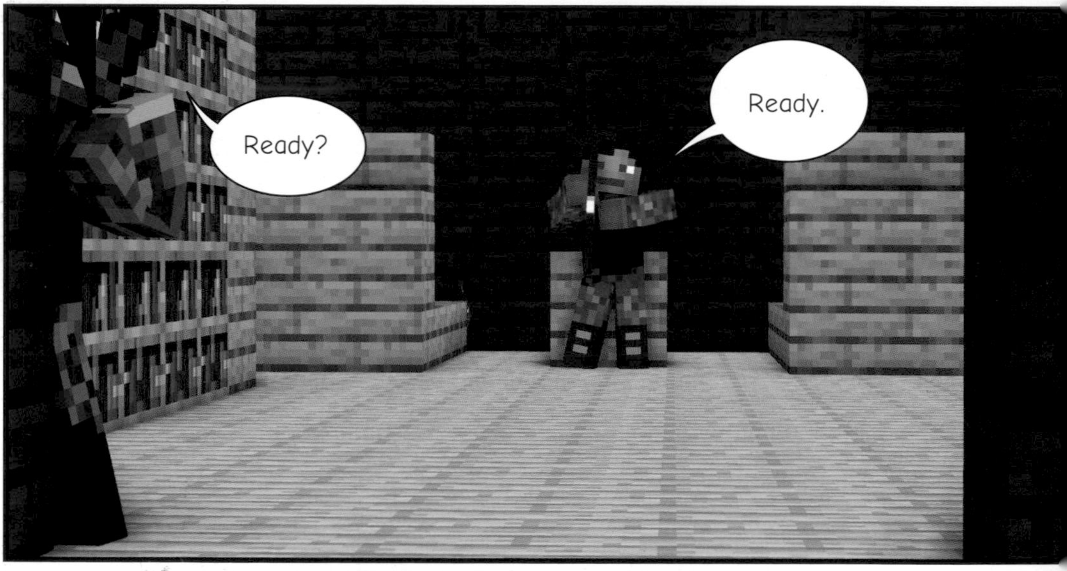
Ready?
Ready.
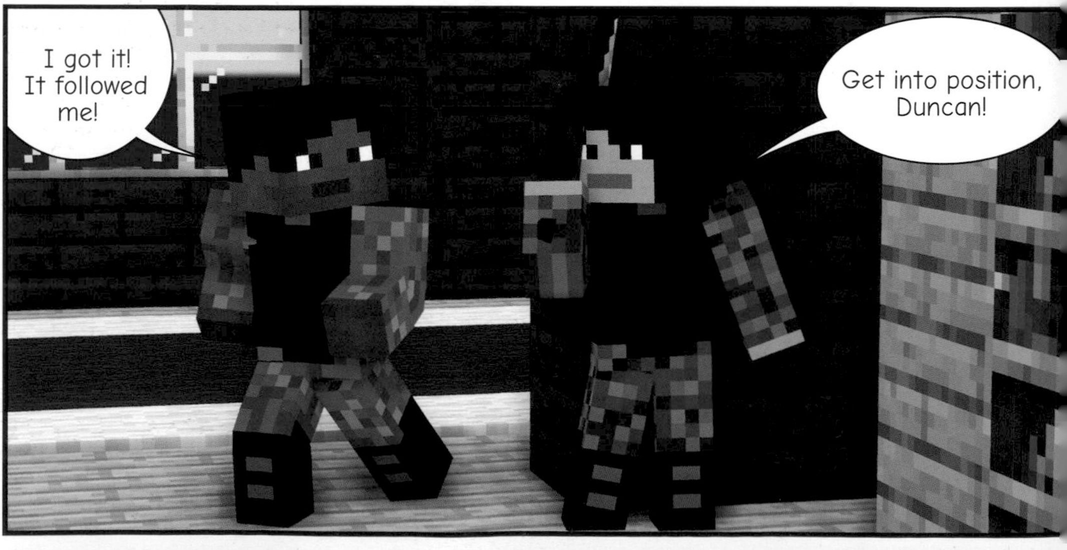
I got it! It followed me!
Get into position, Duncan!

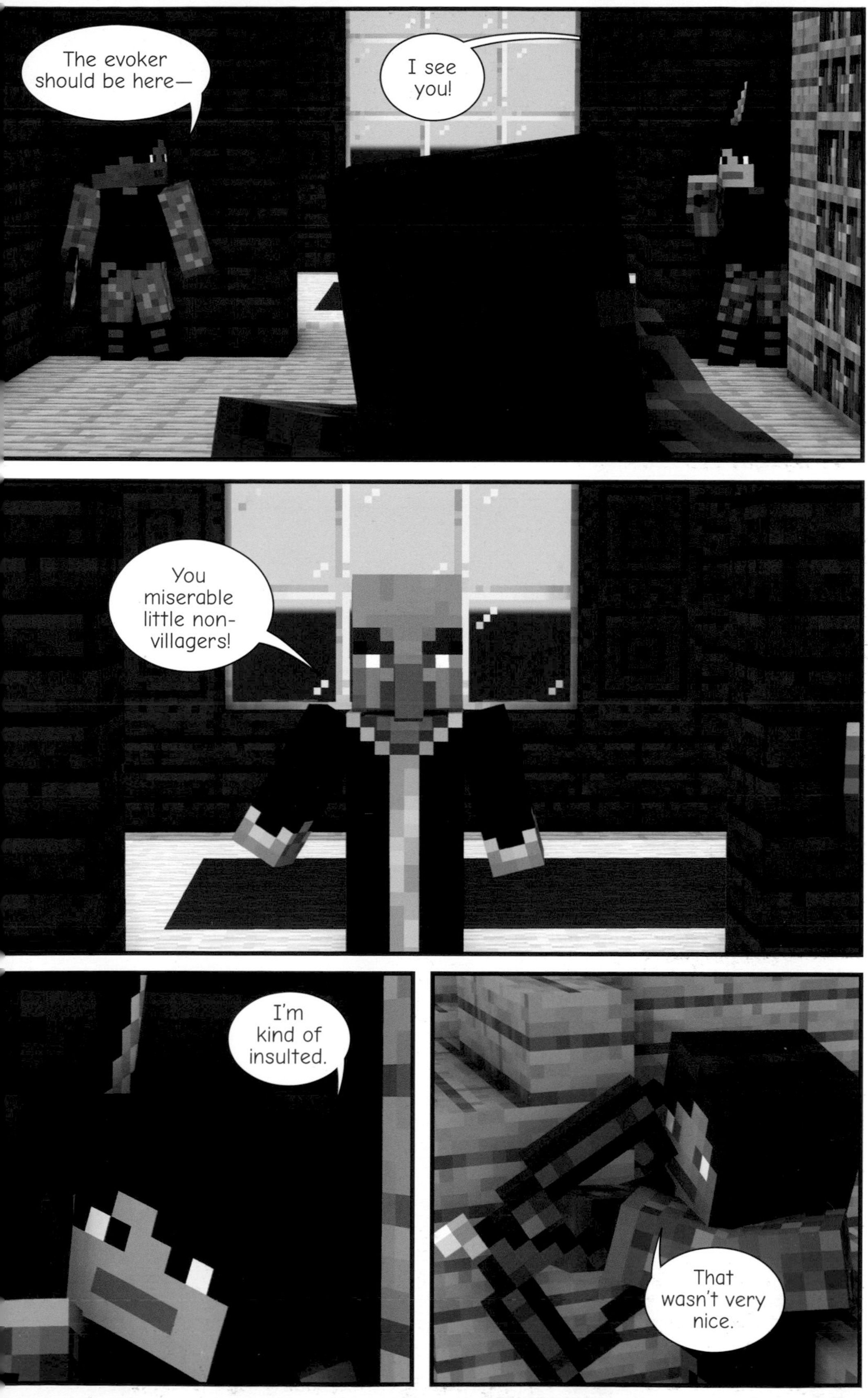
The evoker should be here—
I see you!
You miserable little non-villagers!
I'm kind of insulted.
That wasn't very nice.

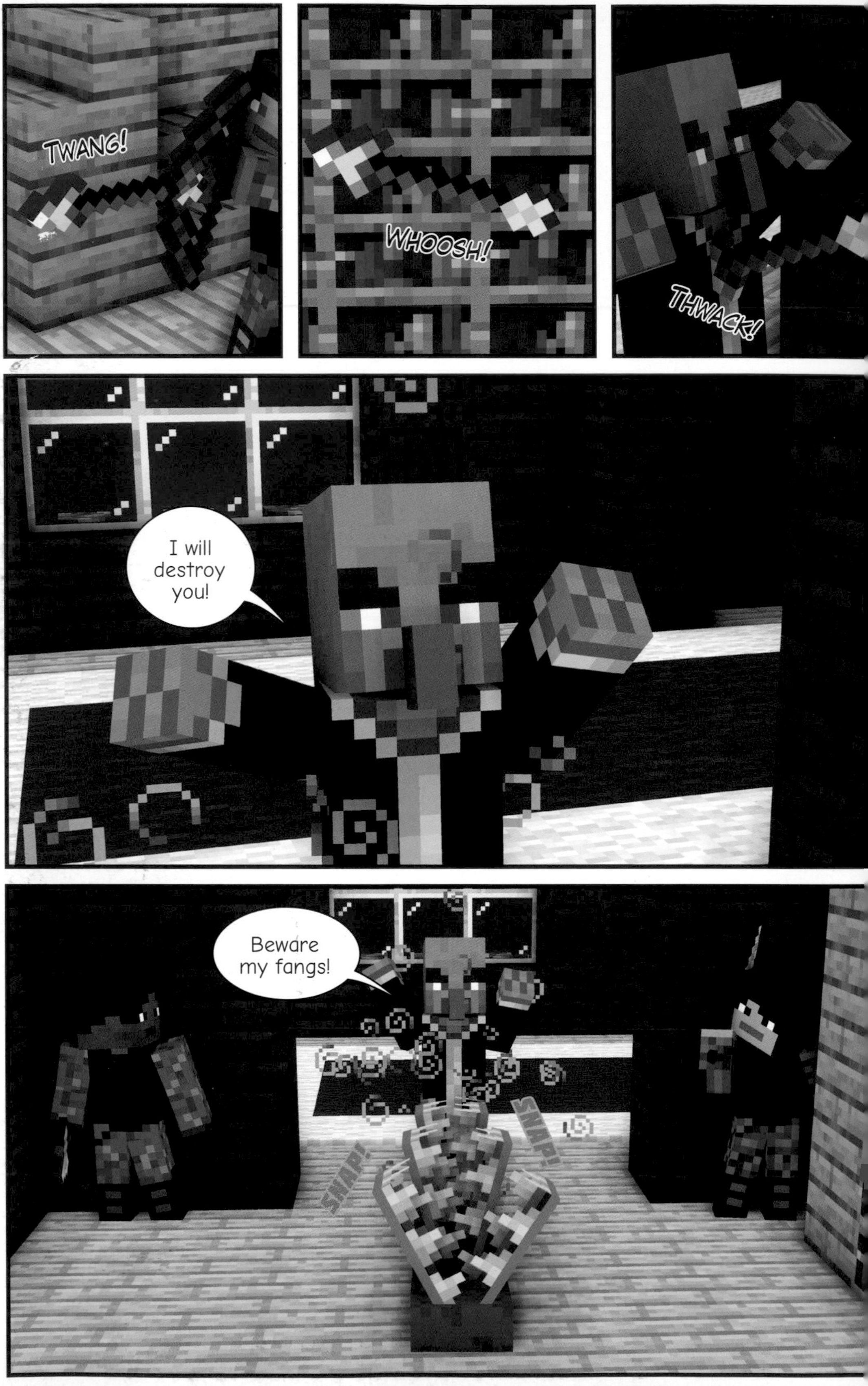
TWANG!
WHOOSH!
THWACK!
I will destroy you!
Beware my fangs!
SNAP!
SNAP!

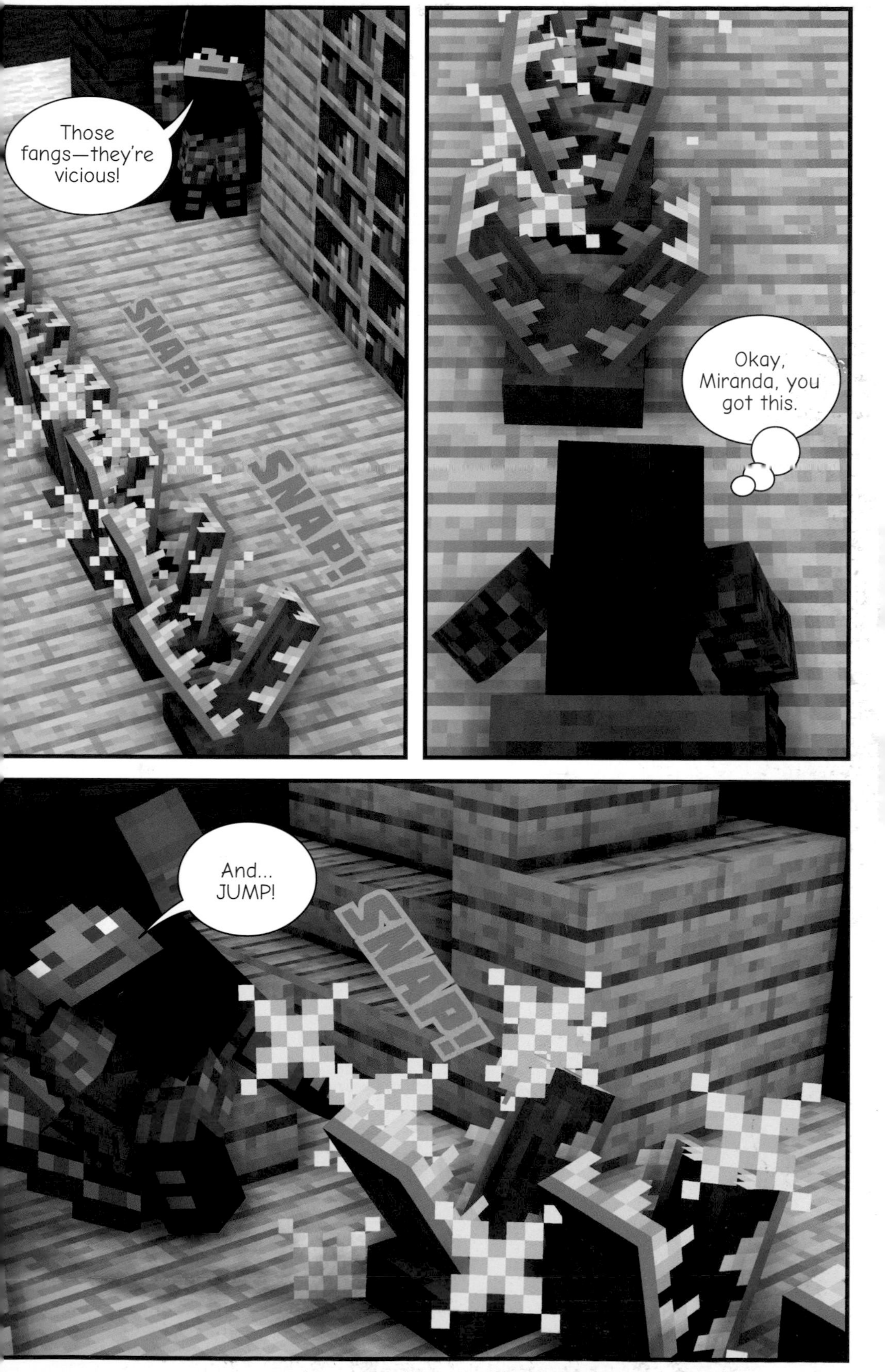
Those fangs—they're vicious!
SNAP!
SNAP!
Okay, Miranda, you got this.
And... JUMP!
SNAP!

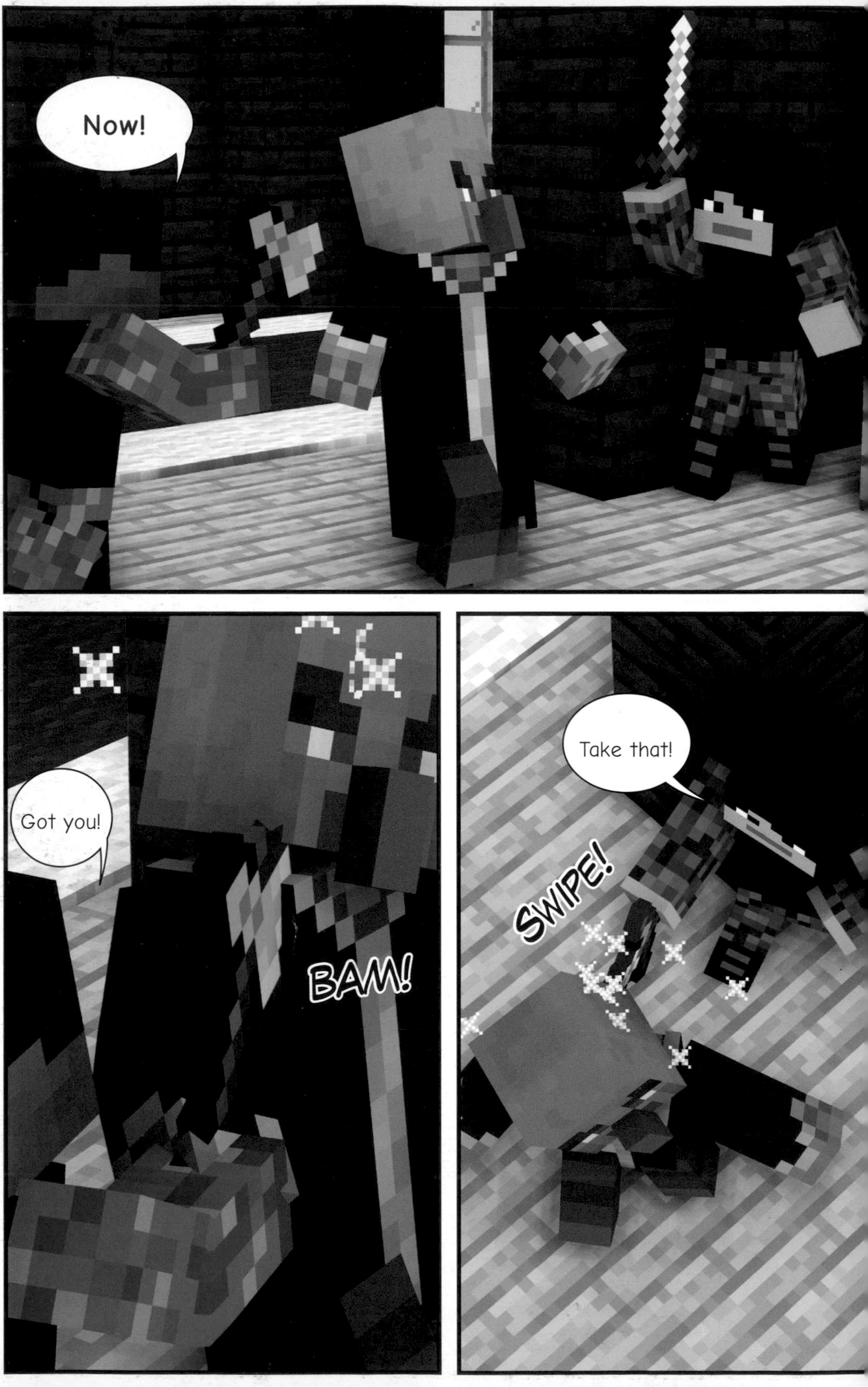
Now!
Got you!
BAM!
Take that!
SWIPE!

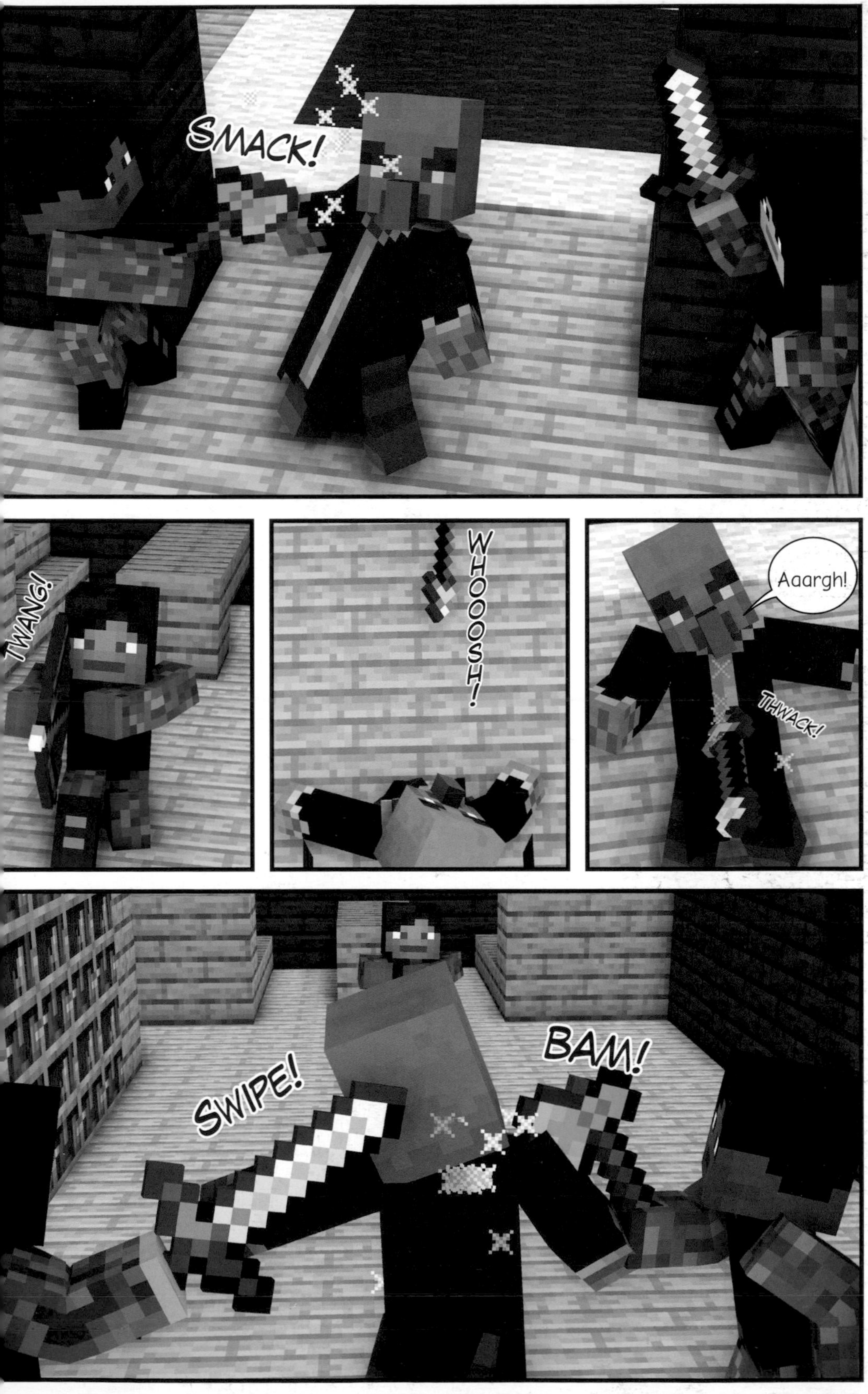
SMACK!
TWANG!
WHOOOSH!
Aaargh!
THWACK!
SWIPE!
BAM!

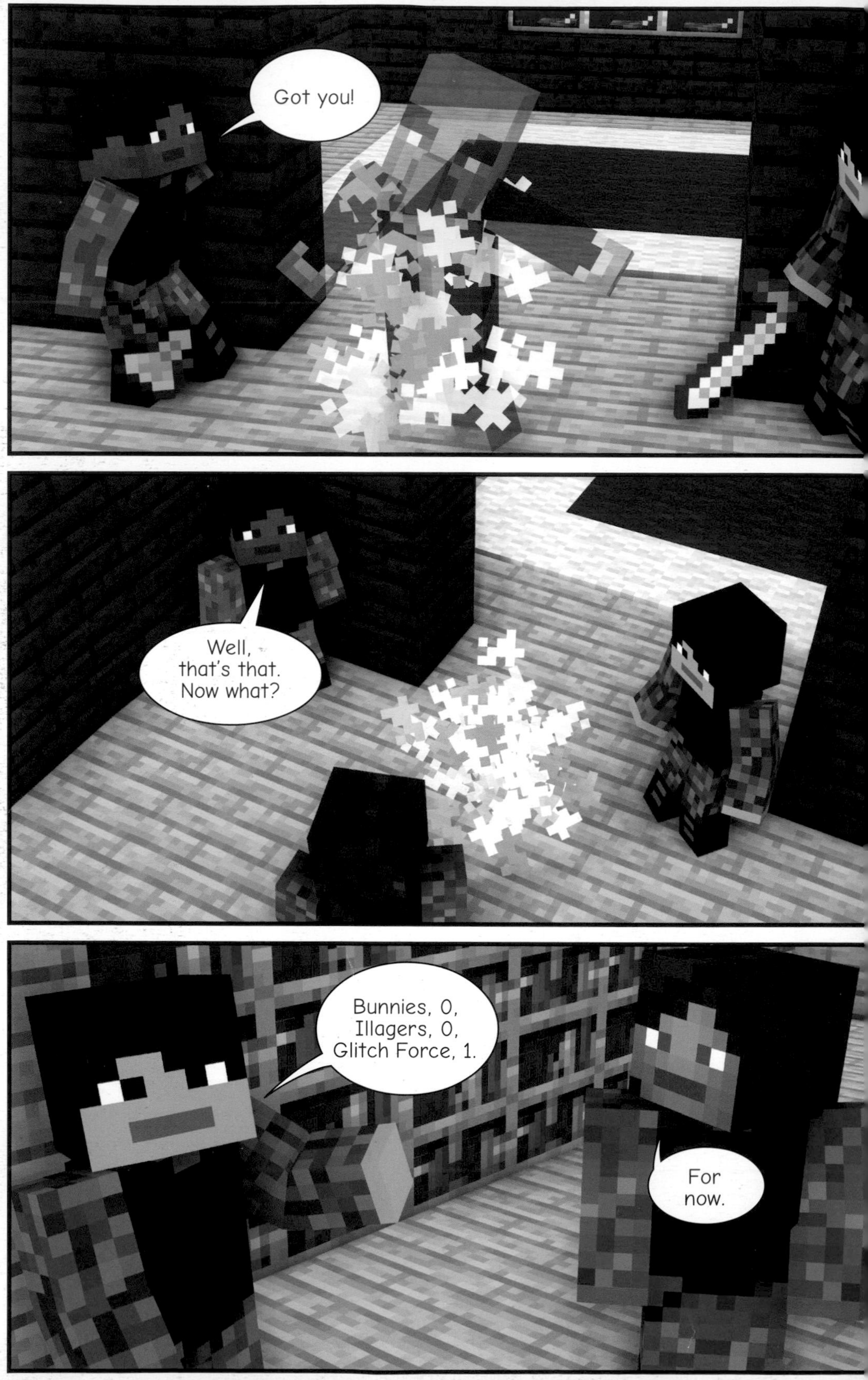
Got you!
Well, that's that. Now what?
Bunnies, 0, Illagers, 0, Glitch Force, 1.
For now.

CHAPTER 3: WOOL

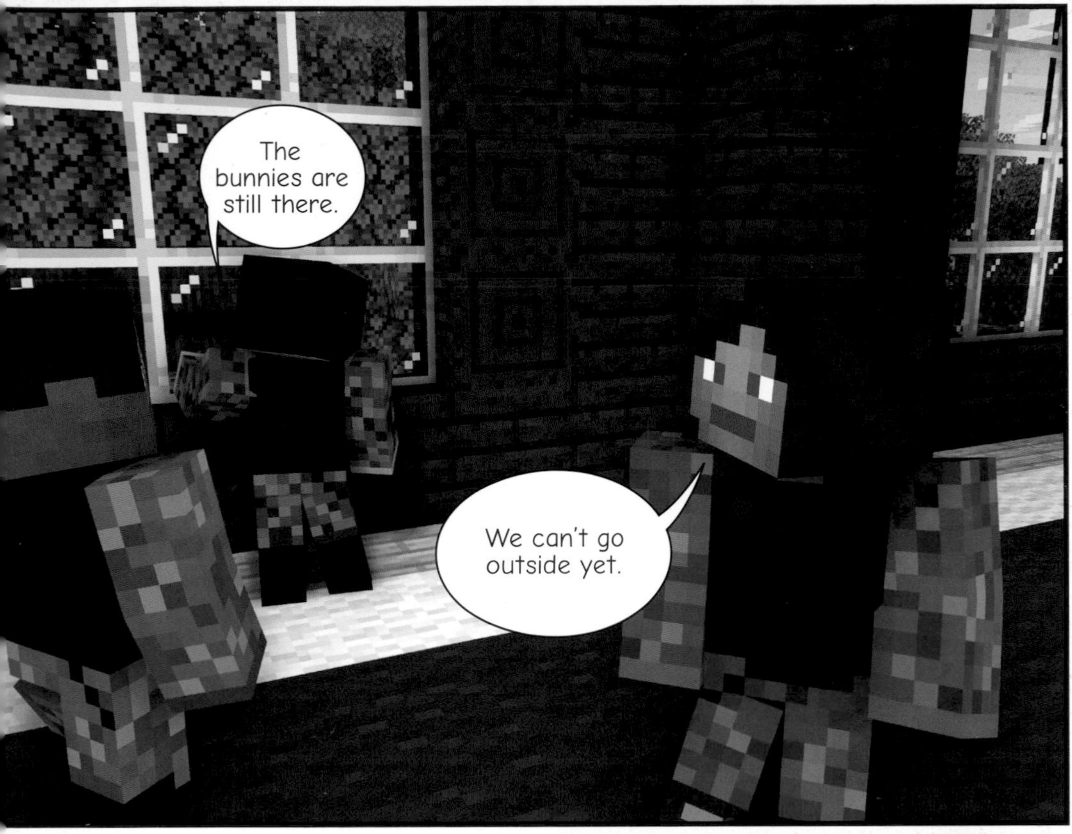
The bunnies are still there.
We can't go outside yet.

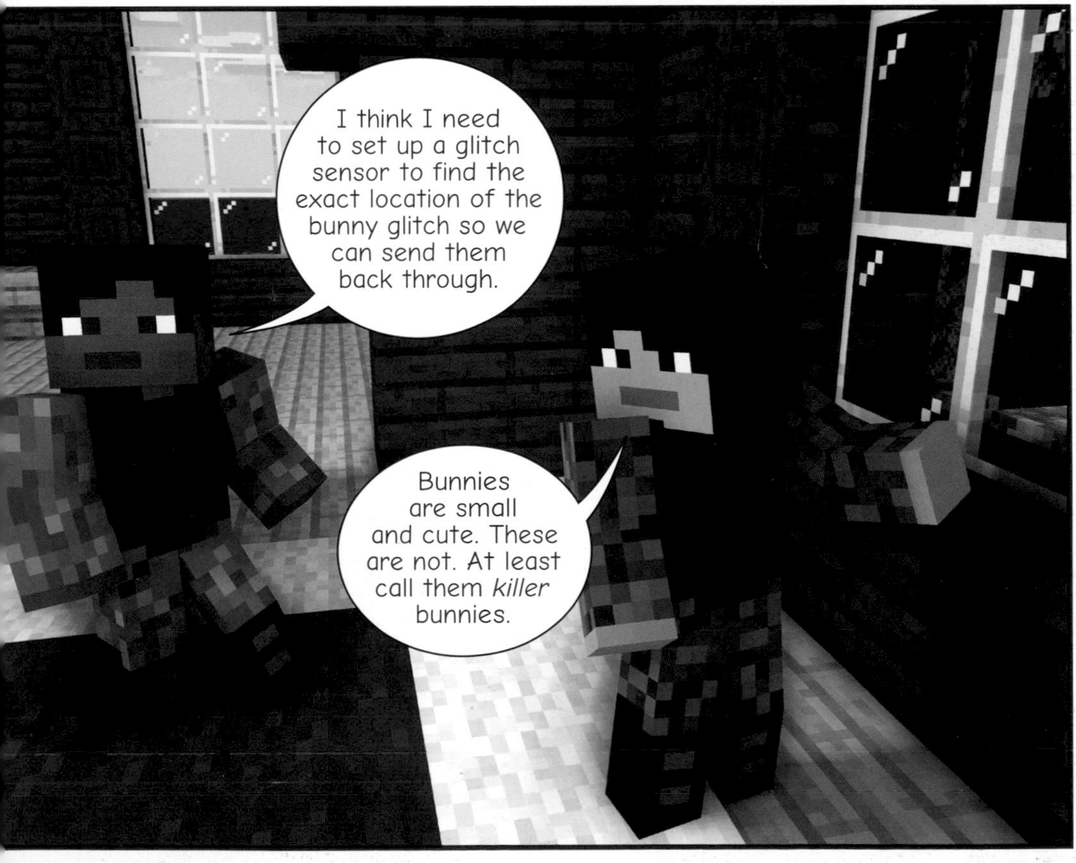
I think I need to set up a glitch sensor to find the exact location of the bunny glitch so we can send them back through.
Bunnies are small and cute. These are not. At least call them *killer* bunnies.

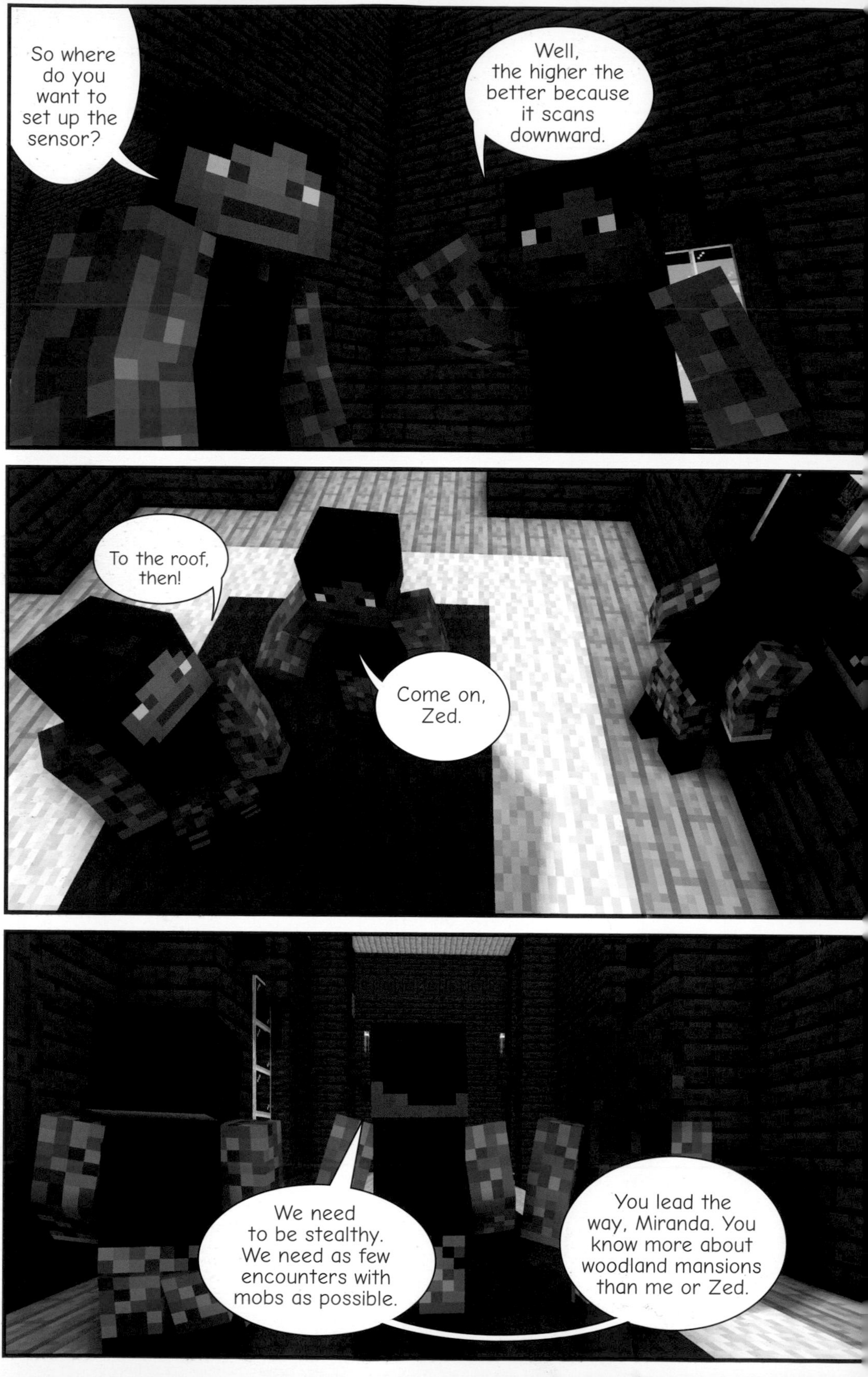
So where do you want to set up the sensor?
Well, the higher the better because it scans downward.
To the roof, then!
Come on, Zed.
We need to be stealthy. We need as few encounters with mobs as possible.
You lead the way, Miranda. You know more about woodland mansions than me or Zed.

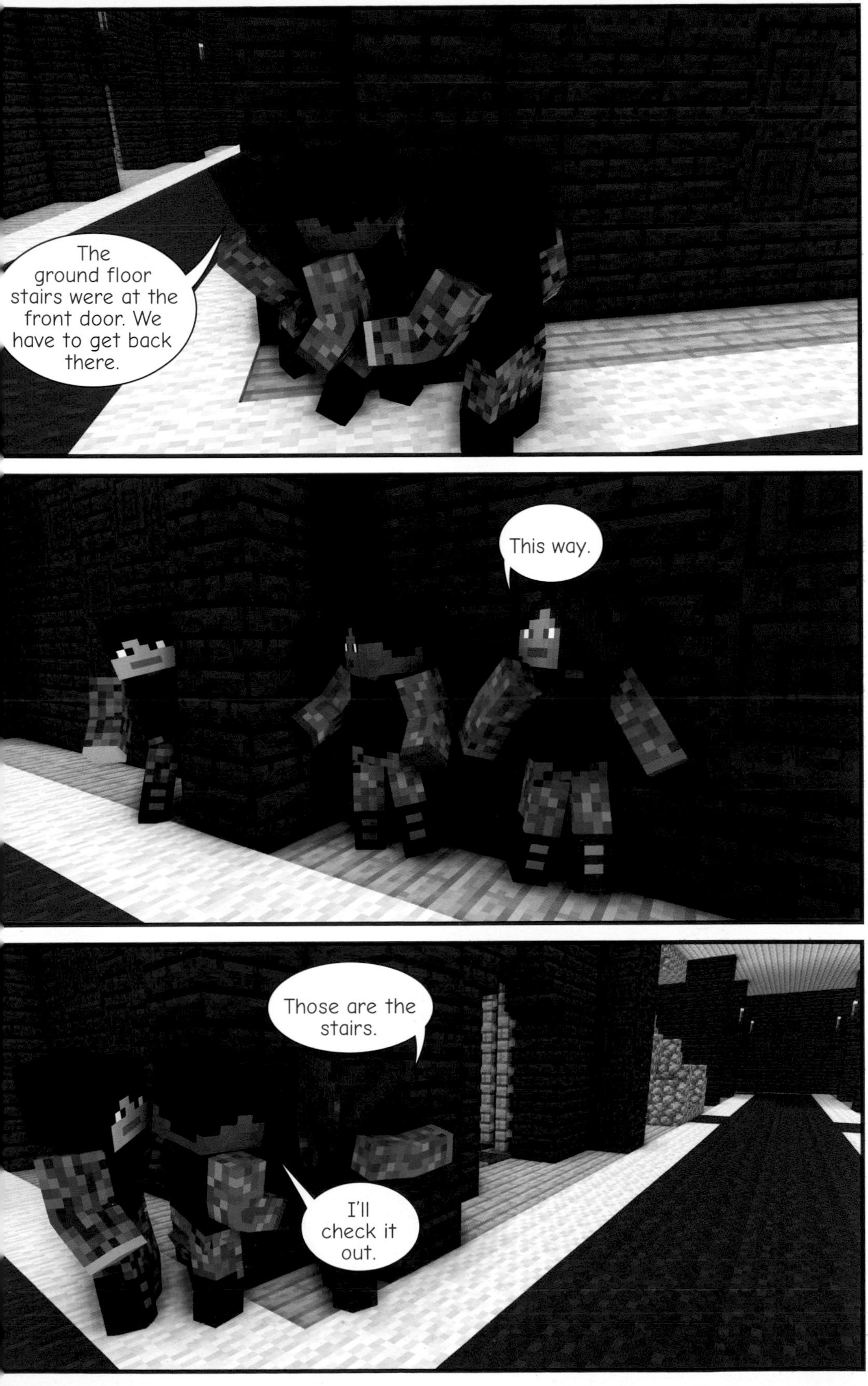
The ground floor stairs were at the front door. We have to get back there.
This way.
Those are the stairs.
I'll check it out.

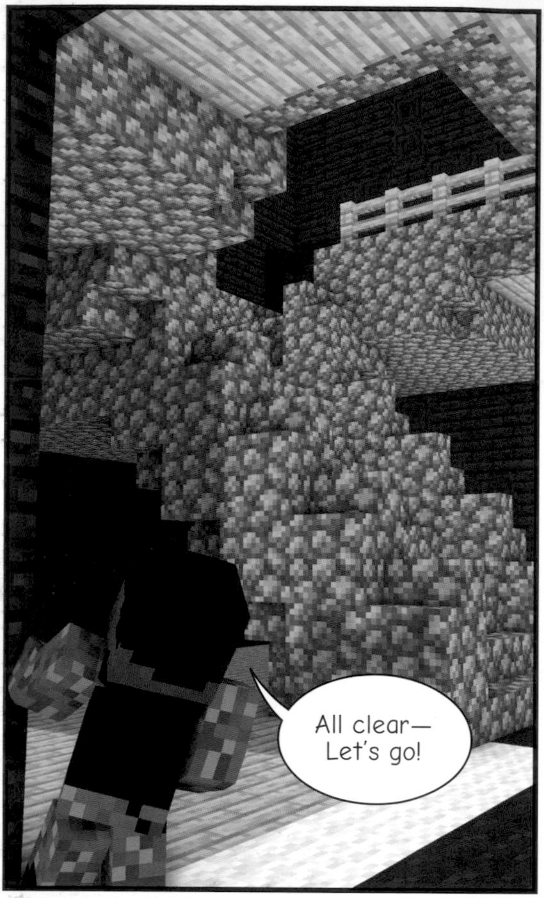
All clear—
Let's go!
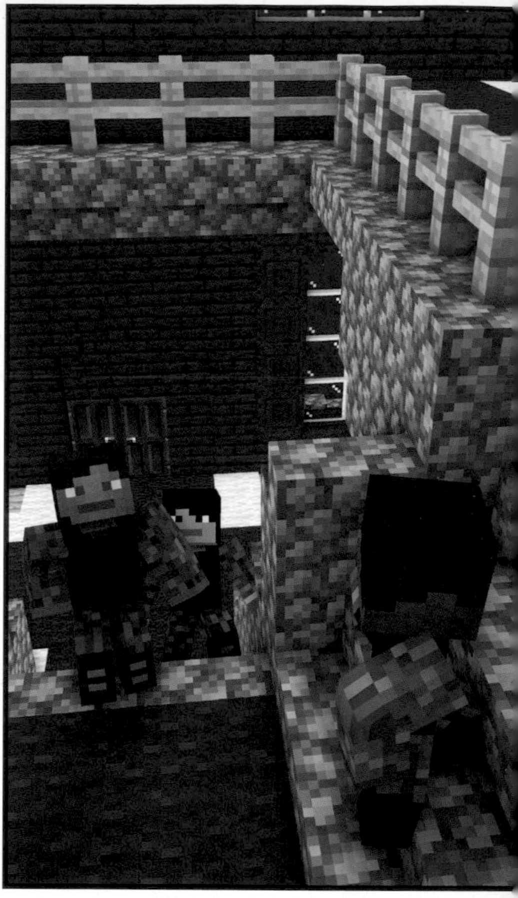
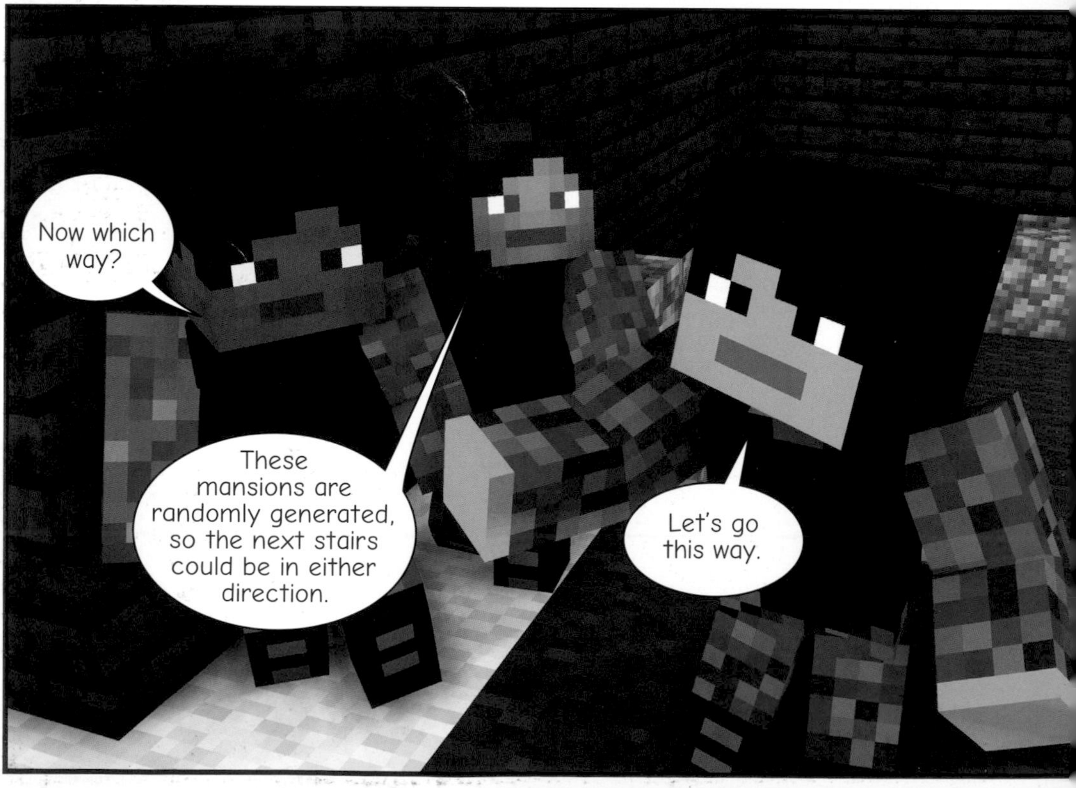
Now which way?
These mansions are randomly generated, so the next stairs could be in either direction.
Let's go this way.

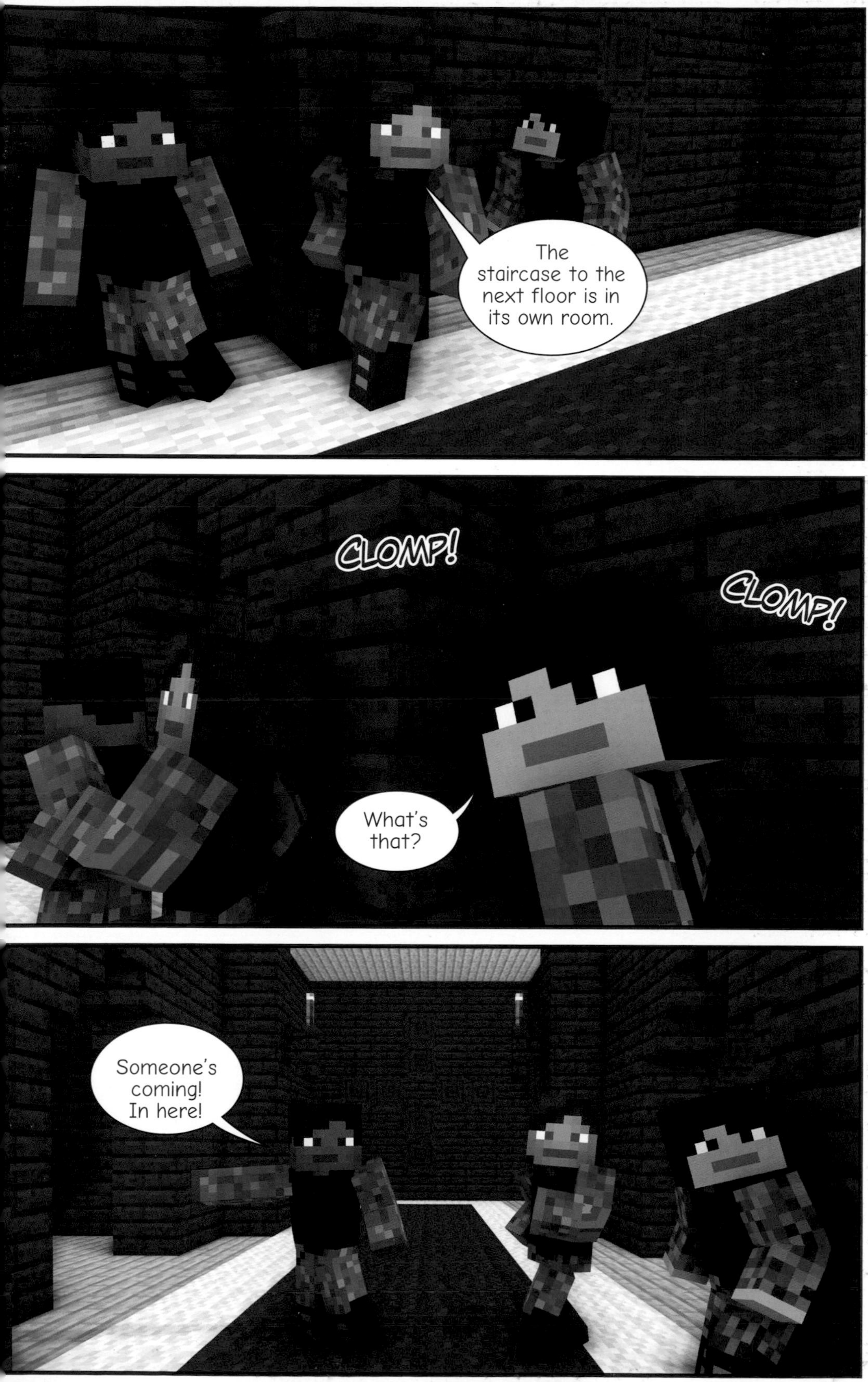
The staircase to the next floor is in its own room.
CLOMP!
CLOMP!
What's that?
Someone's coming! In here!

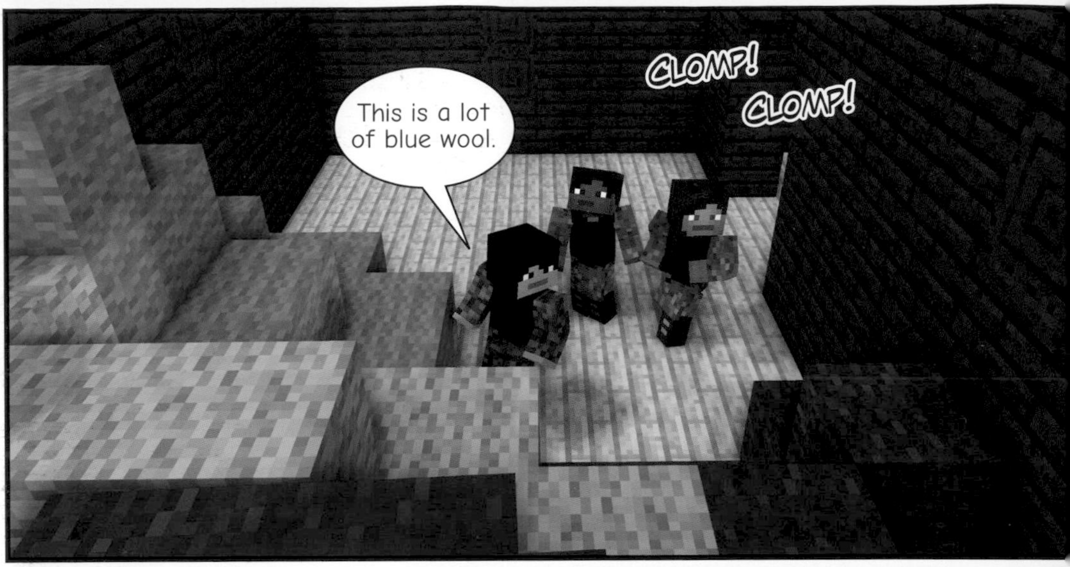
This is a lot of blue wool.
CLOMP!
CLOMP!

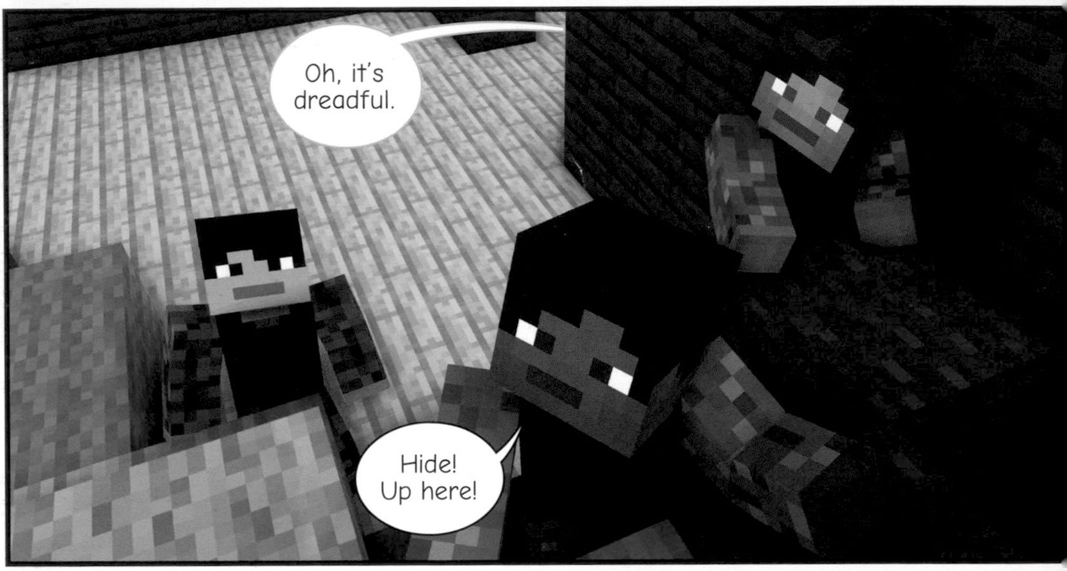
Oh, it's dreadful.
Hide! Up here!

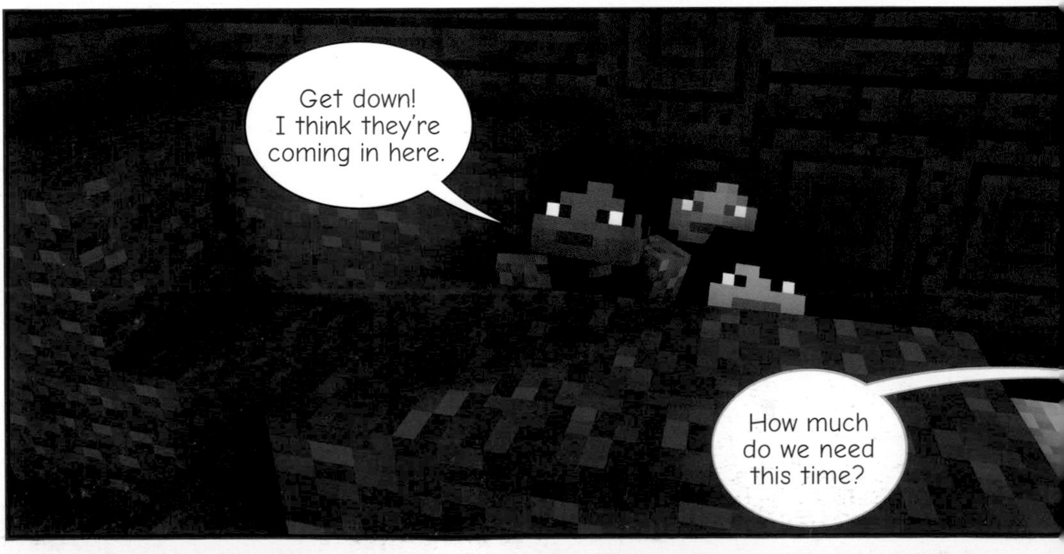
Get down! I think they're coming in here.
How much do we need this time?

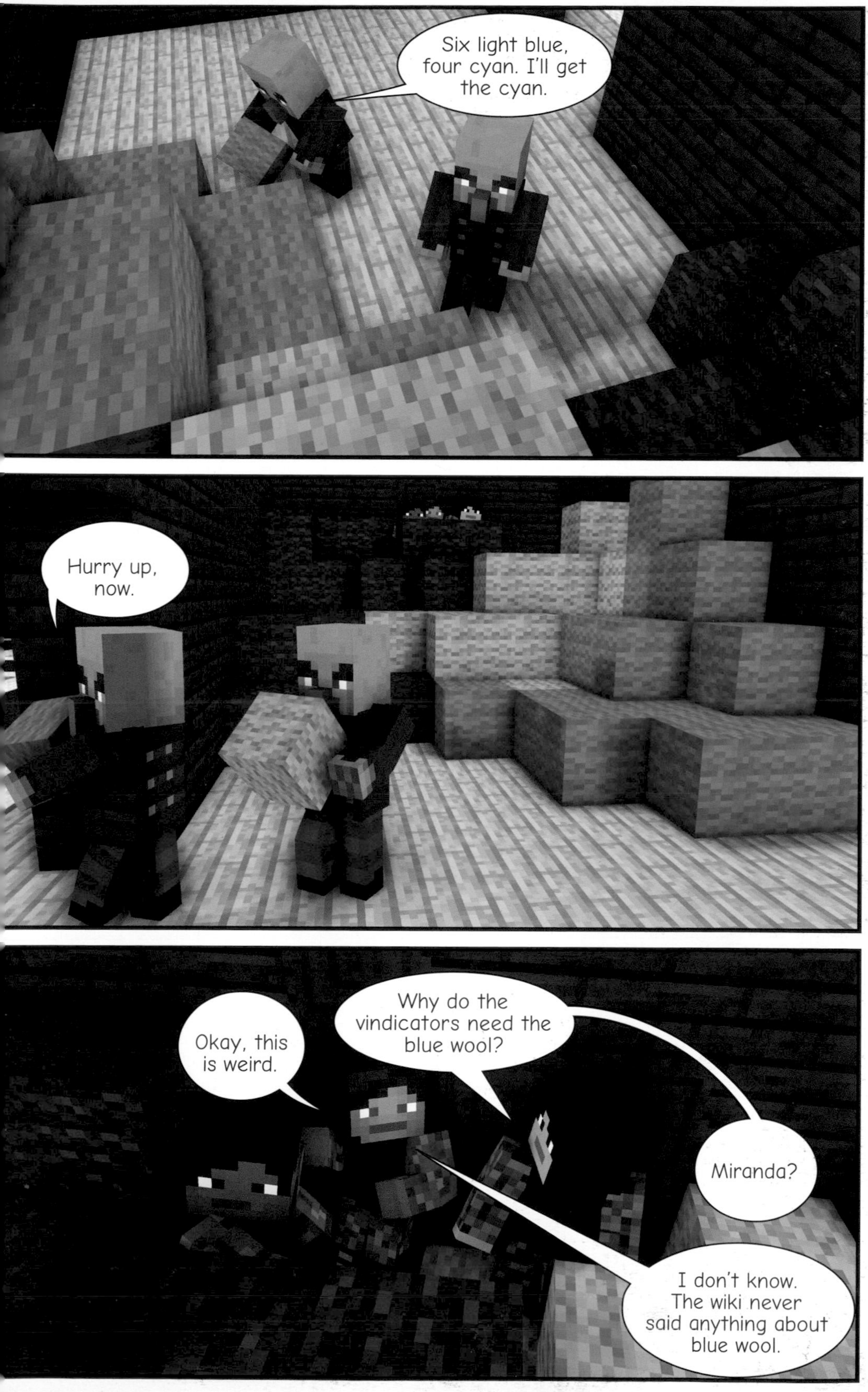
Six light blue, four cyan. I'll get the cyan.
Hurry up, now.
Okay, this is weird.
Why do the vindicators need the blue wool?
Miranda?
I don't know. The wiki never said anything about blue wool.

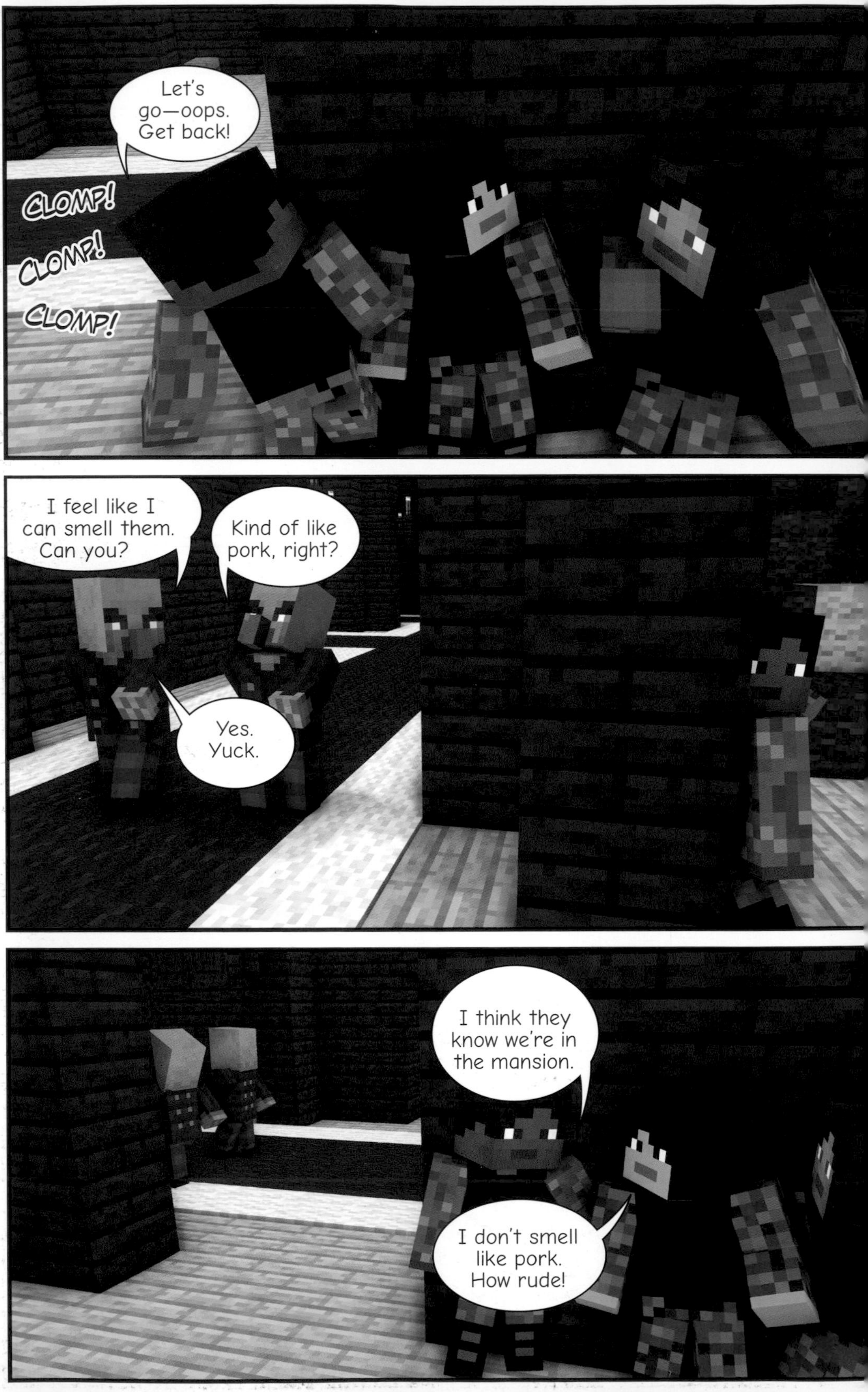
Let's go—oops. Get back!
CLOMP!
CLOMP!
CLOMP!
I feel like I can smell them. Can you?
Kind of like pork, right?
Yes. Yuck.
I think they know we're in the mansion.
I don't smell like pork. How rude!

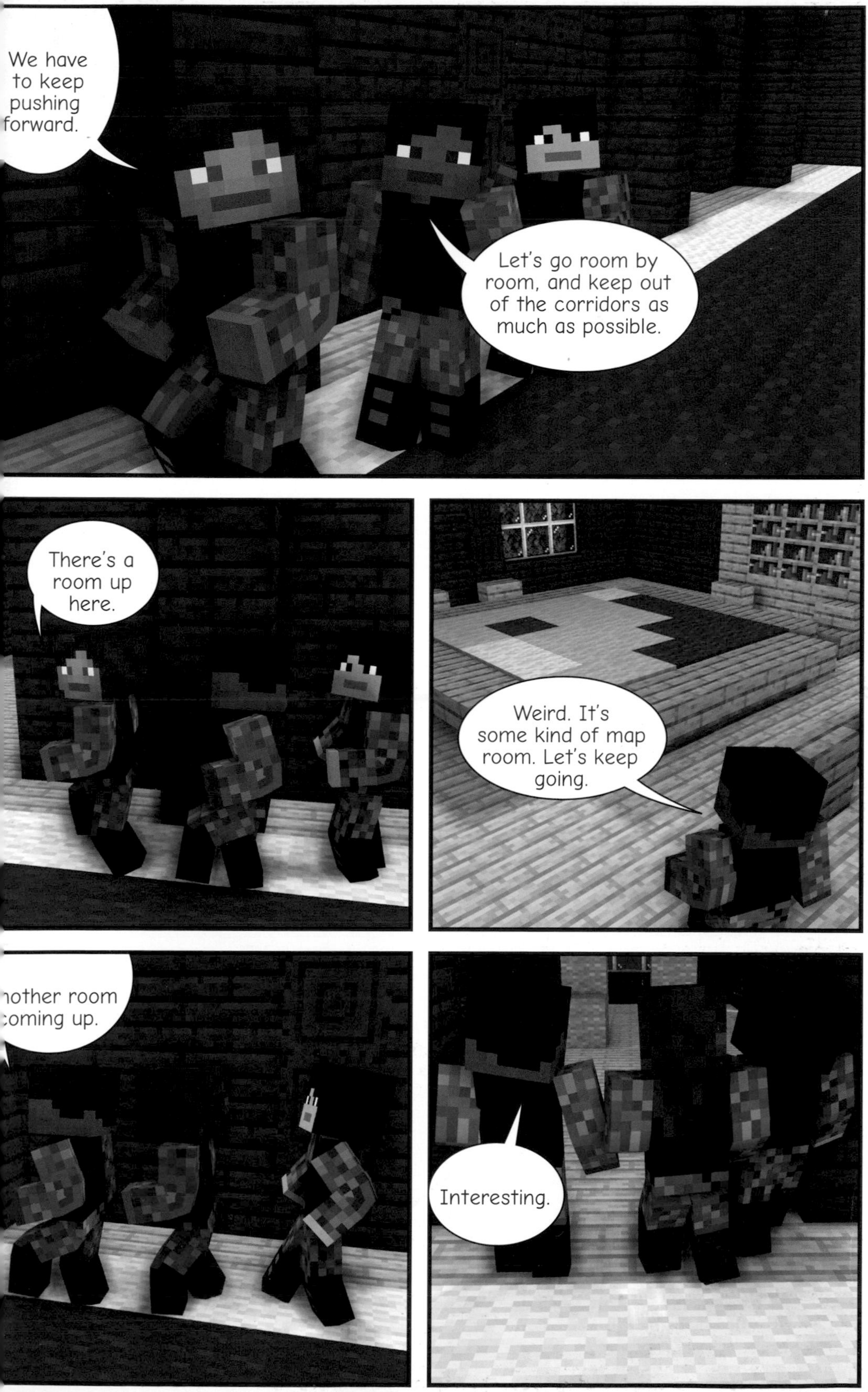
We have to keep pushing forward.
Let's go room by room, and keep out of the corridors as much as possible.
There's a room up here.
Weird. It's some kind of map room. Let's keep going.
nother room coming up.
Interesting.

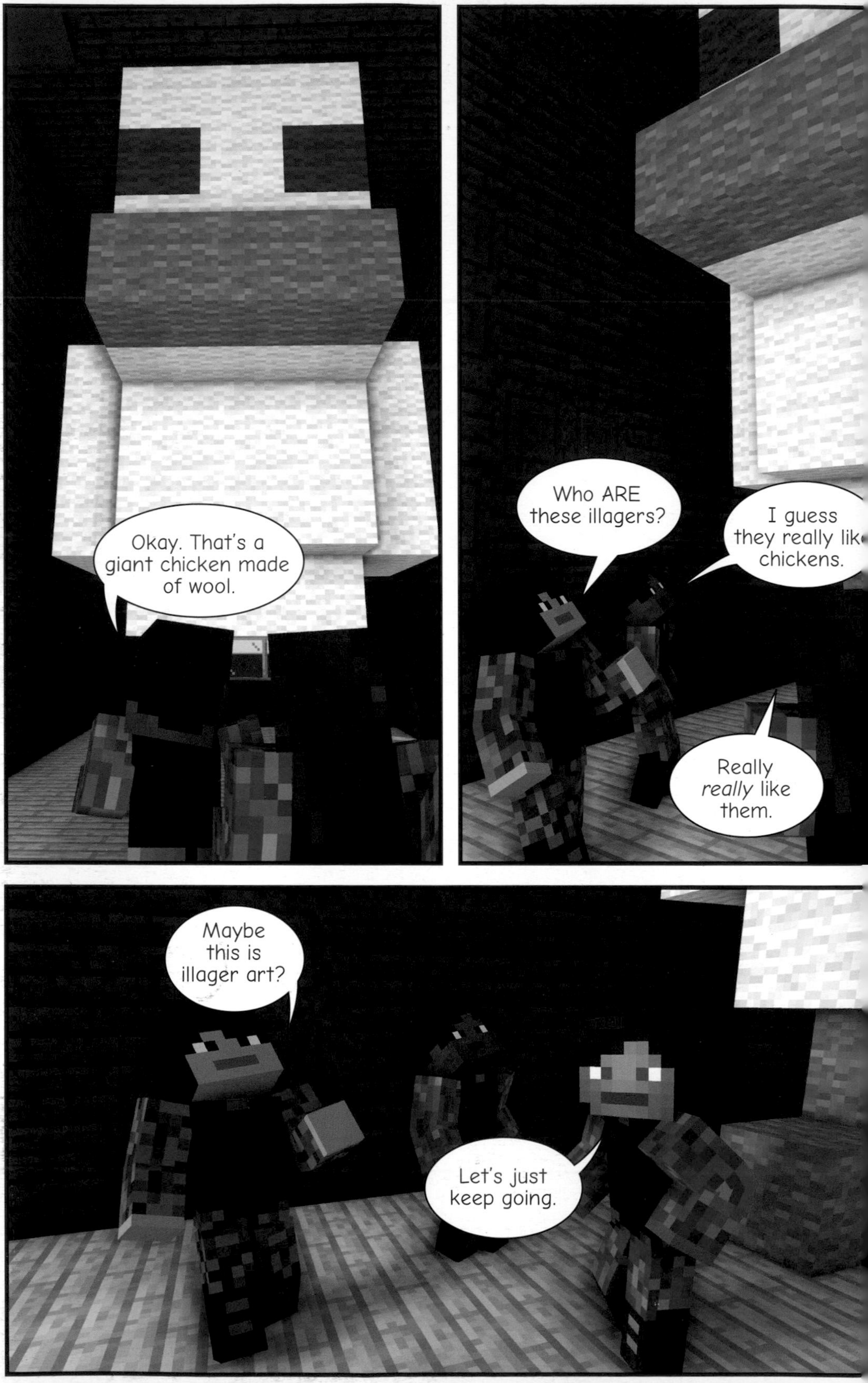
Okay. That's a giant chicken made of wool.
Who ARE these illagers?
I guess they really lik
chickens.
Really *really* like them.
Maybe this is illager art?
Let's just keep going.

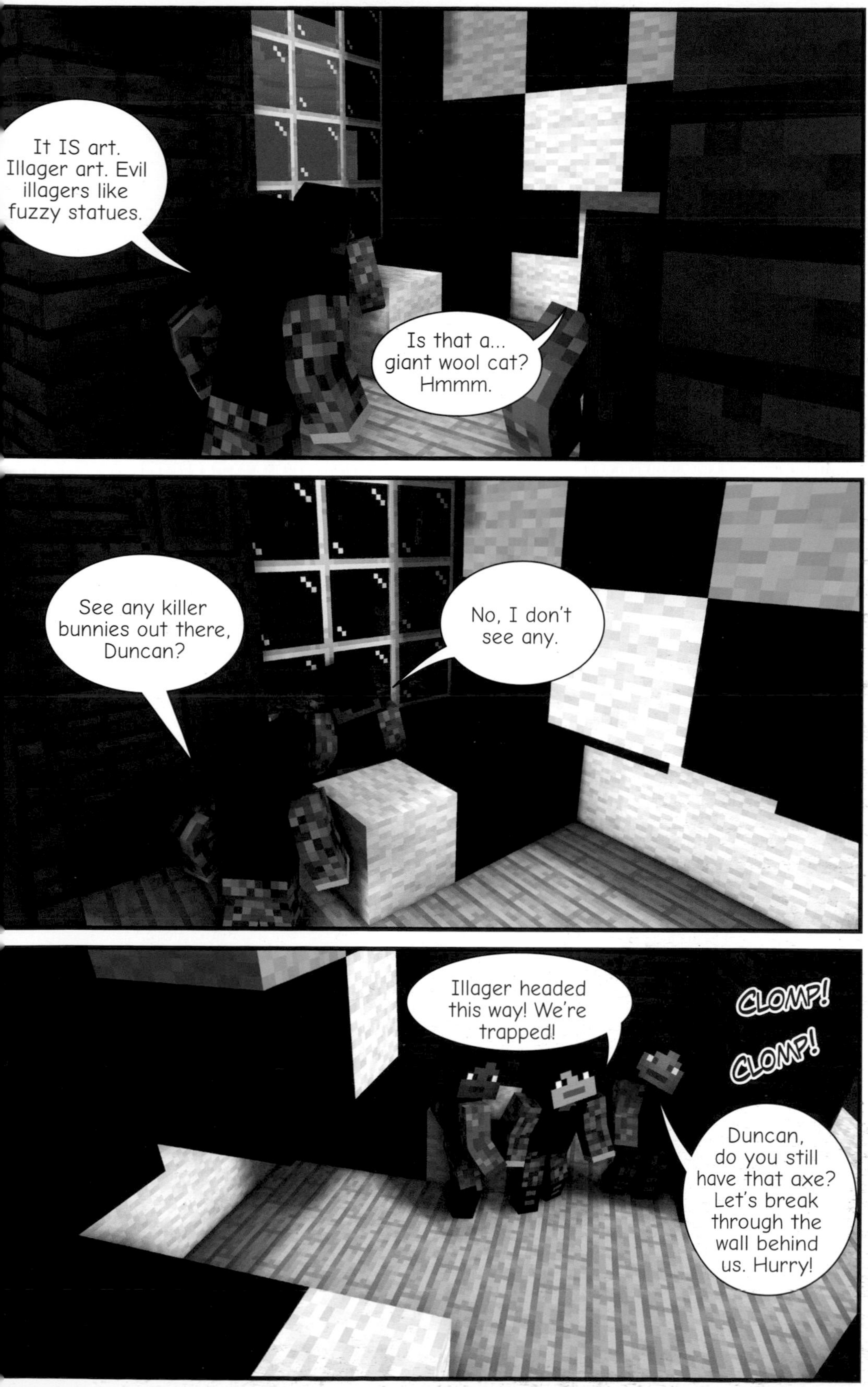
It IS art. Illager art. Evil illagers like fuzzy statues.
Is that a... giant wool cat? Hmmm.
See any killer bunnies out there, Duncan?
No, I don't see any.
Illager headed this way! We're trapped!
CLOMP!
CLOMP!
Duncan, do you still have that axe? Let's break through the wall behind us. Hurry!

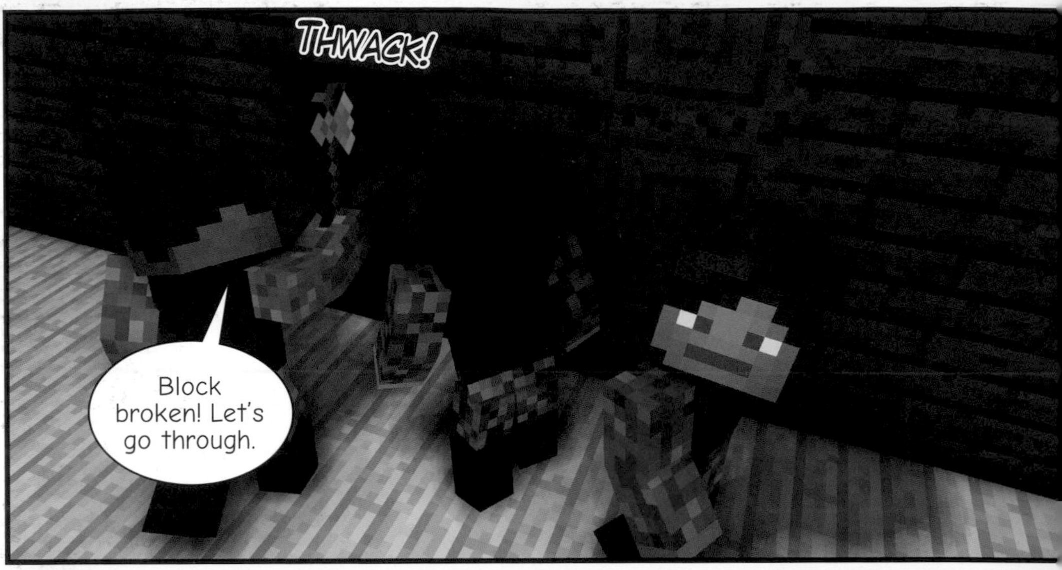
THWACK!
Block broken! Let's go through.

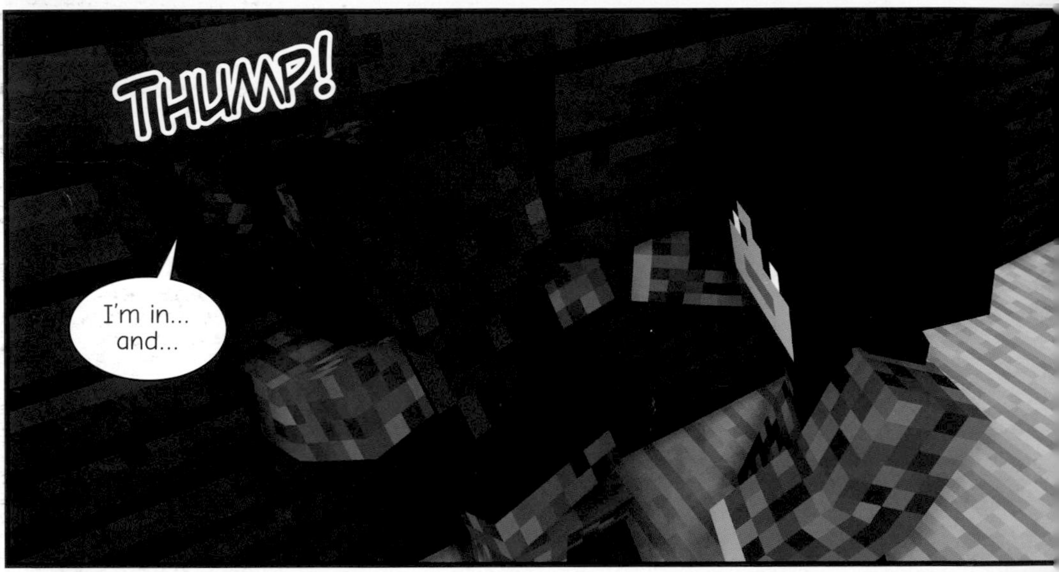
THUMP!
I'm in... and...

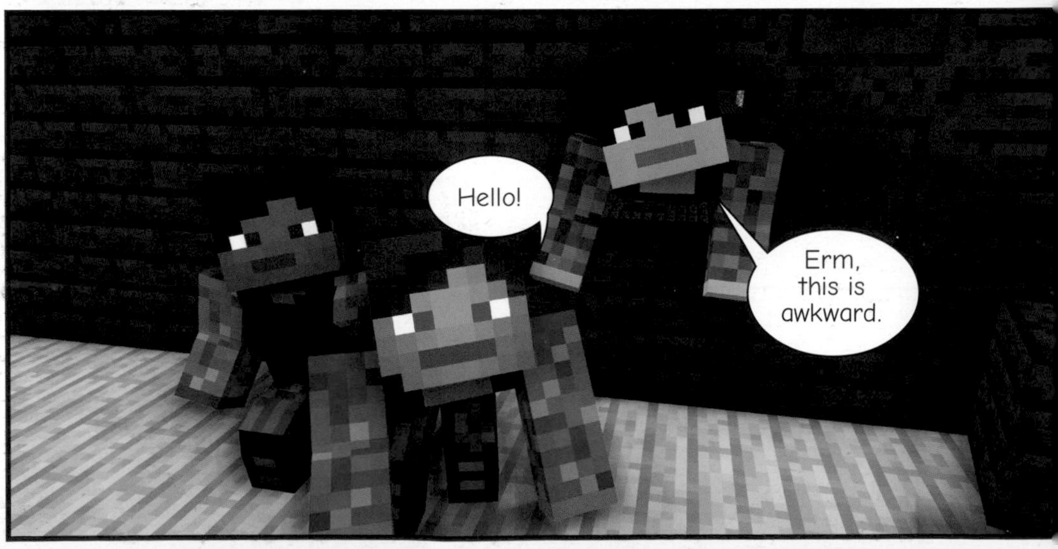
Hello!
Erm, this is awkward.

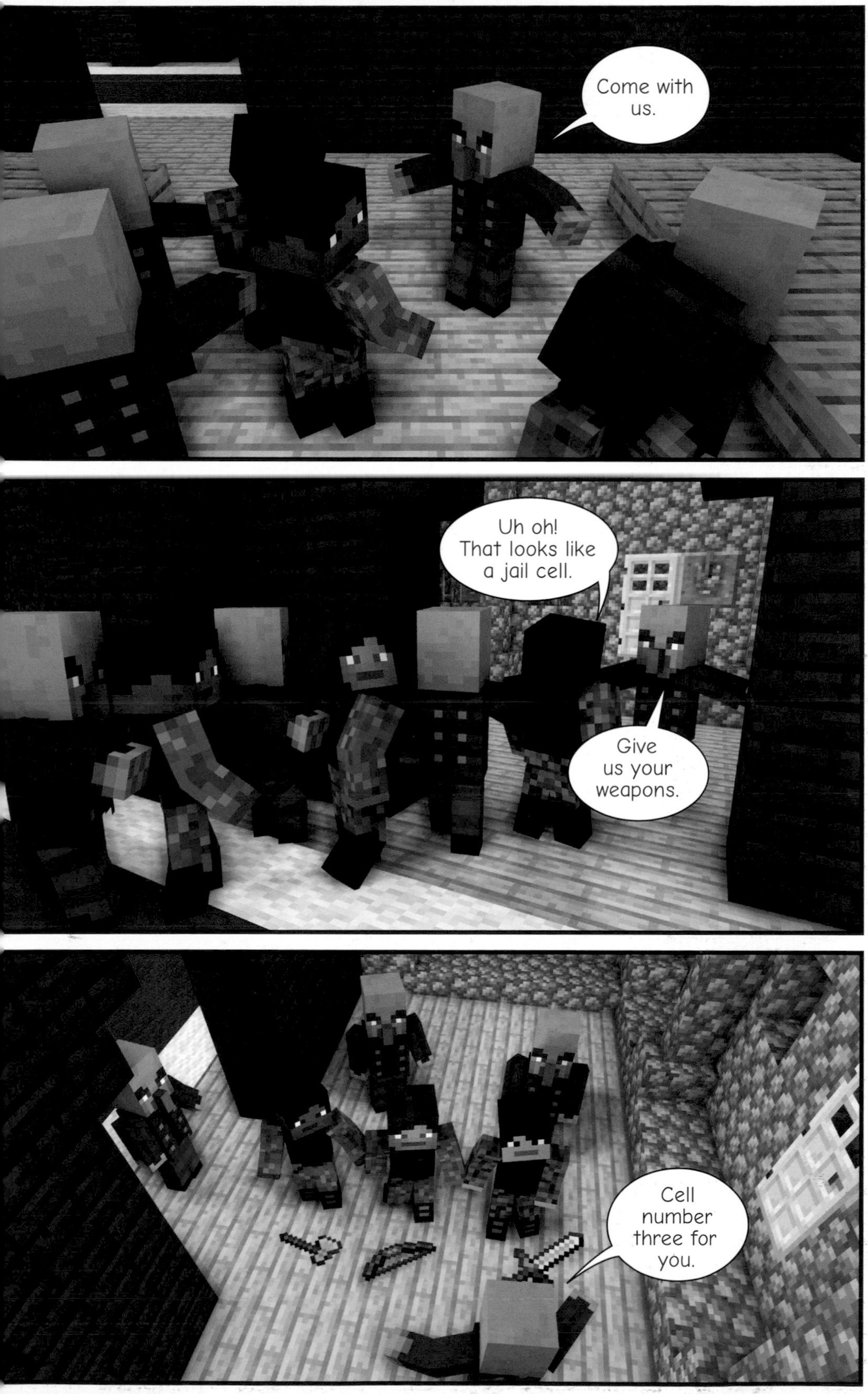
Come with us.
Uh oh! That looks like a jail cell.
Give us your weapons.
Cell number three for you.

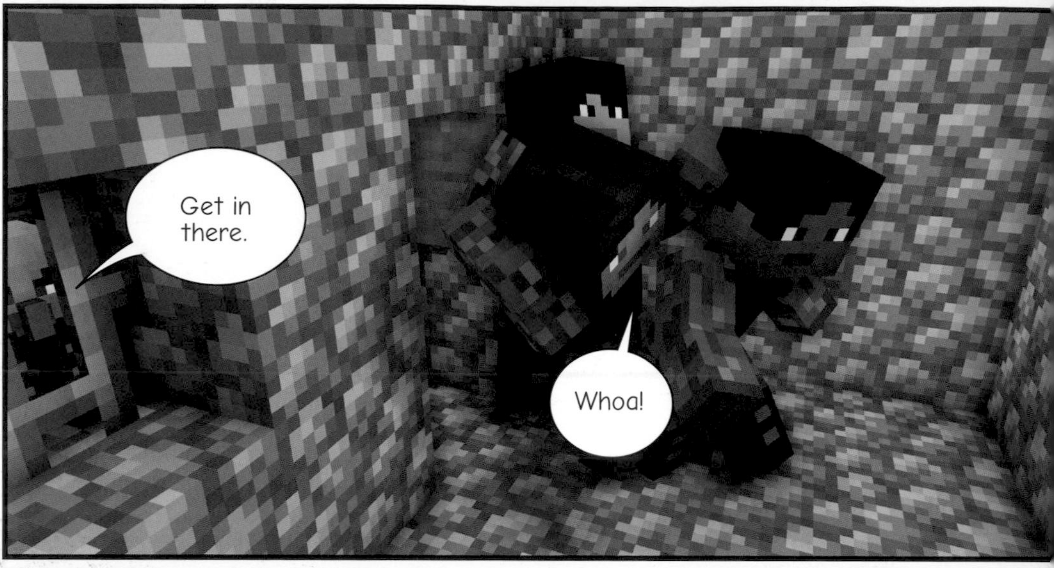
Get in there.
Whoa!
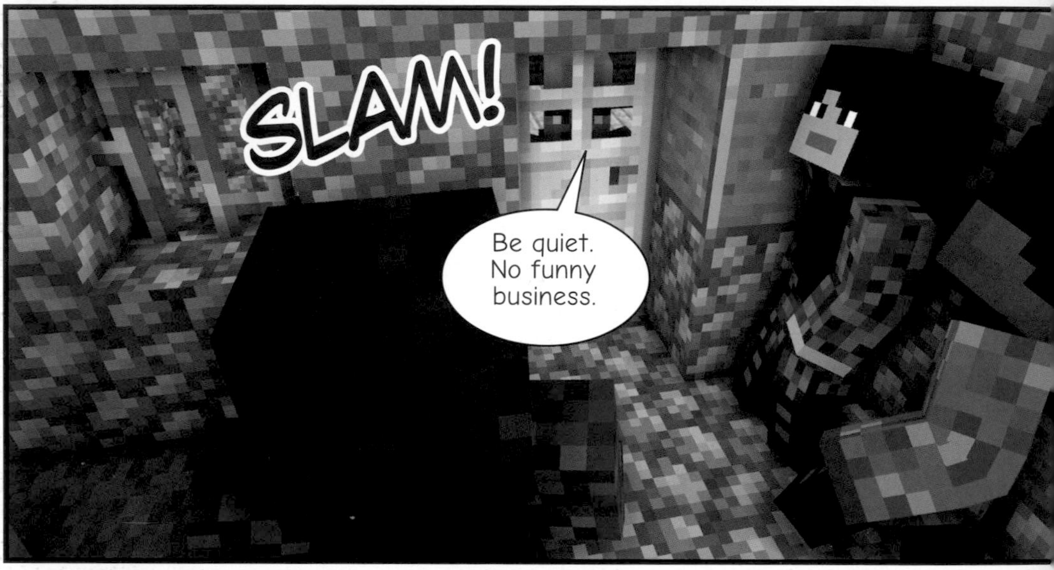
SLAM!
Be quiet. No funny business.
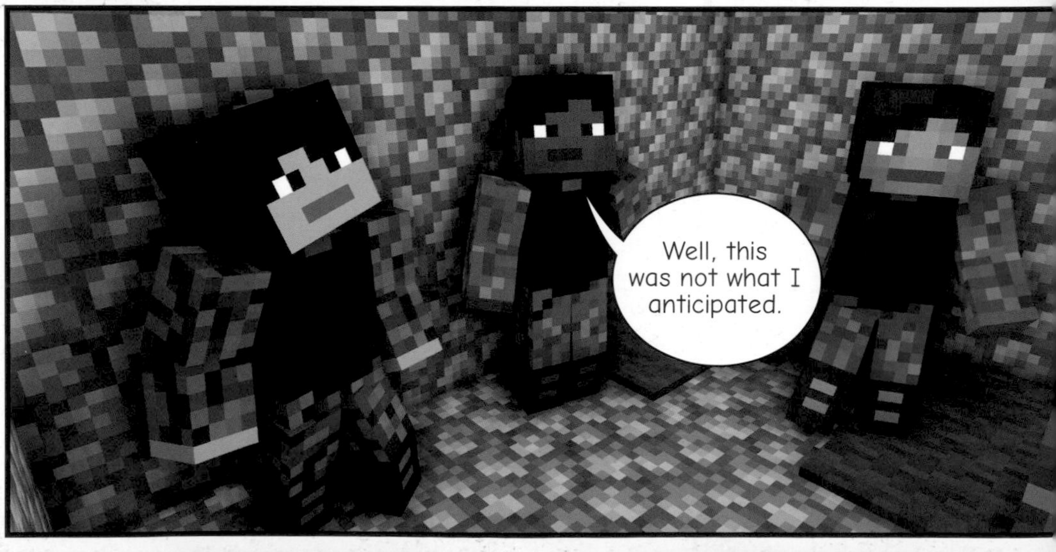
Well, this was not what I anticipated.

CHAPTER 4:
LOOT

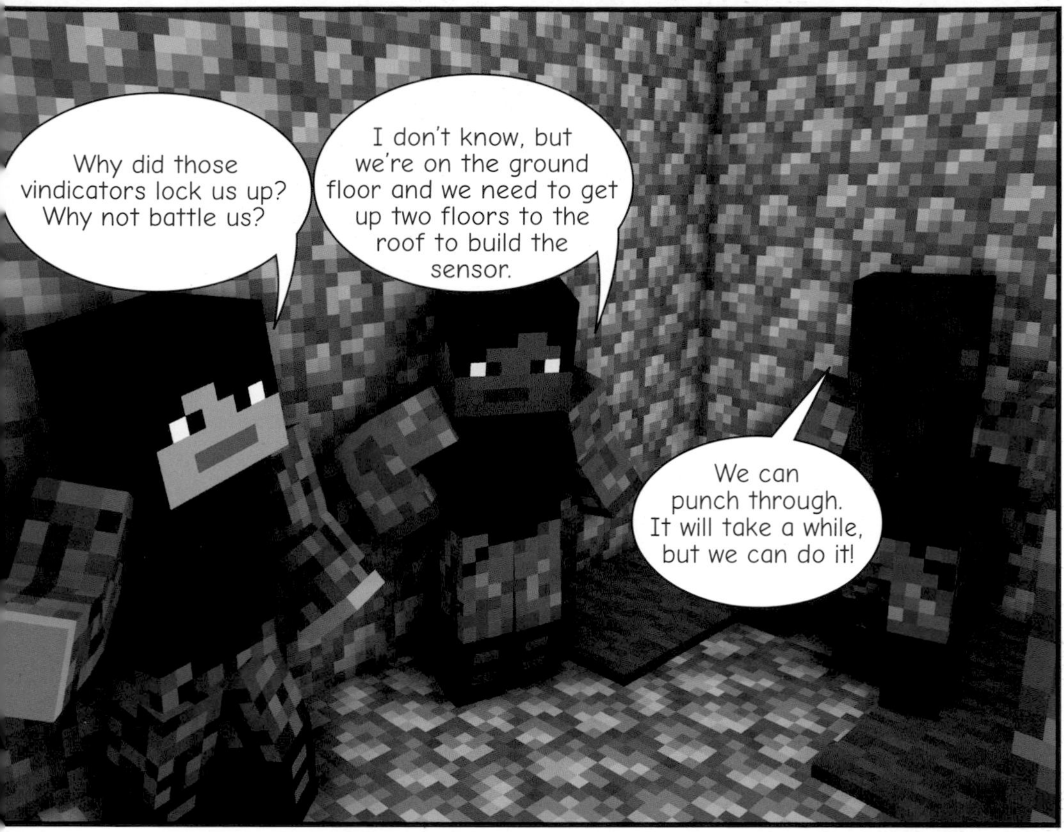
Why did those vindicators lock us up? Why not battle us?
I don't know, but we're on the ground floor and we need to get up two floors to the roof to build the sensor.
We can punch through. It will take a while, but we can do it!

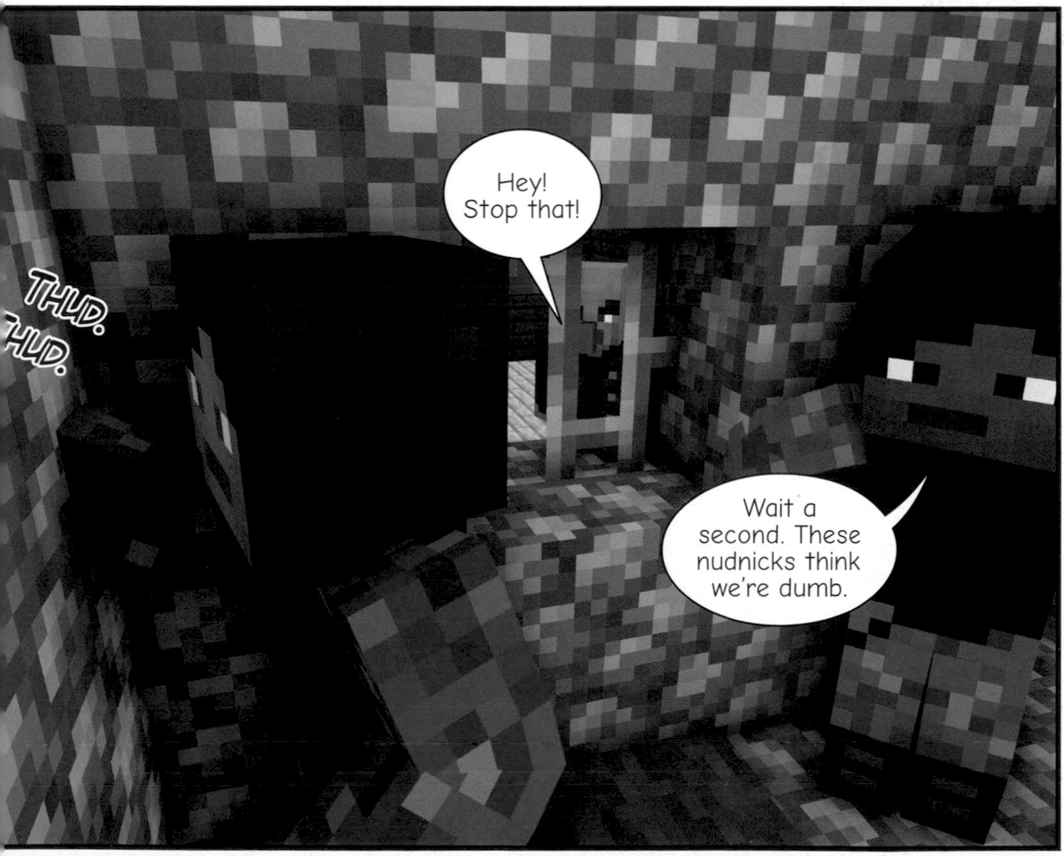
THUD.
Hey! Stop that!
Wait a second. These nudnicks think we're dumb.

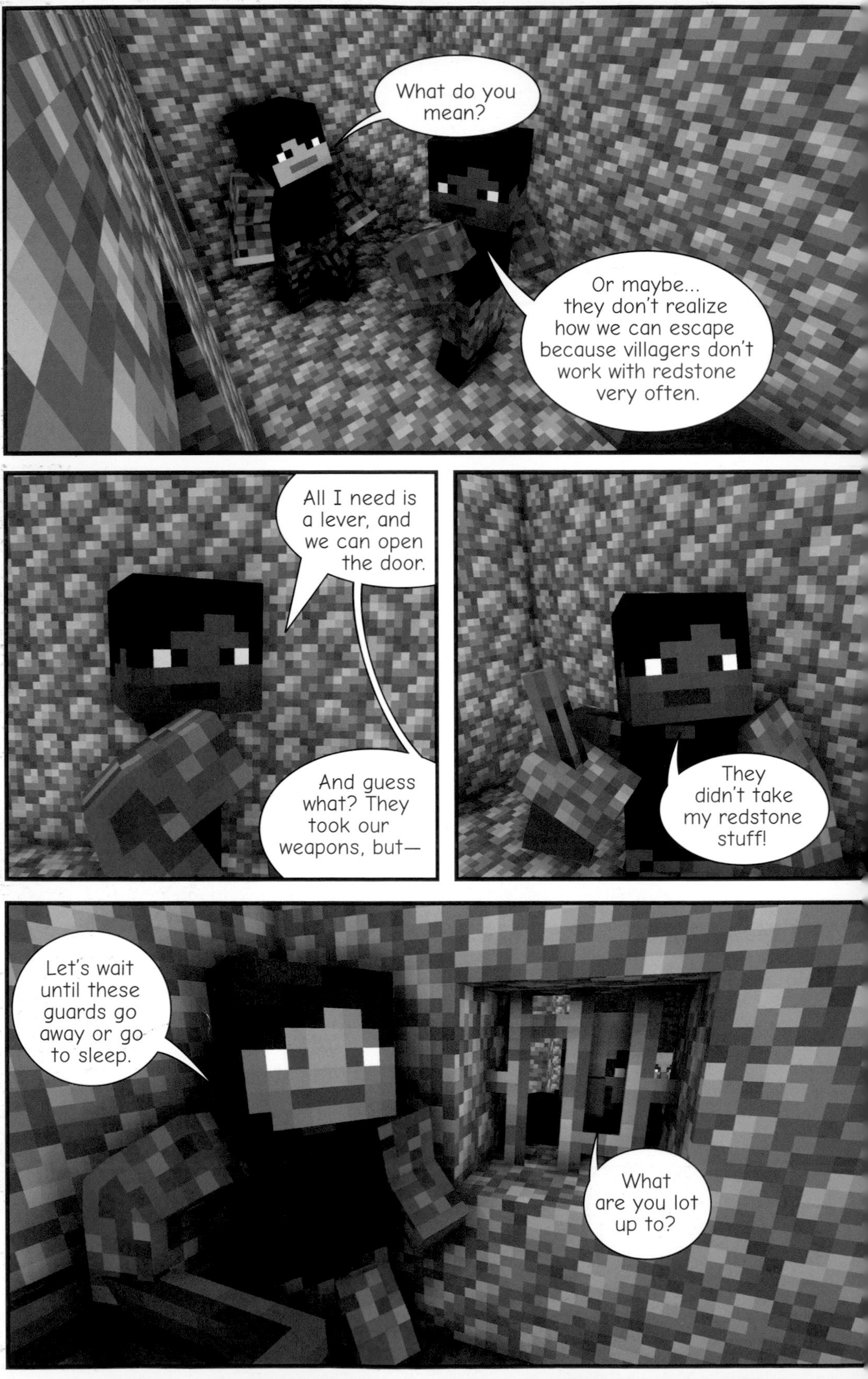
What do you mean?
Or maybe... they don't realize how we can escape because villagers don't work with redstone very often.
All I need is a lever, and we can open the door.
And guess what? They took our weapons, but—
They didn't take my redstone stuff!
Let's wait until these guards go away or go to sleep.
What are you lot up to?

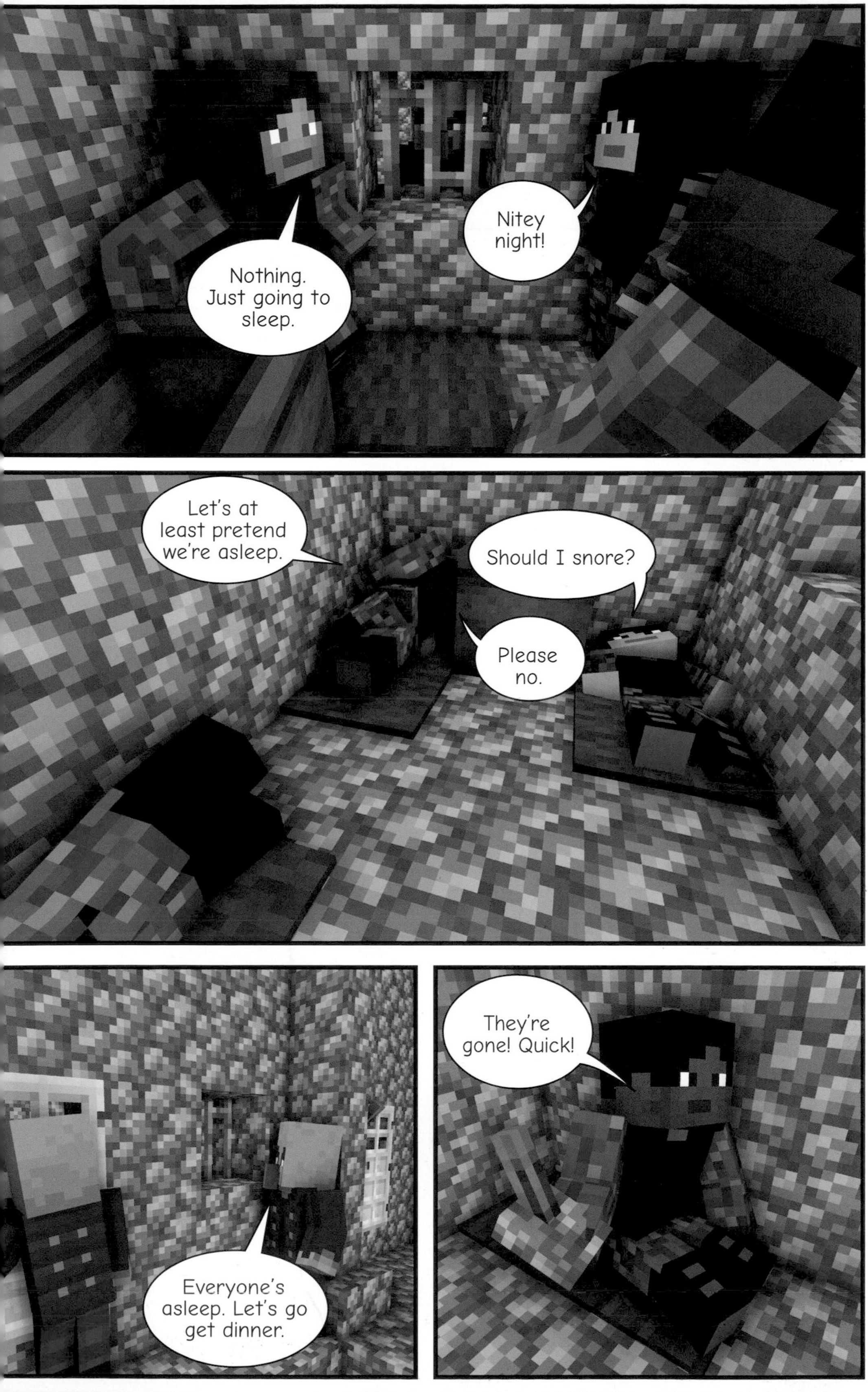
Nothing. Just going to sleep.
Nitey night!
Let's at least pretend we're asleep.
Should I snore?
Please no.
Everyone's asleep. Let's go get dinner.
They're gone! Quick!

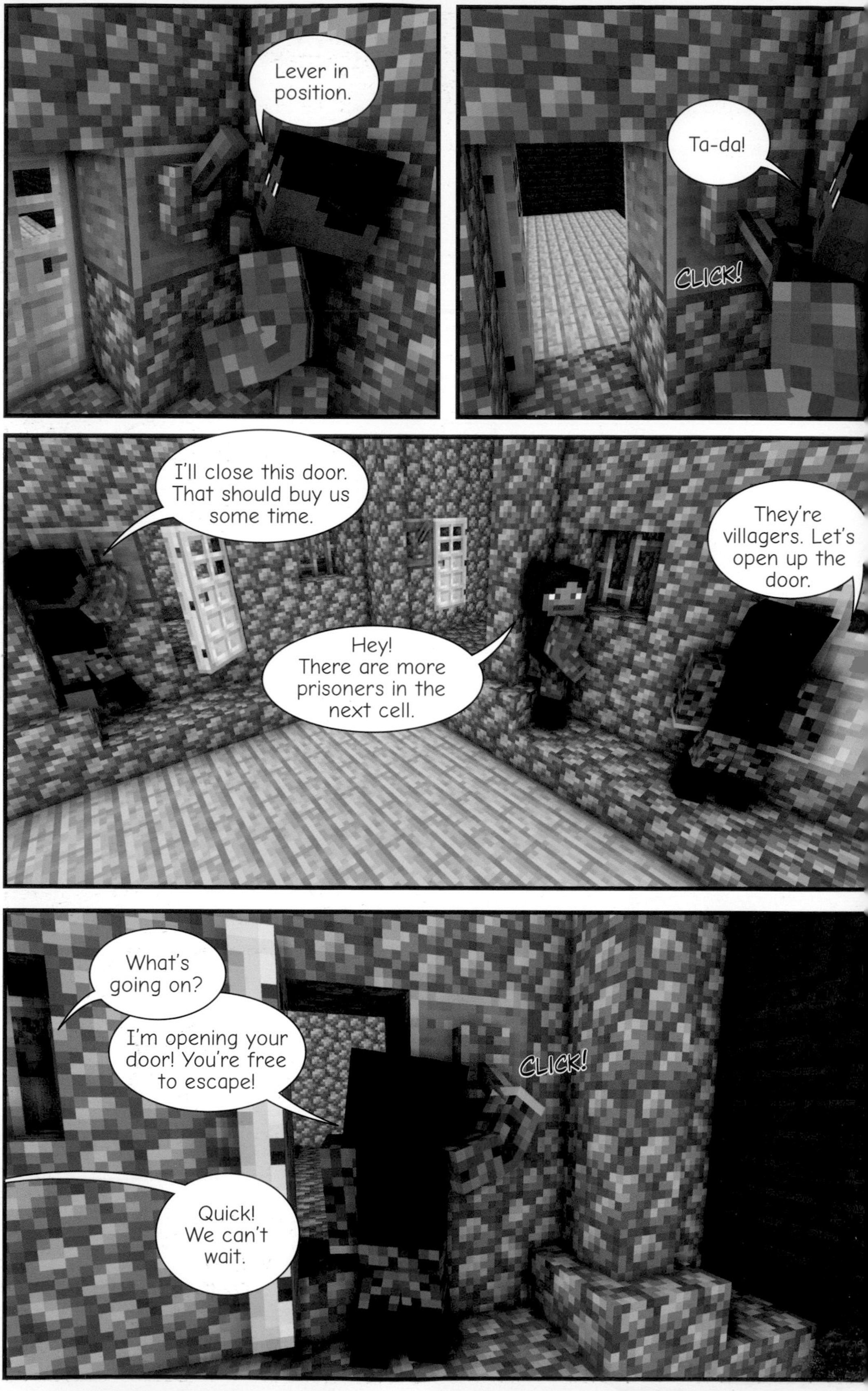
Lever in position.
Ta-da!
CLICK!
I'll close this door. That should buy us some time.
Hey! There are more prisoners in the next cell.
They're villagers. Let's open up the door.
What's going on?
I'm opening your door! You're free to escape!
CLICK!
Quick! We can't wait.

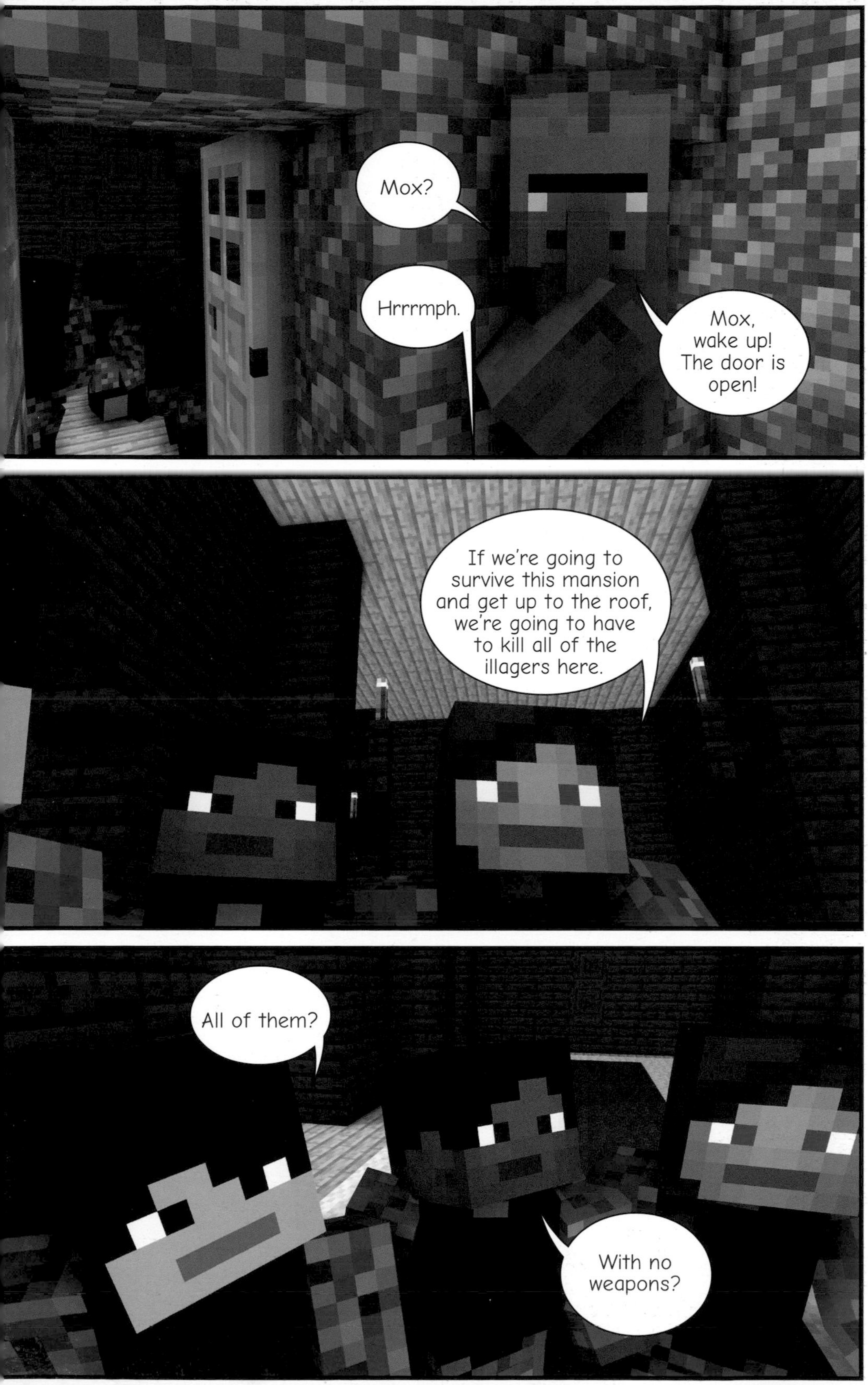
Mox?
Hrrrmph.
Mox, wake up! The door is open!
If we're going to survive this mansion and get up to the roof, we're going to have to kill all of the illagers here.
All of them?
With no weapons?

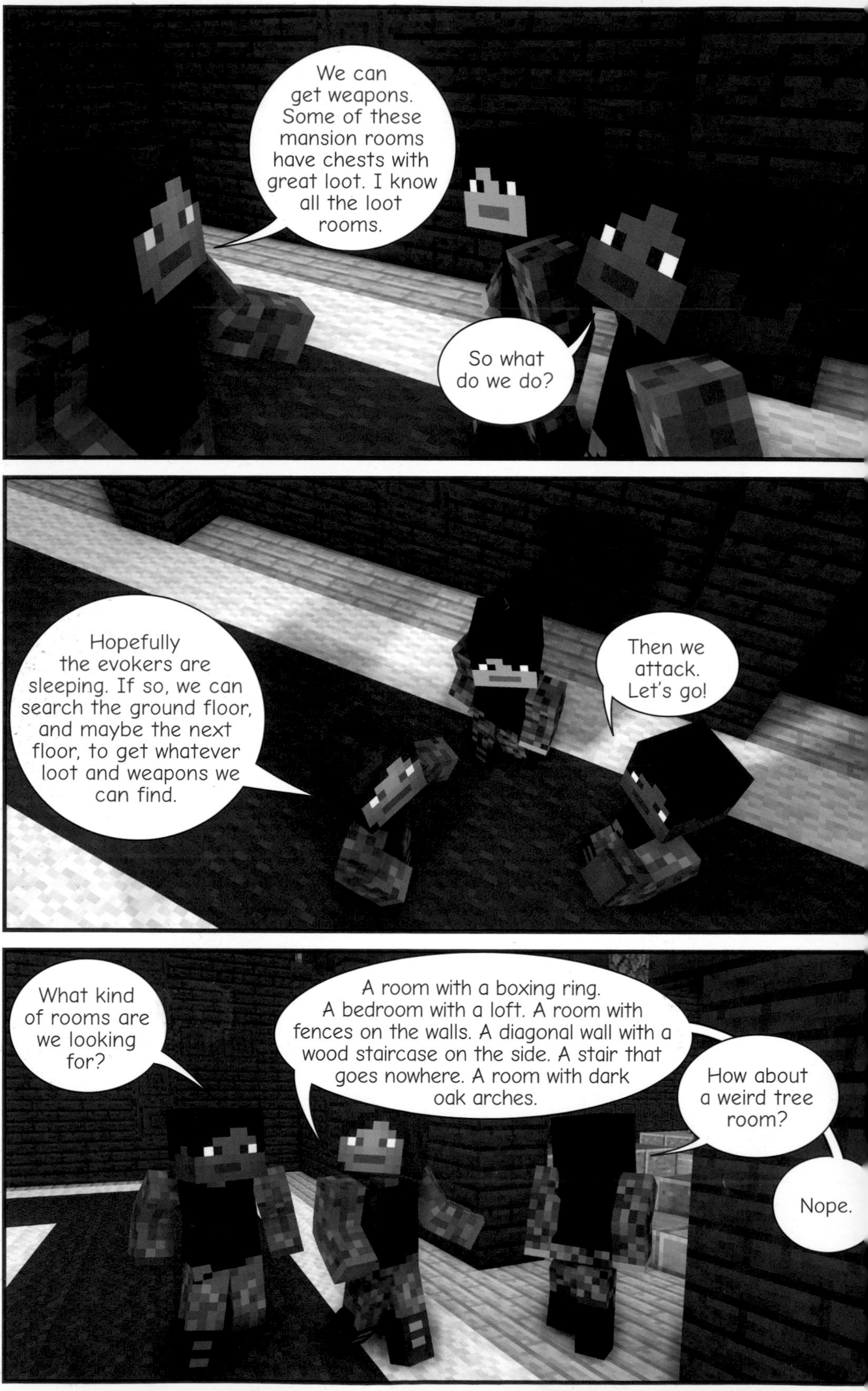
We can get weapons. Some of these mansion rooms have chests with great loot. I know all the loot rooms.
So what do we do?
Hopefully the evokers are sleeping. If so, we can search the ground floor, and maybe the next floor, to get whatever loot and weapons we can find.
Then we attack. Let's go!
What kind of rooms are we looking for?
A room with a boxing ring. A bedroom with a loft. A room with fences on the walls. A diagonal wall with a wood staircase on the side. A stair that goes nowhere. A room with dark oak arches.
How about a weird tree room?
Nope.

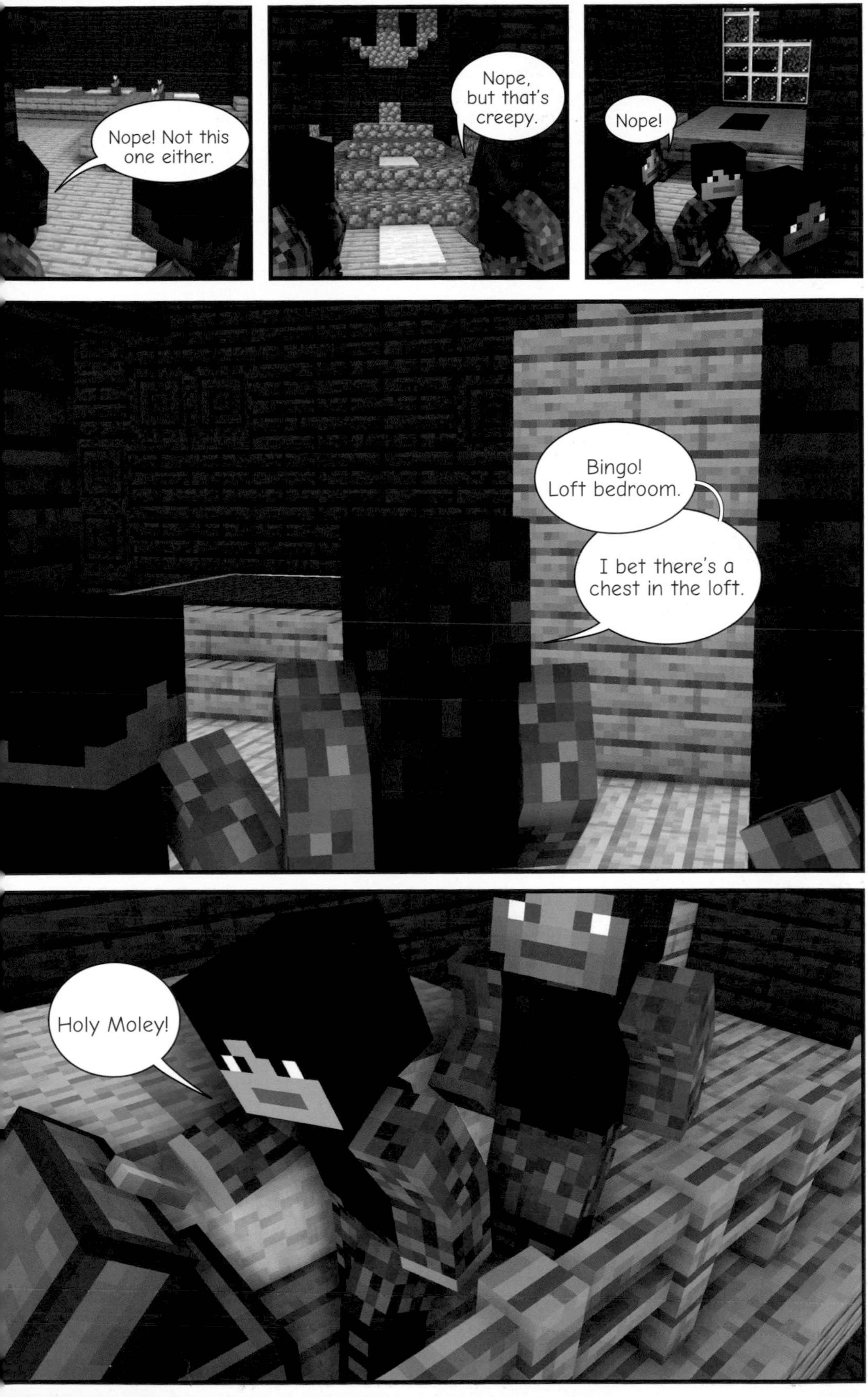
Nope! Not this one either.
Nope, but that's creepy.
Nope!
Bingo! Loft bedroom.
I bet there's a chest in the loft.
Holy Moley!

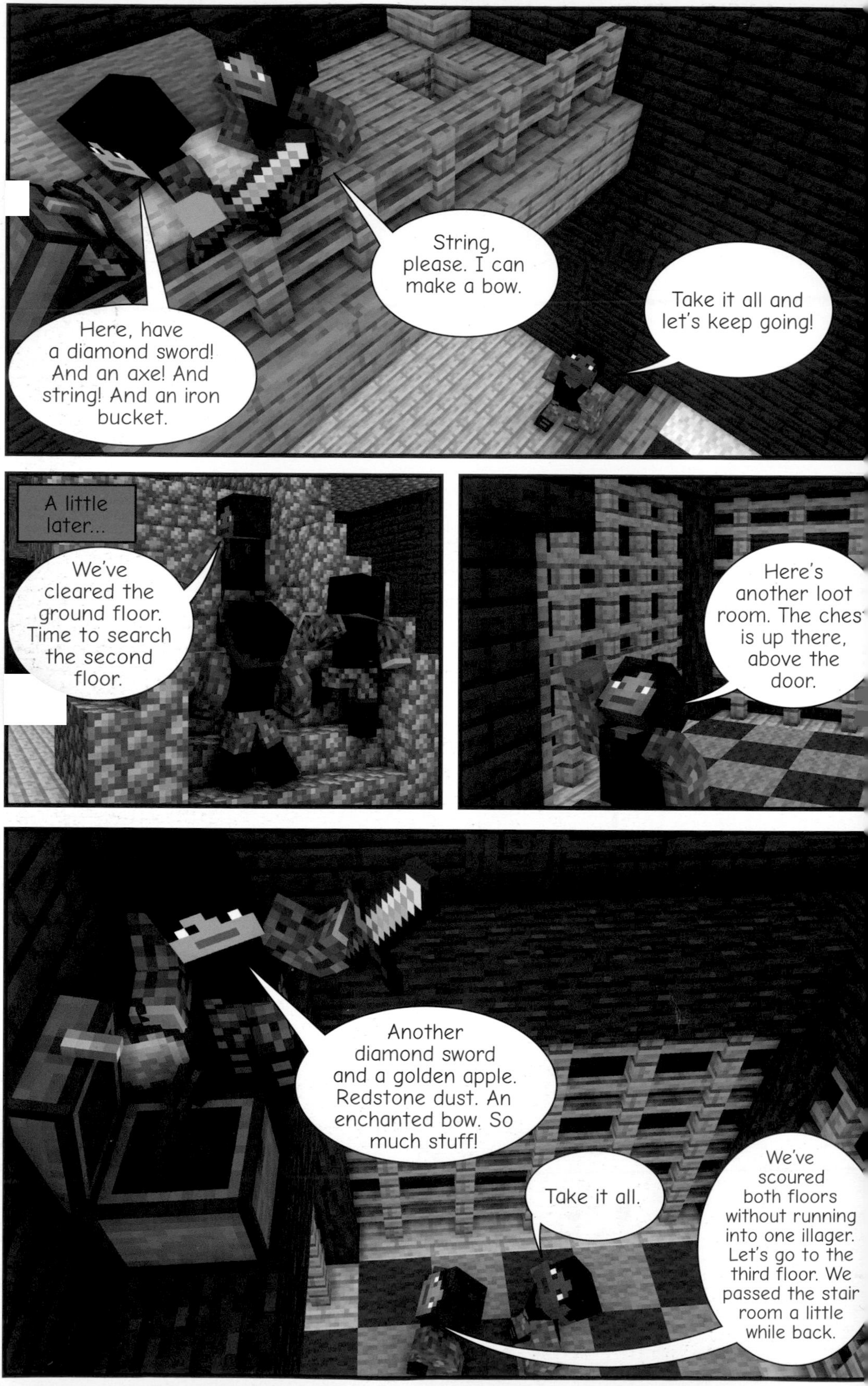

Here, have a diamond sword! And an axe! And string! And an iron bucket.
String, please. I can make a bow.
Take it all and let's keep going!
A little later...
We've cleared the ground floor. Time to search the second floor.
Here's another loot room. The ches is up there, above the door.
Another diamond sword and a golden apple. Redstone dust. An enchanted bow. So much stuff!
Take it all.
We've scoured both floors without running into one illager. Let's go to the third floor. We passed the stair room a little while back.

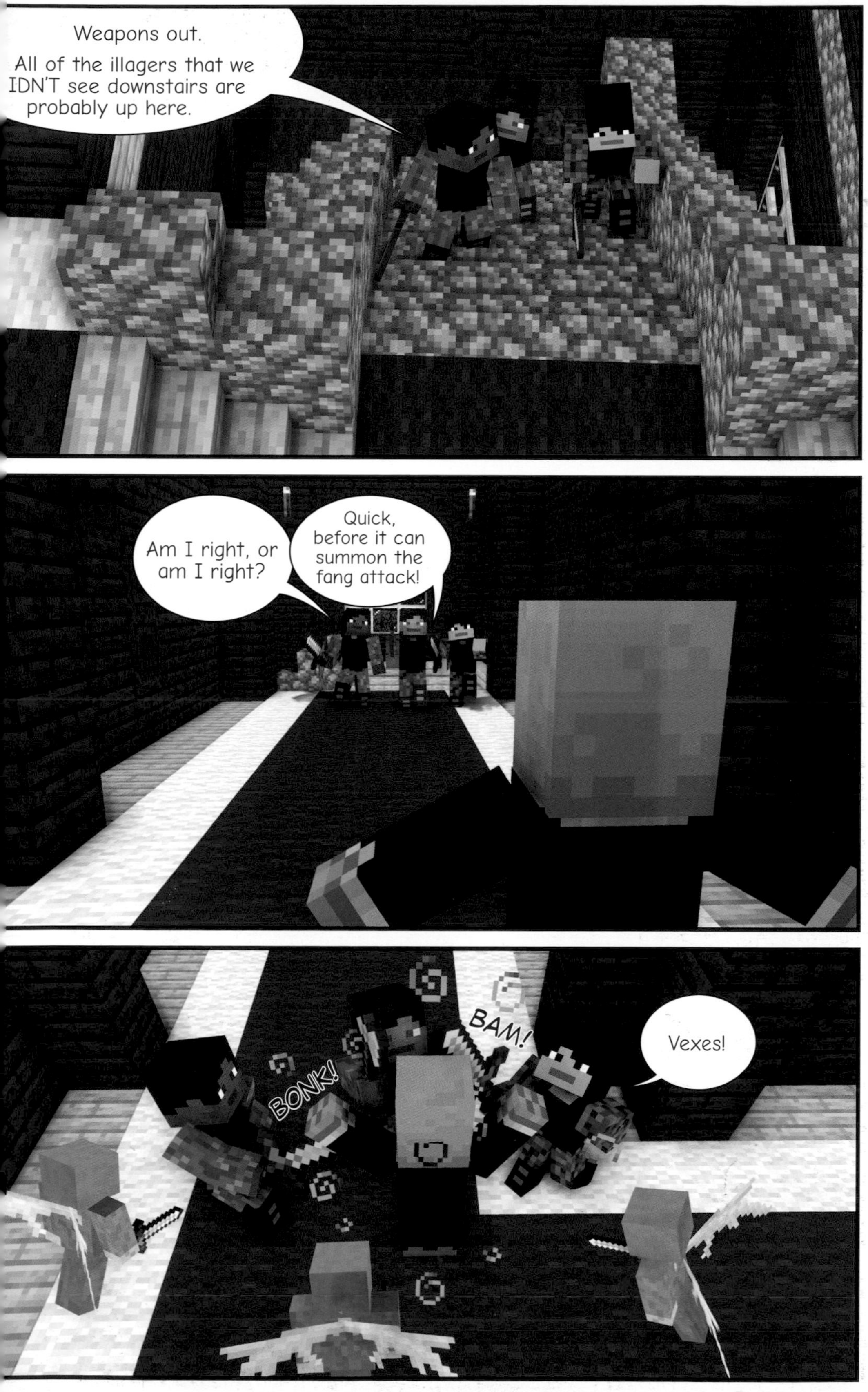
Weapons out.
All of the illagers that we IDN'T see downstairs are probably up here.
Am I right, or am I right?
Quick, before it can summon the fang attack!
BONK!
BAM!
Vexes!

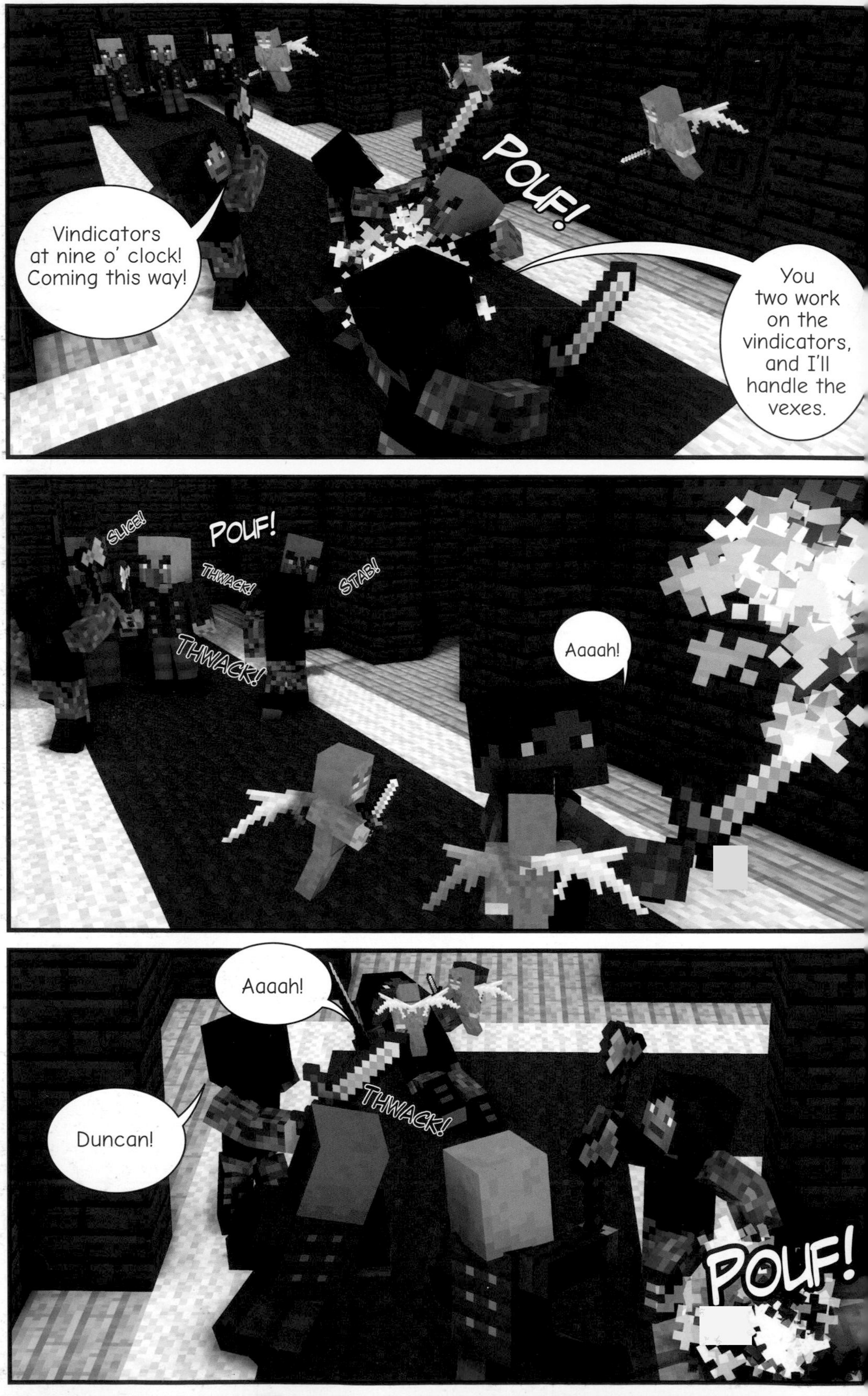
Vindicators at nine o' clock! Coming this way!
POUF!
You two work on the vindicators, and I'll handle the vexes.
SLICE!
POUF!
THWACK!
STAB!
THWACK!
Aaaah!
Aaaah!
THWACK!
Duncan!
POUF!

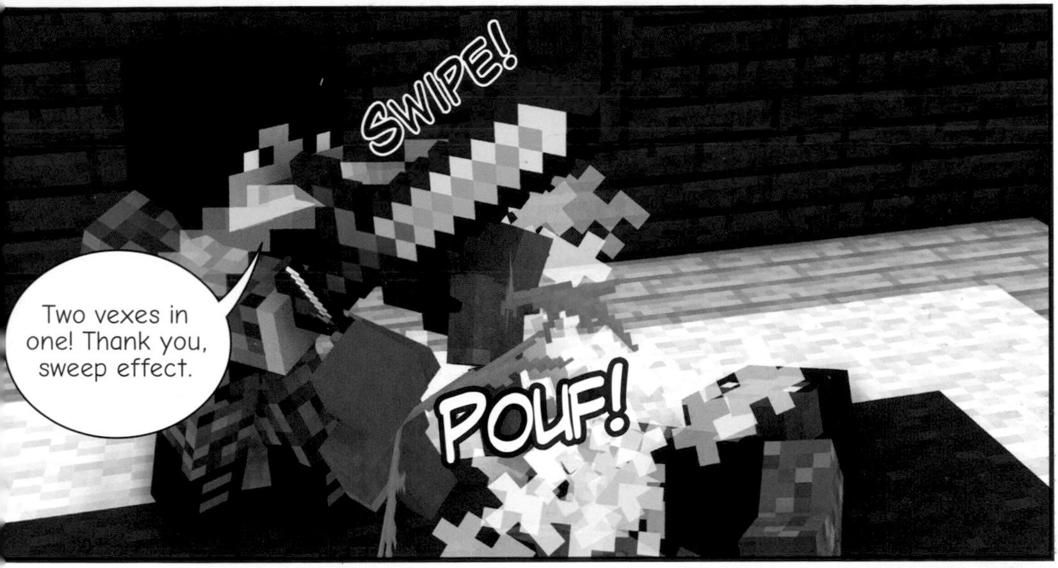
SWIPE!
Two vexes in one! Thank you, sweep effect.
POUF!

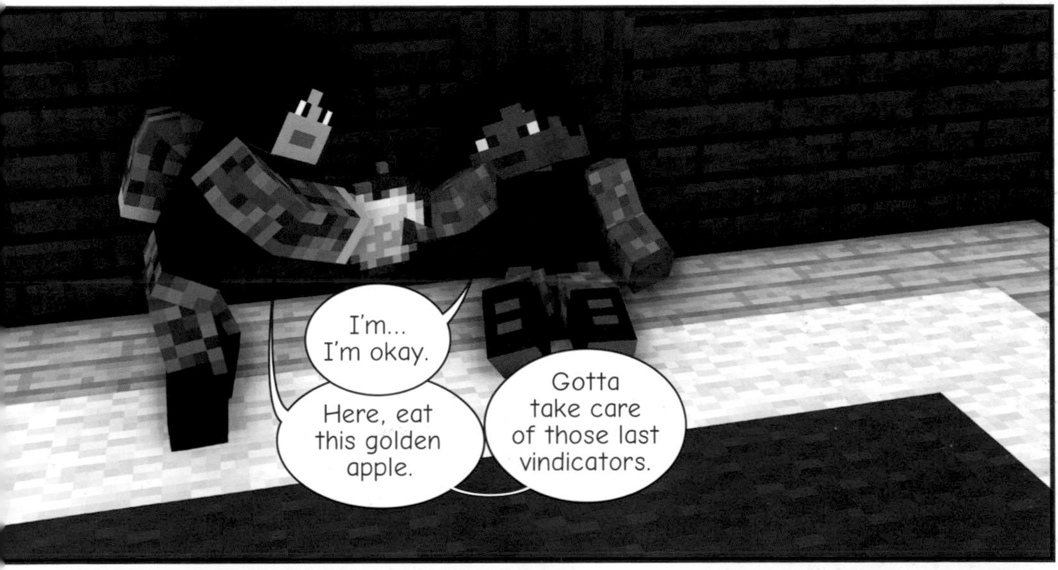
I'm... I'm okay.
Here, eat this golden apple.
Gotta take care of those last vindicators.

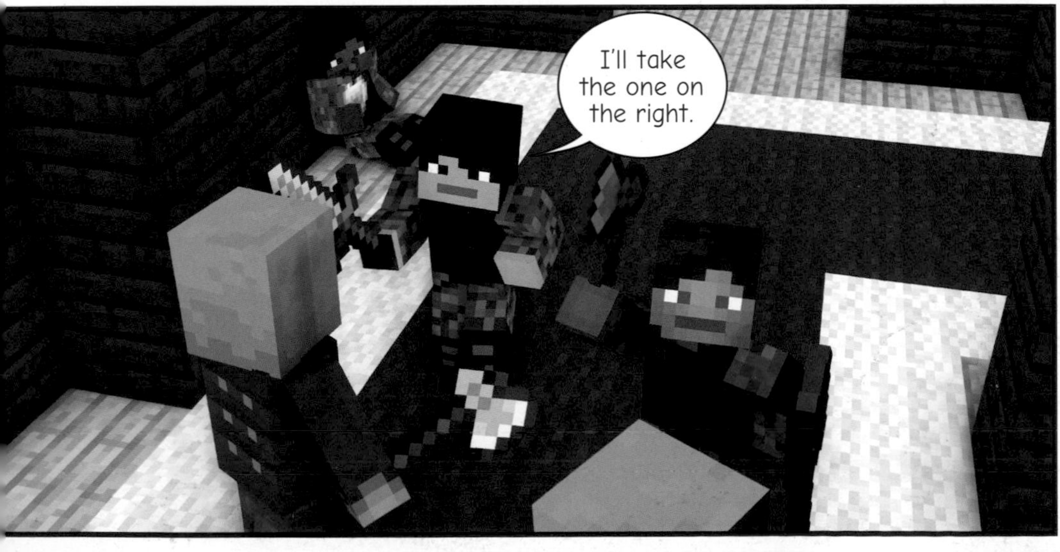
I'll take the one on the right.

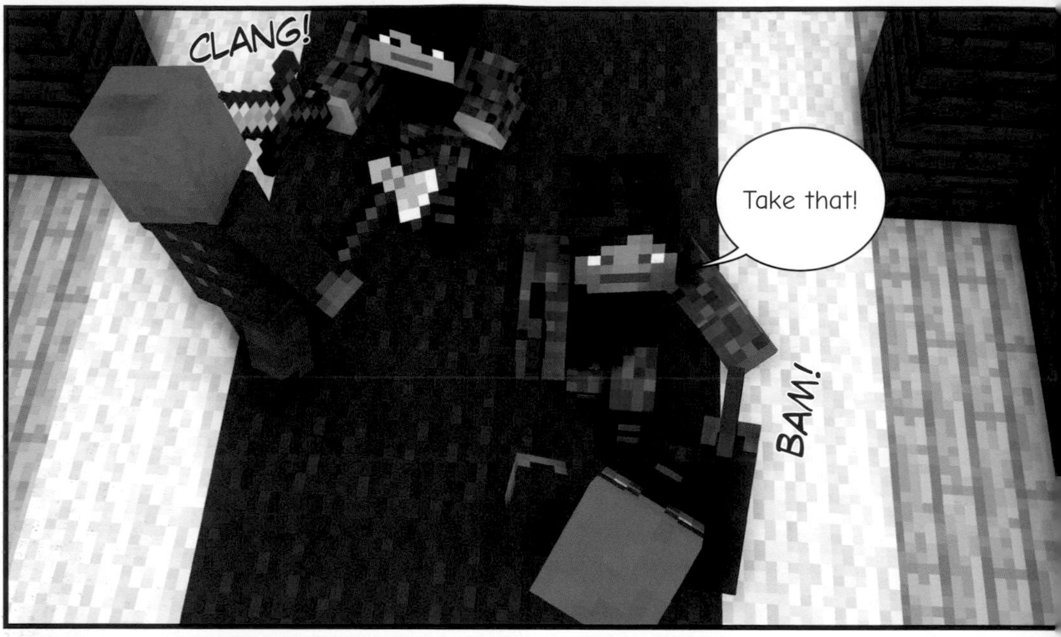
CLANG!
Take that!
BAM!

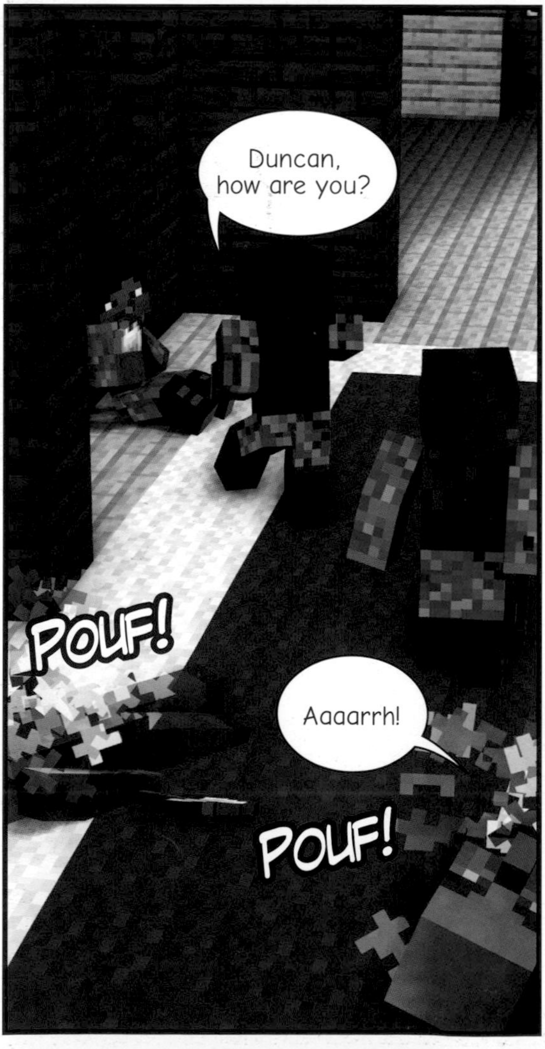
Duncan, how are you?
POUF!
Aaaarrh!
POUF!

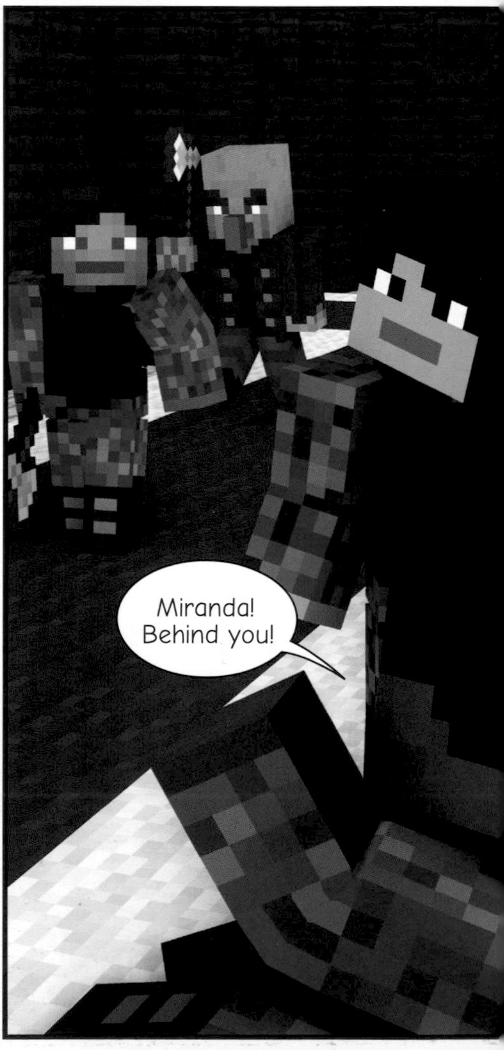
Miranda! Behind you!

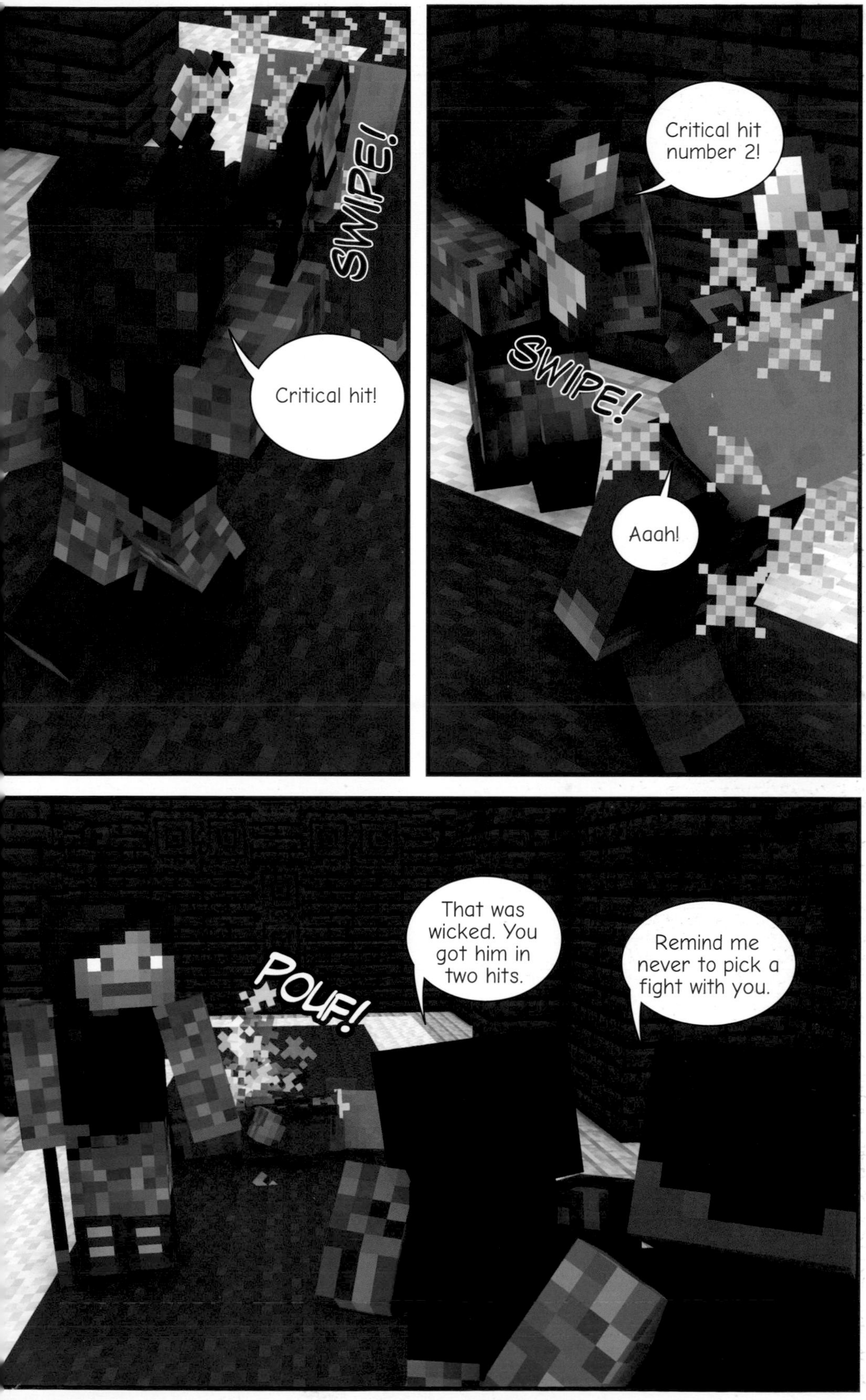
SWIPE!
Critical hit!
Critical hit number 2!
SWIPE!
Aaah!
POUF!
That was wicked. You got him in two hits.
Remind me never to pick a fight with you.

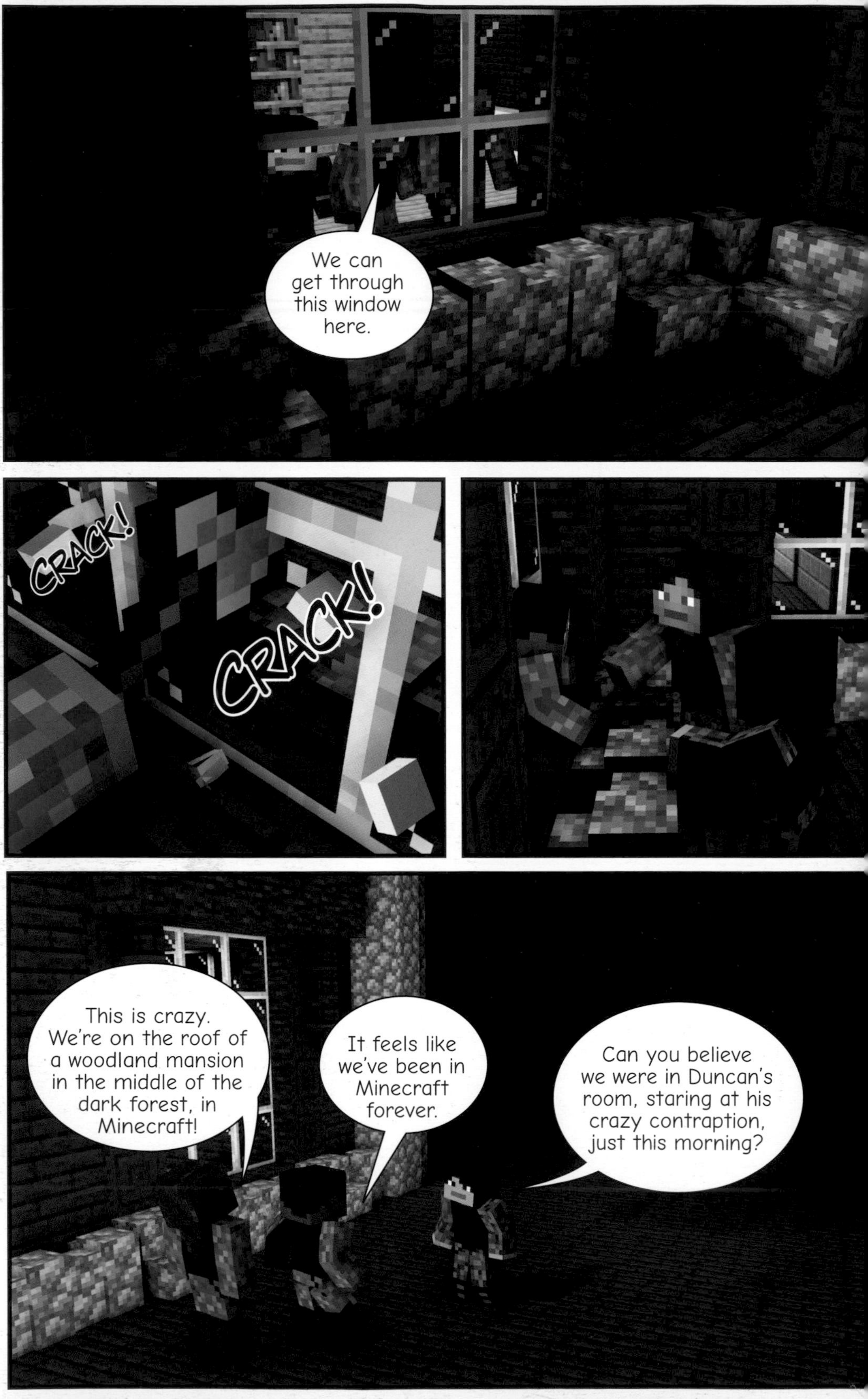
We can get through this window here.
CRACK!
CRACK!
This is crazy. We're on the roof of a woodland mansion in the middle of the dark forest, in Minecraft!
It feels like we've been in Minecraft forever.
Can you believe we were in Duncan's room, staring at his crazy contraption, just this morning?

Chapter 5:
Back to the
Beginning

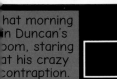

hat morning
in Duncan's
room, staring
at his crazy
contraption.

Select World

You guys
ready?

You sure
this is going
to work?

3, 2, 1.

Glitch World 1
Glitch World 1 (4/5/22, 10:37 AM)
Creative Mode, Cheats, Version: 1.18.2

Redstone
Redstone (4/5/22, 10:27 AM)
Creative Mode, Cheats, Version: 1.18.2

Glitch test
Glitch test (4/5/22, 10:19 AM)
Creative Mode, Cheats, Version: 1.18.2

Snapshots

Play Selected World   **Create New World**

Edit   Delete   Re-Create   Cancel

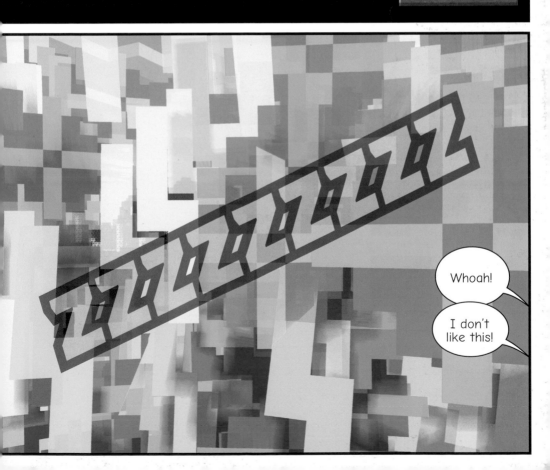

Whoah!

I don't
like this!

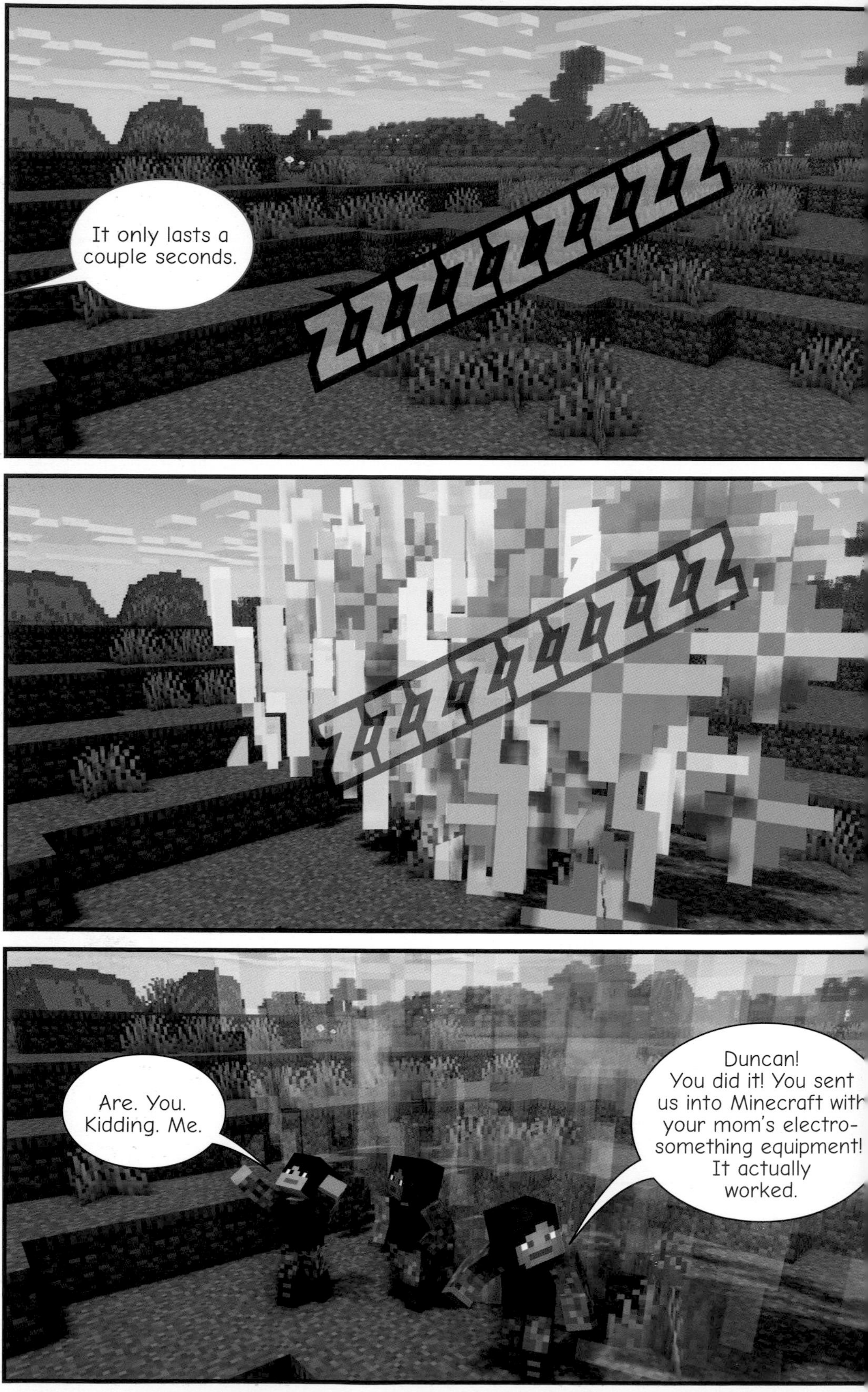

It only lasts a couple seconds.
ZZZZZZZZZZ
ZZZZZZZZZZ
Are. You. Kidding. Me.
Duncan! You did it! You sent us into Minecraft with your mom's electro-something equipment! It actually worked.

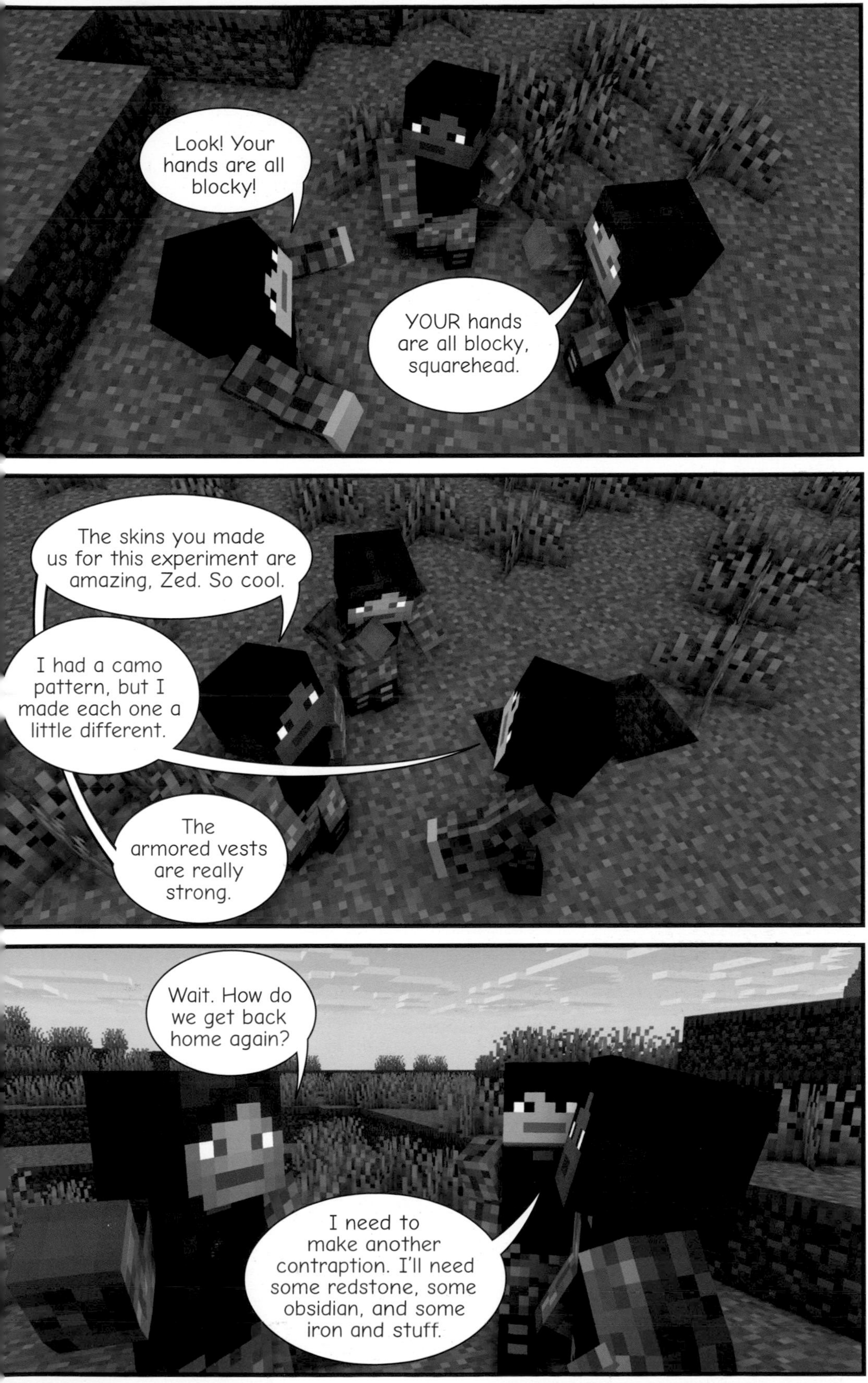
Look! Your hands are all blocky!
YOUR hands are all blocky, squarehead.
The skins you made us for this experiment are amazing, Zed. So cool.
I had a camo pattern, but I made each one a little different.
The armored vests are really strong.
Wait. How do we get back home again?
I need to make another contraption. I'll need some redstone, some obsidian, and some iron and stuff.

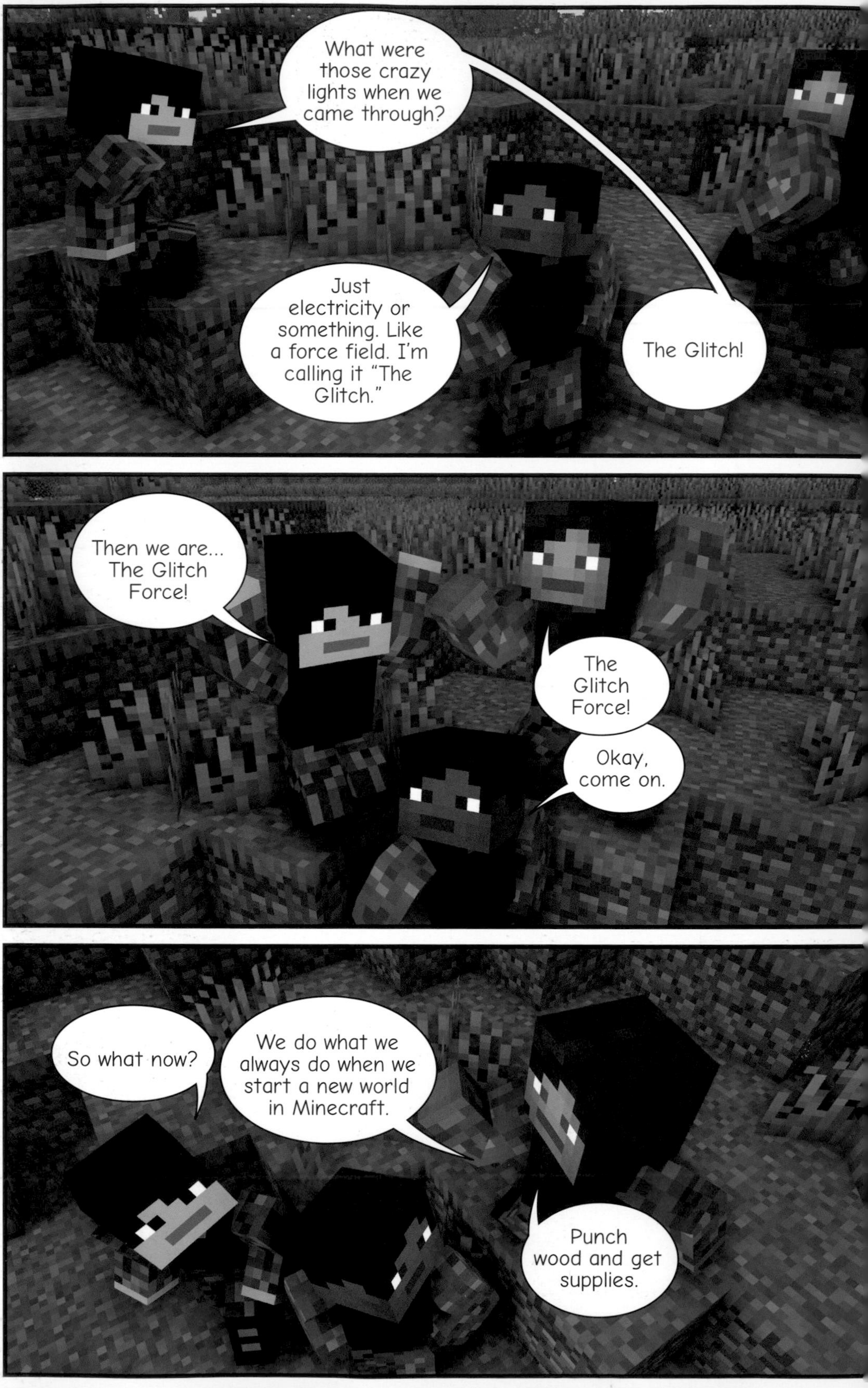
What were those crazy lights when we came through?
Just electricity or something. Like a force field. I'm calling it "The Glitch."
The Glitch!
Then we are... The Glitch Force!
The Glitch Force!
Okay, come on.
So what now?
We do what we always do when we start a new world in Minecraft.
Punch wood and get supplies.

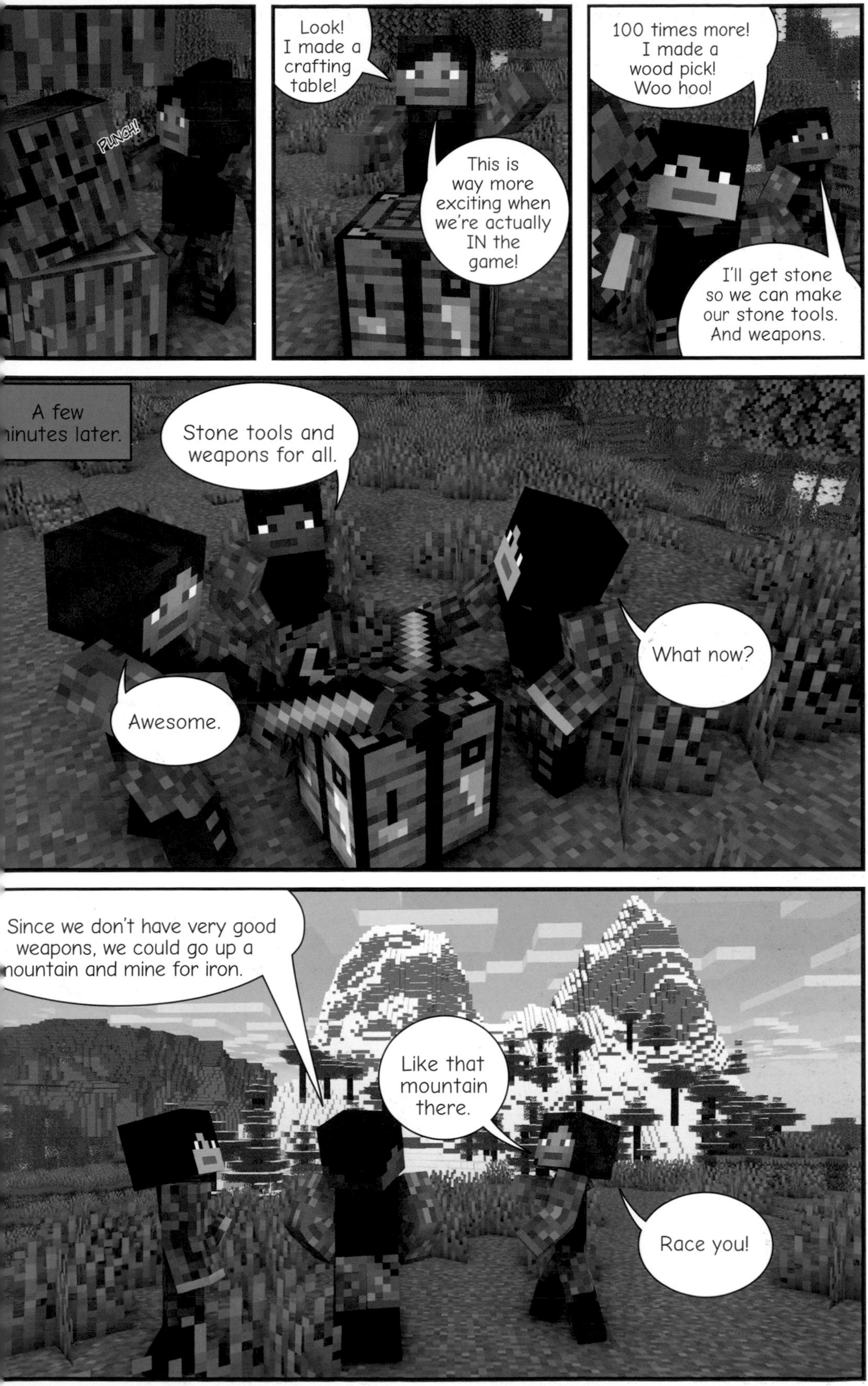
PUNCH!!
Look! I made a crafting table!
This is way more exciting when we're actually IN the game!
100 times more! I made a wood pick! Woo hoo!
I'll get stone so we can make our stone tools. And weapons.
A few
inutes later.
Stone tools and weapons for all.
Awesome.
What now?
Since we don't have very good weapons, we could go up a
nountain and mine for iron.
Like that mountain there.
Race you!

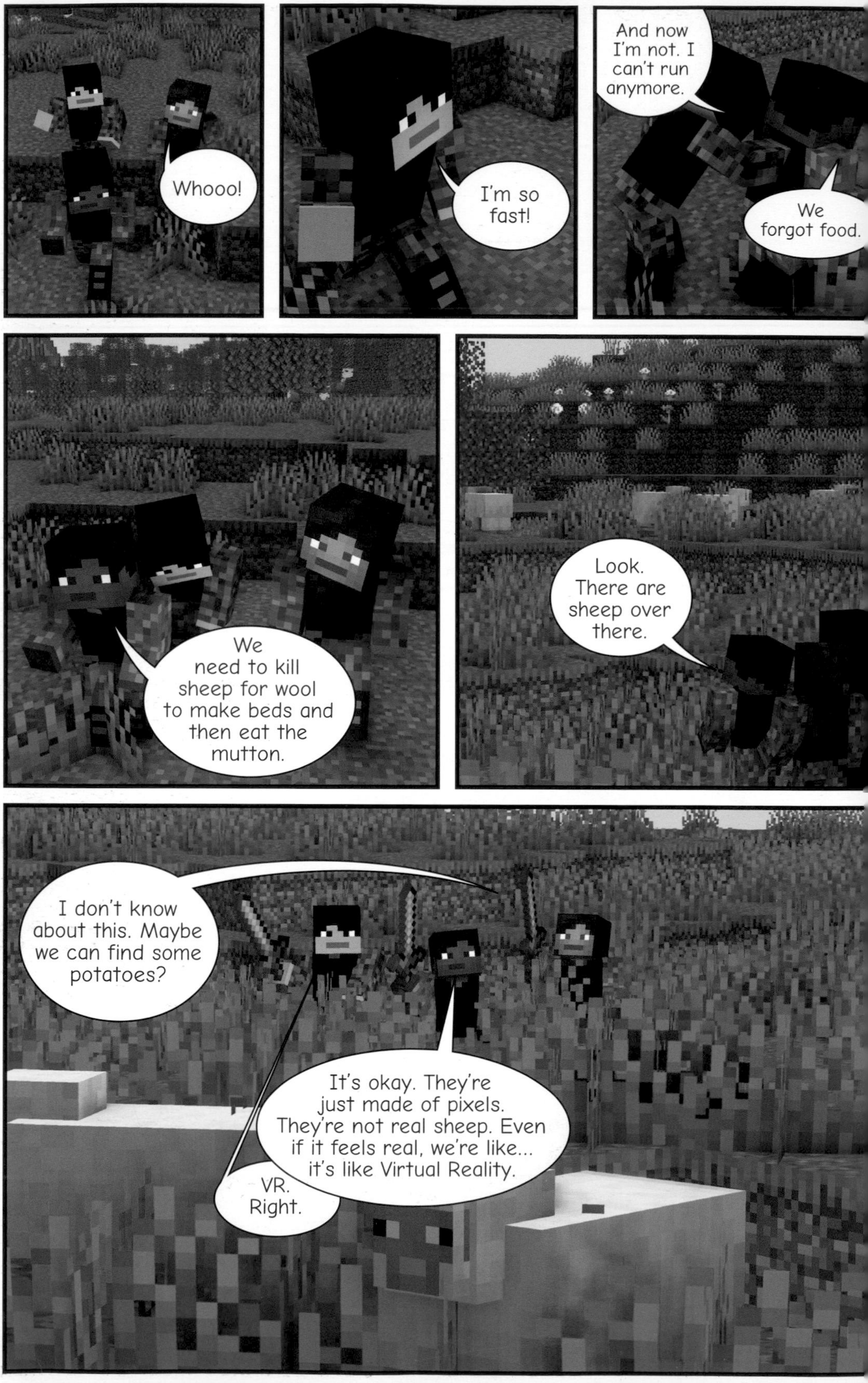
Whooo!
I'm so fast!
And now I'm not. I can't run anymore.
We forgot food.
We need to kill sheep for wool to make beds and then eat the mutton.
Look. There are sheep over there.
I don't know about this. Maybe we can find some potatoes?
It's okay. They're just made of pixels. They're not real sheep. Even if it feels real, we're like... it's like Virtual Reality.
VR. Right.

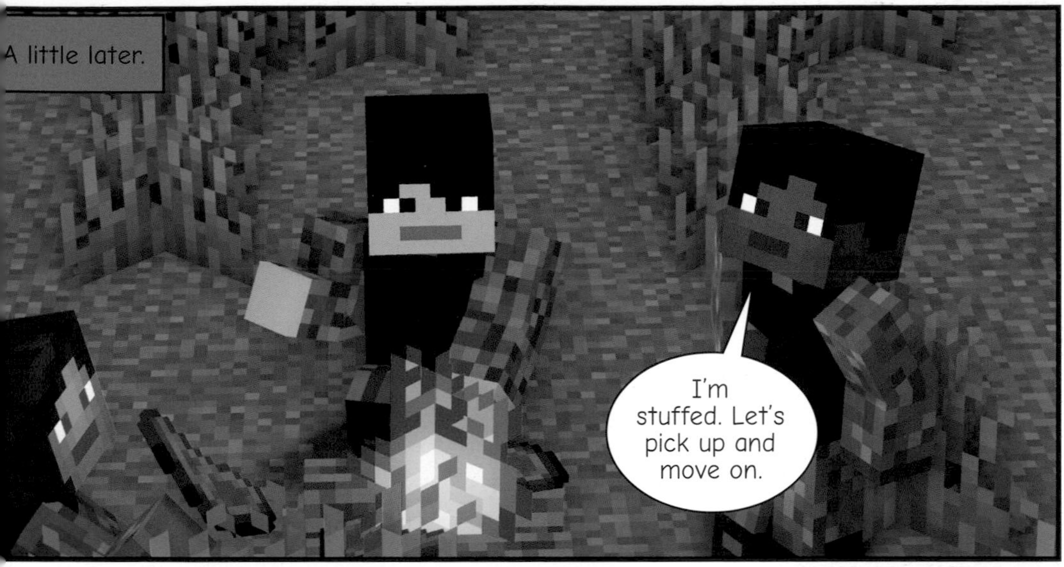
A little later.
I'm stuffed. Let's pick up and move on.
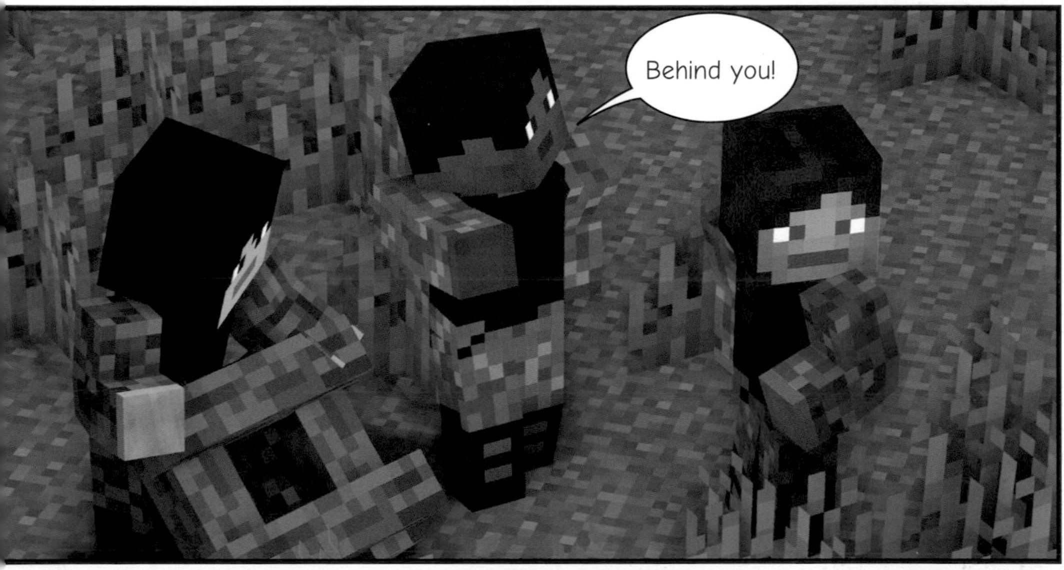
Behind you!
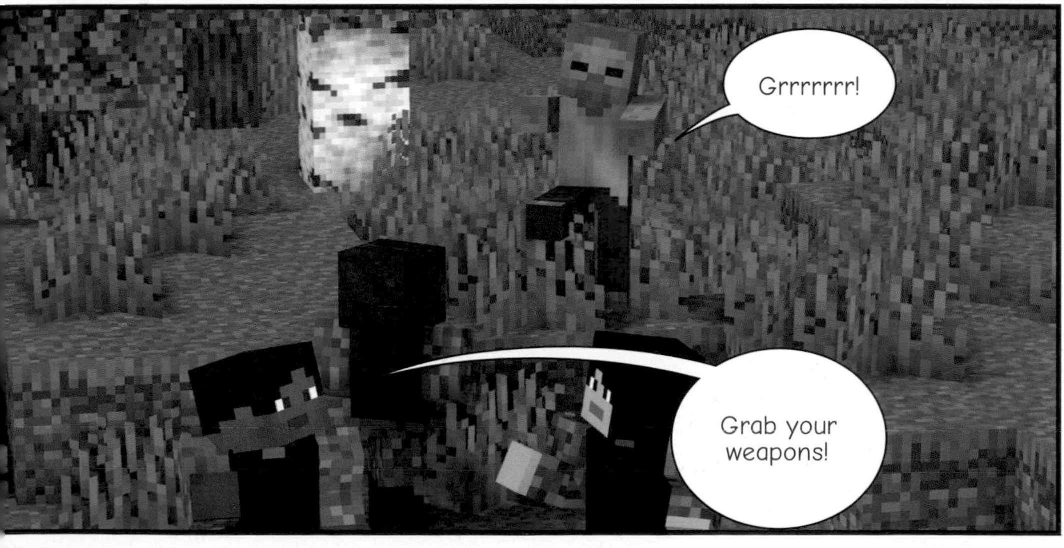
Grrrrrrr!
Grab your weapons!

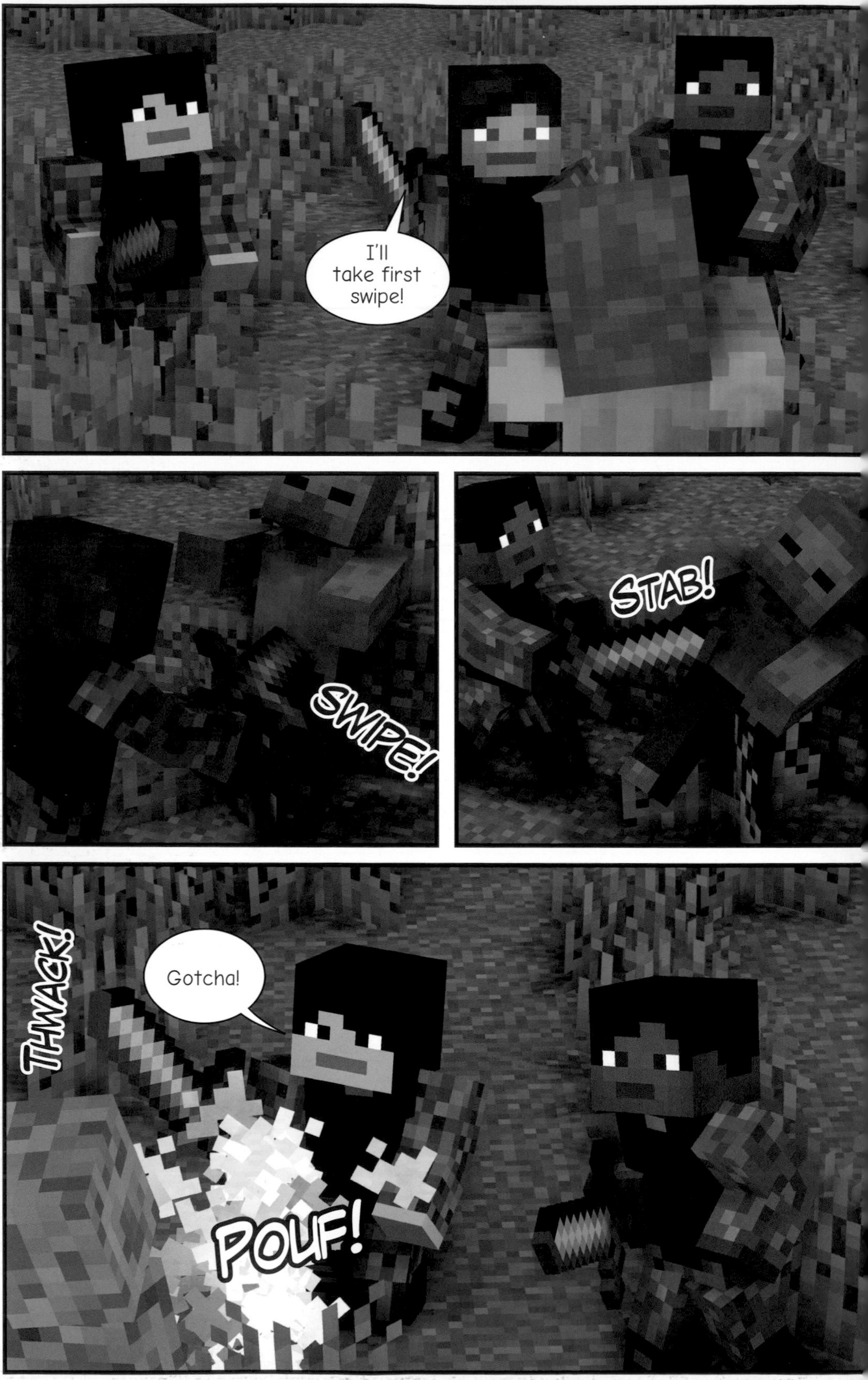
I'll take first swipe!
SWIPE!
STAB!
THWACK!
Gotcha!
POUF!

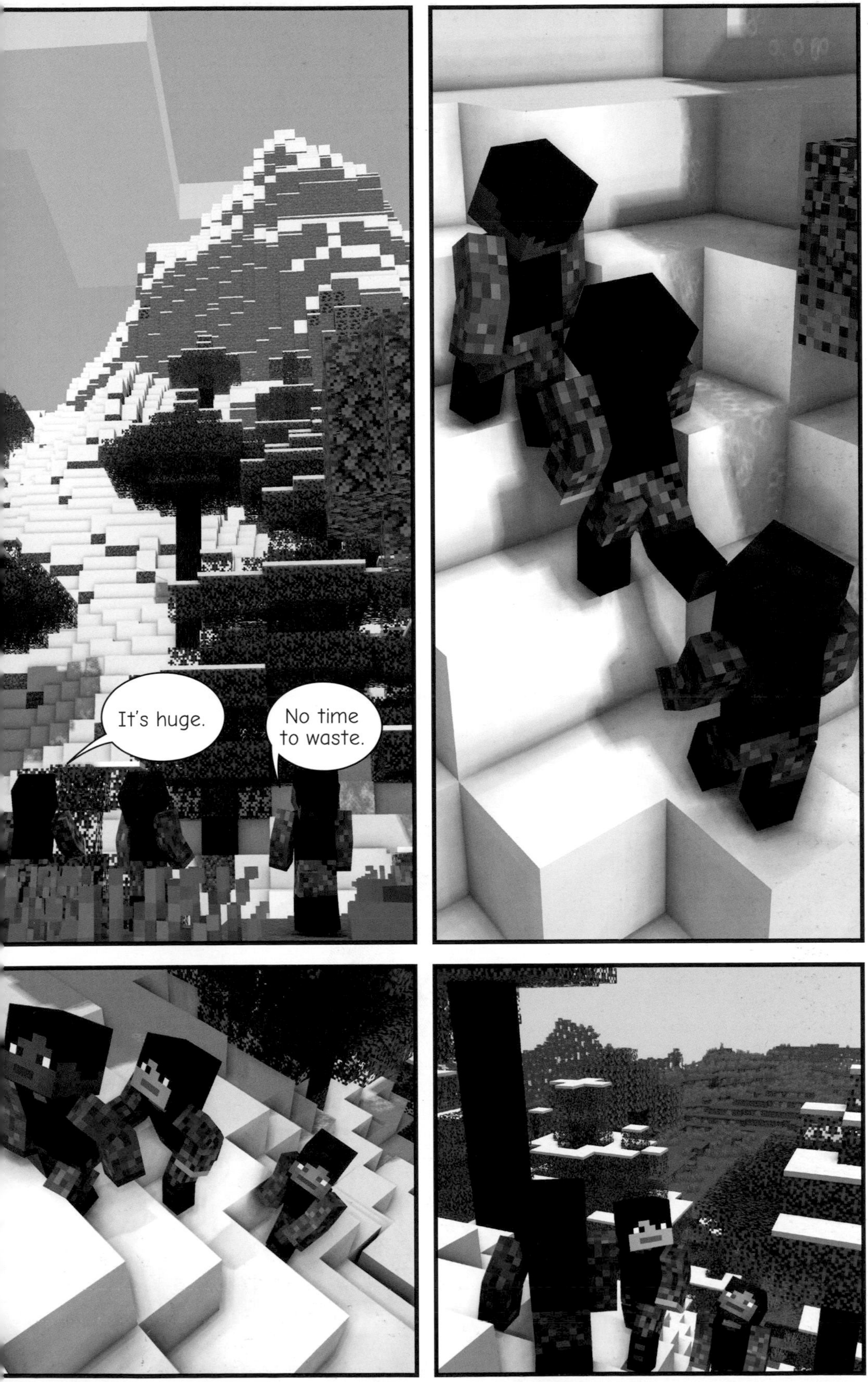
It's huge.
No time to waste.

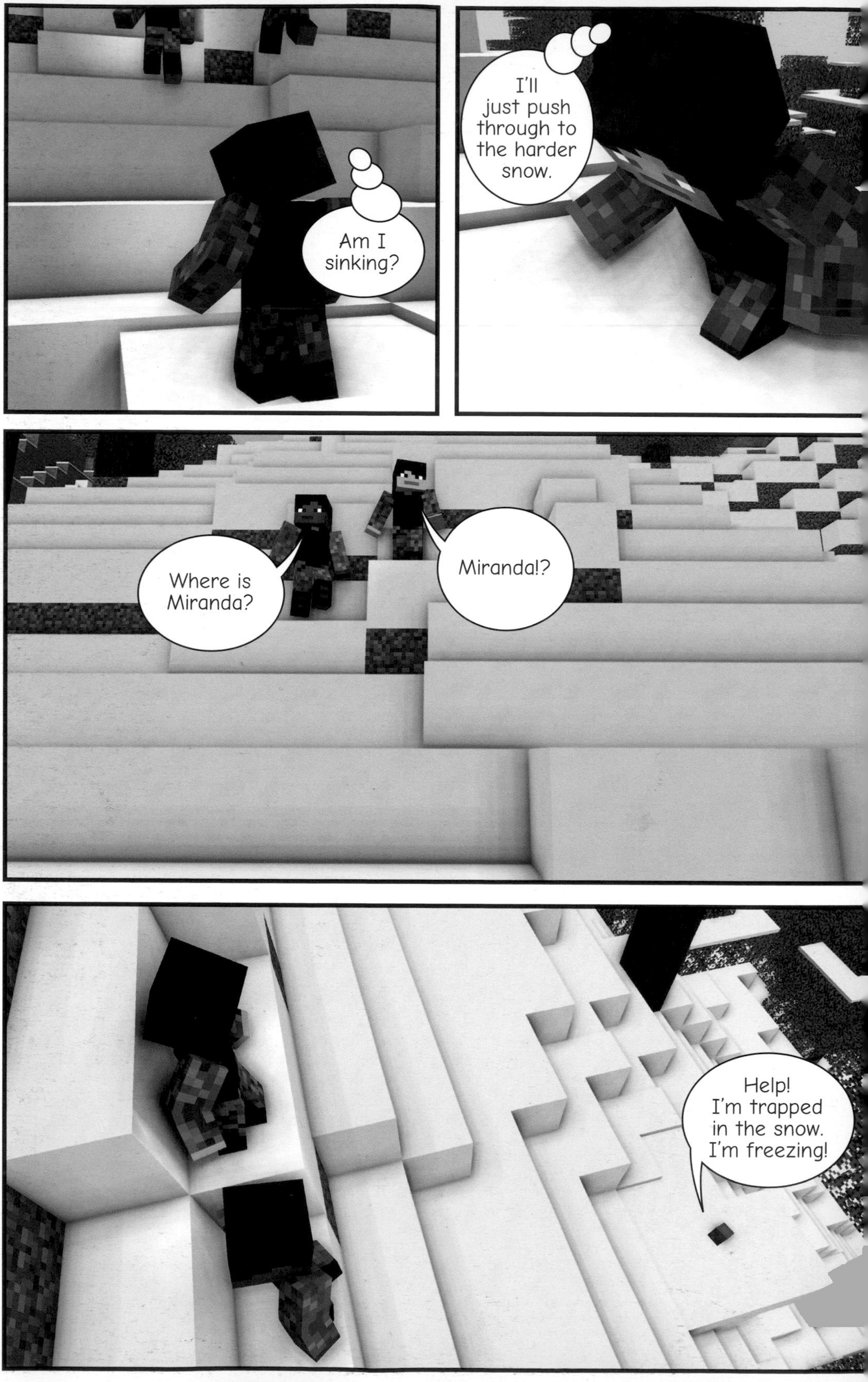
Am I sinking?
I'll just push through to the harder snow.
Where is Miranda?
Miranda!?
Help! I'm trapped in the snow. I'm freezing!

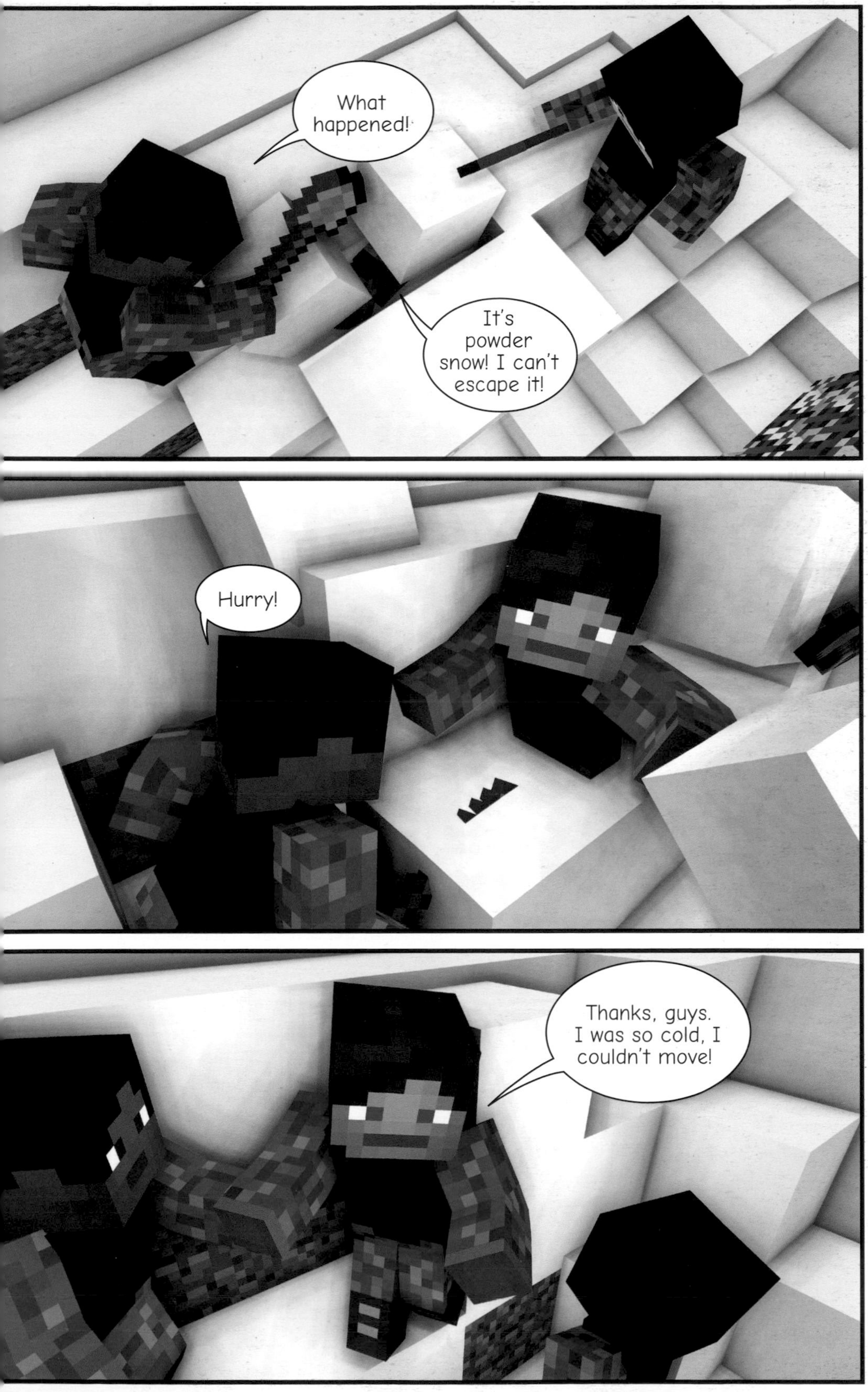
What happened!
It's powder snow! I can't escape it!
Hurry!
Thanks, guys. I was so cold, I couldn't move!

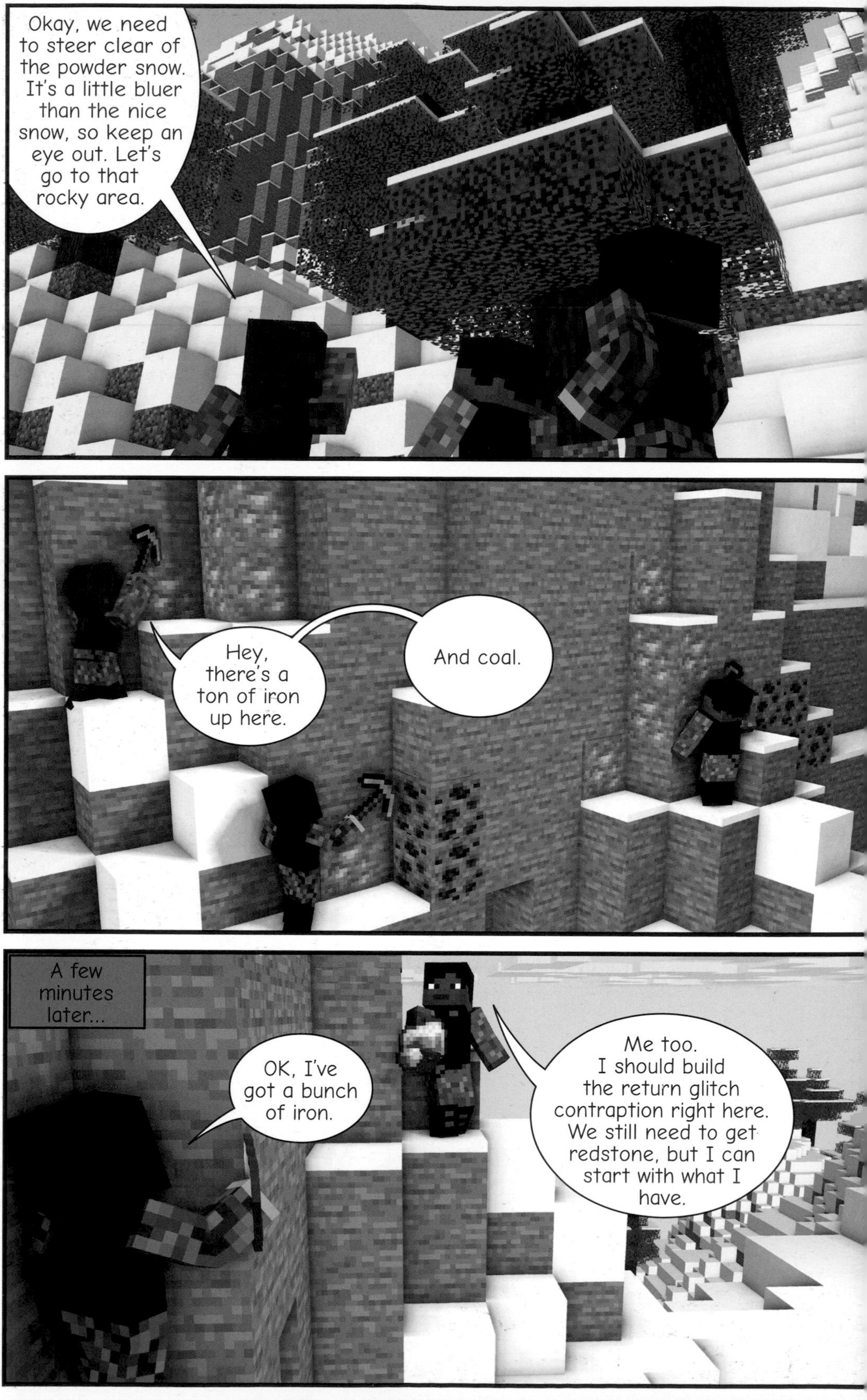
Okay, we need to steer clear of the powder snow. It's a little bluer than the nice snow, so keep an eye out. Let's go to that rocky area.
Hey, there's a ton of iron up here.
And coal.
A few minutes later...
OK, I've got a bunch of iron.
Me too. I should build the return glitch contraption right here. We still need to get redstone, but I can start with what I have.

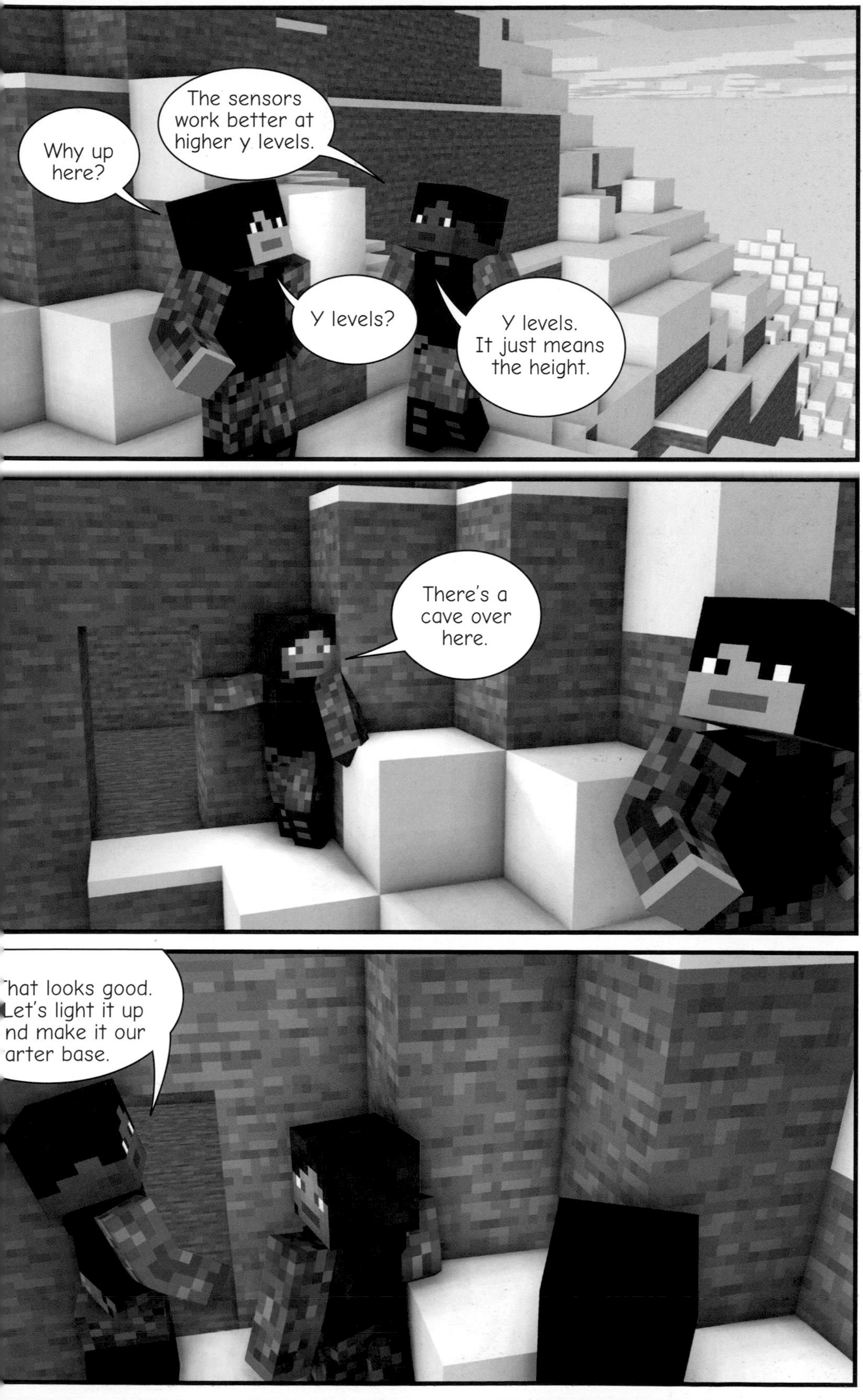

Why up here?
The sensors work better at higher y levels.
Y levels?
Y levels. It just means the height.
There's a cave over here.
hat looks good. et's light it up nd make it our arter base.

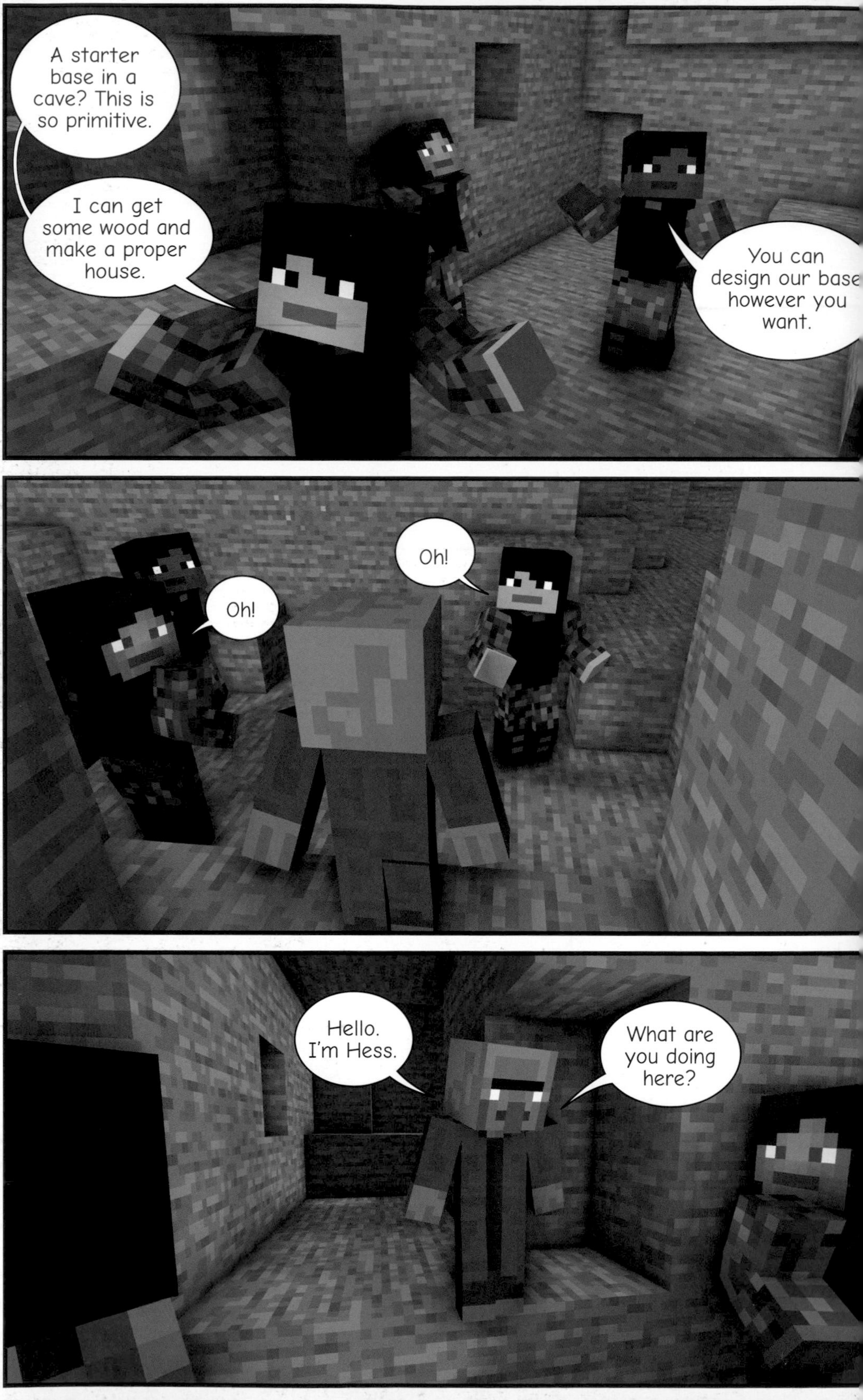
A starter base in a cave? This is so primitive.
I can get some wood and make a proper house.
You can design our base however you want.
Oh!
Oh!
Hello. I'm Hess.
What are you doing here?

CHAPTER 6:

HESS

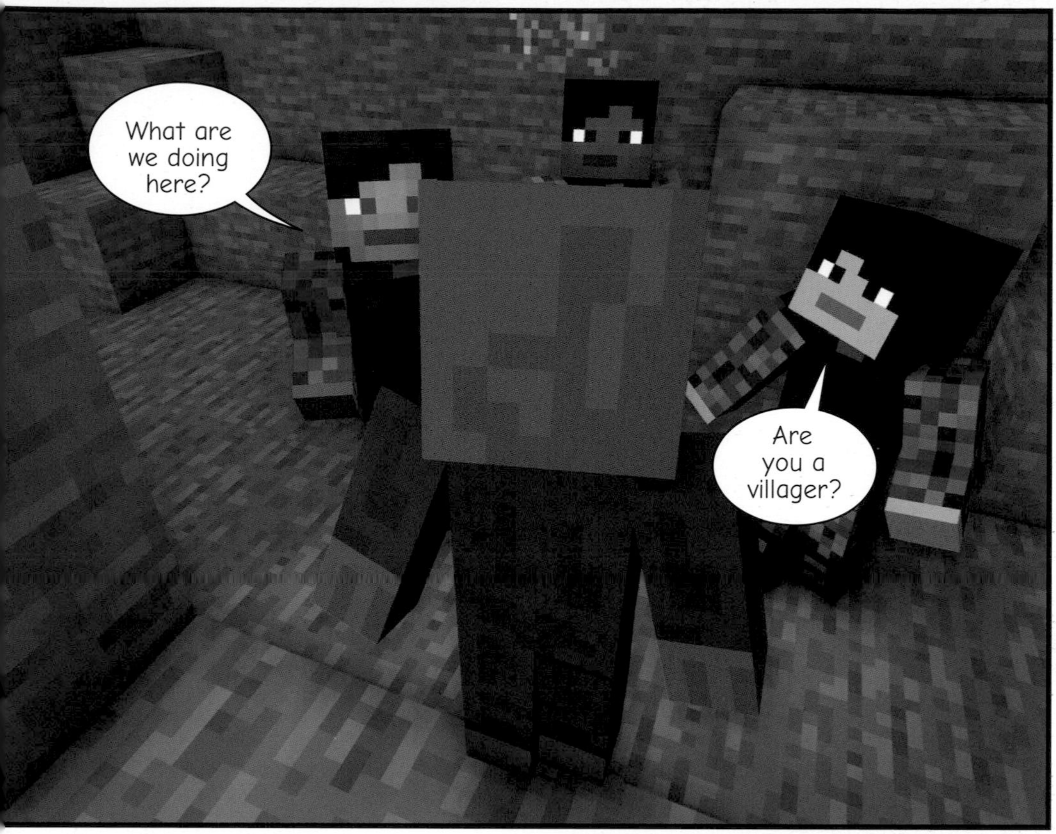
What are we doing here?
Are you a villager?

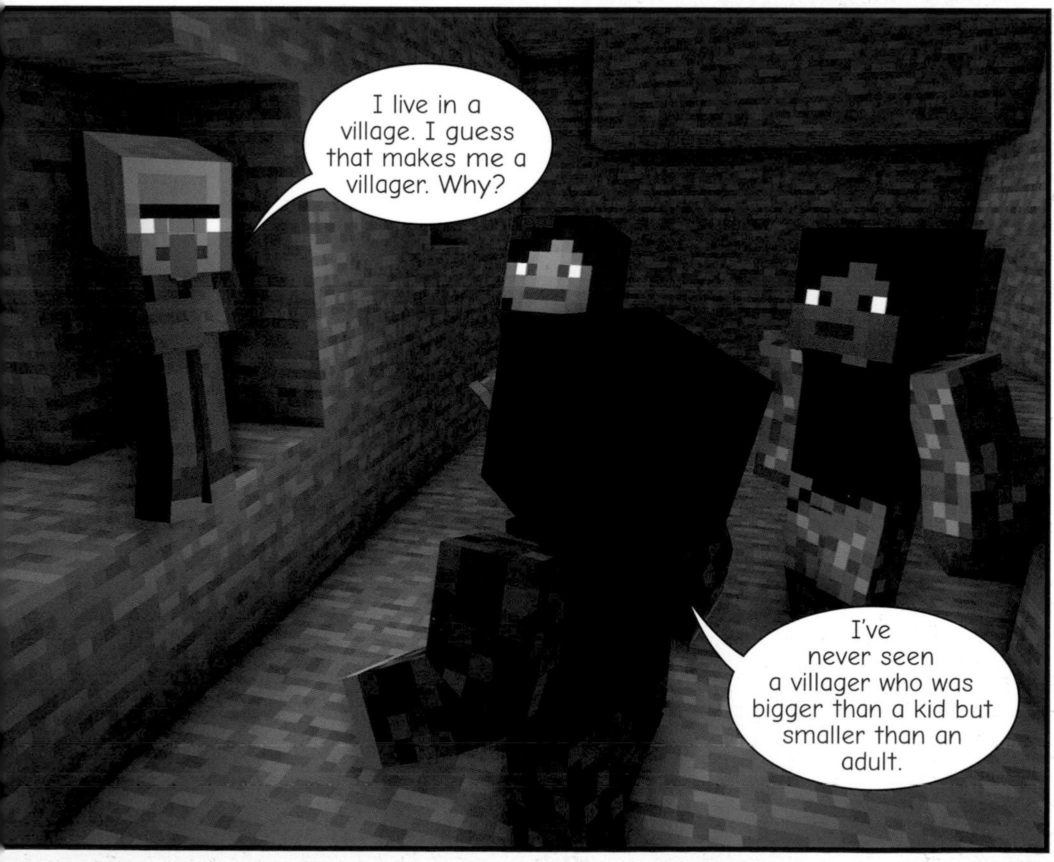
I live in a village. I guess that makes me a villager. Why?
I've never seen a villager who was bigger than a kid but smaller than an adult.

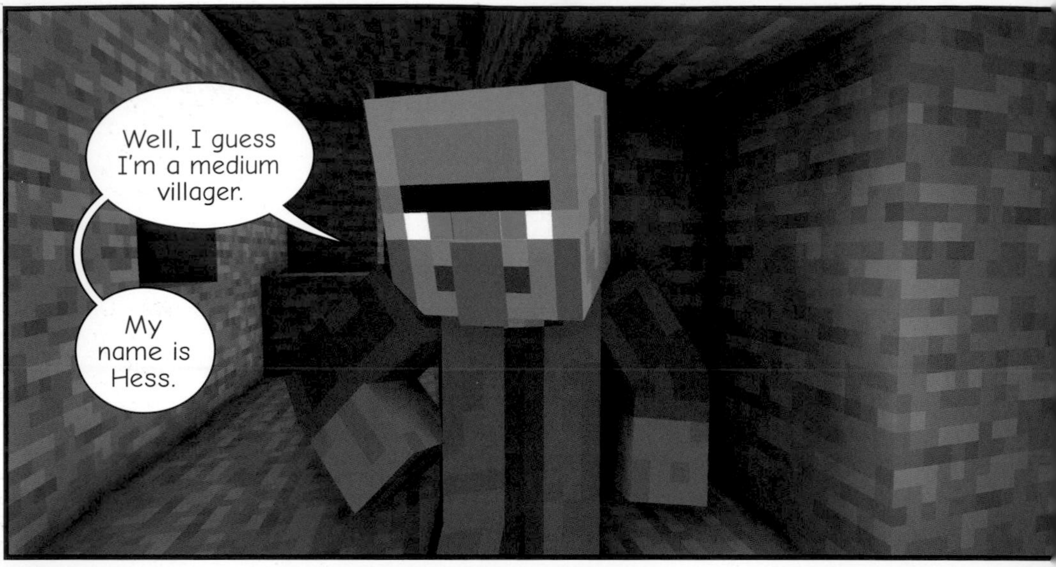
Well, I guess I'm a medium villager.
My name is Hess.

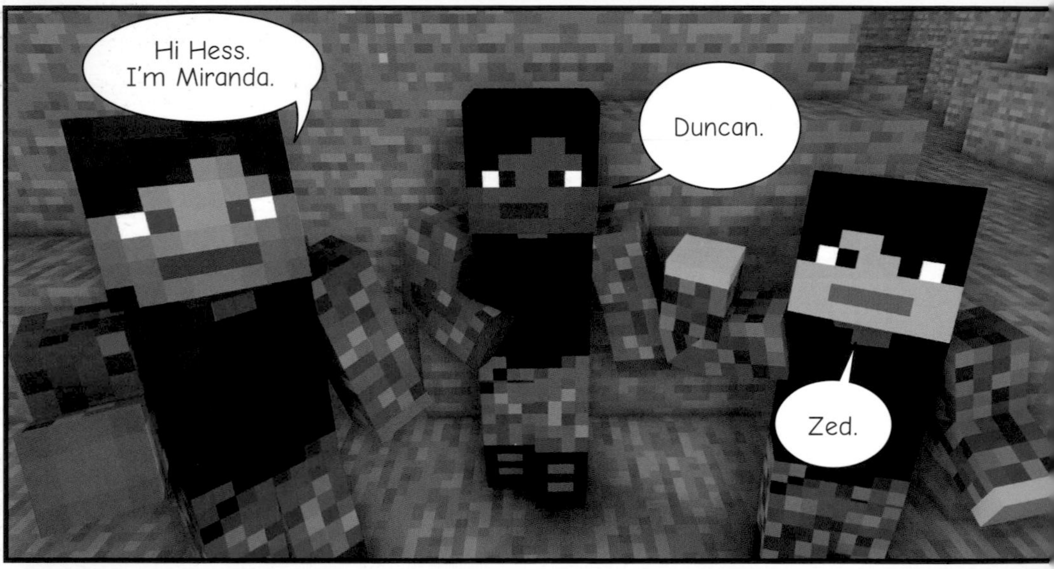
Hi Hess. I'm Miranda.
Duncan.
Zed.

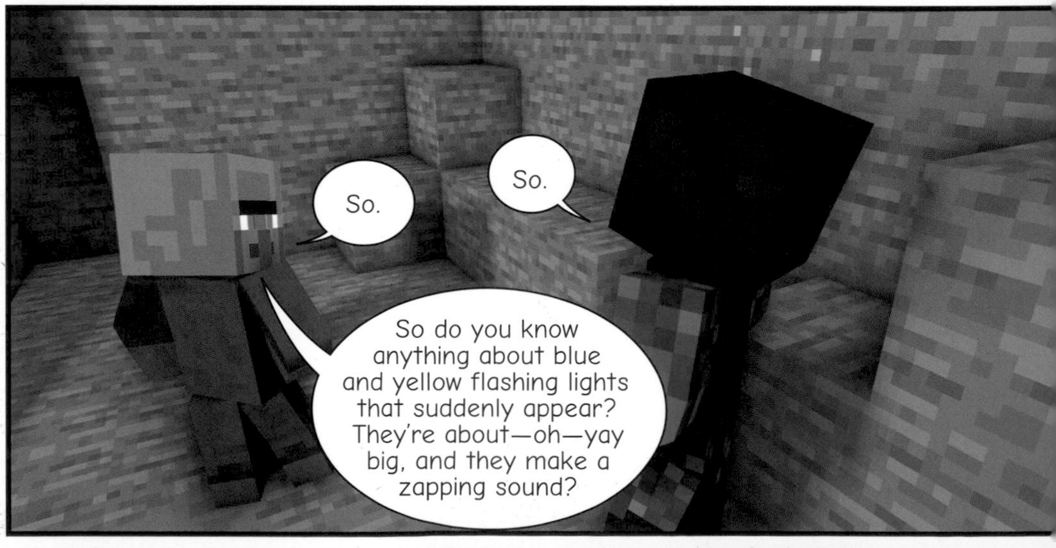
So.
So.
So do you know anything about blue and yellow flashing lights that suddenly appear? They're about—oh—yay big, and they make a zapping sound?

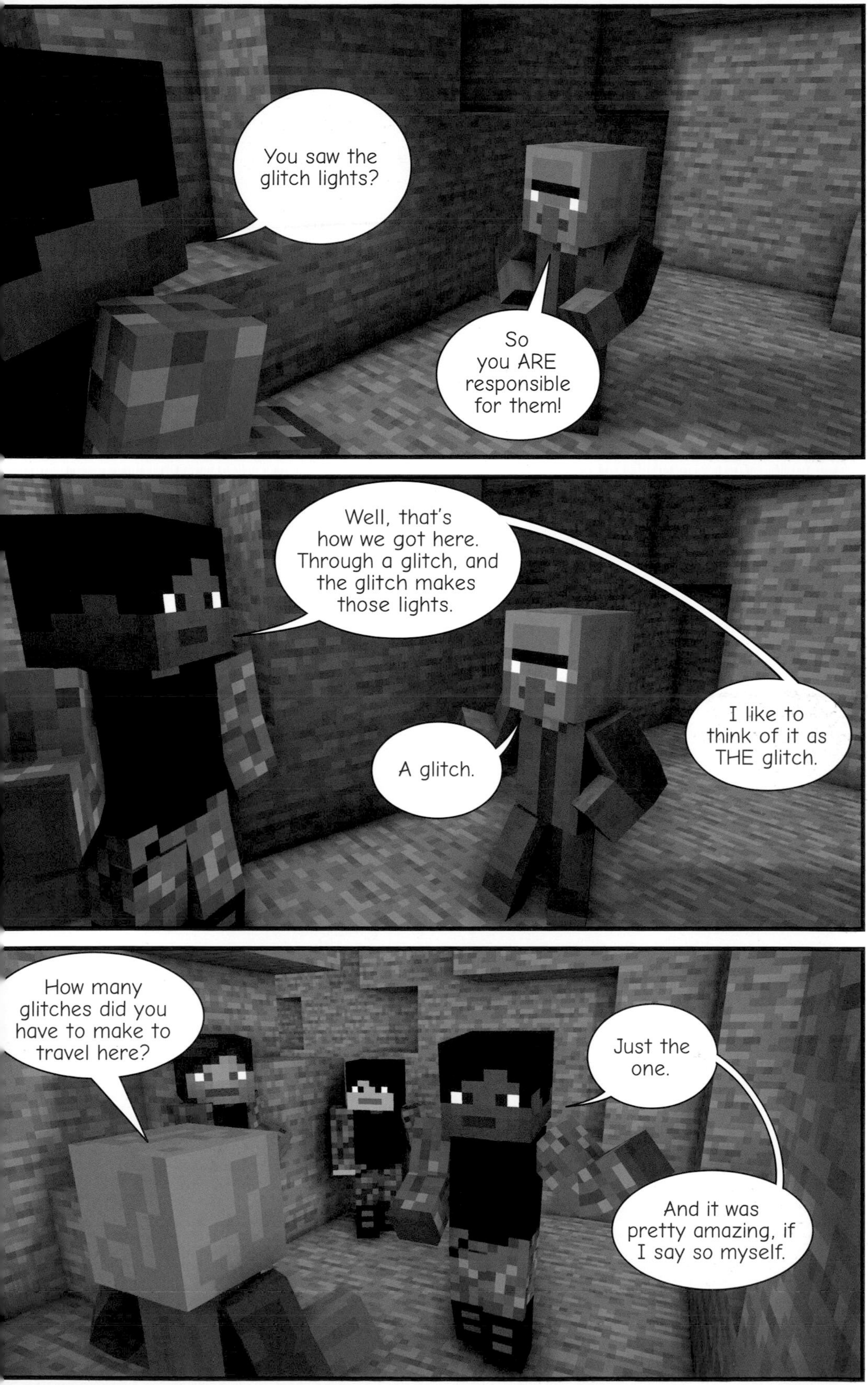
You saw the glitch lights?
So you ARE responsible for them!
Well, that's how we got here. Through a glitch, and the glitch makes those lights.
A glitch.
I like to think of it as THE glitch.
How many glitches did you have to make to travel here?
Just the one.
And it was pretty amazing, if I say so myself.

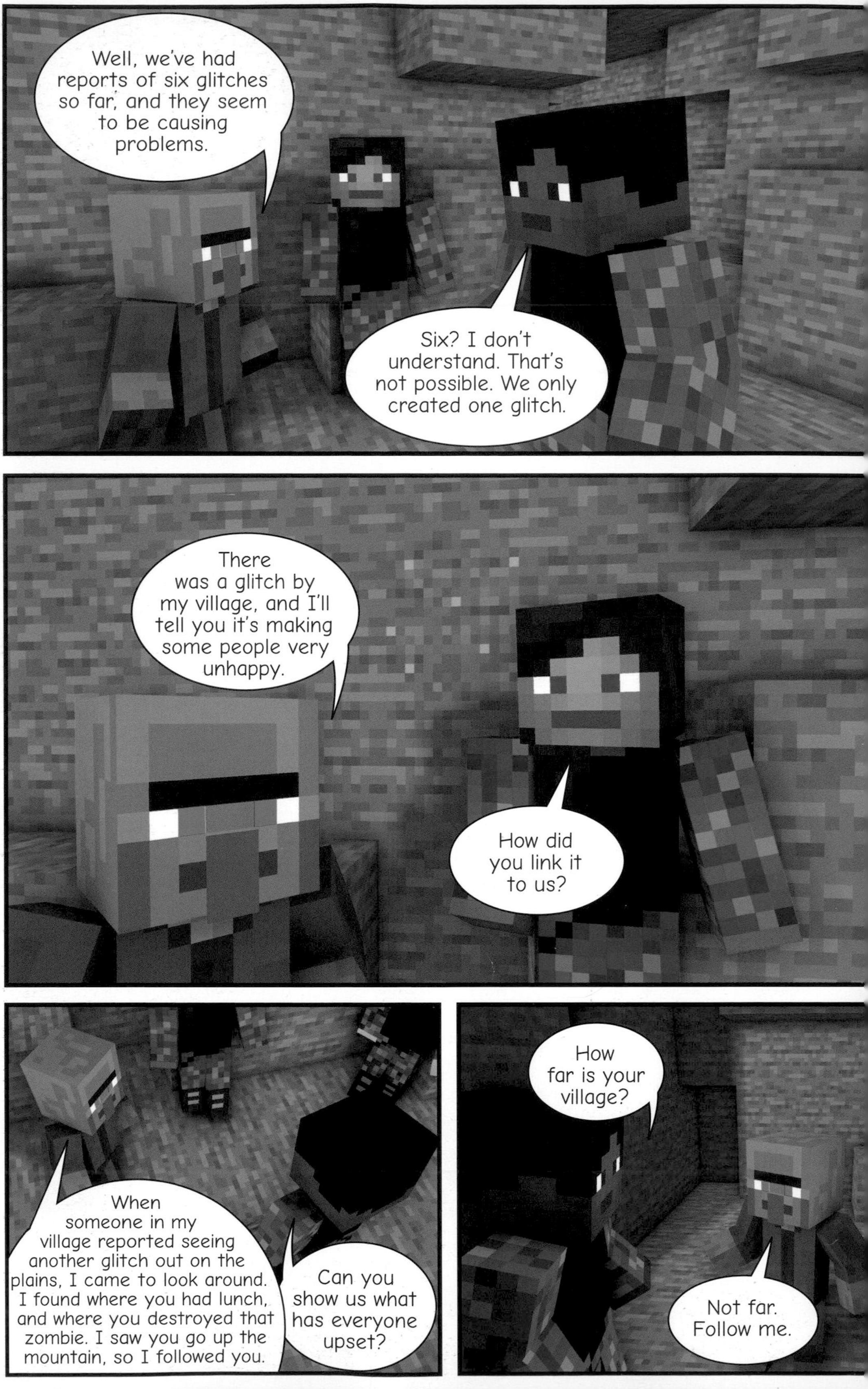
Well, we've had reports of six glitches so far, and they seem to be causing problems.
Six? I don't understand. That's not possible. We only created one glitch.
There was a glitch by my village, and I'll tell you it's making some people very unhappy.
How did you link it to us?
When someone in my village reported seeing another glitch out on the plains, I came to look around. I found where you had lunch, and where you destroyed that zombie. I saw you go up the mountain, so I followed you.
Can you show us what has everyone upset?
How far is your village?
Not far. Follow me.

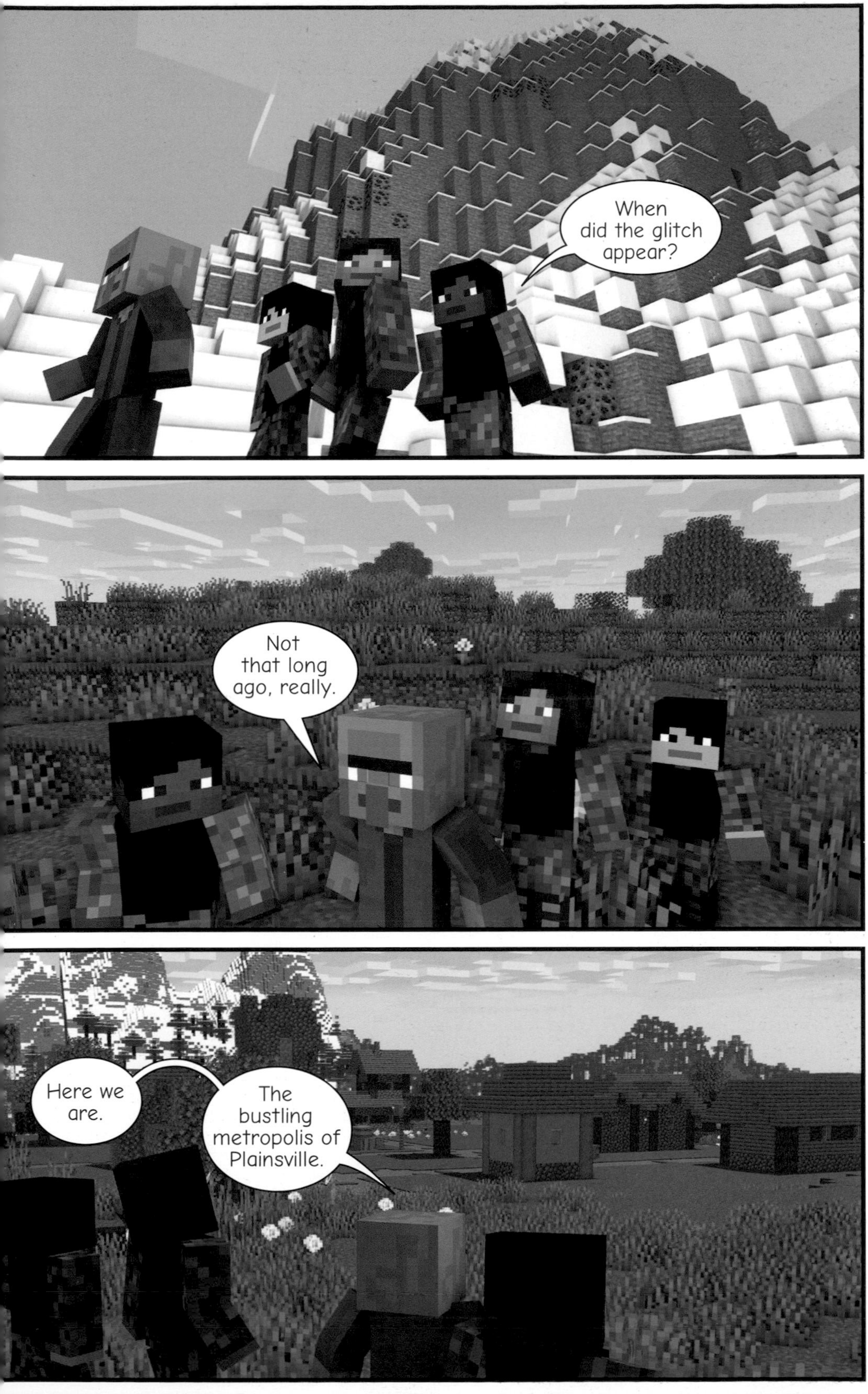
When did the glitch appear?
Not that long ago, really.
Here we are.
The bustling metropolis of Plainsville.

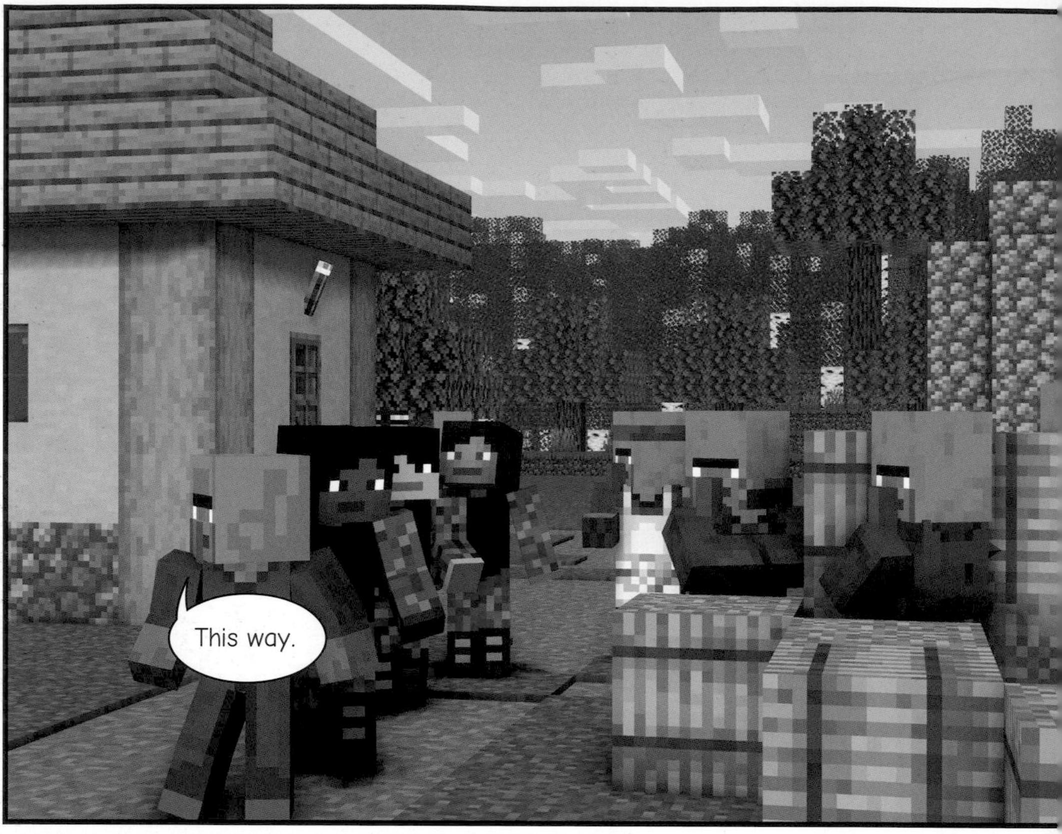
This way.

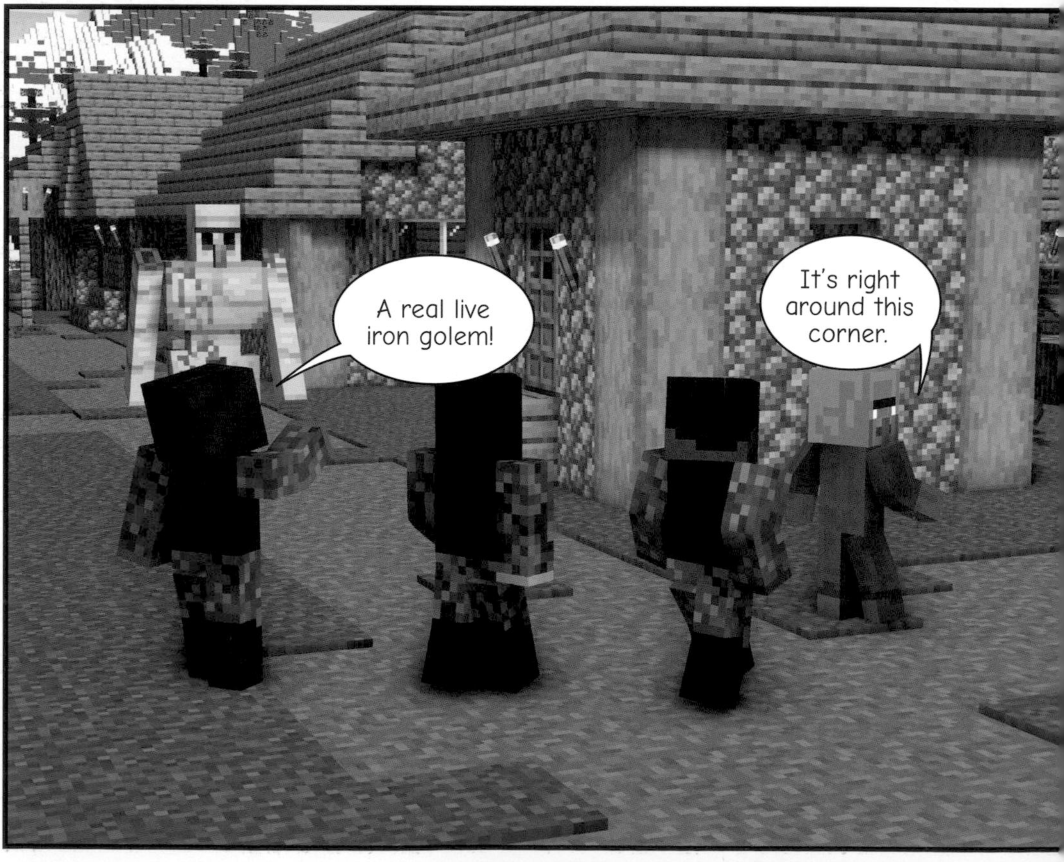
A real live
iron golem!
It's right
around this
corner.

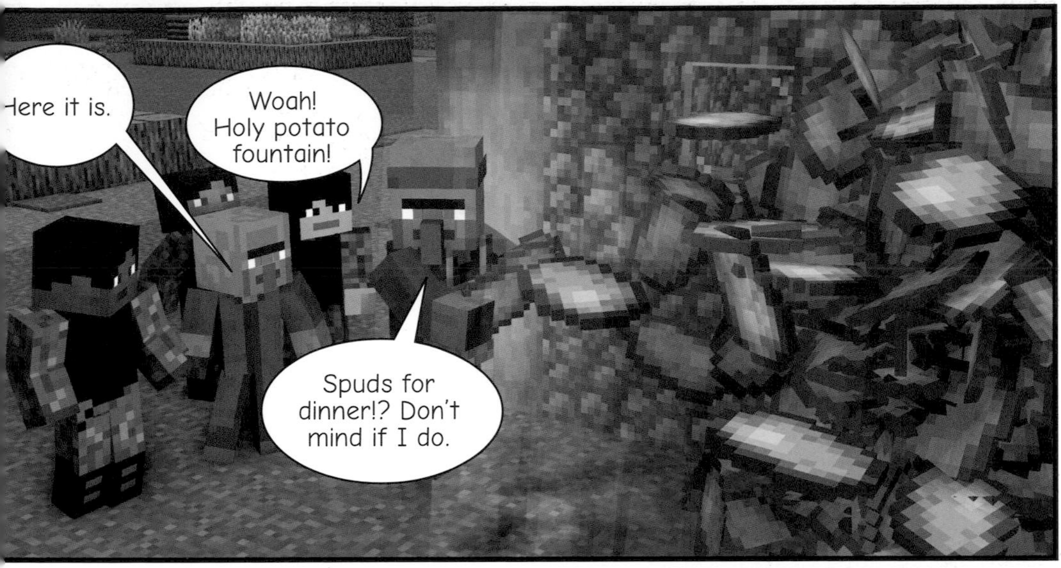
Here it is.
Woah! Holy potato fountain!
Spuds for dinner!? Don't mind if I do.

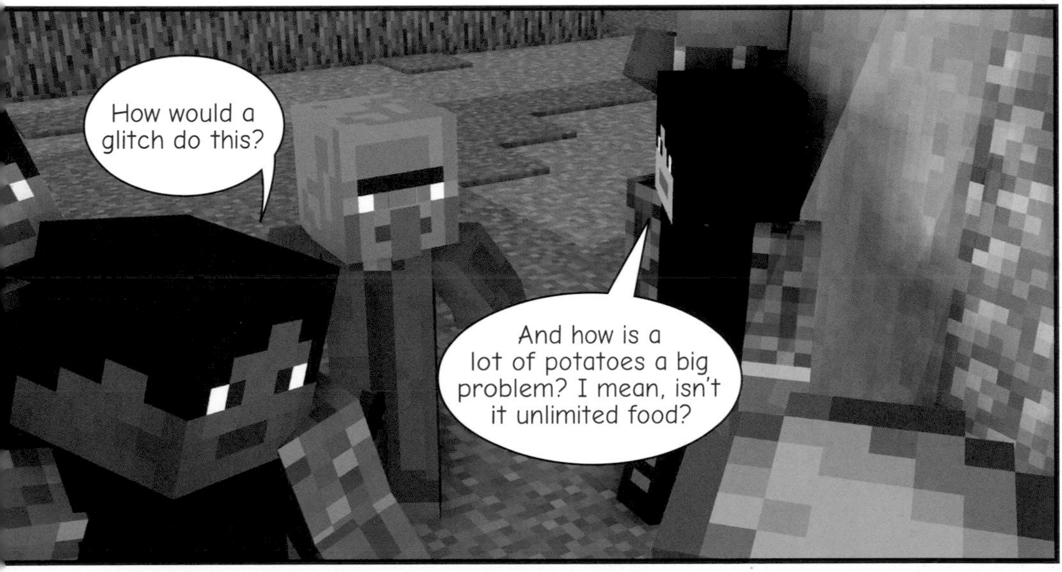
How would a glitch do this?
And how is a lot of potatoes a big problem? I mean, isn't it unlimited food?

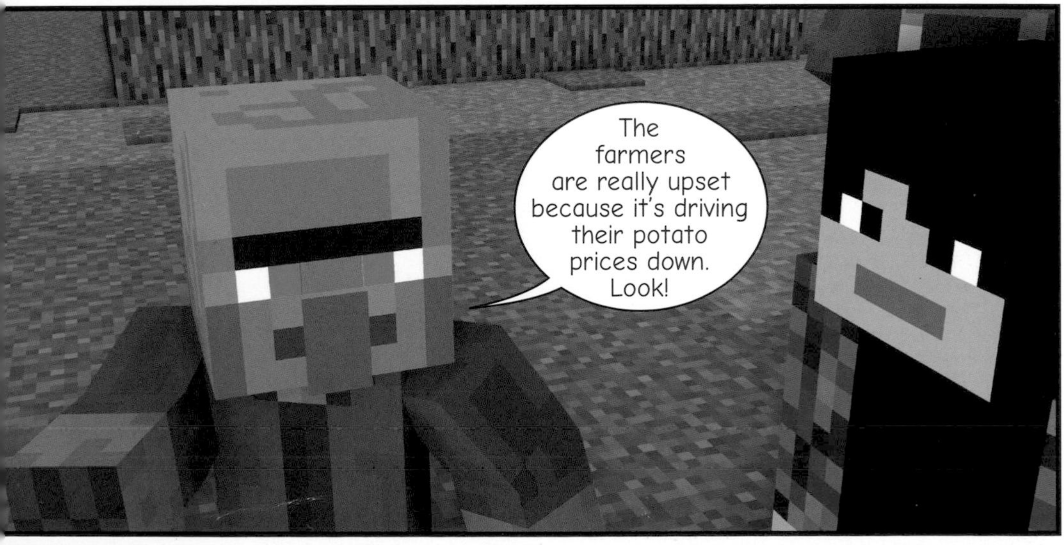
The farmers are really upset because it's driving their potato prices down. Look!

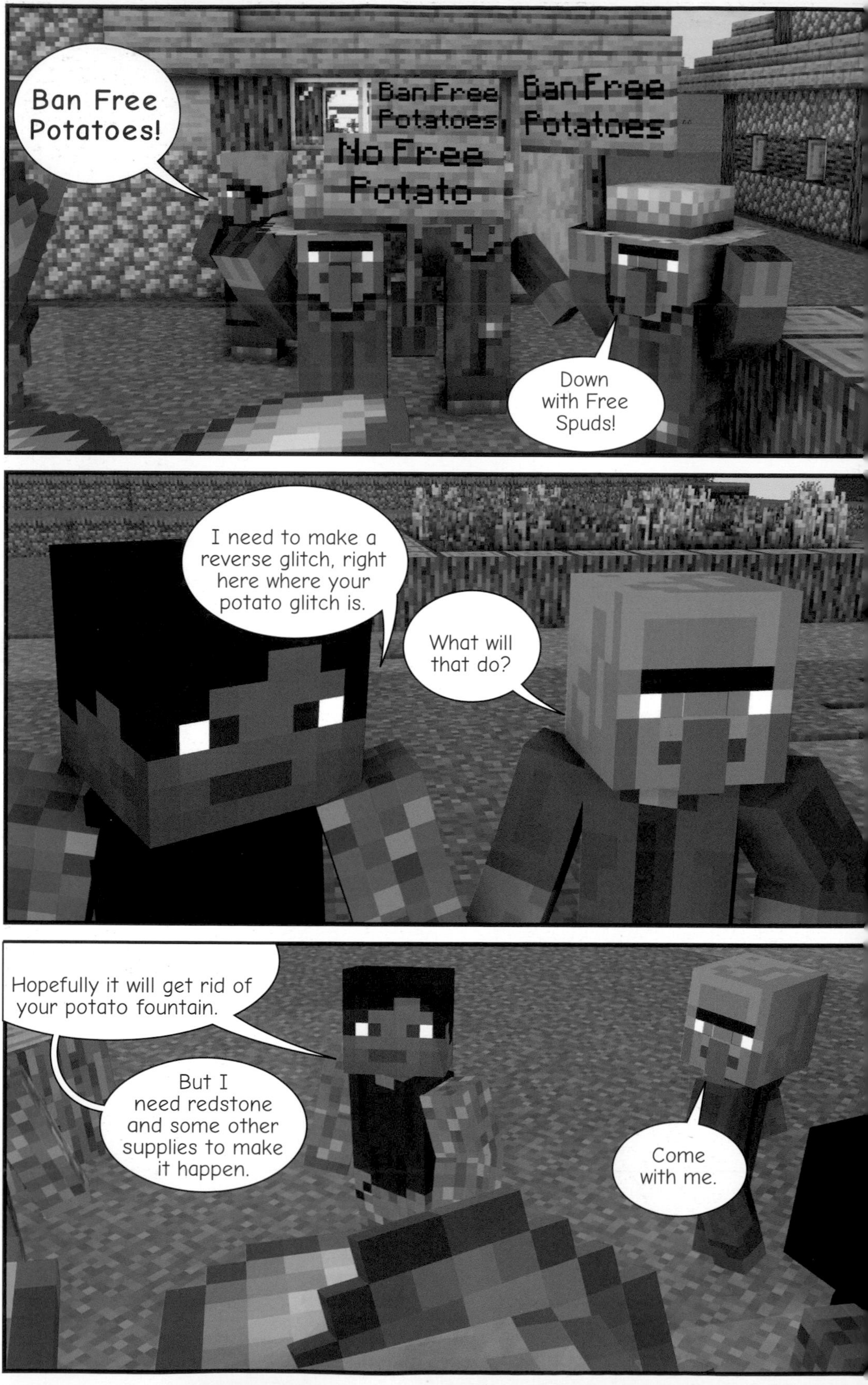

Ban Free Potatoes!
Ban Free Potatoes
No Free Potato
Ban Free Potatoes
Down with Free Spuds!
I need to make a reverse glitch, right here where your potato glitch is.
What will that do?
Hopefully it will get rid of your potato fountain.
But I need redstone and some other supplies to make it happen.
Come with me.

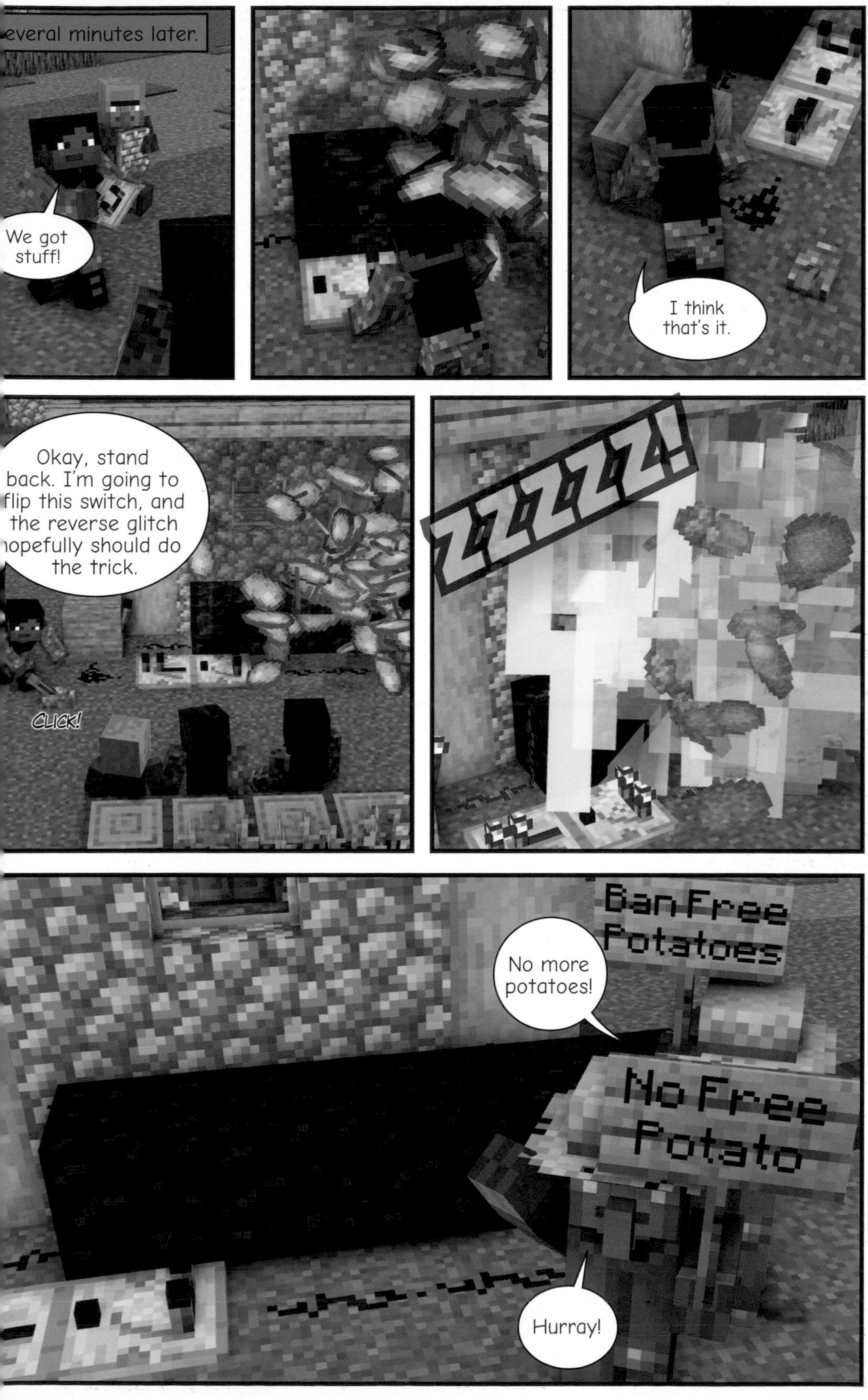
everal minutes later.
We got stuff!
I think that's it.
Okay, stand back. I'm going to flip this switch, and the reverse glitch hopefully should do the trick.
CLICK!
ZZZZZZ!
Ban Free Potatoes
No more potatoes!
No Free Potato
Hurray!

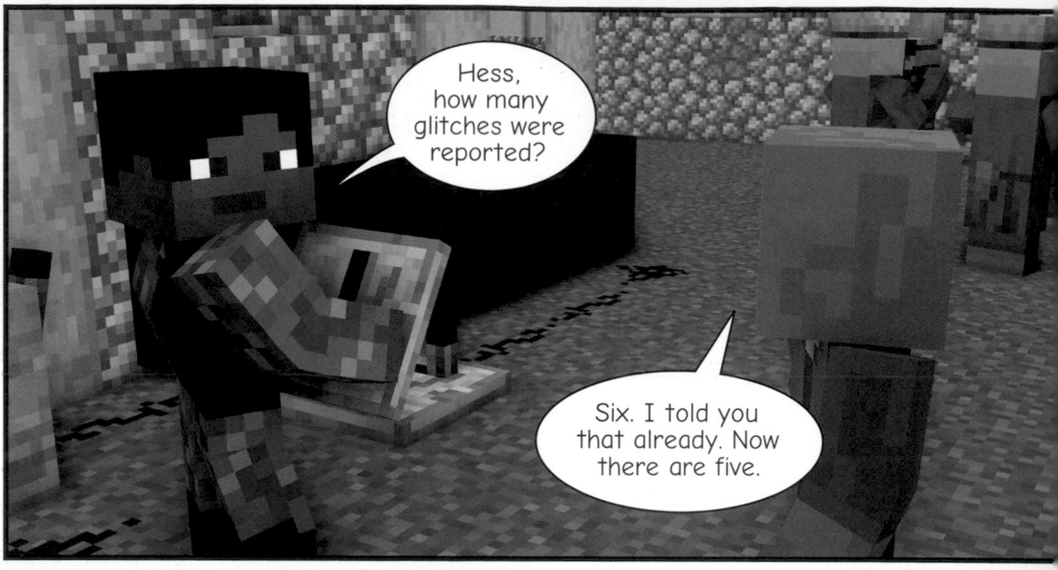
Hess, how many glitches were reported?
Six. I told you that already. Now there are five.

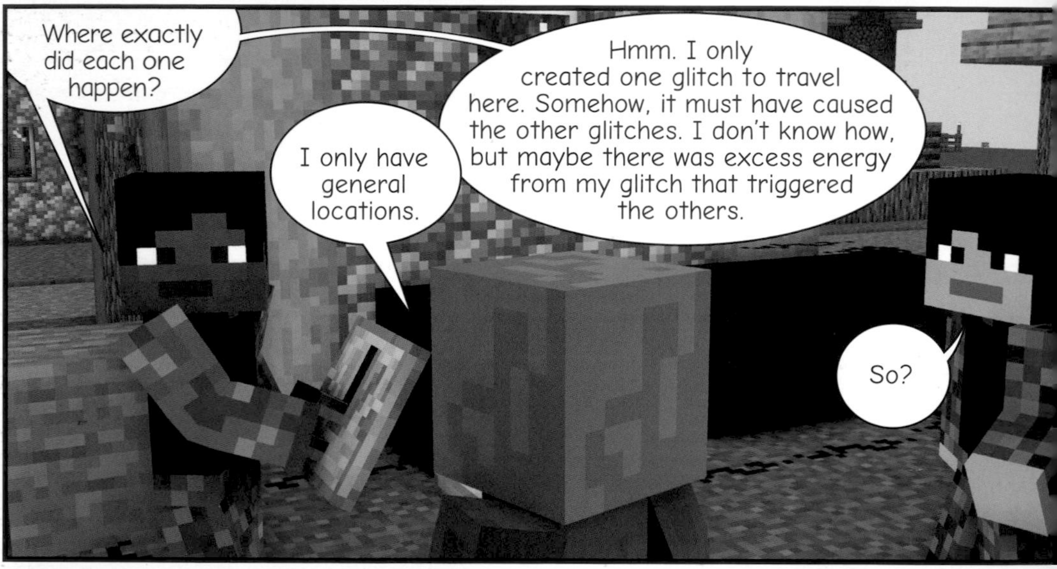
Where exactly did each one happen?
I only have general locations.
Hmm. I only created one glitch to travel here. Somehow, it must have caused the other glitches. I don't know how, but maybe there was excess energy from my glitch that triggered the others.
So?

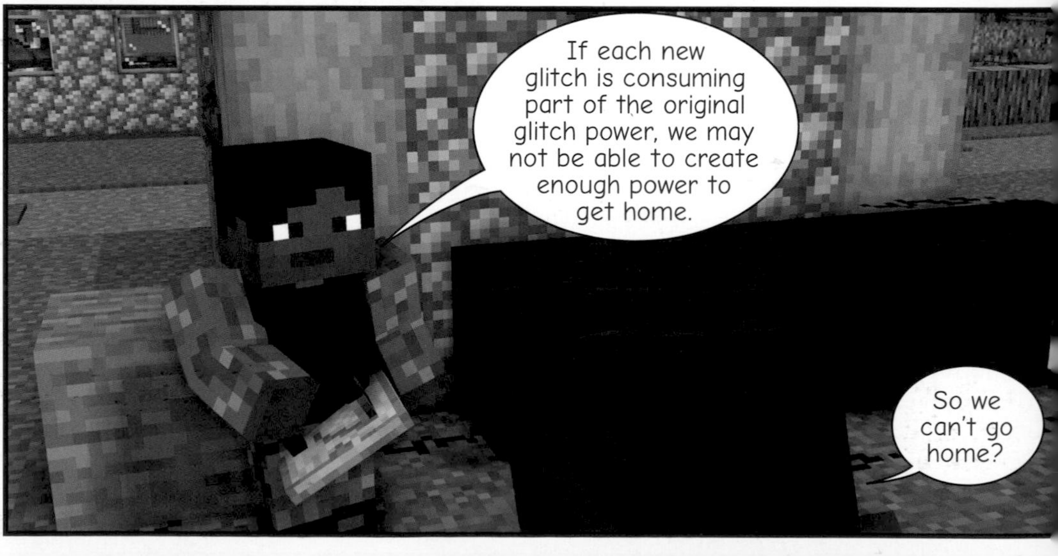
If each new glitch is consuming part of the original glitch power, we may not be able to create enough power to get home.
So we can't go home?

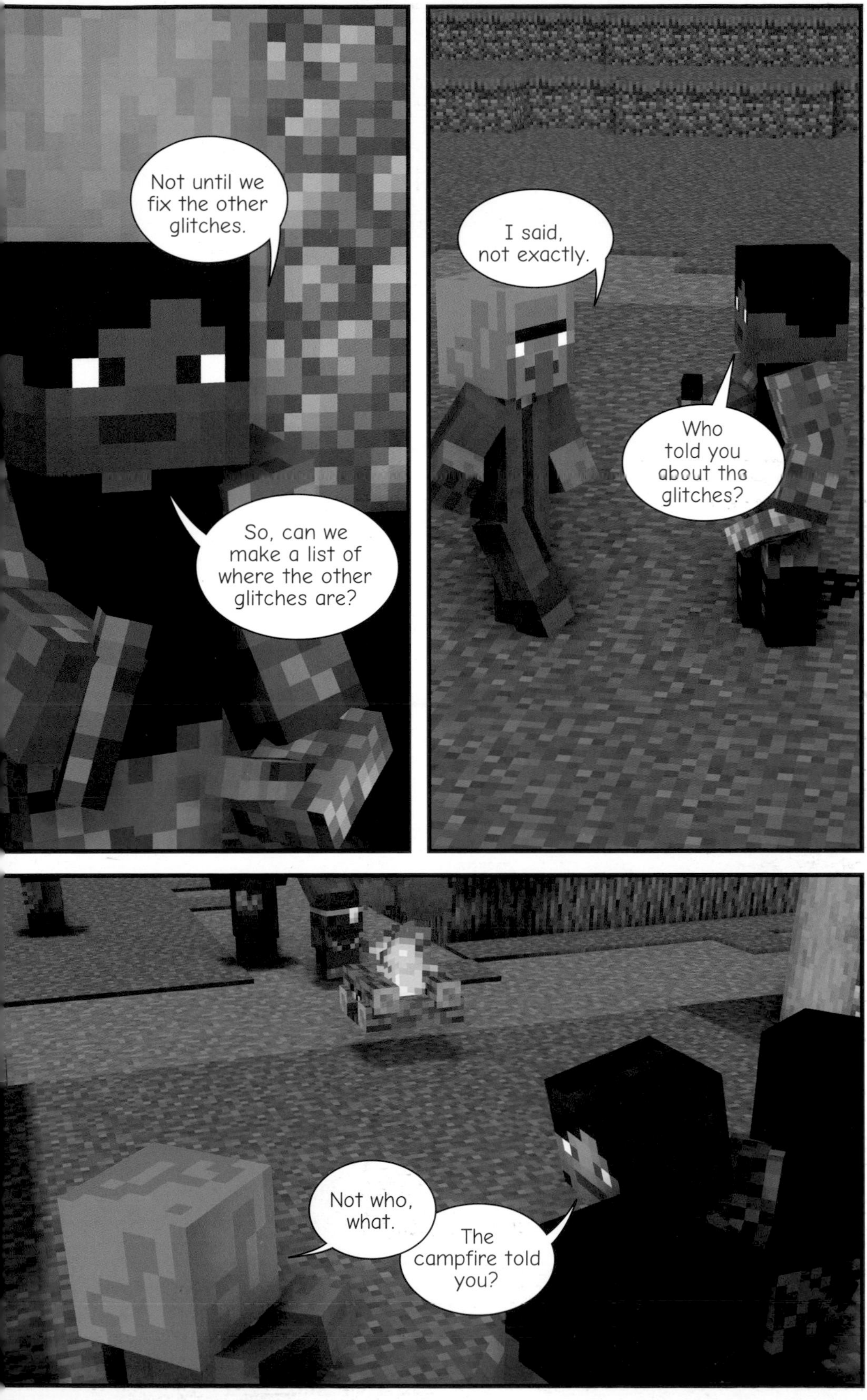
Not until we fix the other glitches.
So, can we make a list of where the other glitches are?
I said, not exactly.
Who told you about the glitches?
Not who, what.
The campfire told you?

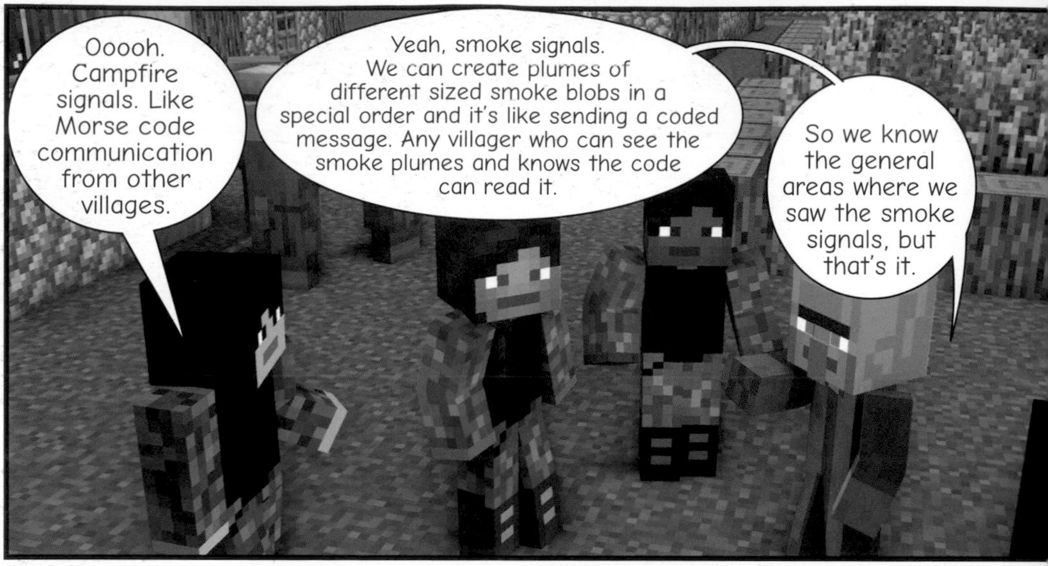
Ooooh. Campfire signals. Like Morse code communication from other villages.
Yeah, smoke signals. We can create plumes of different sized smoke blobs in a special order and it's like sending a coded message. Any villager who can see the smoke plumes and knows the code can read it.
So we know the general areas where we saw the smoke signals, but that's it.

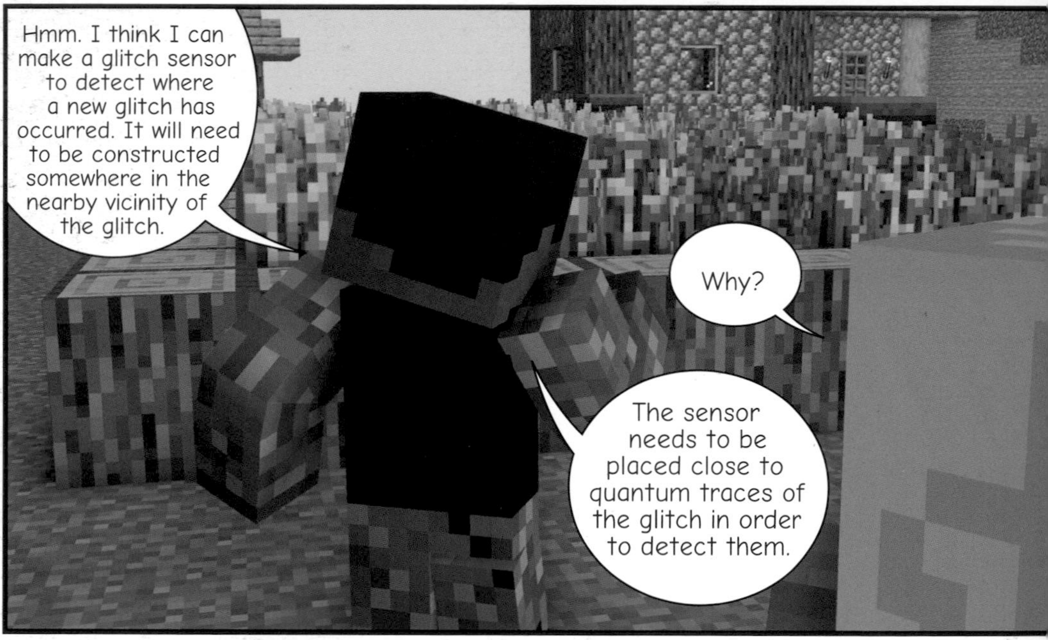
Hmm. I think I can make a glitch sensor to detect where a new glitch has occurred. It will need to be constructed somewhere in the nearby vicinity of the glitch.
Why?
The sensor needs to be placed close to quantum traces of the glitch in order to detect them.

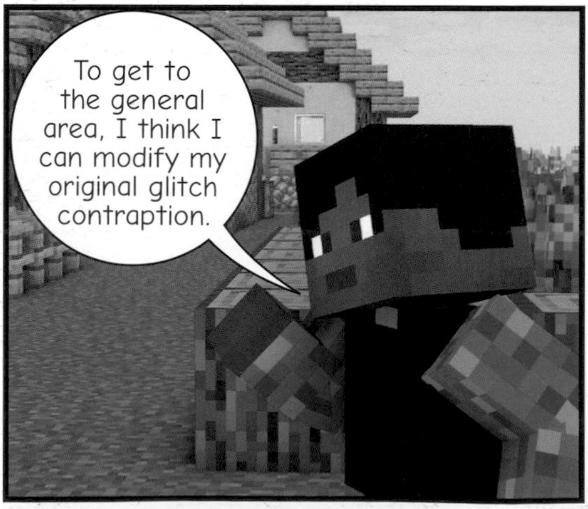
To get to the general area, I think I can modify my original glitch contraption.

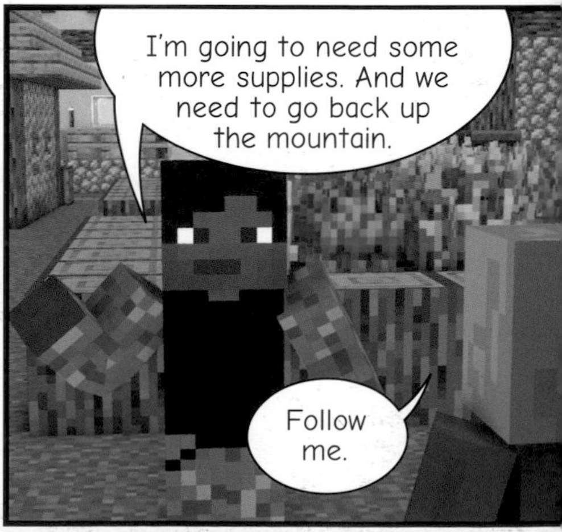
I'm going to need some more supplies. And we need to go back up the mountain.
Follow me.

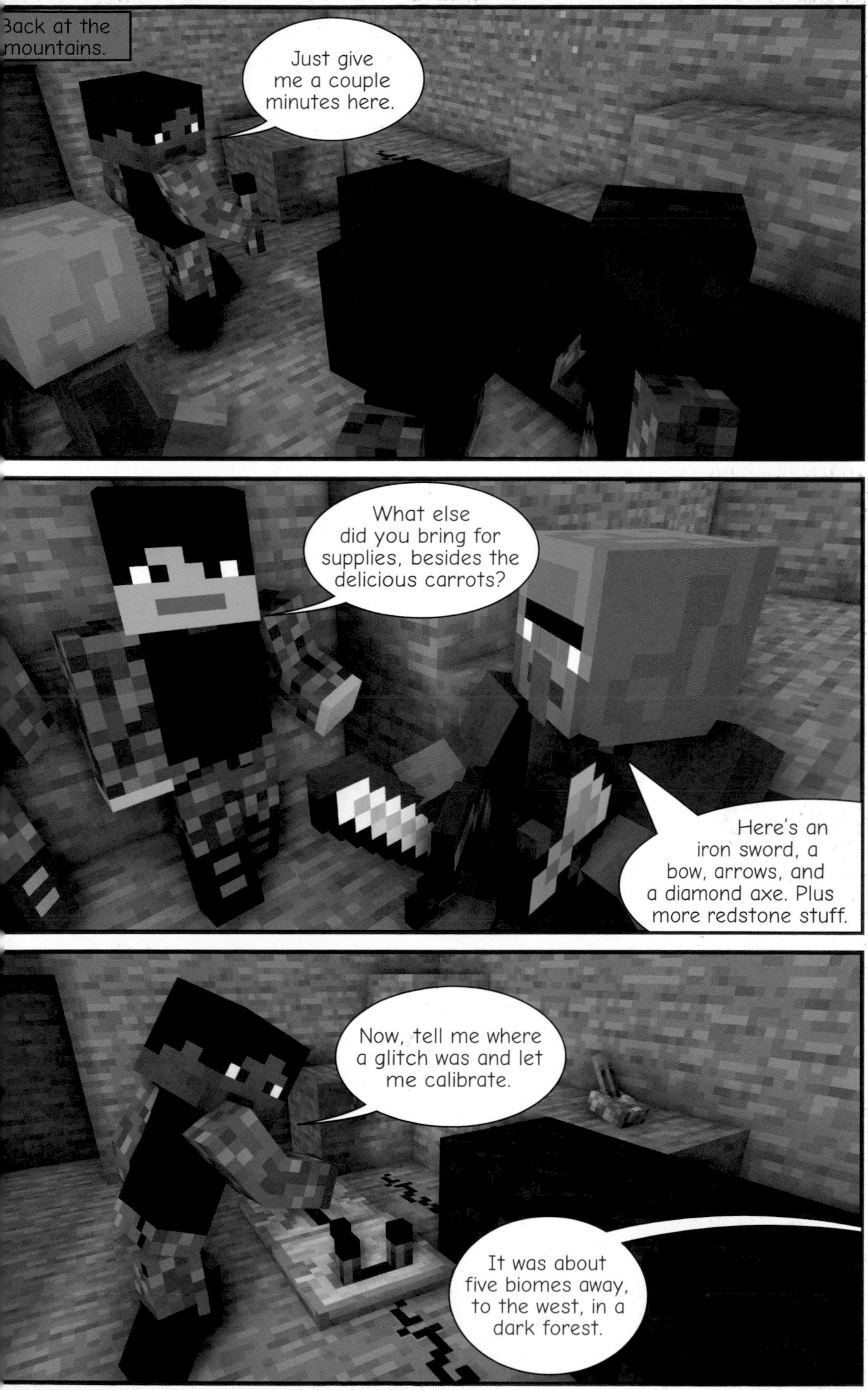
Back at the mountains.
Just give me a couple minutes here.
What else did you bring for supplies, besides the delicious carrots?
Here's an iron sword, a bow, arrows, and a diamond axe. Plus more redstone stuff.
Now, tell me where a glitch was and let me calibrate.
It was about five biomes away, to the west, in a dark forest.

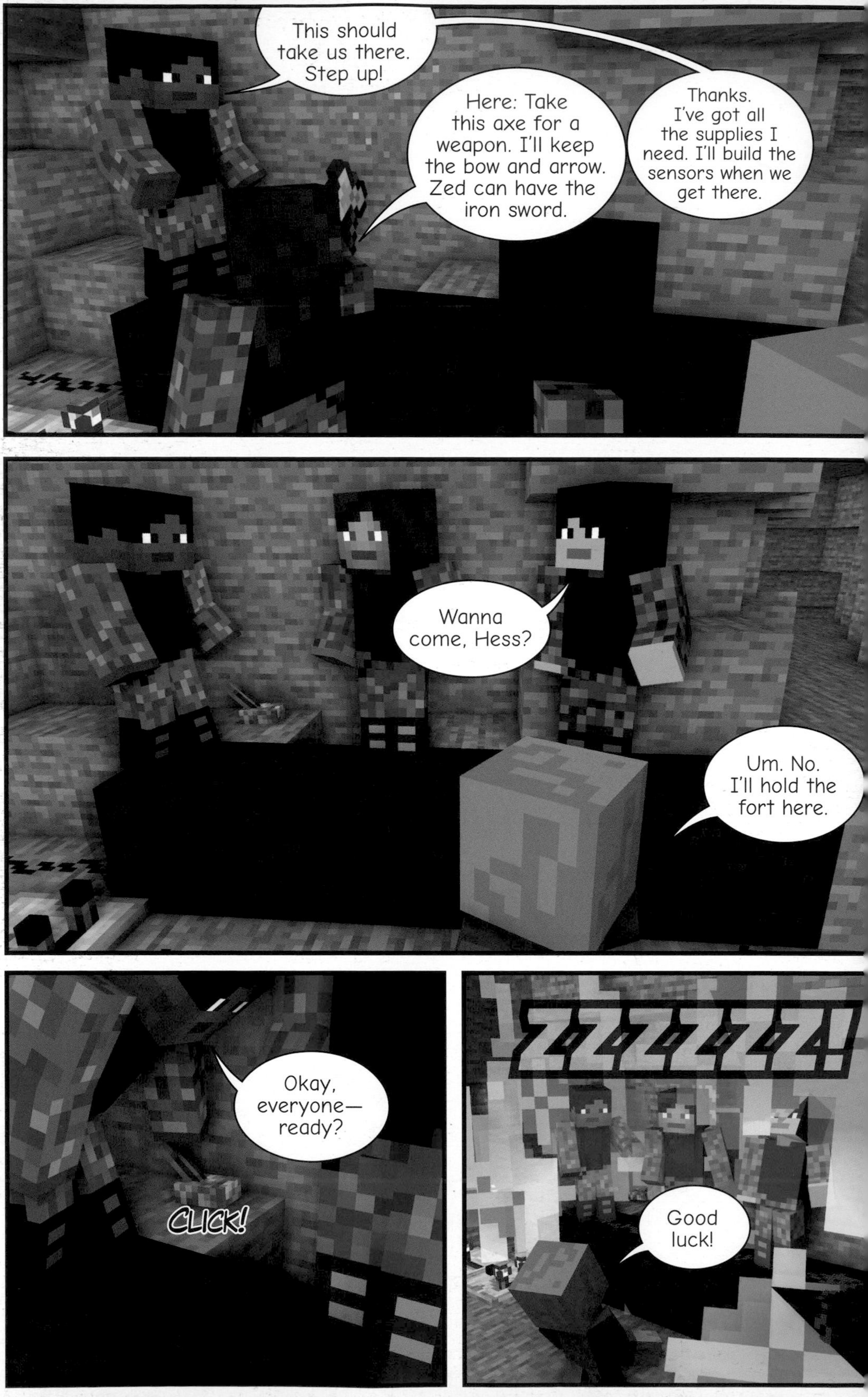
This should take us there. Step up!
Here: Take this axe for a weapon. I'll keep the bow and arrow. Zed can have the iron sword.
Thanks. I've got all the supplies I need. I'll build the sensors when we get there.
Wanna come, Hess?
Um. No. I'll hold the fort here.
Okay, everyone—ready?
CLICK!
ZZZZZZZ!
Good luck!

CHAPTER 7:
GRAVEL

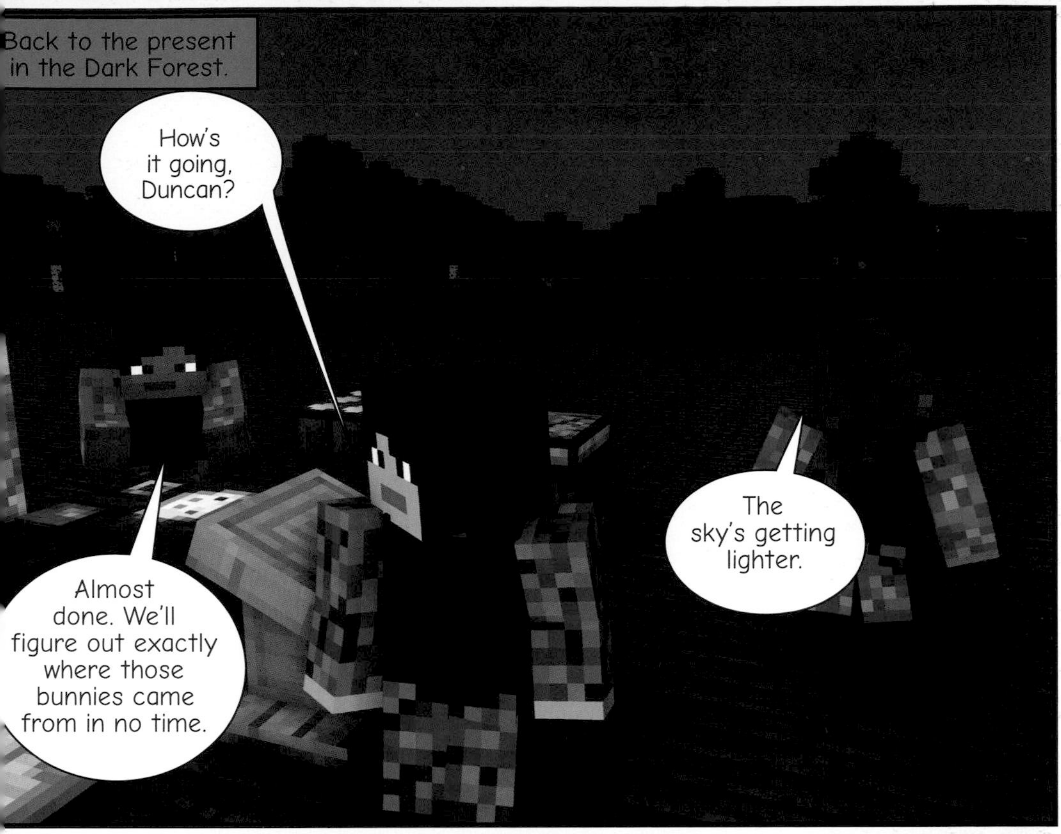
Back to the present in the Dark Forest.
How's it going, Duncan?
The sky's getting lighter.
Almost done. We'll figure out exactly where those bunnies came from in no time.

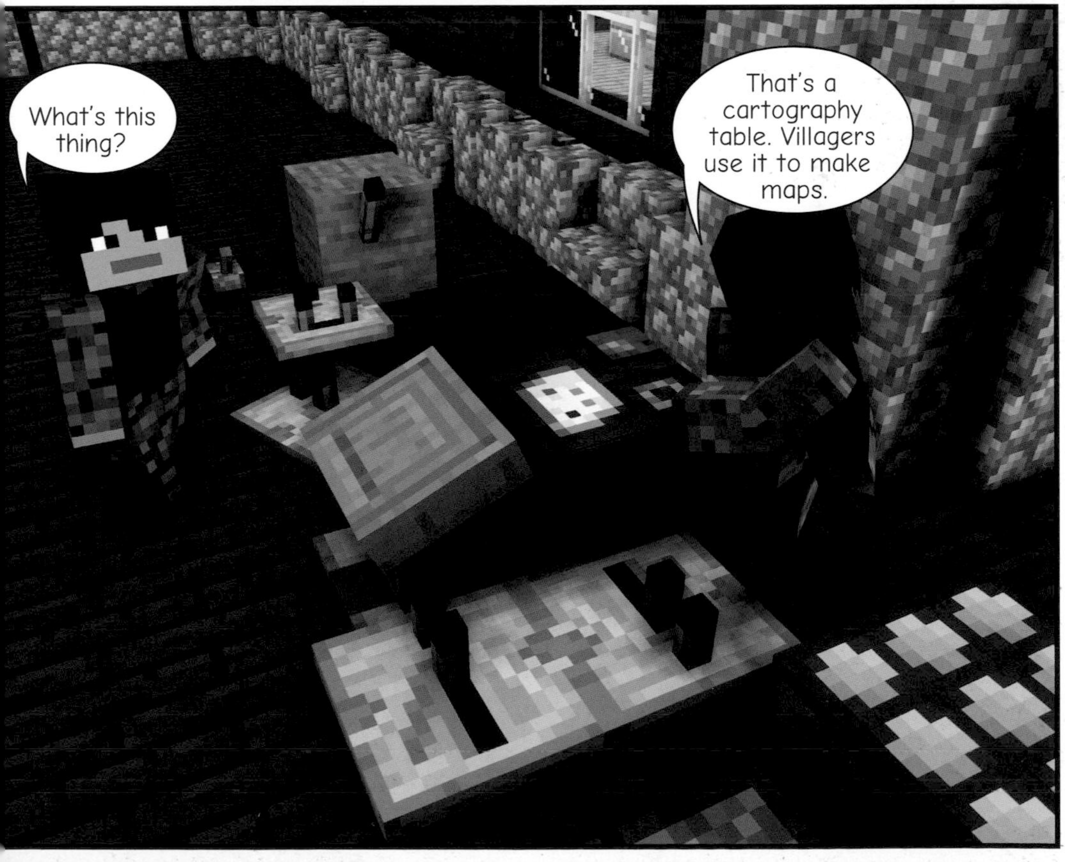
What's this thing?
That's a cartography table. Villagers use it to make maps.

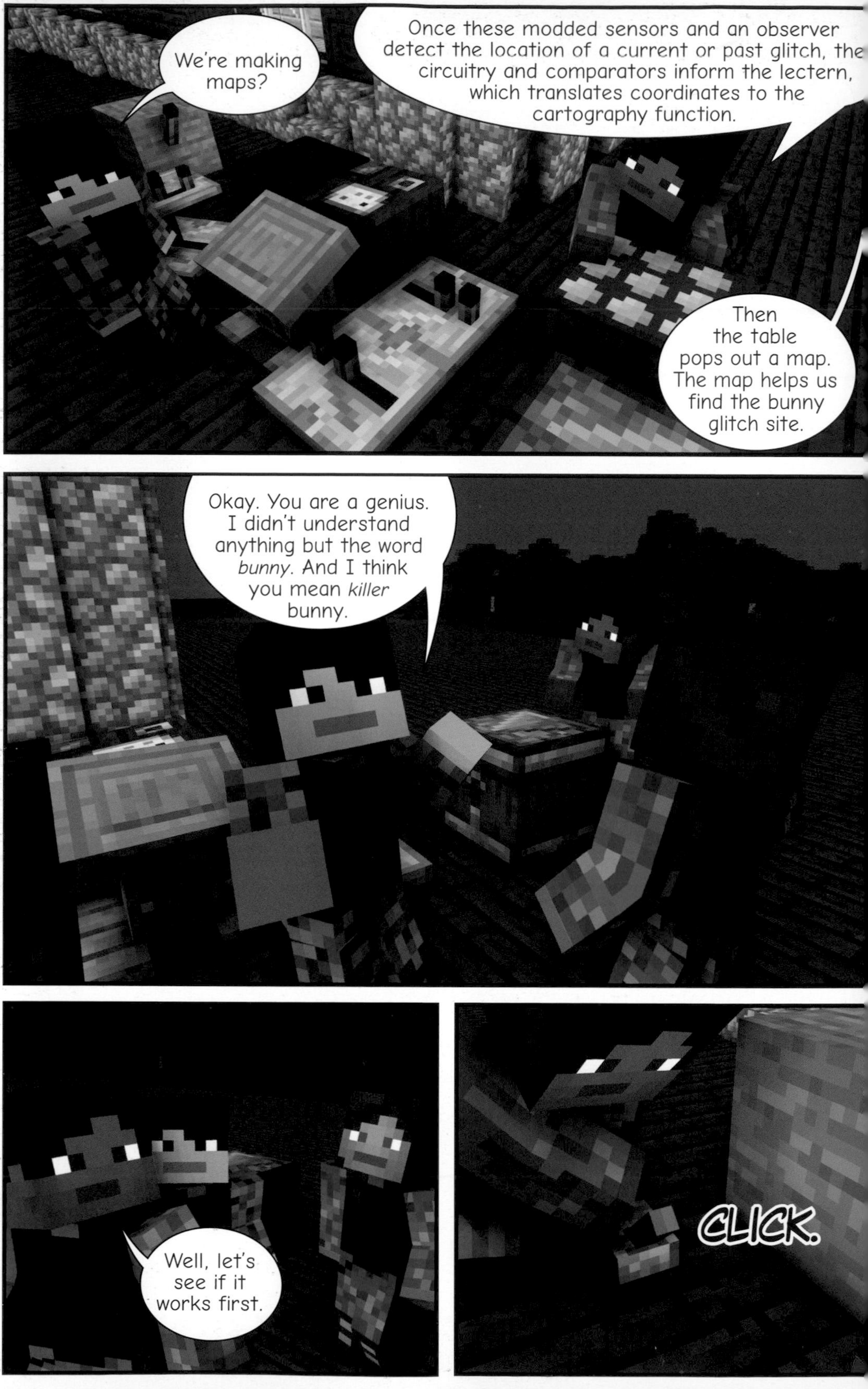
We're making maps?
Once these modded sensors and an observer detect the location of a current or past glitch, the circuitry and comparators inform the lectern, which translates coordinates to the cartography function.
Then the table pops out a map. The map helps us find the bunny glitch site.
Okay. You are a genius. I didn't understand anything but the word *bunny*. And I think you mean *killer* bunny.
Well, let's see if it works first.
CLICK.

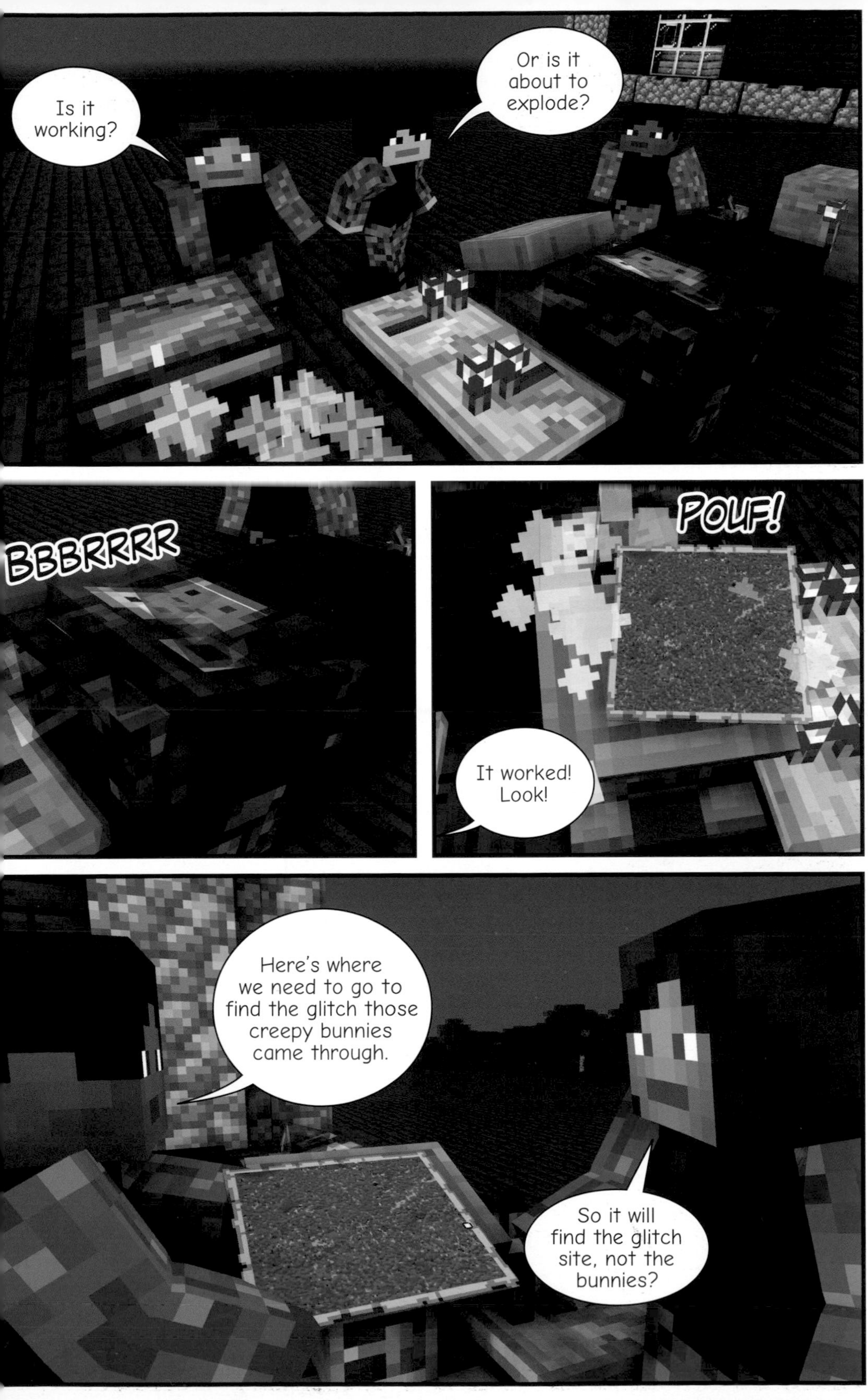
Is it working?
Or is it about to explode?
BBBRRRR
POUF!
It worked! Look!
Here's where we need to go to find the glitch those creepy bunnies came through.
So it will find the glitch site, not the bunnies?

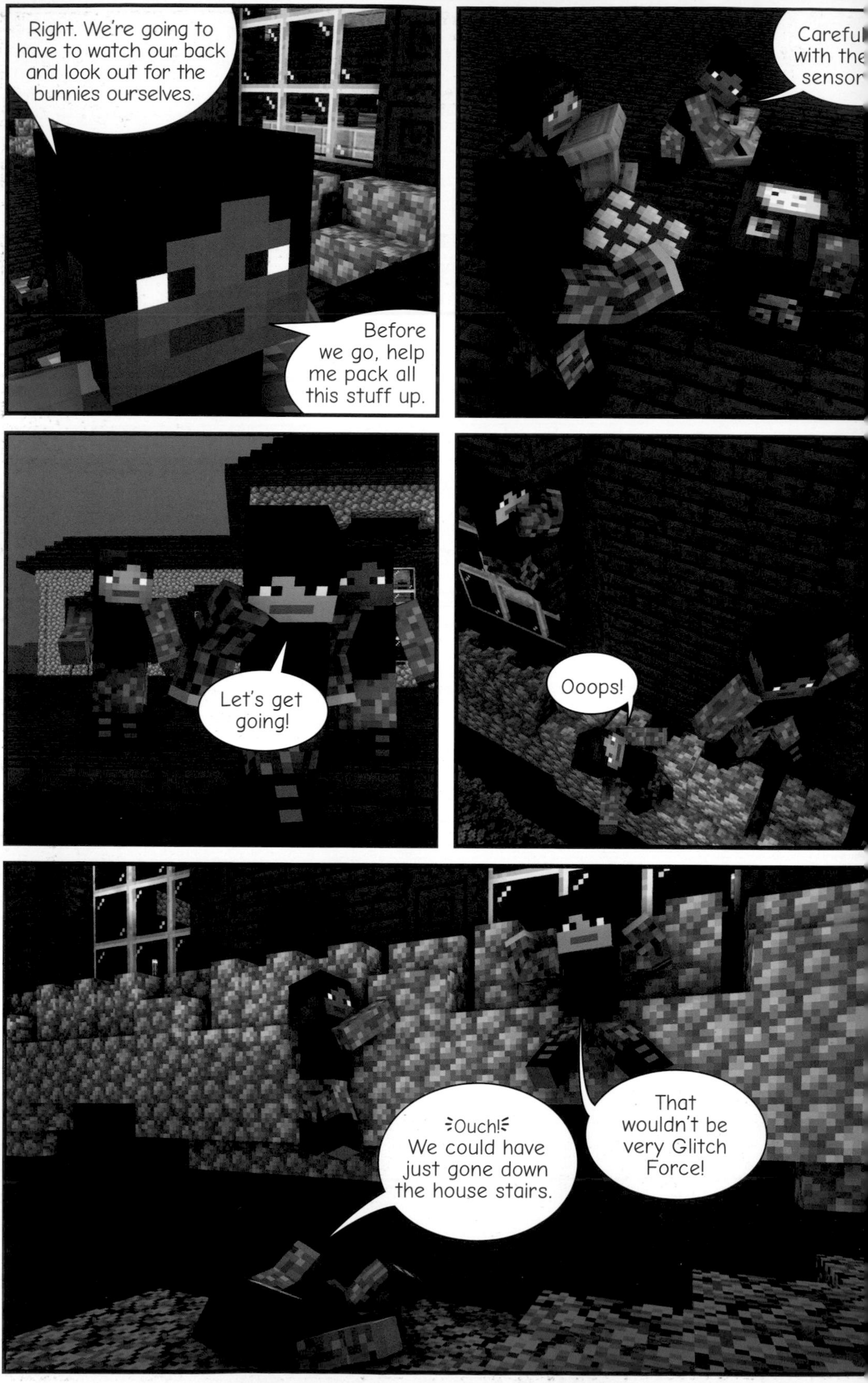
Right. We're going to have to watch our back and look out for the bunnies ourselves.
Before we go, help me pack all this stuff up.
Careful with the sensor
Let's get going!
Ooops!
Ouch! We could have just gone down the house stairs.
That wouldn't be very Glitch Force!

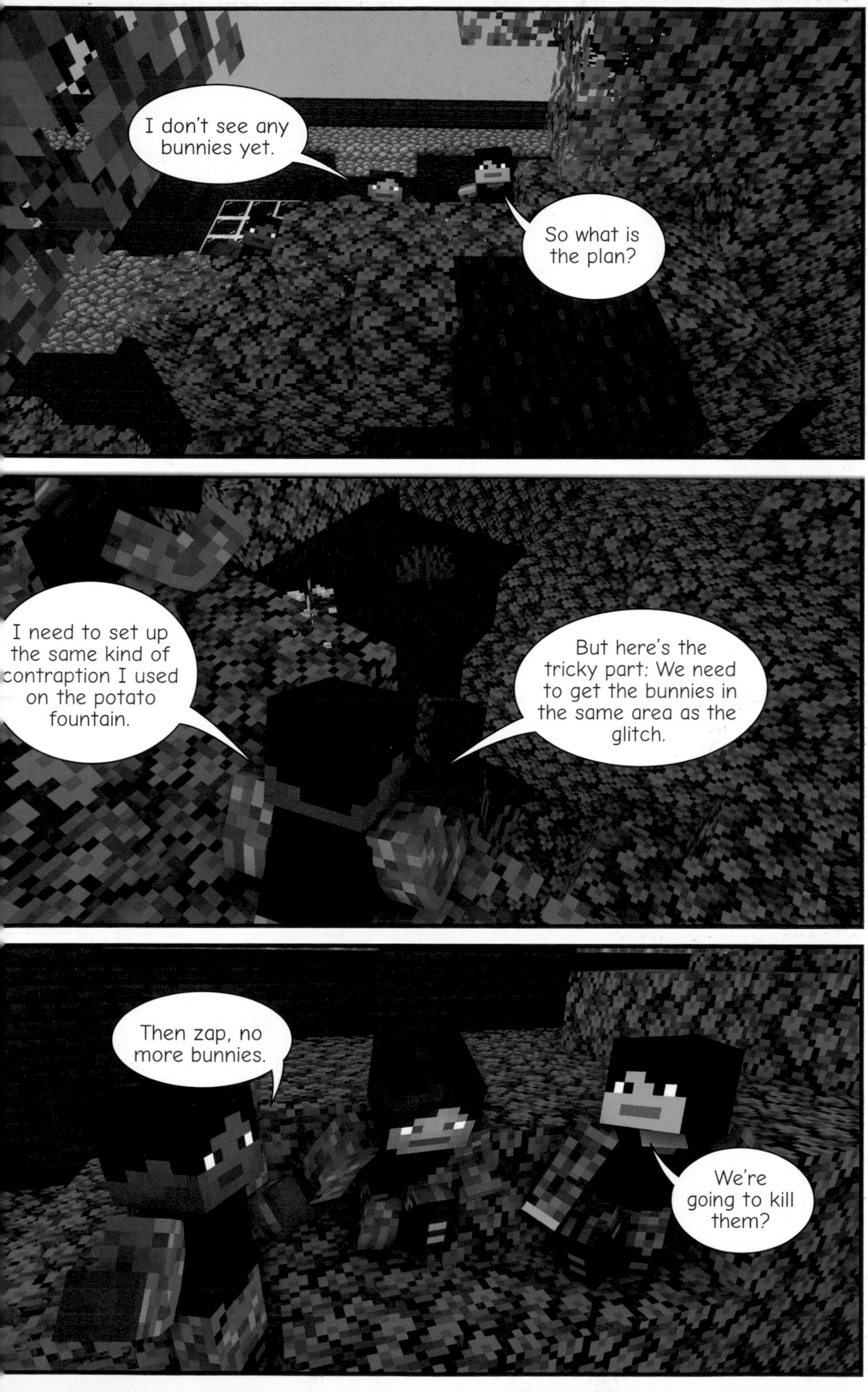
I don't see any bunnies yet.
So what is the plan?
I need to set up the same kind of contraption I used on the potato fountain.
But here's the tricky part: We need to get the bunnies in the same area as the glitch.
Then zap, no more bunnies.
We're going to kill them?

If it's an energy imbalance that caused this problem, we need to send about the same amount of energy and mass that came in through the glitch out of the glitch.

No, just send them back to wherever they came from. Like the potatoes.

Look. Gravel.

So what?

I want to get some flint so we can have a flint and steel. It's a good tool to have in our arsenal for making fire or lighting a portal or setting enemies on fire, or whatever. Plus, I need it if I need to make more arrows.

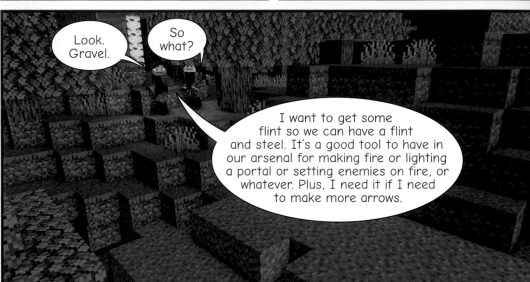

Good idea. We should all have a flint and steel.

Hold on. The gravel is collapsing!

FSFSFSSFS

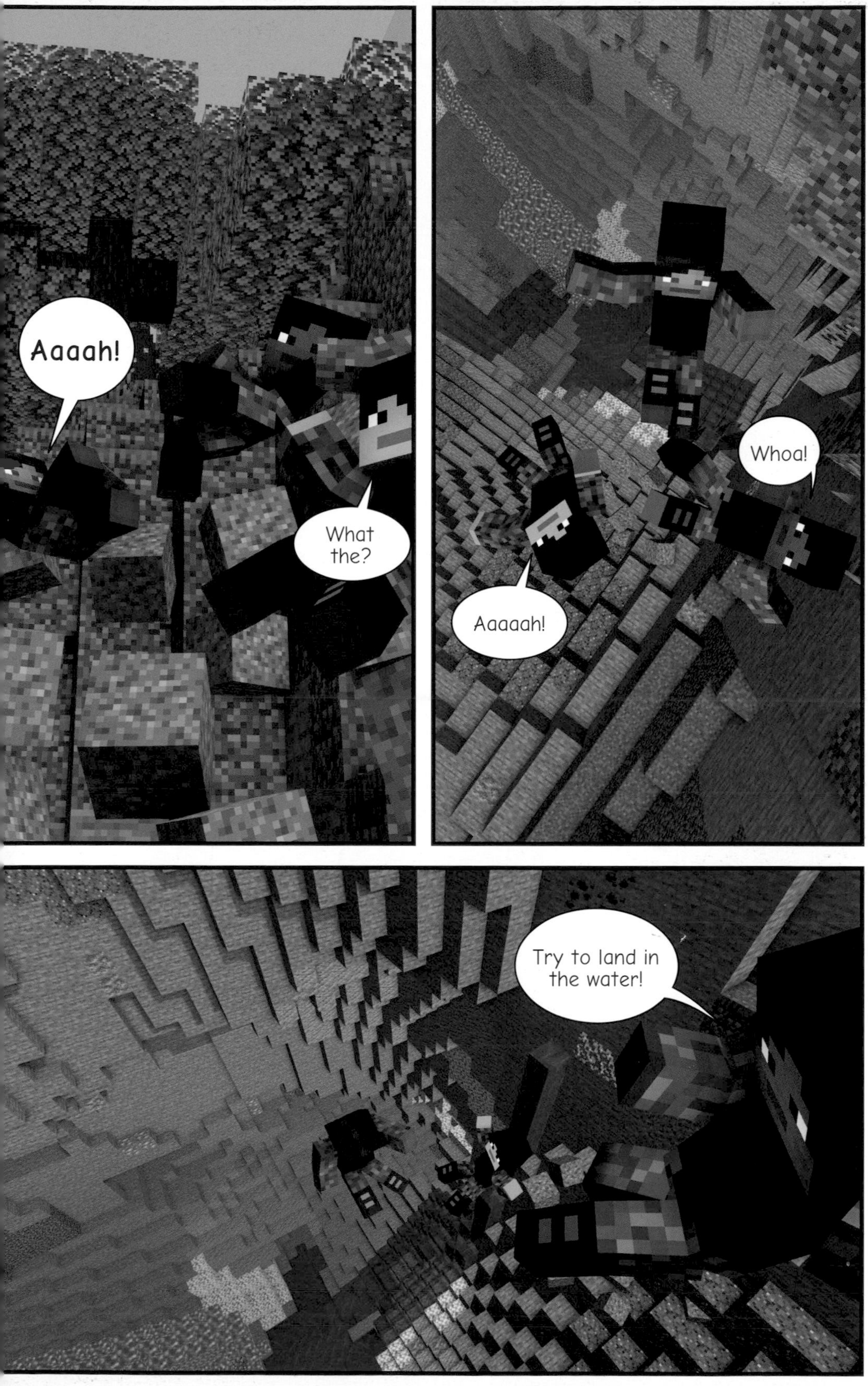
Aaaah!
What the?
Whoa!
Aaaaah!
Try to land in the water!

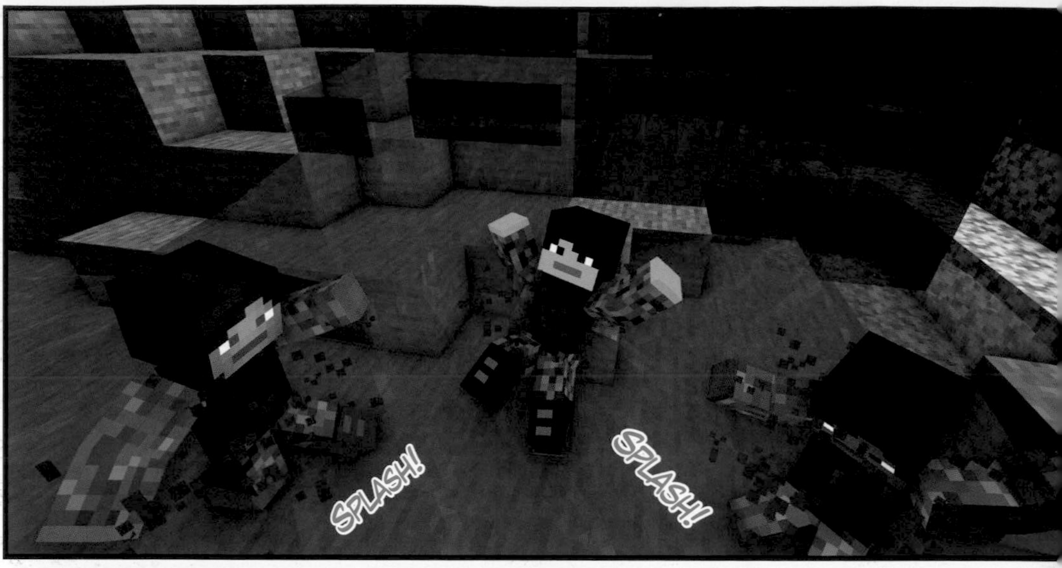
SPLASH!
SPLASH!

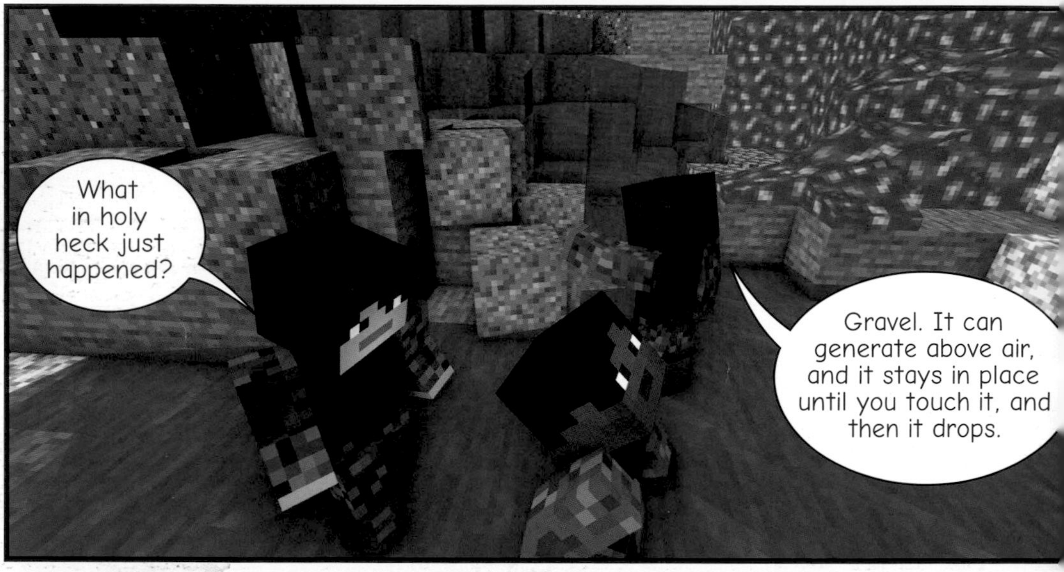
What in holy heck just happened?
Gravel. It can generate above air, and it stays in place until you touch it, and then it drops.

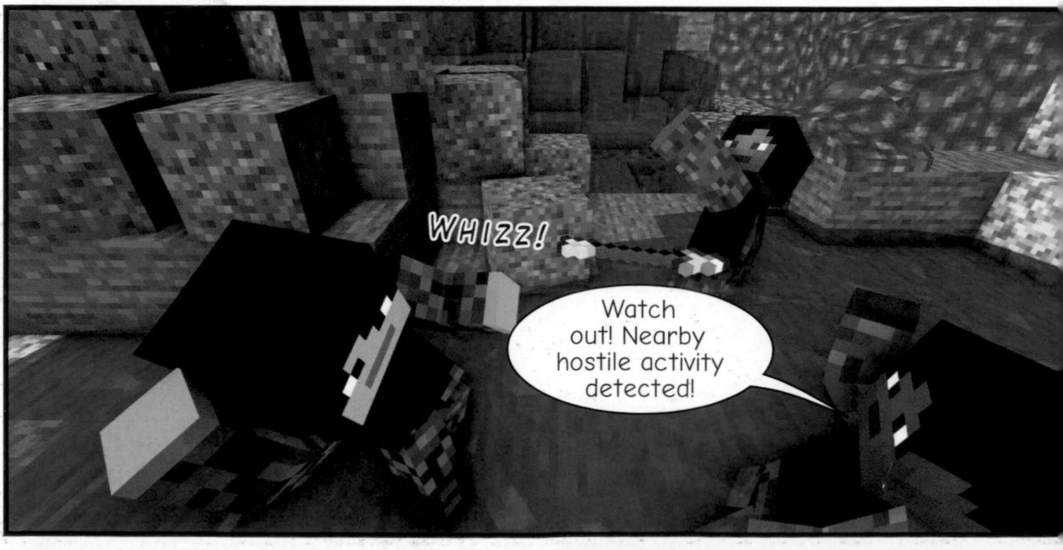
WHIZZ!
Watch out! Nearby hostile activity detected!

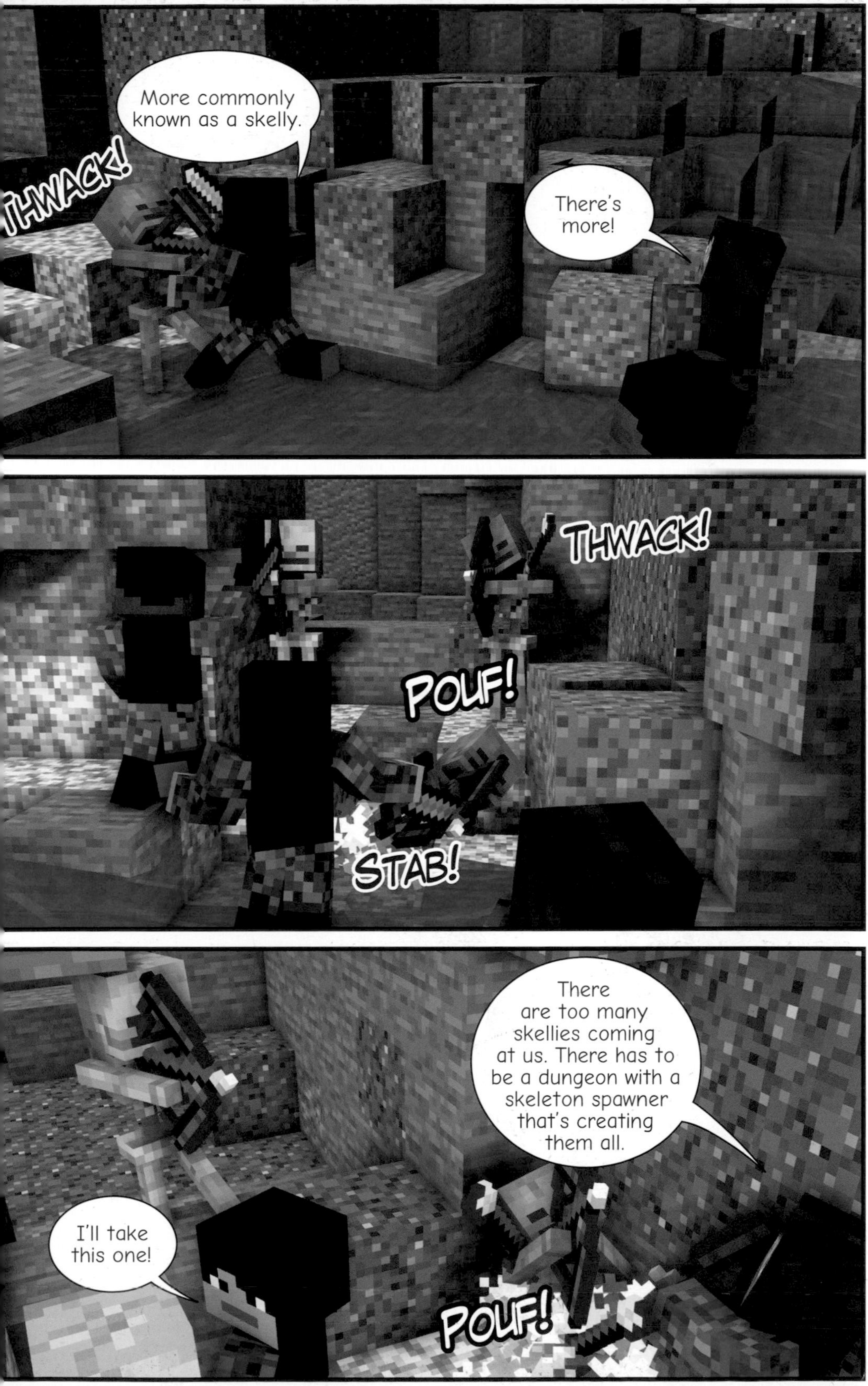

More commonly known as a skelly.
THWACK!
There's more!
THWACK!
POUF!
STAB!
There are too many skellies coming at us. There has to be a dungeon with a skeleton spawner that's creating them all.
I'll take this one!
POUF!

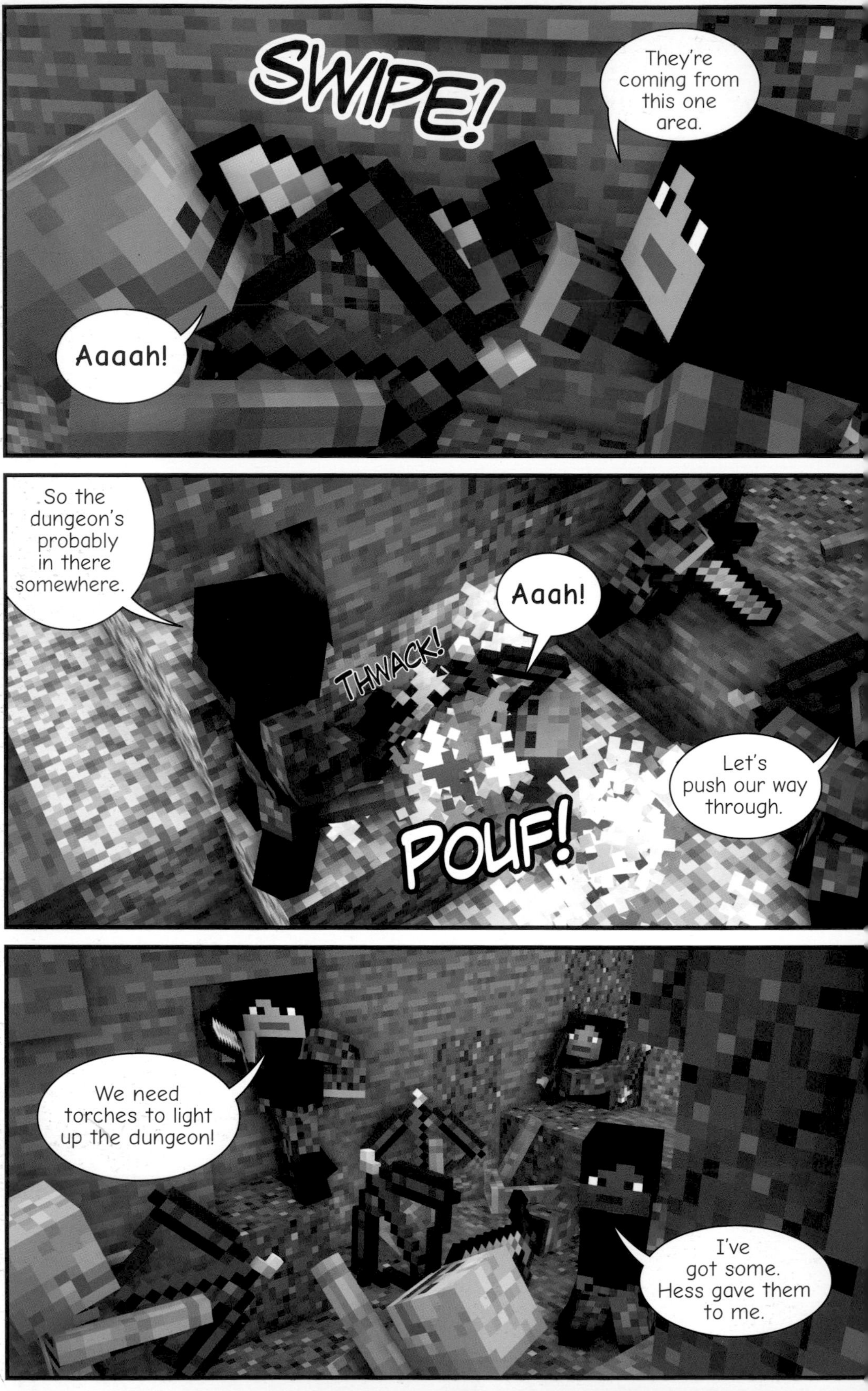
SWIPE!
They're coming from this one area.
Aaaah!
So the dungeon's probably in there somewhere.
Aaah!
THWACK!
Let's push our way through.
POUF!
We need torches to light up the dungeon!
I've got some. Hess gave them to me.

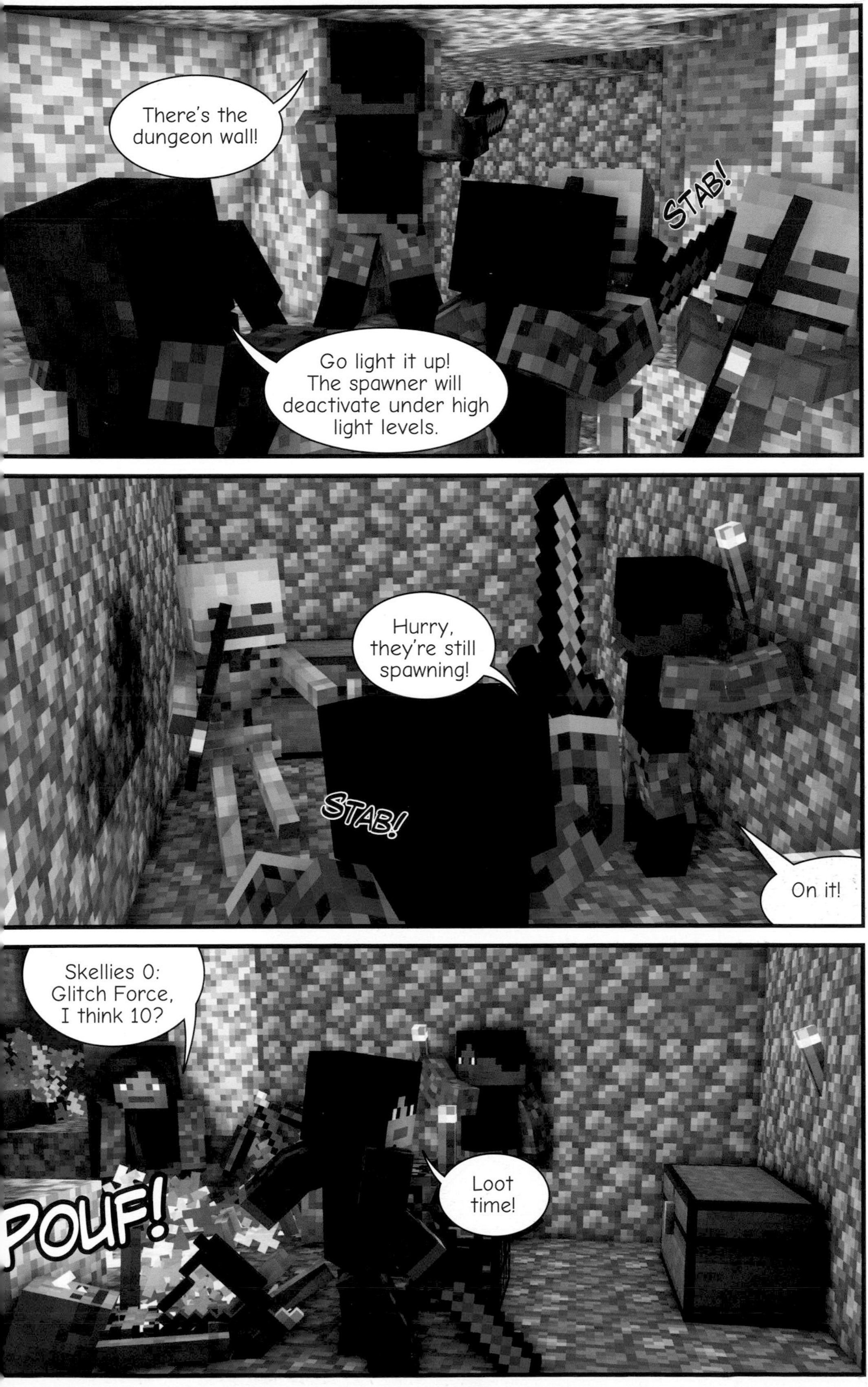
There's the dungeon wall!
STAB!
Go light it up! The spawner will deactivate under high light levels.
Hurry, they're still spawning!
STAB!
On it!
Skellies 0: Glitch Force, I think 10?
POUF!
Loot time!

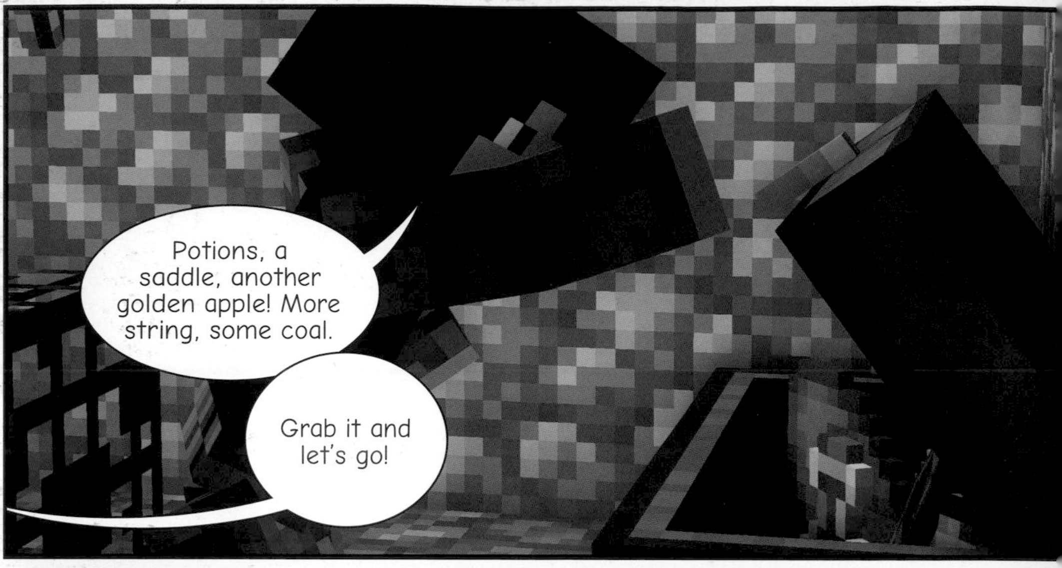
Potions, a saddle, another golden apple! More string, some coal.
Grab it and let's go!

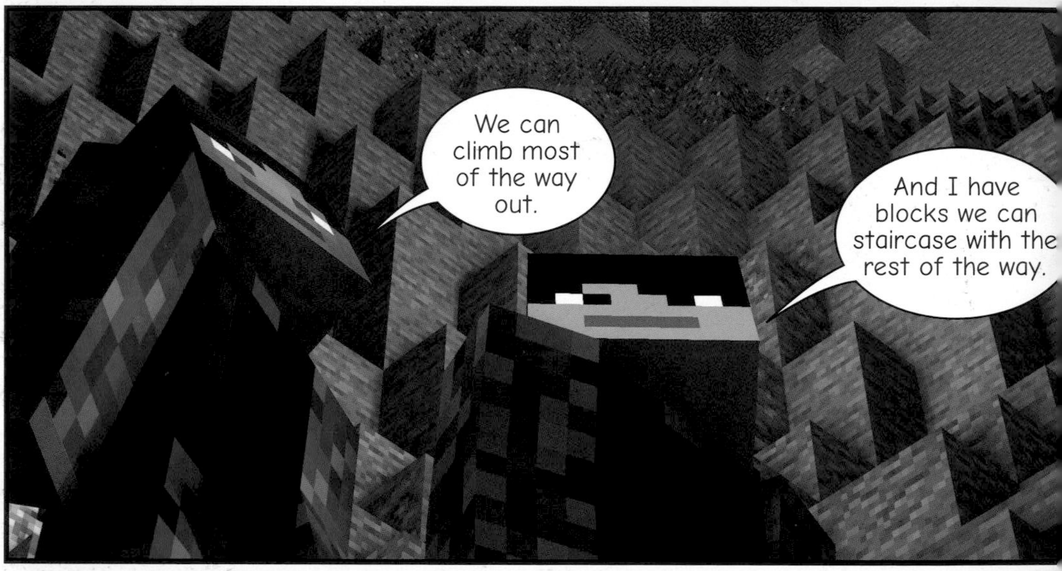
We can climb most of the way out.
And I have blocks we can staircase with the rest of the way.

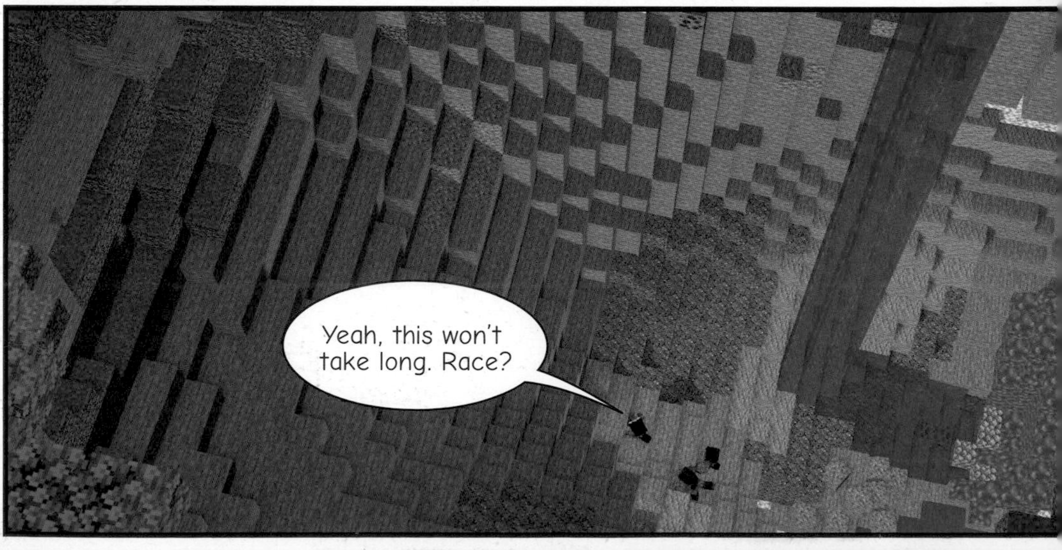
Yeah, this won't take long. Race?

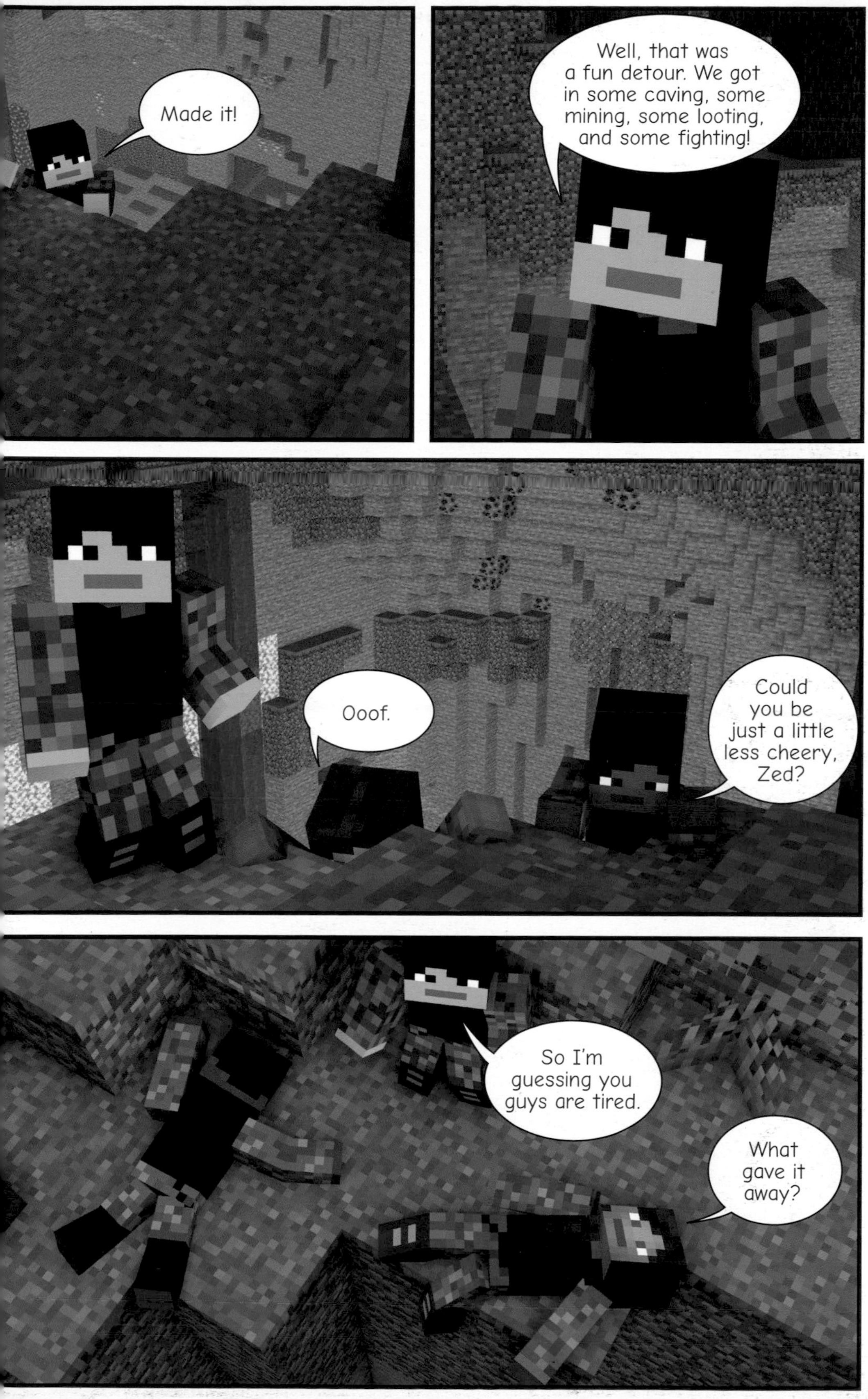
Made it!
Well, that was a fun detour. We got in some caving, some mining, some looting, and some fighting!
Ooof.
Could you be just a little less cheery, Zed?
So I'm guessing you guys are tired.
What gave it away?

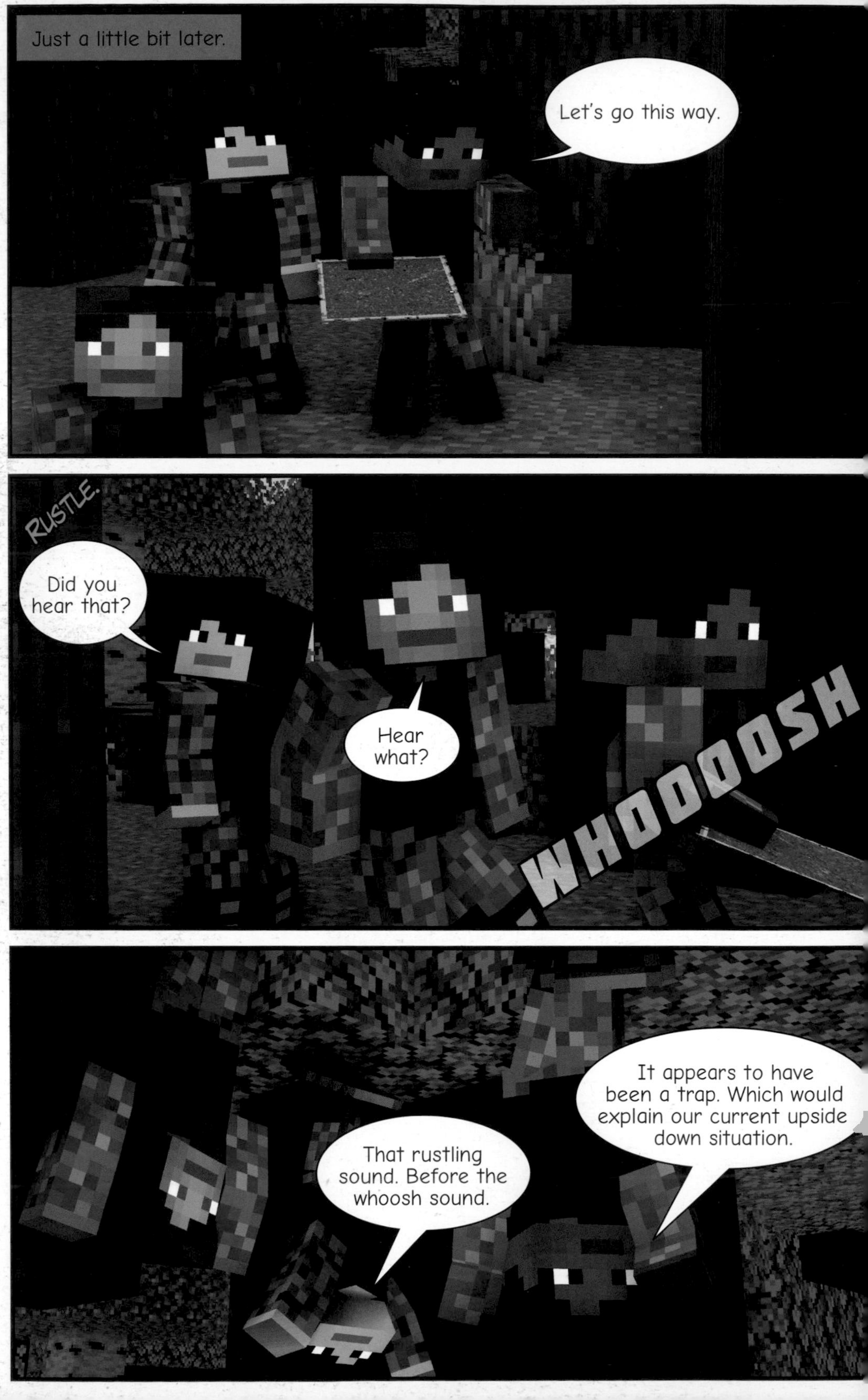
Just a little bit later.
Let's go this way.
RUSTLE.
Did you hear that?
Hear what?
WHOOOOOSH
That rustling sound. Before the whoosh sound.
It appears to have been a trap. Which would explain our current upside down situation.

CHAPTER 8:
HUNGRY

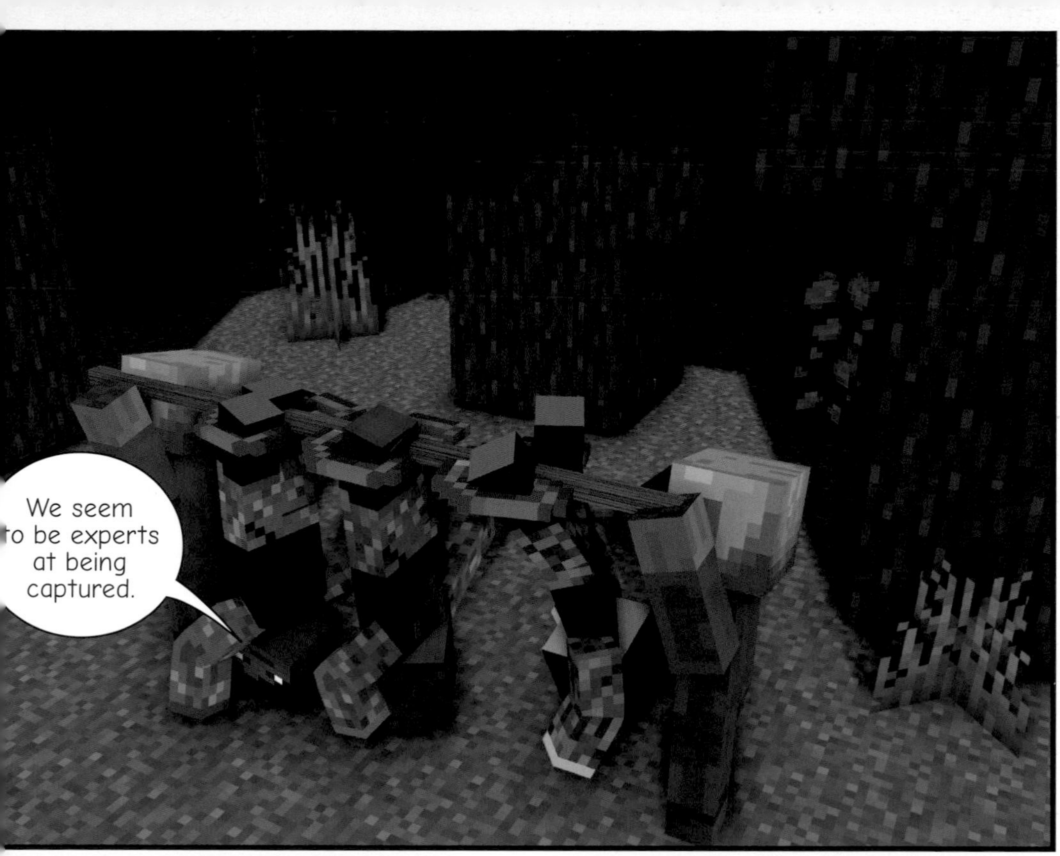
We seem to be experts at being captured.

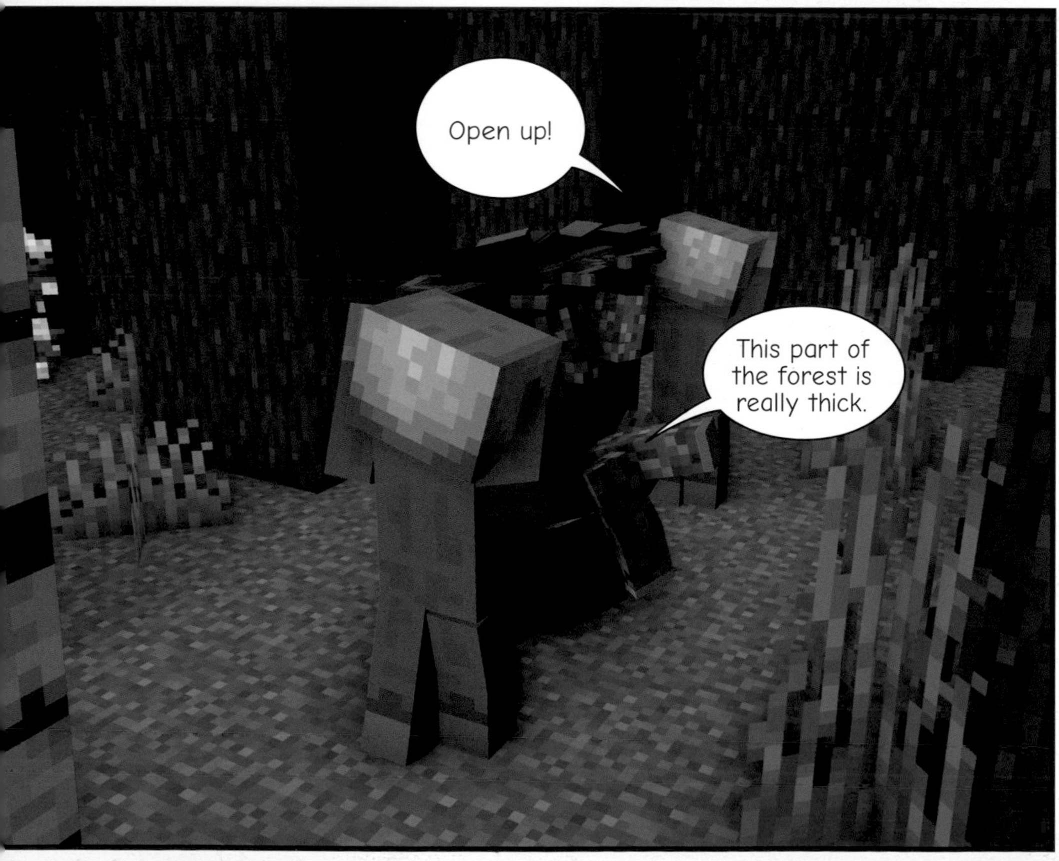
Open up!
This part of the forest is really thick.

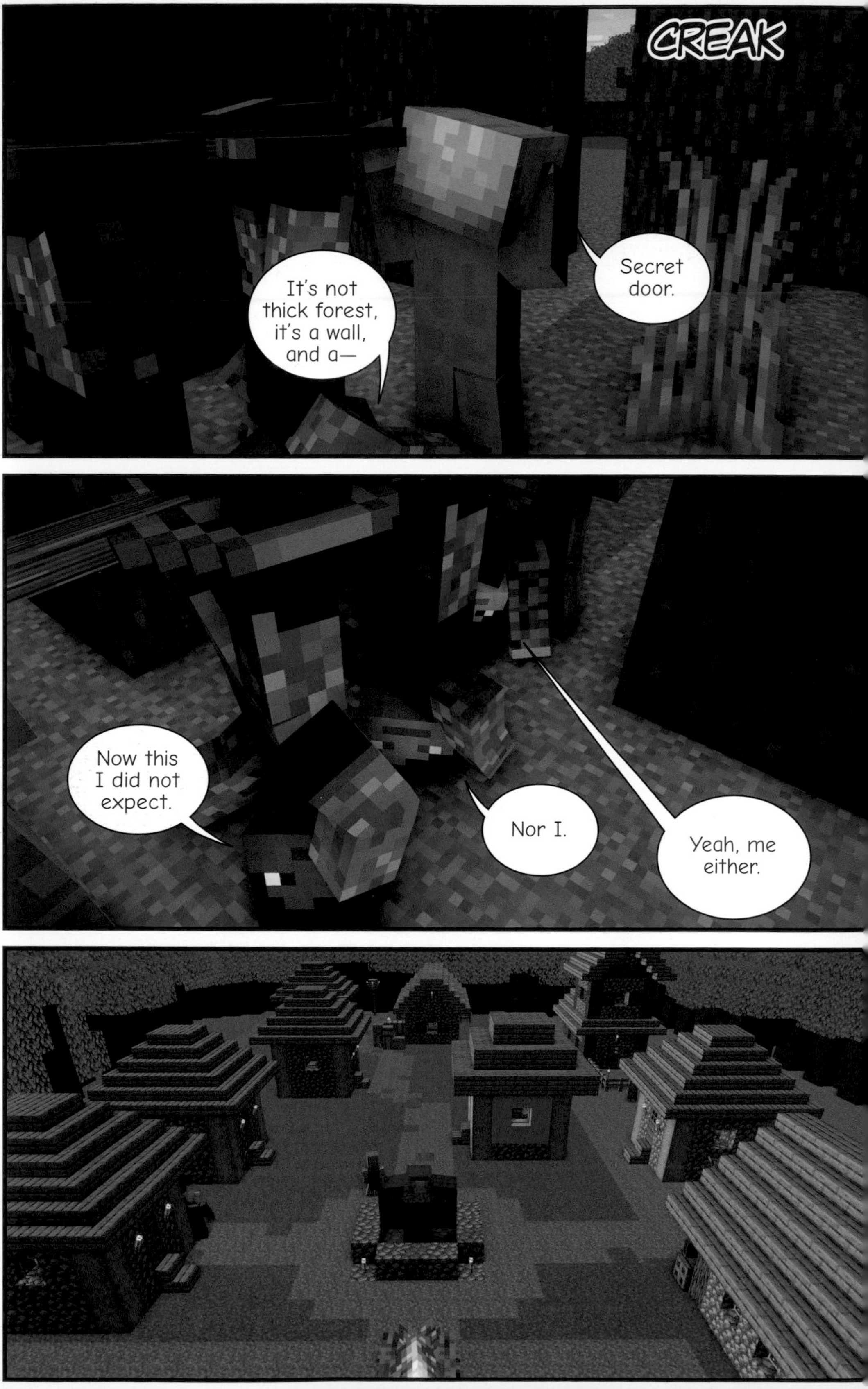
CREAK
It's not thick forest, it's a wall, and a—
Secret door.
Now this I did not expect.
Nor I.
Yeah, me either.

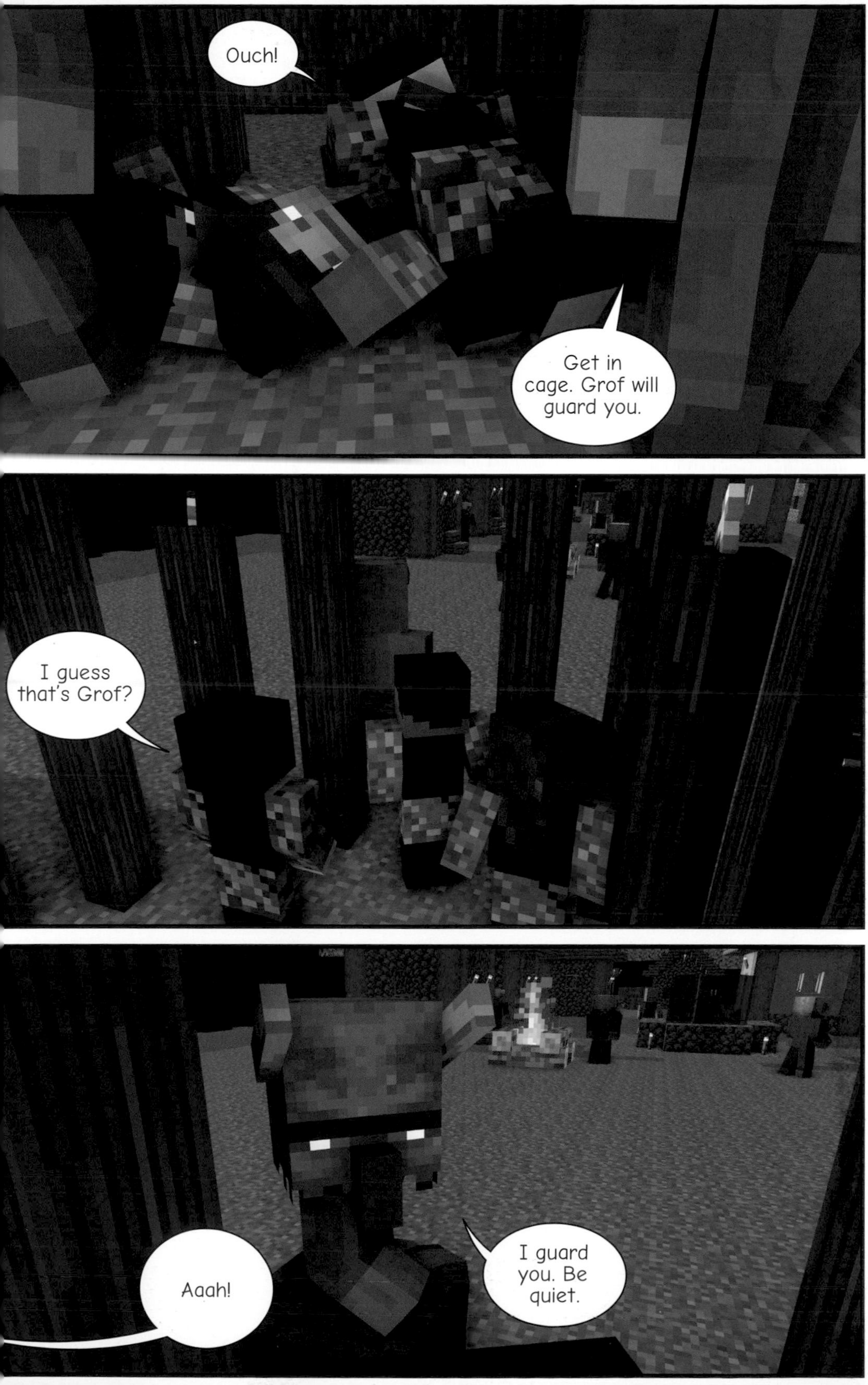
Ouch!
Get in cage. Grof will guard you.
I guess that's Grof?
I guard you. Be quiet.
Aaah!

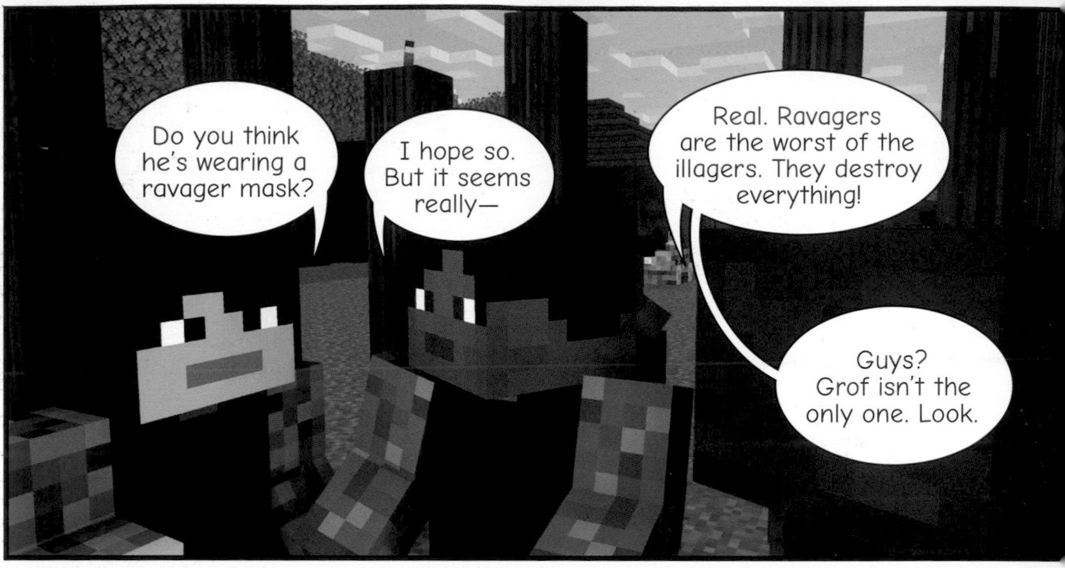
Do you think he's wearing a ravager mask?
I hope so. But it seems really—
Real. Ravagers are the worst of the illagers. They destroy everything!
Guys? Grof isn't the only one. Look.

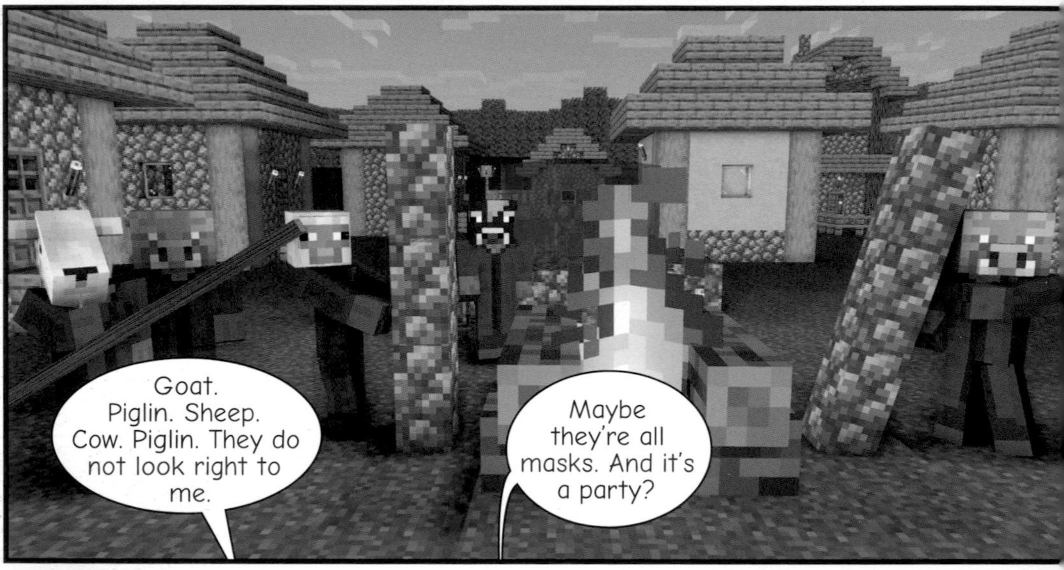
Goat. Piglin. Sheep. Cow. Piglin. They do not look right to me.
Maybe they're all masks. And it's a party?

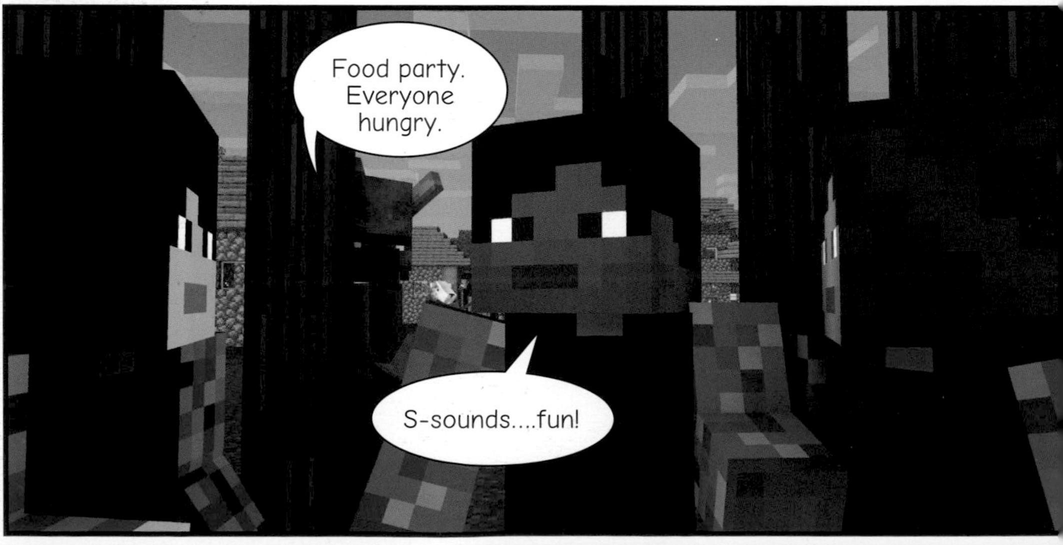
Food party. Everyone hungry.
S-sounds....fun!

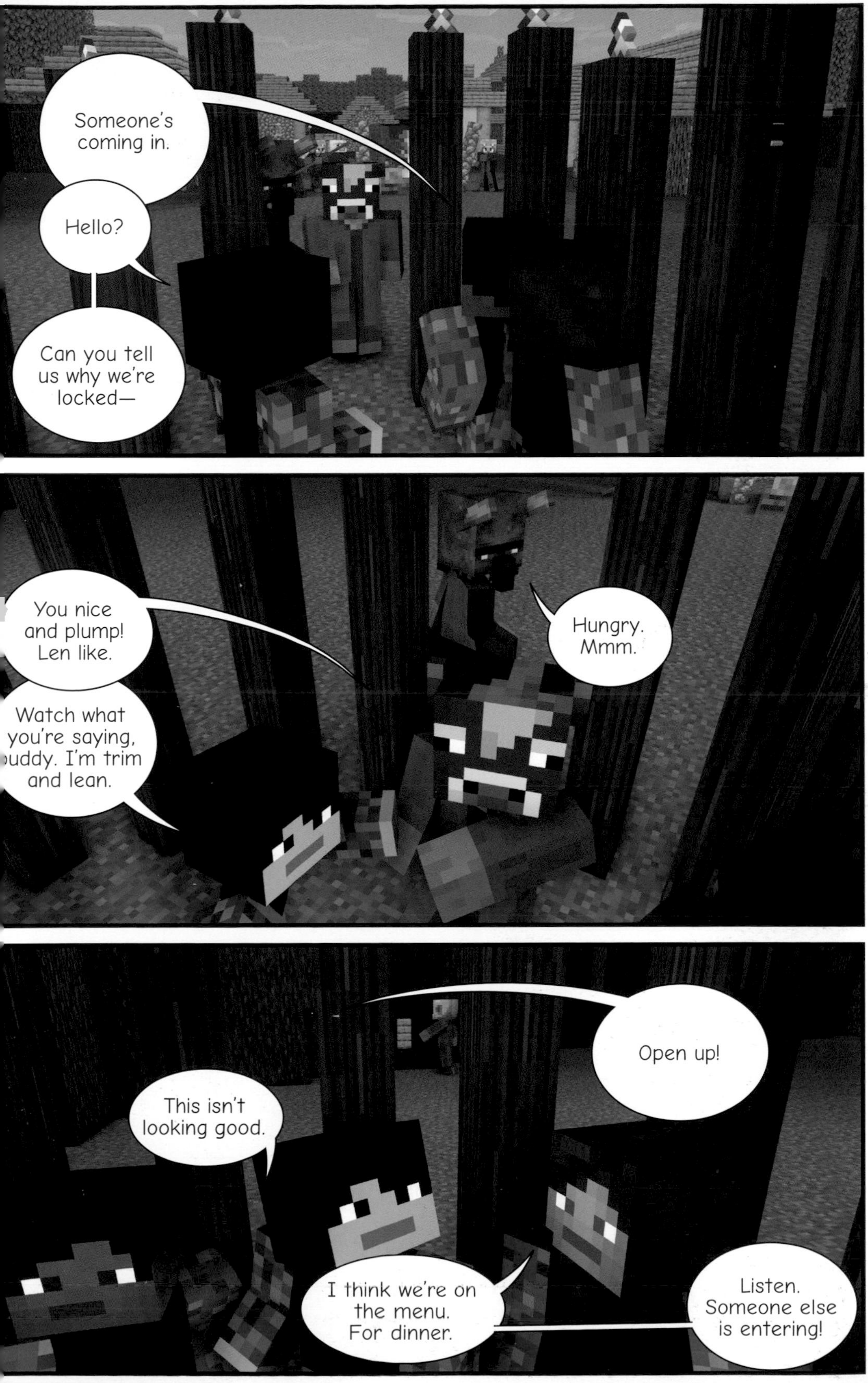
Someone's coming in.
Hello?
Can you tell us why we're locked—
You nice and plump! Len like.
Hungry. Mmm.
Watch what you're saying, buddy. I'm trim and lean.
Open up!
This isn't looking good.
I think we're on the menu. For dinner.
Listen. Someone else is entering!

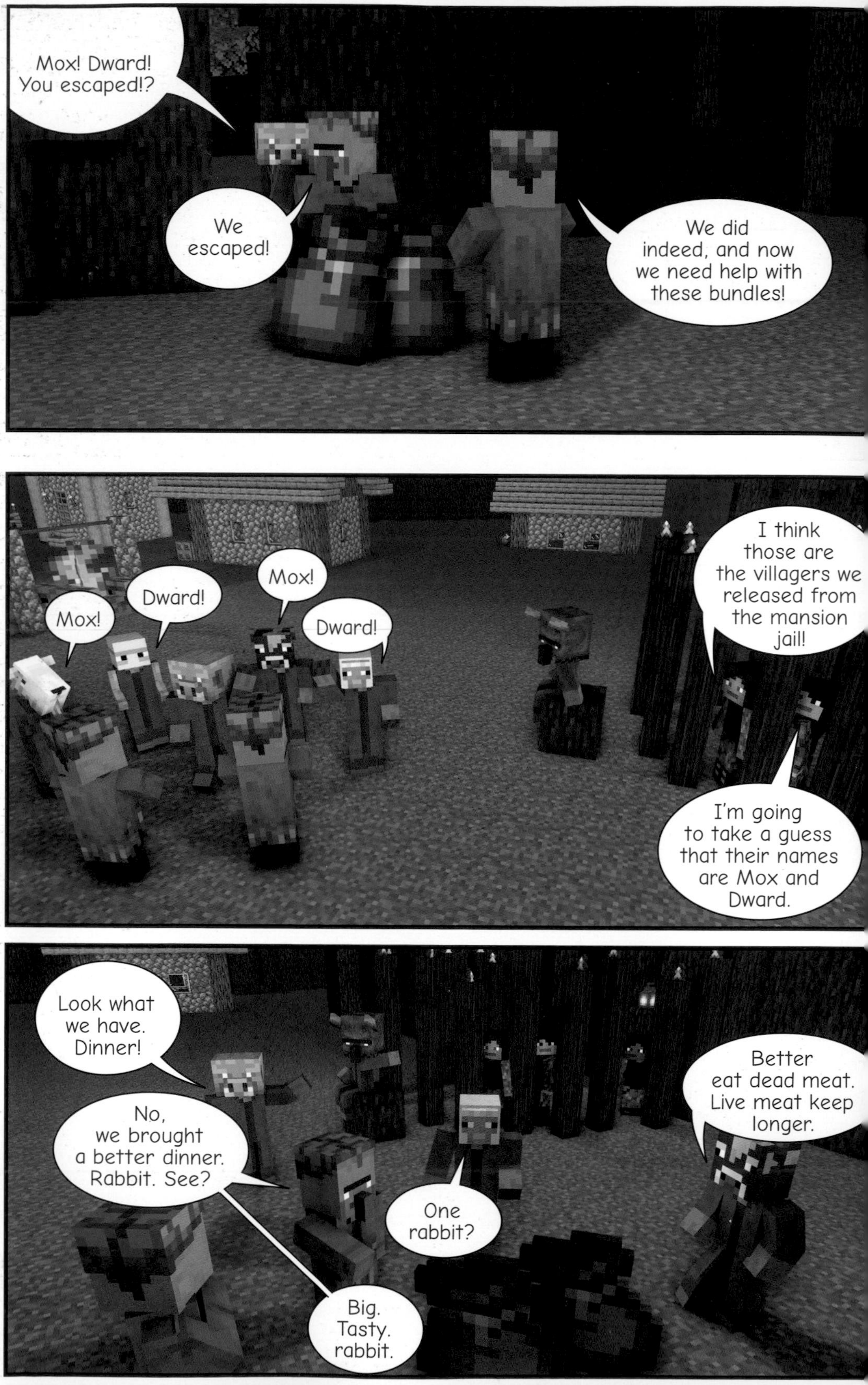
Mox! Dward! You escaped!?
We escaped!
We did indeed, and now we need help with these bundles!
Mox!
Dward!
Mox!
Dward!
I think those are the villagers we released from the mansion jail!
I'm going to take a guess that their names are Mox and Dward.
Look what we have. Dinner!
No, we brought a better dinner. Rabbit. See?
One rabbit?
Big. Tasty. rabbit.
Better eat dead meat. Live meat keep longer.

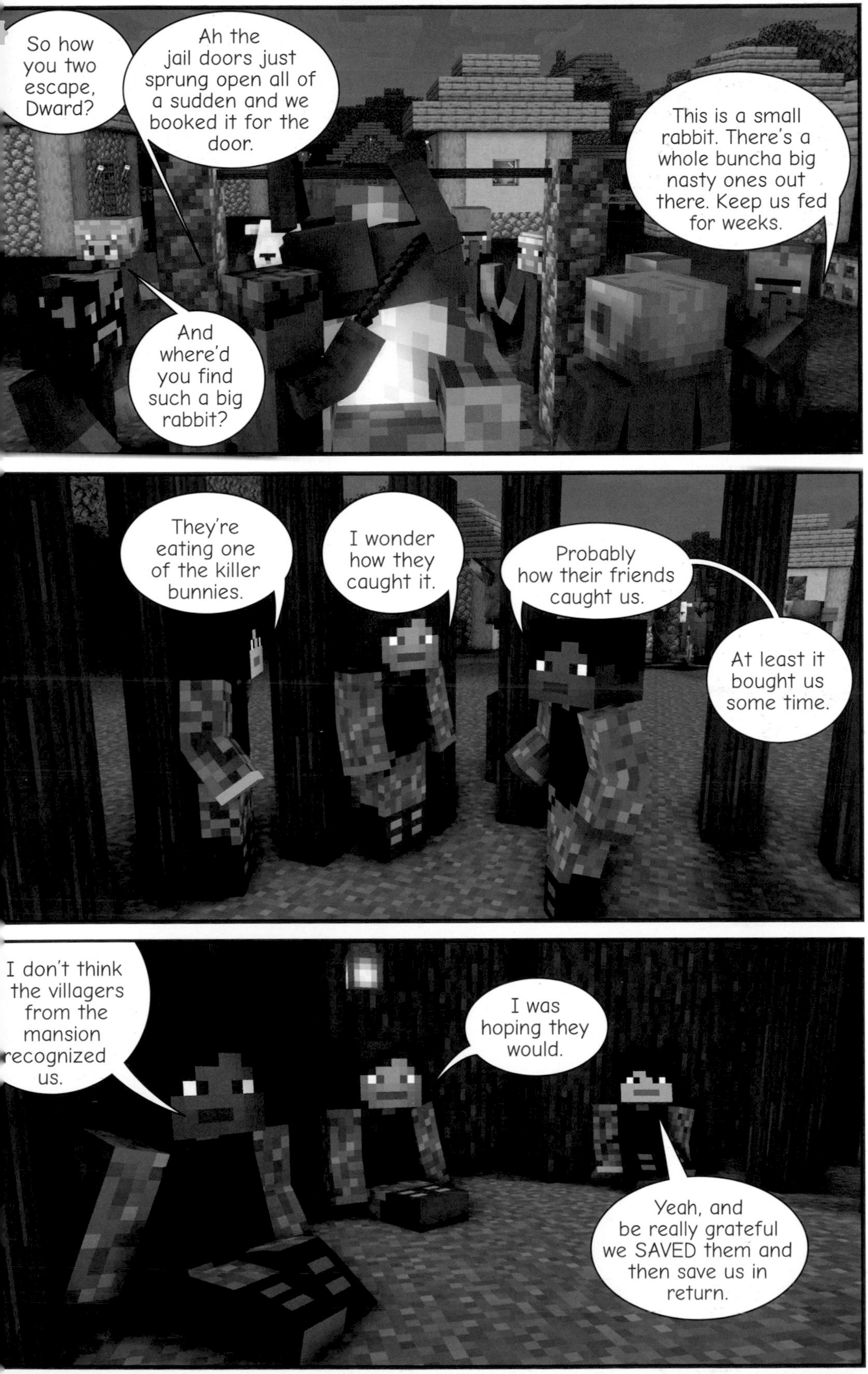
So how you two escape, Dward?
Ah the jail doors just sprung open all of a sudden and we booked it for the door.
And where'd you find such a big rabbit?
This is a small rabbit. There's a whole buncha big nasty ones out there. Keep us fed for weeks.
They're eating one of the killer bunnies.
I wonder how they caught it.
Probably how their friends caught us.
At least it bought us some time.
I don't think the villagers from the mansion recognized us.
I was hoping they would.
Yeah, and be really grateful we SAVED them and then save us in return.

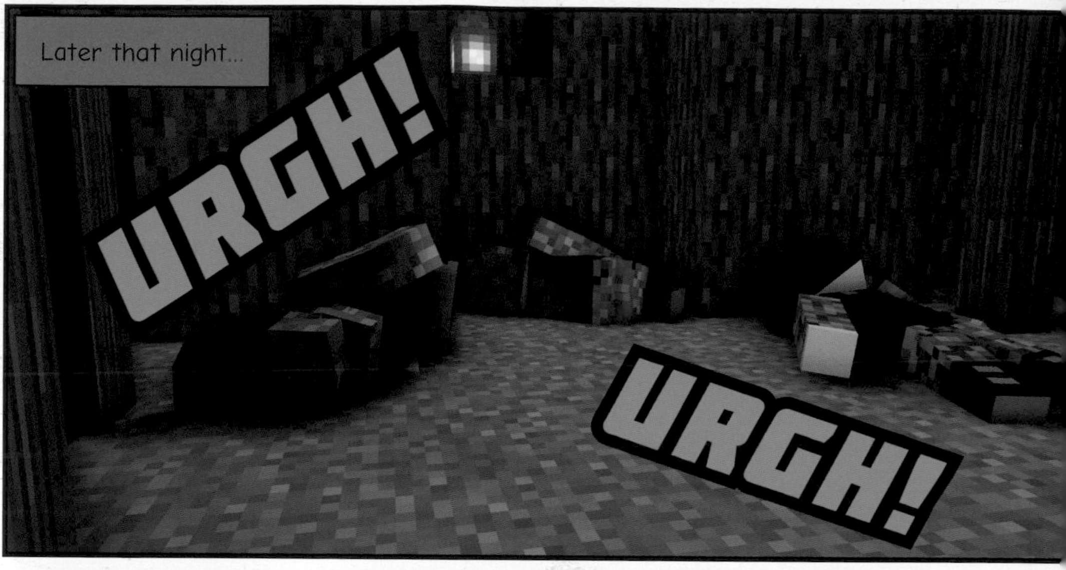
Later that night...
URGH!
URGH!

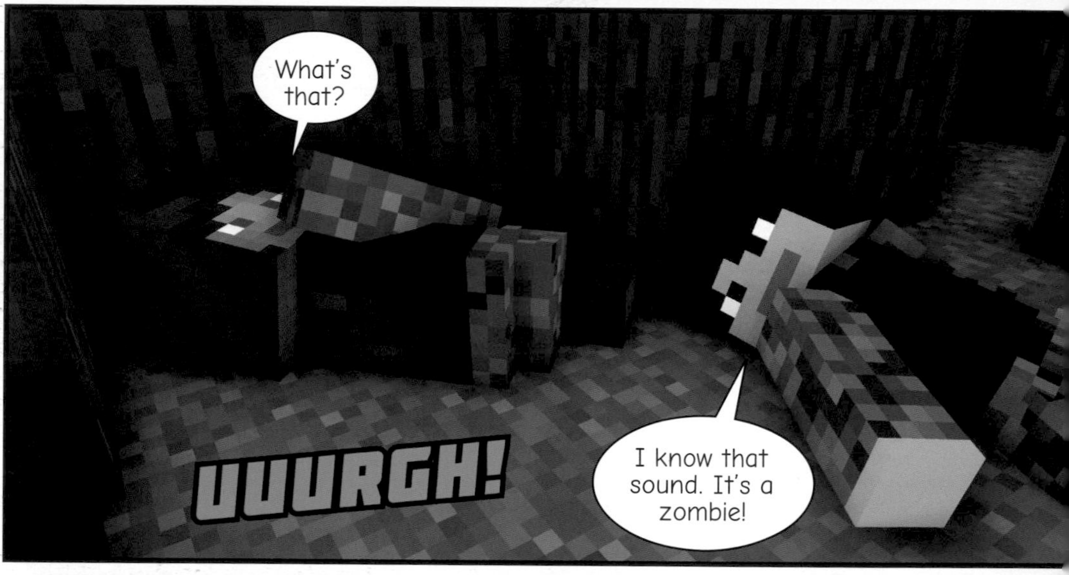
What's that?
UUURGH!
I know that sound. It's a zombie!

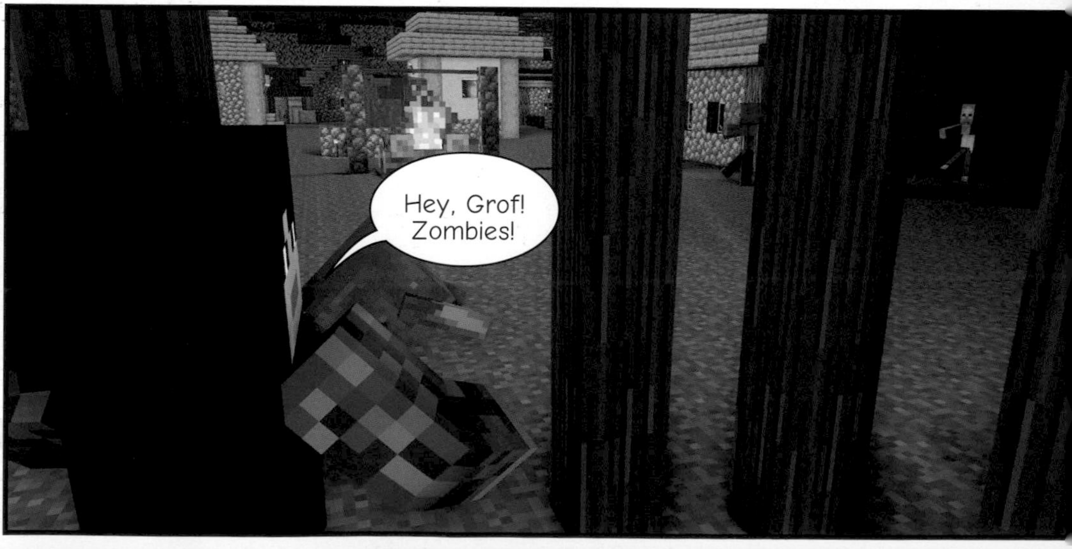
Hey, Grof! Zombies!

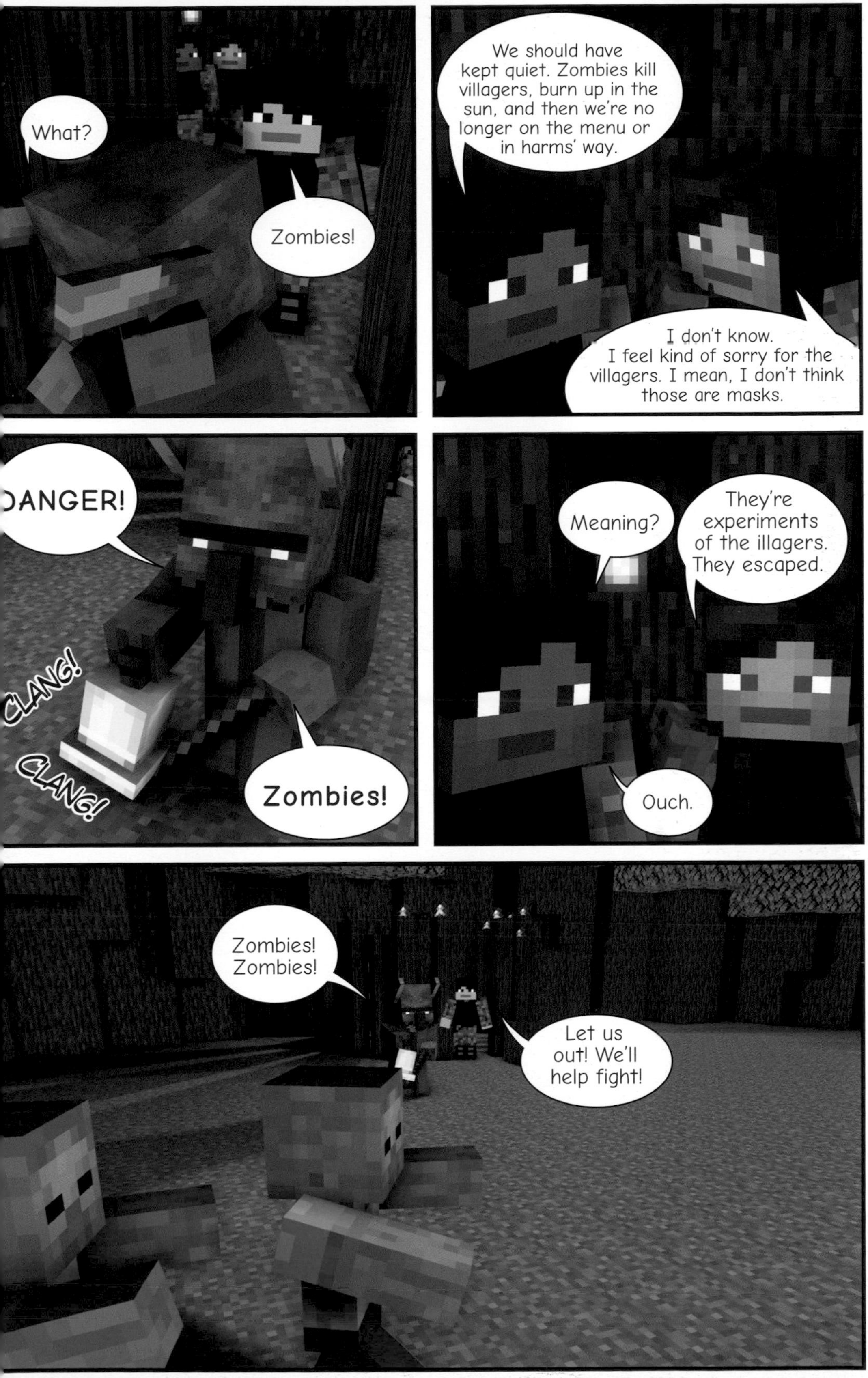

What?
Zombies!
We should have kept quiet. Zombies kill villagers, burn up in the sun, and then we're no longer on the menu or in harms' way.
I don't know. I feel kind of sorry for the villagers. I mean, I don't think those are masks.
ANGER!
CLANG!
CLANG!
Zombies!
Meaning?
They're experiments of the illagers. They escaped.
Ouch.
Zombies! Zombies!
Let us out! We'll help fight!

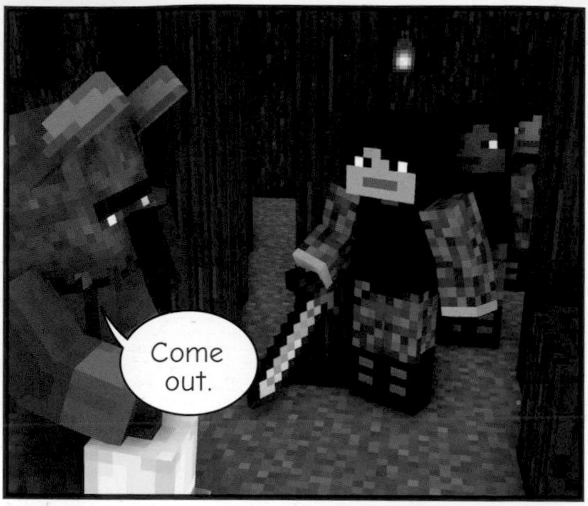
Come out.

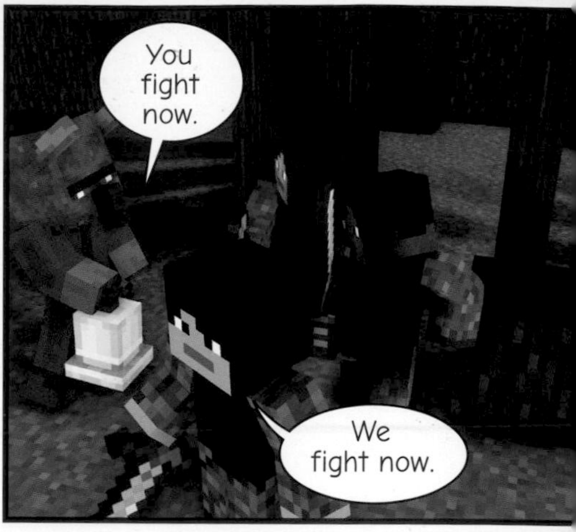
You fight now.
We fight now.

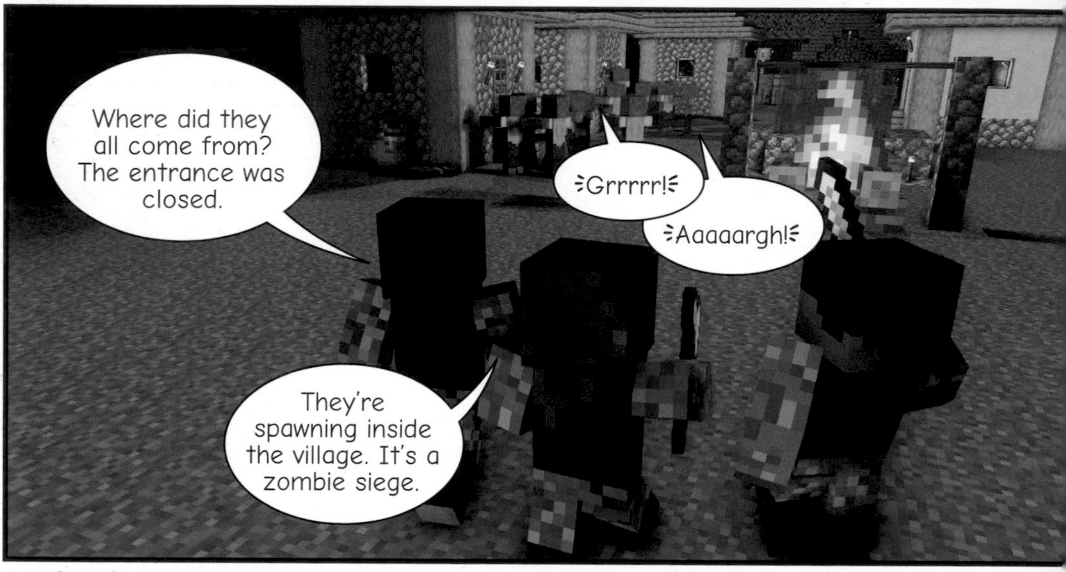
Where did they all come from? The entrance was closed.
Grrrrr!
Aaaaargh!
They're spawning inside the village. It's a zombie siege.

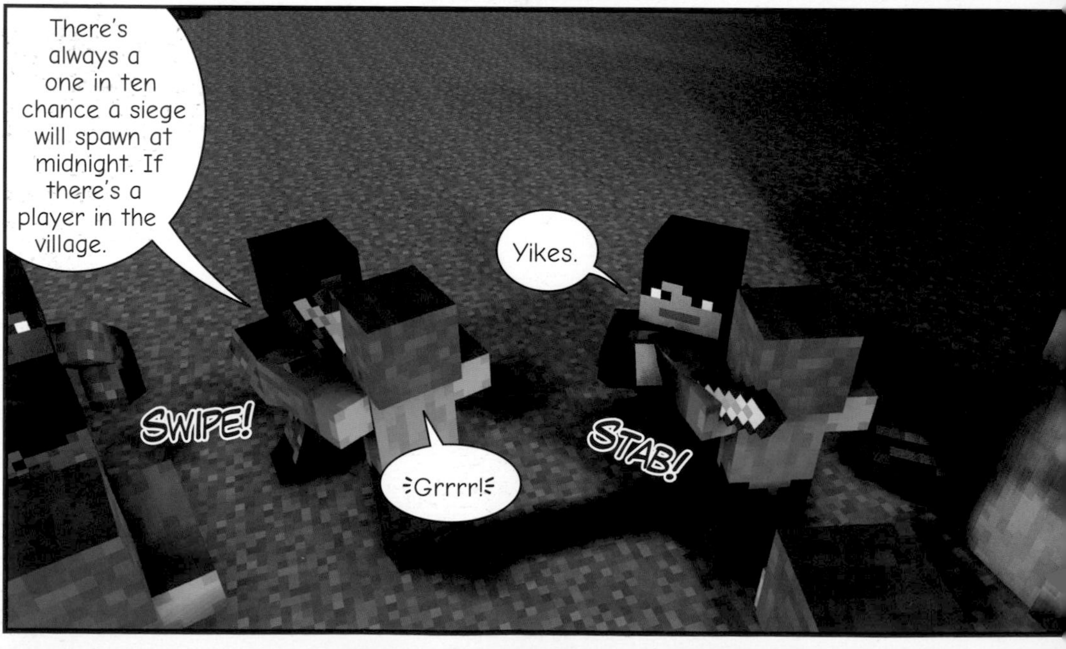
There's always a one in ten chance a siege will spawn at midnight. If there's a player in the village.
Yikes.
SWIPE!
STAB!
Grrrr!

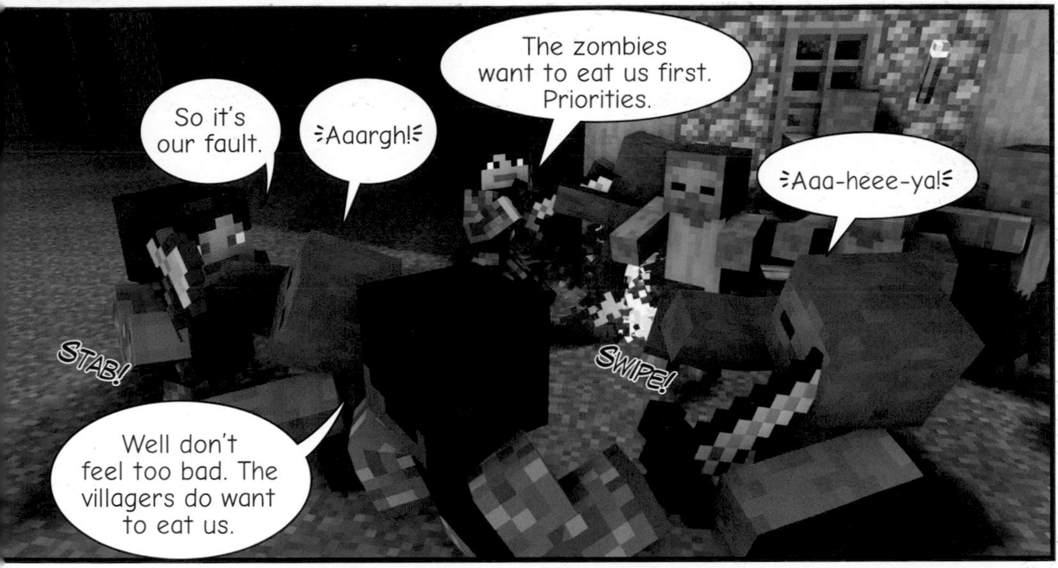
So it's our fault.
Aaargh!
The zombies want to eat us first. Priorities.
Aaa-heee-ya!
STAB!
SWIPE!
Well don't feel too bad. The villagers do want to eat us.

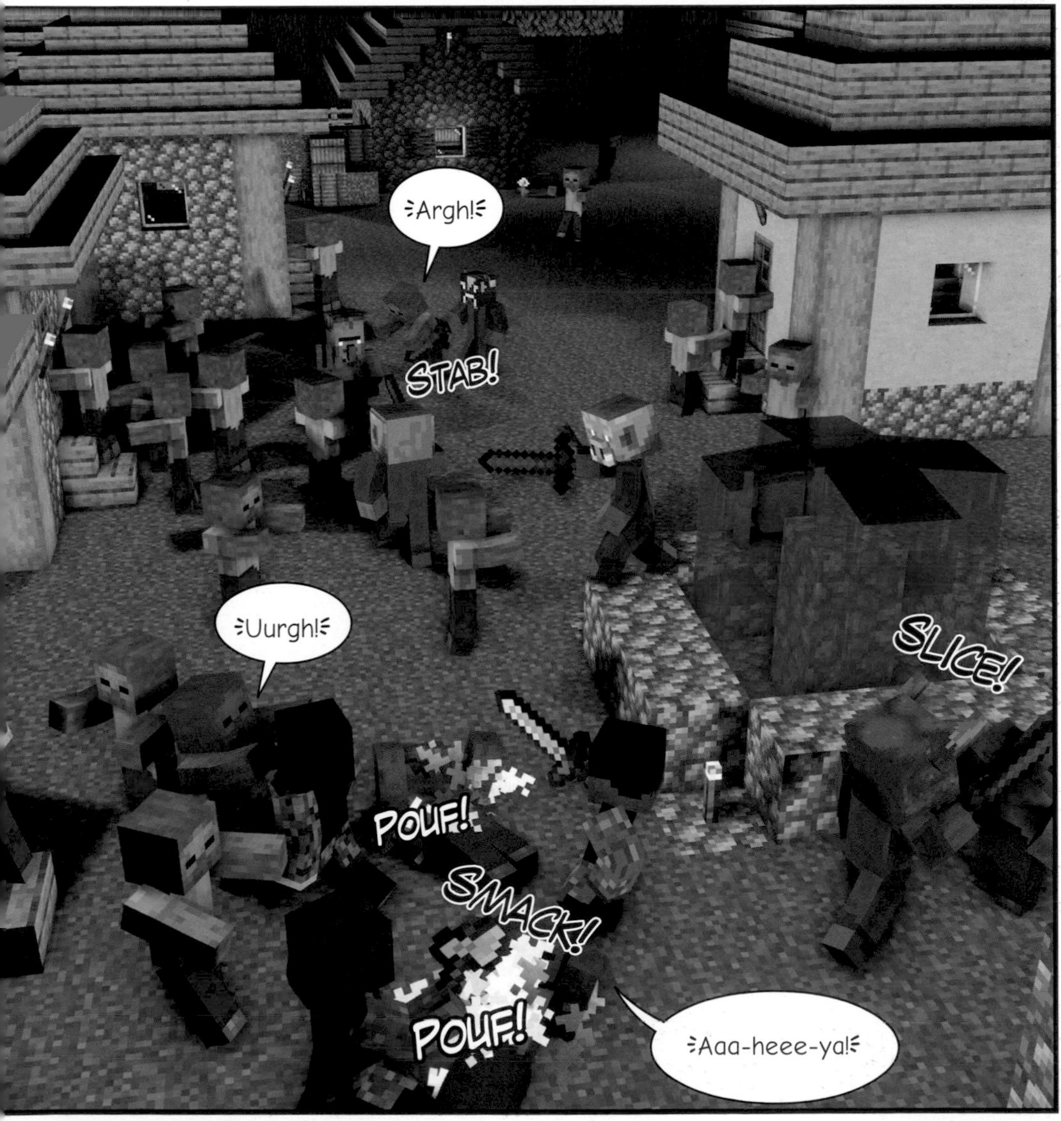
Argh!
STAB!
Uurgh!
SLICE!
POUF!
SMACK!
POUF!
Aaa-heee-ya!

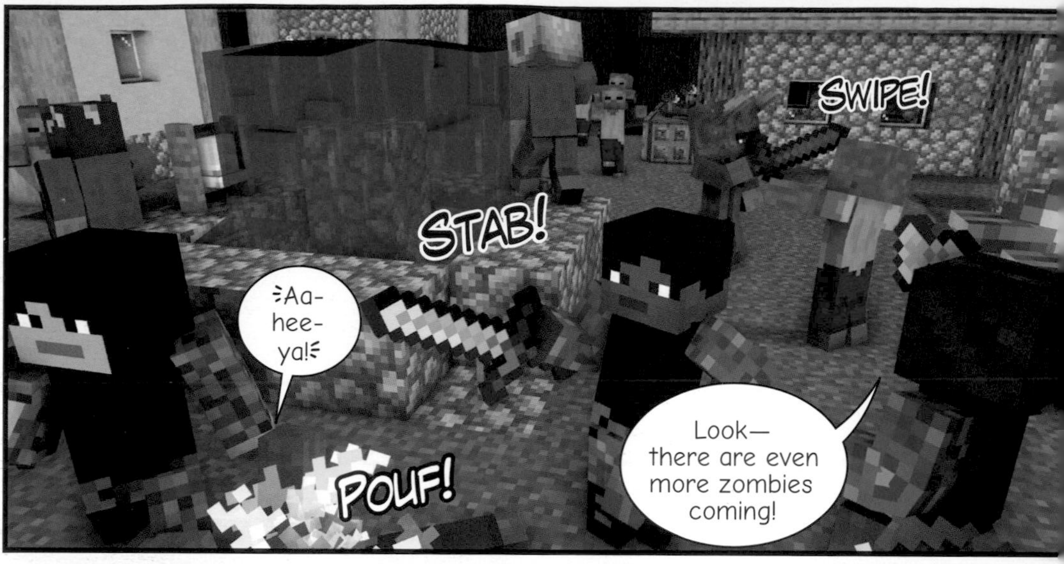
SWIPE!
STAB!
Aa-hee-ya!
POUF!
Look— there are even more zombies coming!

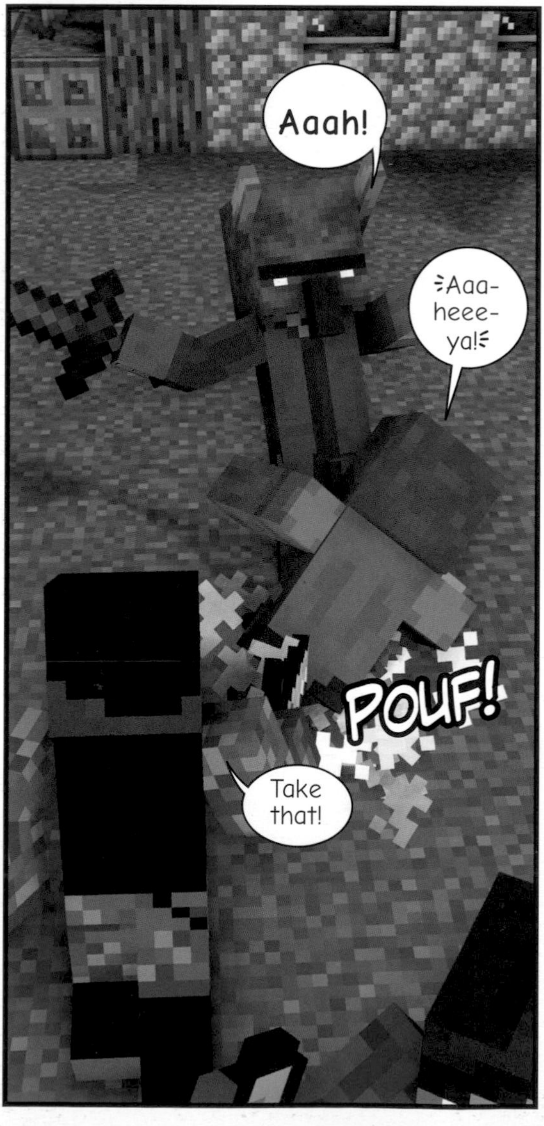
Aaah!
Aaa-heee-ya!
POUF!
Take that!

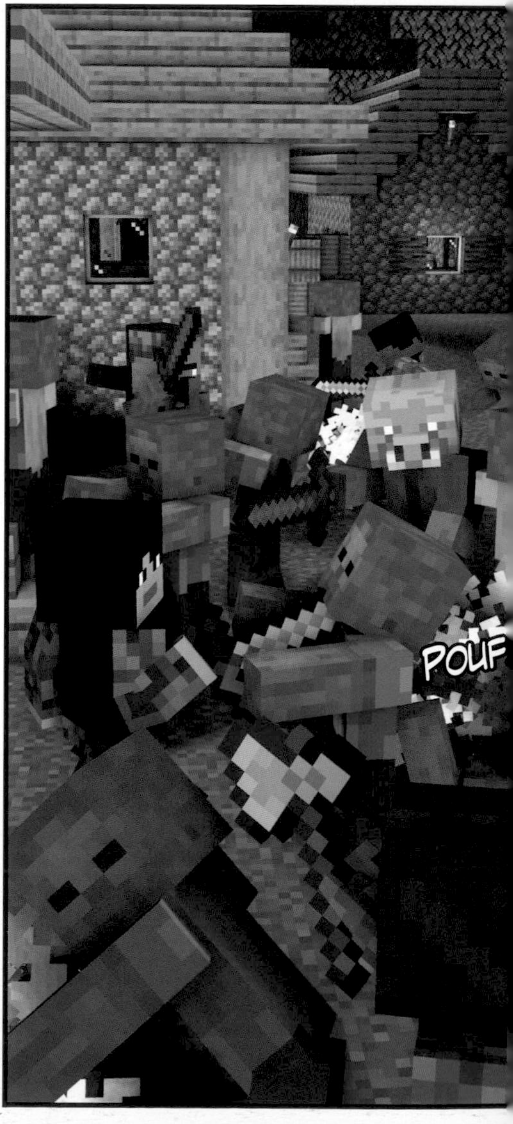
POUF

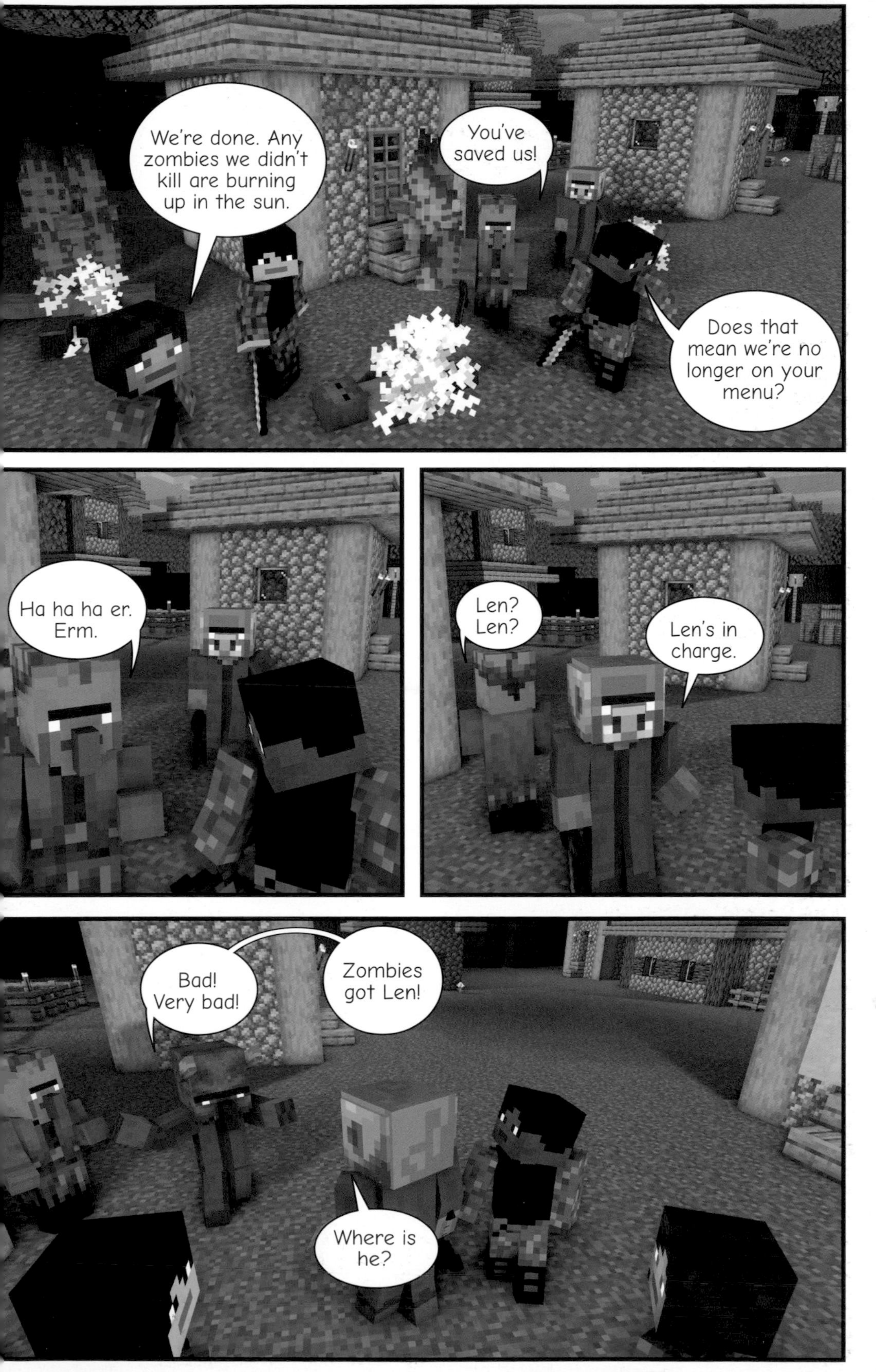
We're done. Any zombies we didn't kill are burning up in the sun.
You've saved us!
Does that mean we're no longer on your menu?
Ha ha ha er. Erm.
Len? Len?
Len's in charge.
Bad! Very bad!
Zombies got Len!
Where is he?

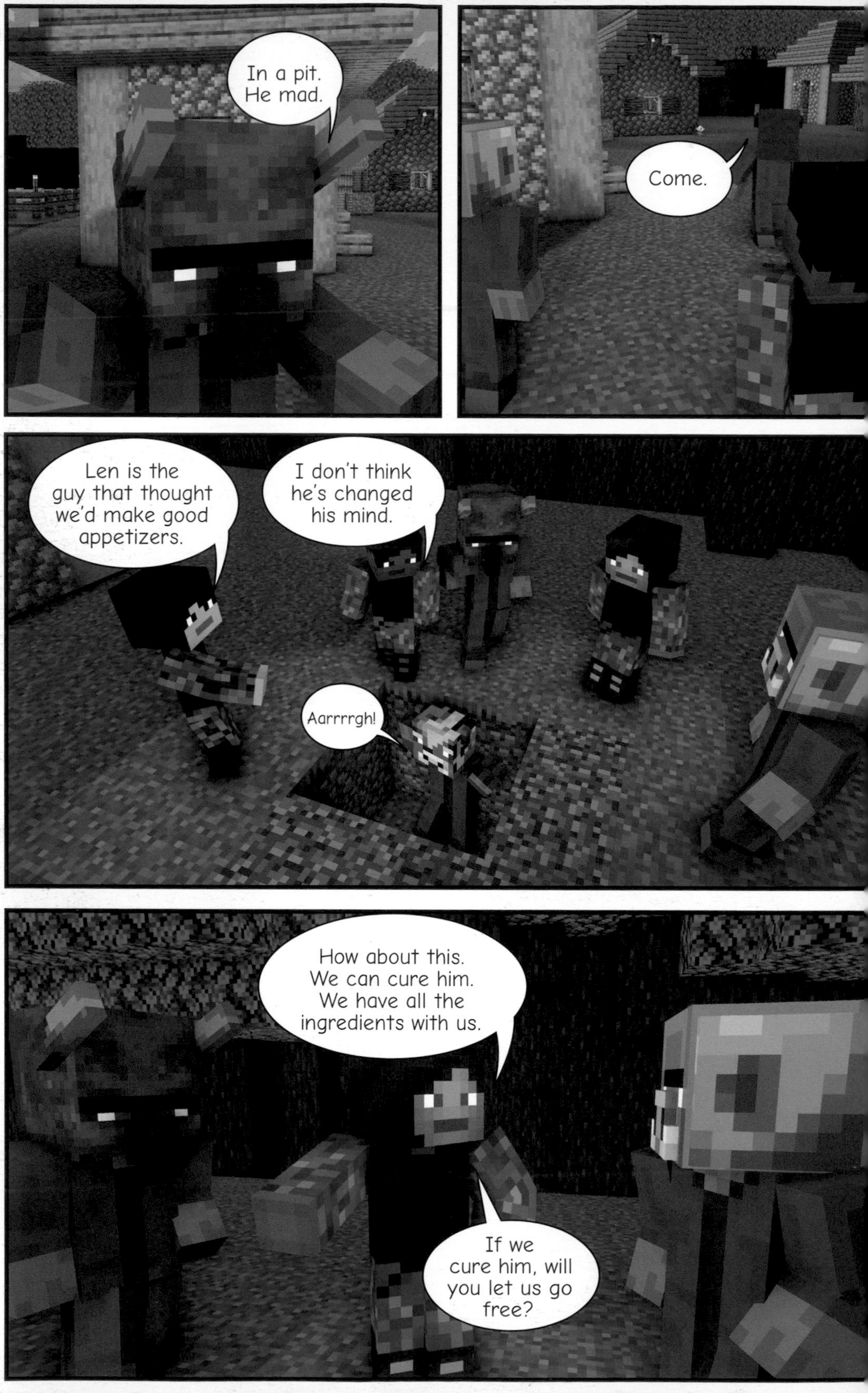
In a pit. He mad.
Come.
Len is the guy that thought we'd make good appetizers.
I don't think he's changed his mind.
Aarrrrgh!
How about this. We can cure him. We have all the ingredients with us.
If we cure him, will you let us go free?

Chapter 9:
Hunt

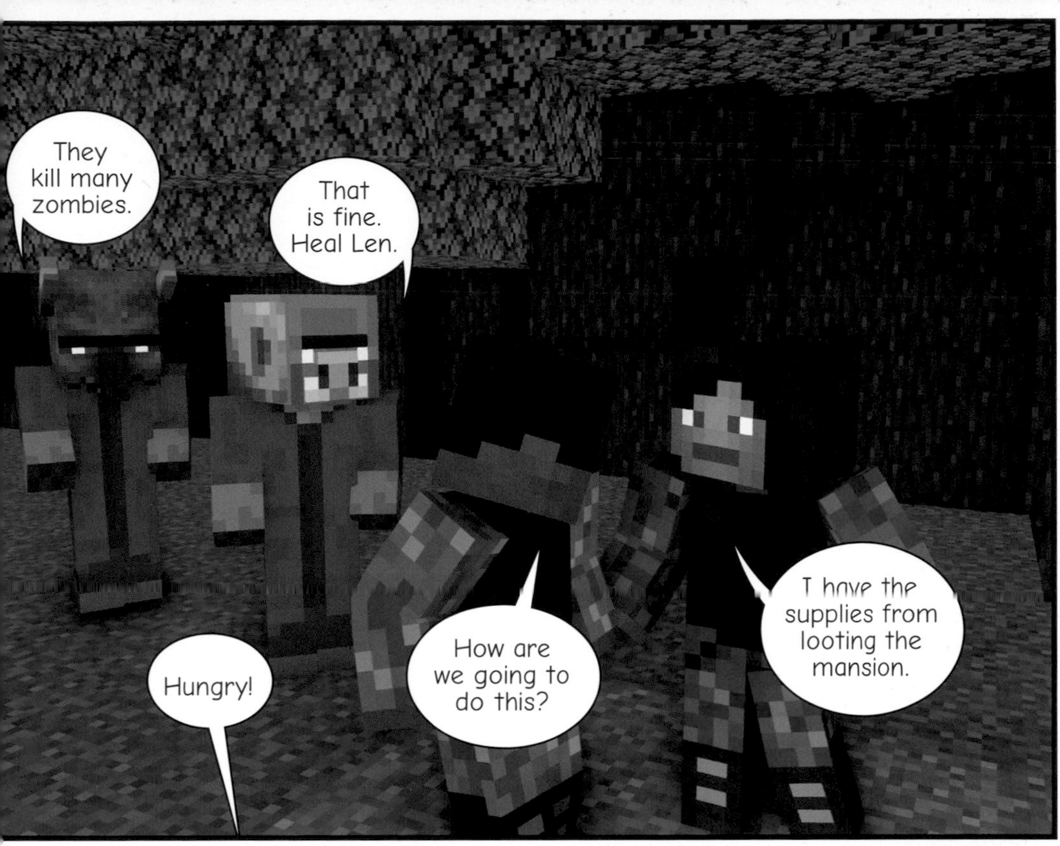
They kill many zombies.
That is fine. Heal Len.
Hungry!
How are we going to do this?
I have the supplies from looting the mansion.

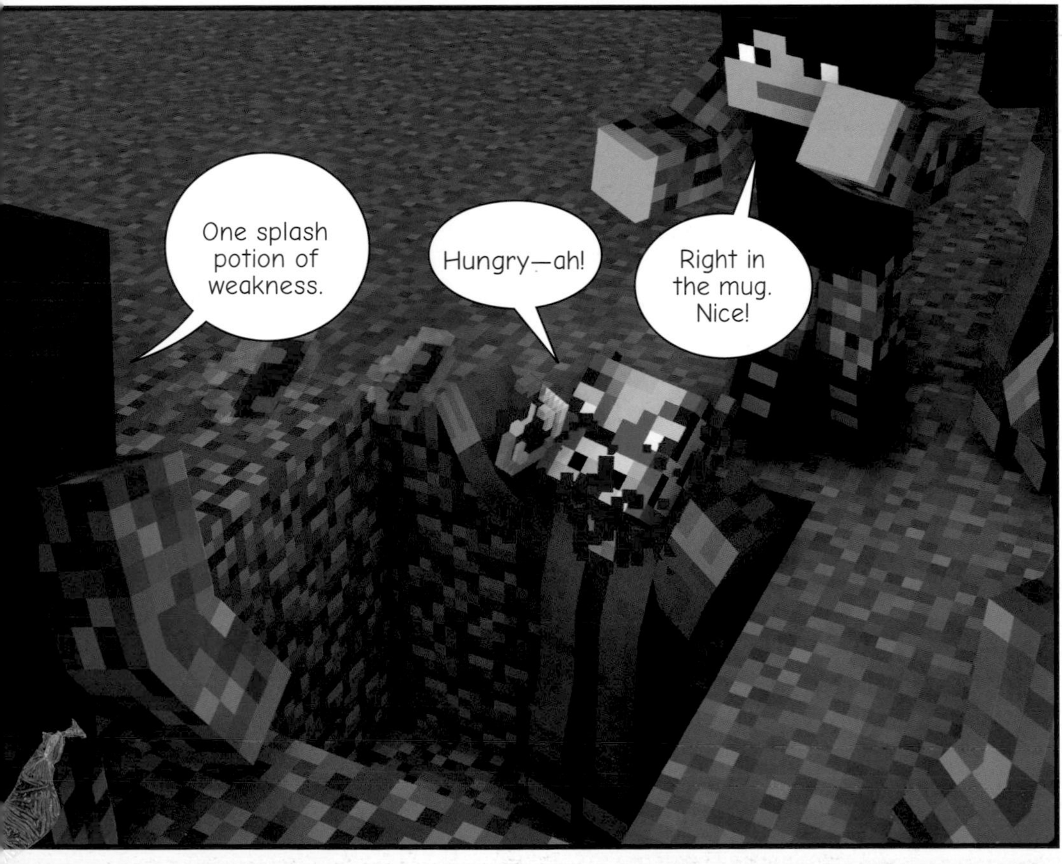
One splash potion of weakness.
Hungry—ah!
Right in the mug. Nice!

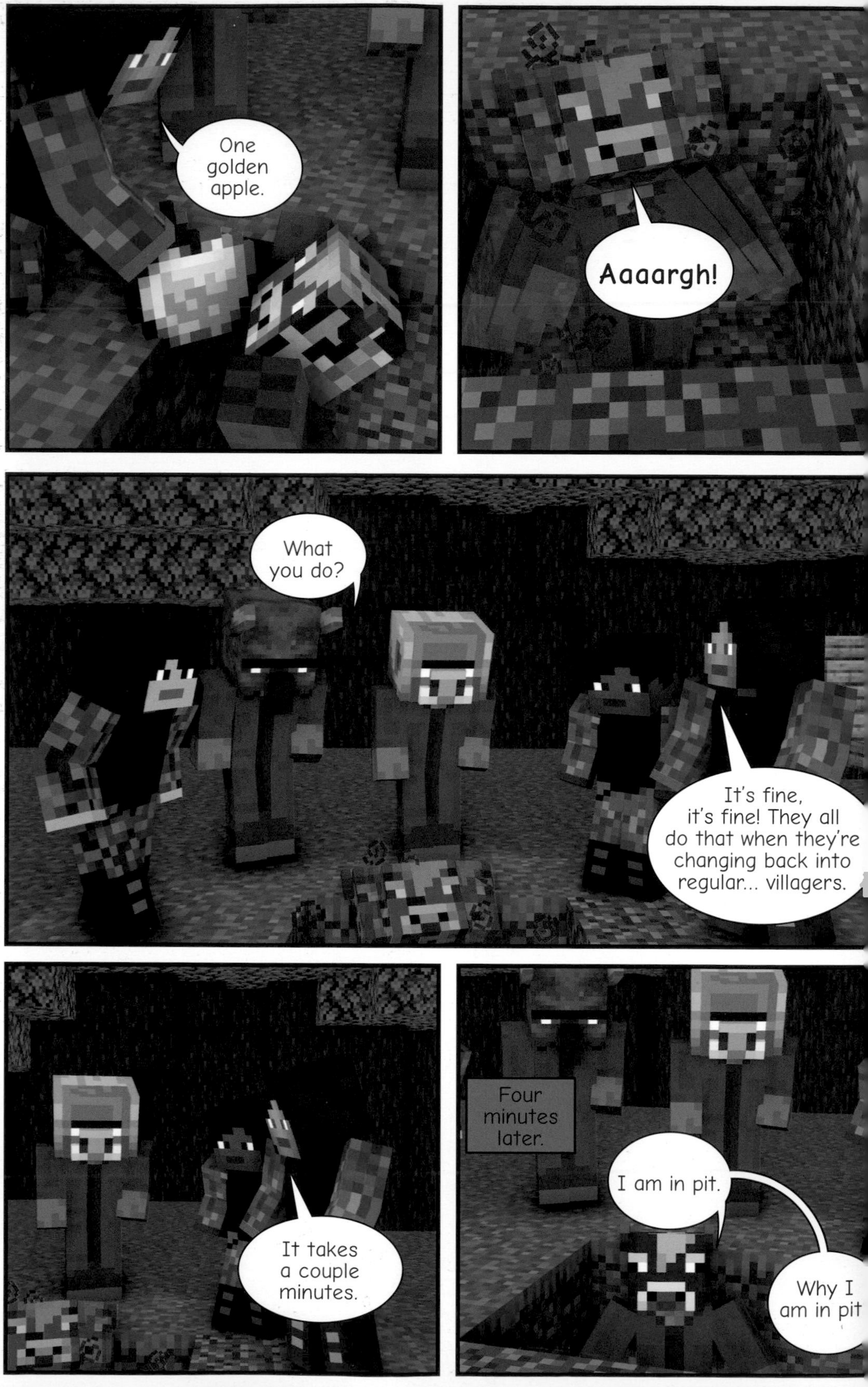
One golden apple.
Aaaargh!
What you do?
It's fine, it's fine! They all do that when they're changing back into regular... villagers.
It takes a couple minutes.
Four minutes later.
I am in pit.
Why I am in pit

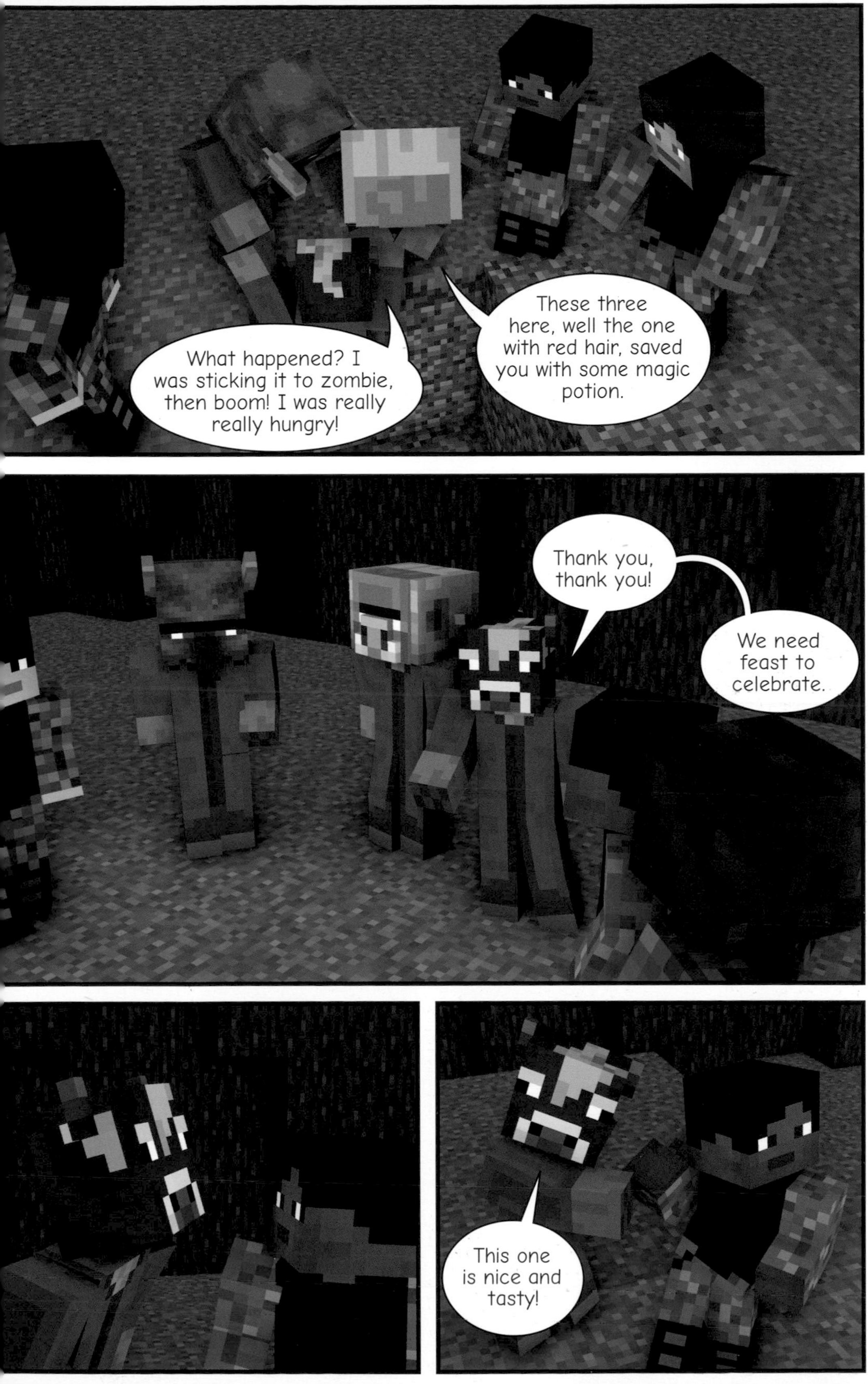
What happened? I was sticking it to zombie, then boom! I was really really hungry!
These three here, well the one with red hair, saved you with some magic potion.
Thank you, thank you!
We need feast to celebrate.
This one is nice and tasty!

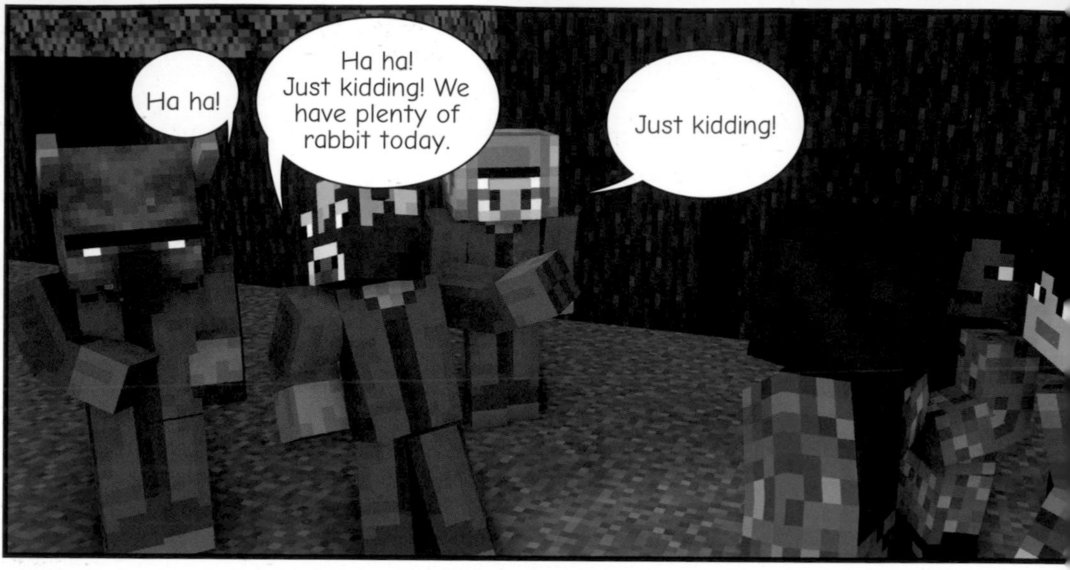
Ha ha!
Ha ha! Just kidding! We have plenty of rabbit today.
Just kidding!

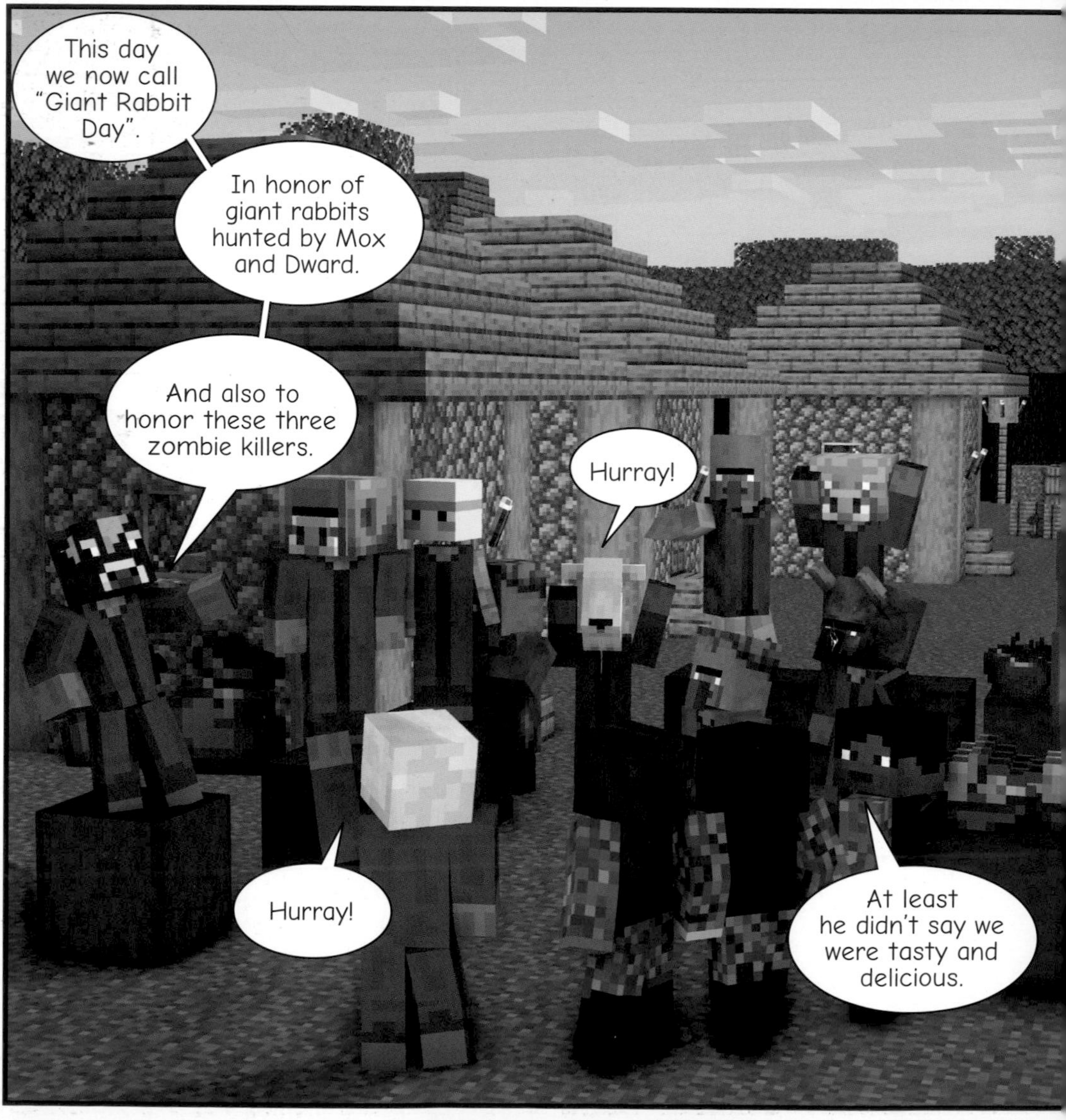
This day we now call "Giant Rabbit Day".
In honor of giant rabbits hunted by Mox and Dward.
And also to honor these three zombie killers.
Hurray!
Hurray!
At least he didn't say we were tasty and delicious.

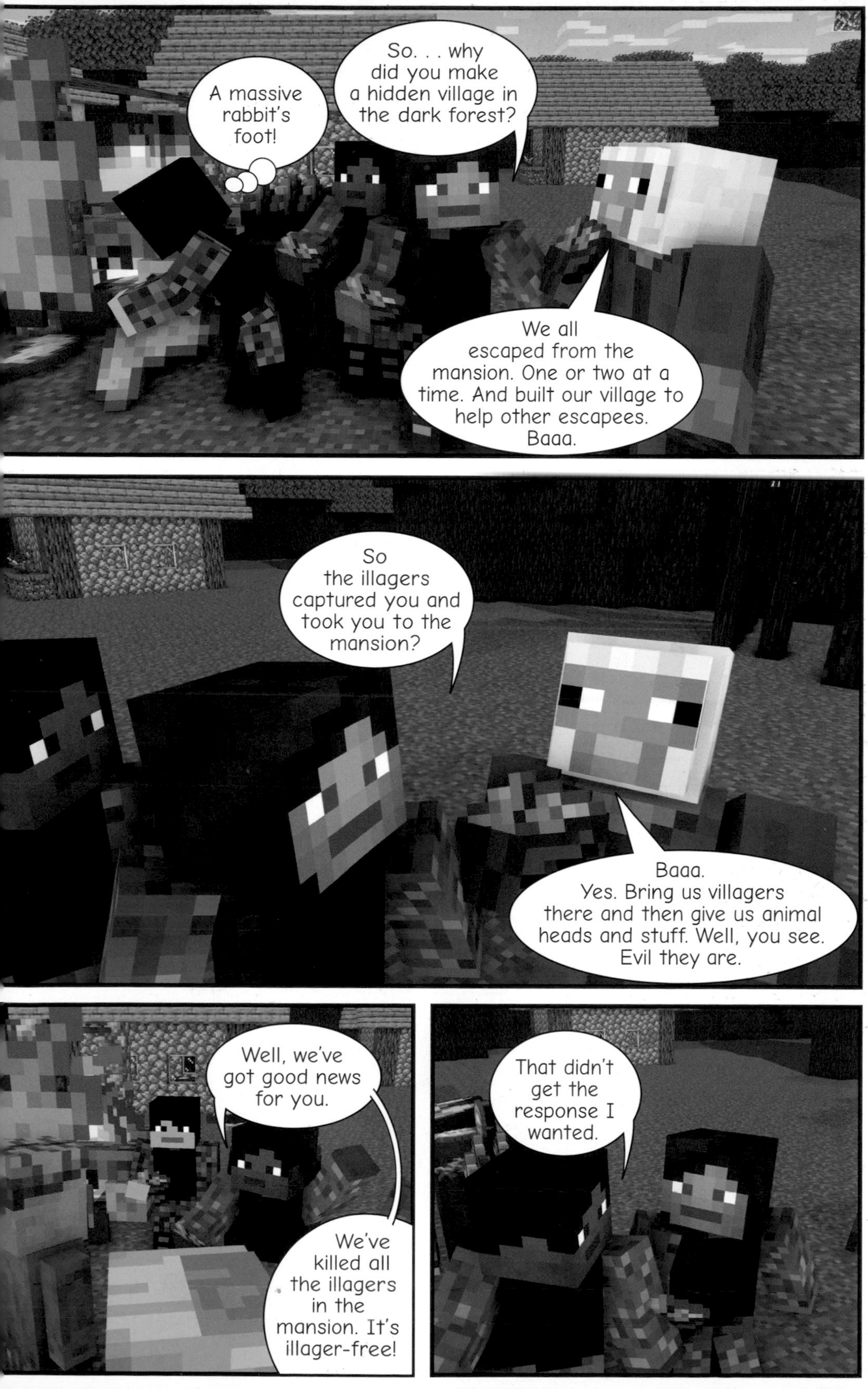

A massive rabbit's foot!
So. . . why did you make a hidden village in the dark forest?
We all escaped from the mansion. One or two at a time. And built our village to help other escapees. Baaa.
So the illagers captured you and took you to the mansion?
Baaa. Yes. Bring us villagers there and then give us animal heads and stuff. Well, you see. Evil they are.
Well, we've got good news for you.
We've killed all the illagers in the mansion. It's illager-free!
That didn't get the response I wanted.

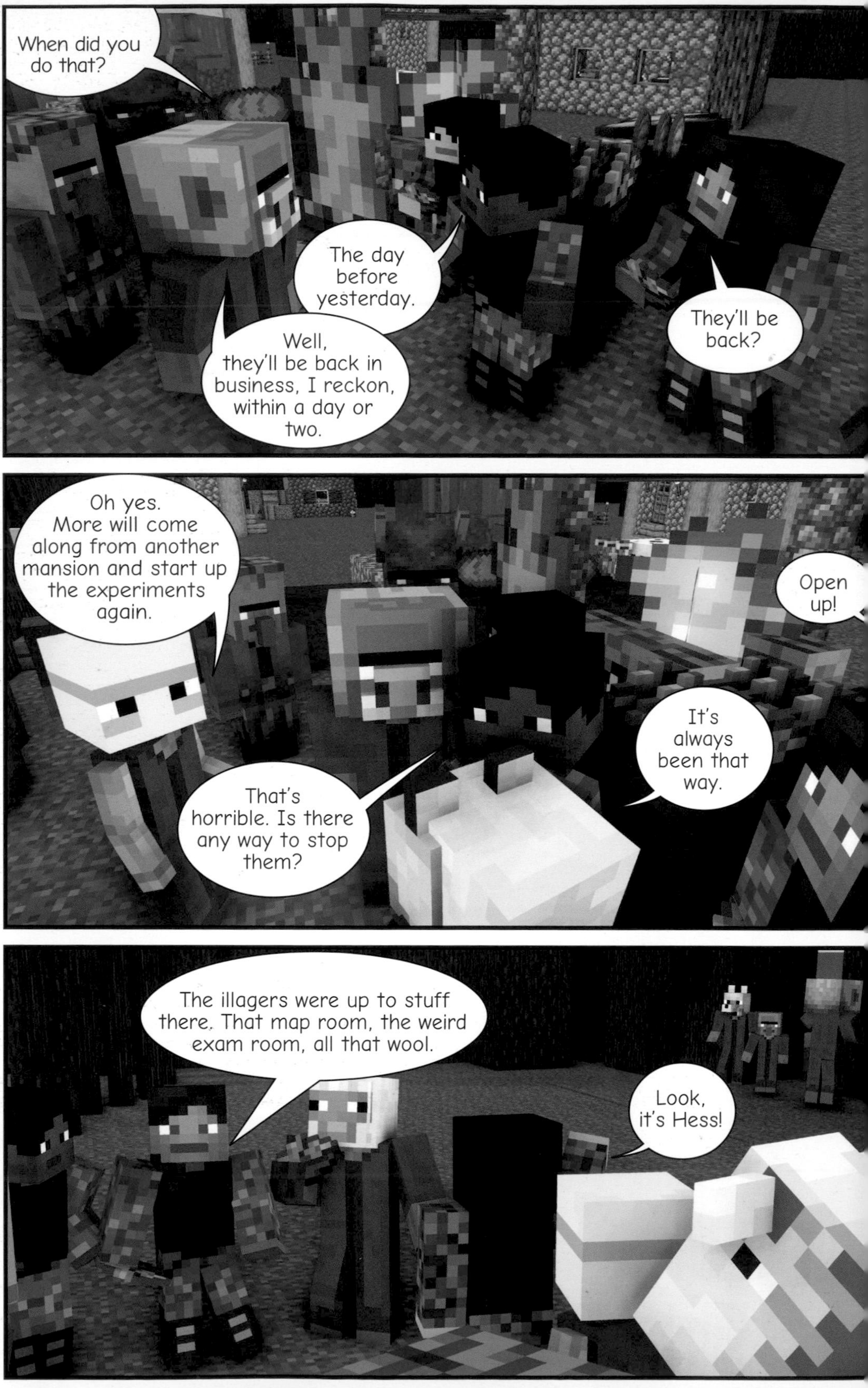

When did you do that?
The day before yesterday.
Well, they'll be back in business, I reckon, within a day or two.
They'll be back?
Oh yes. More will come along from another mansion and start up the experiments again.
Open up!
That's horrible. Is there any way to stop them?
It's always been that way.
The illagers were up to stuff there. That map room, the weird exam room, all that wool.
Look, it's Hess!

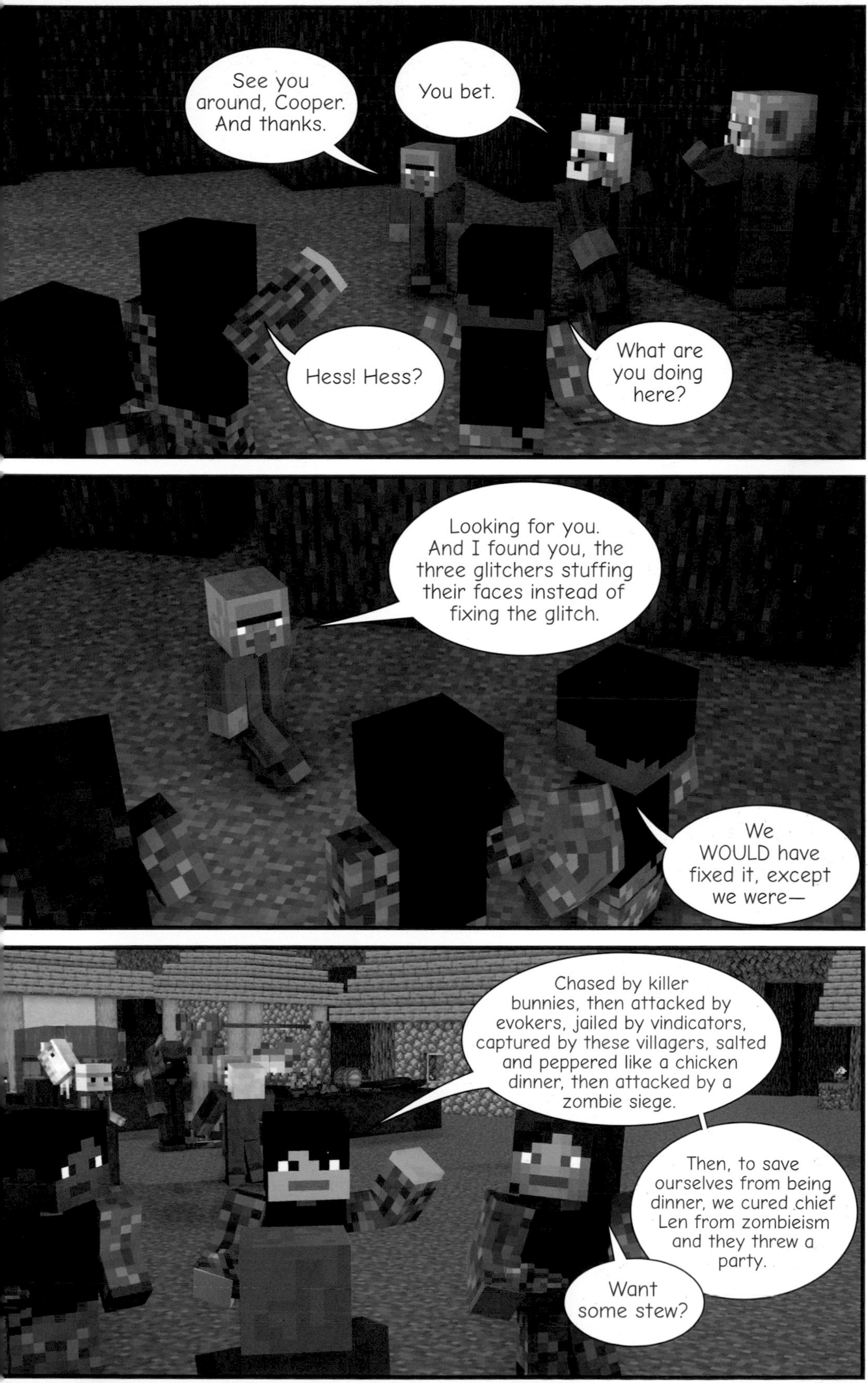

See you around, Cooper. And thanks.
You bet.
Hess! Hess?
What are you doing here?
Looking for you. And I found you, the three glitchers stuffing their faces instead of fixing the glitch.
We WOULD have fixed it, except we were—
Chased by killer bunnies, then attacked by evokers, jailed by vindicators, captured by these villagers, salted and peppered like a chicken dinner, then attacked by a zombie siege.
Then, to save ourselves from being dinner, we cured chief Len from zombieism and they threw a party.
Want some stew?

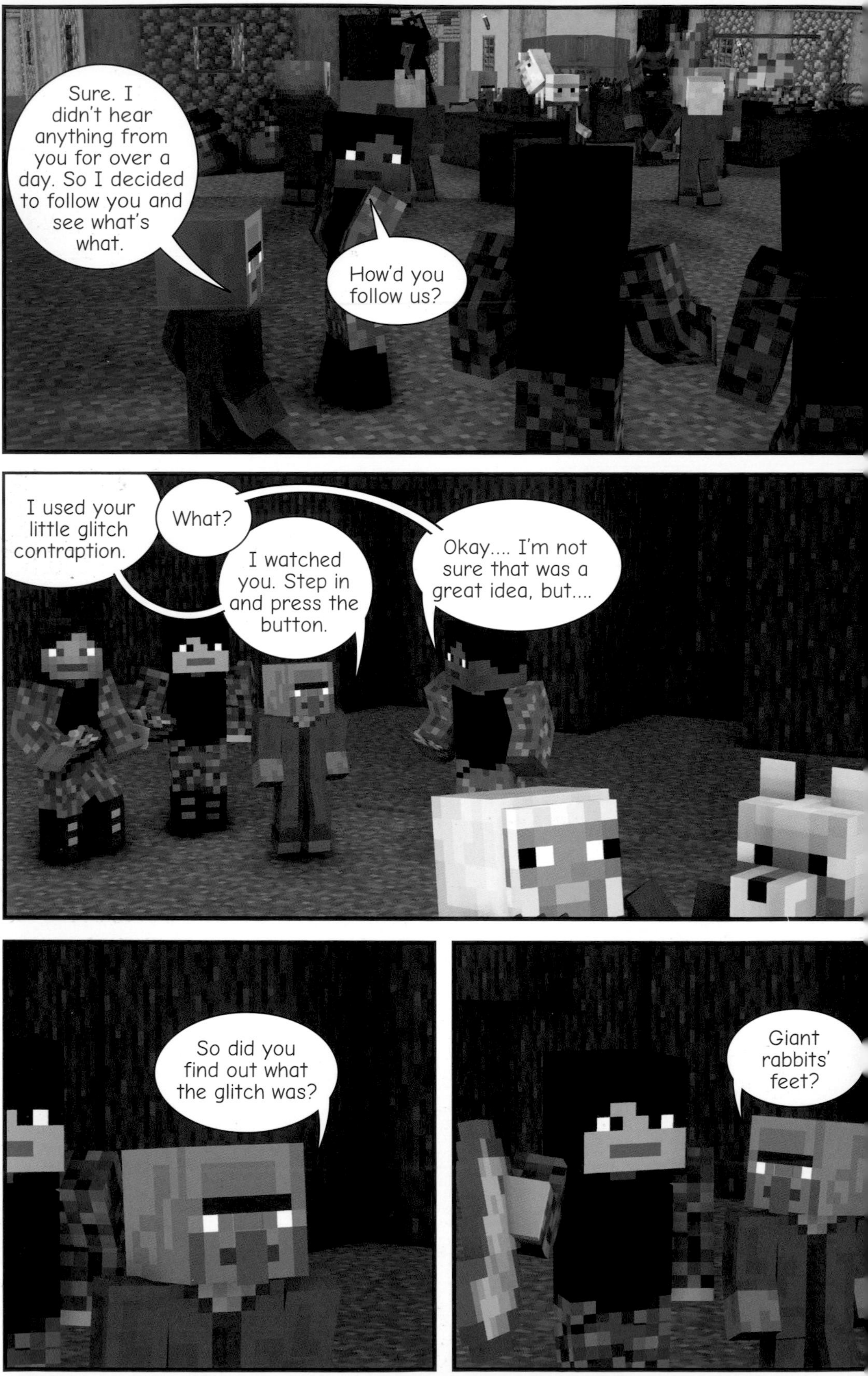

Sure. I didn't hear anything from you for over a day. So I decided to follow you and see what's what.
How'd you follow us?
I used your little glitch contraption.
What?
I watched you. Step in and press the button.
Okay.... I'm not sure that was a great idea, but....
So did you find out what the glitch was?
Giant rabbits' feet?

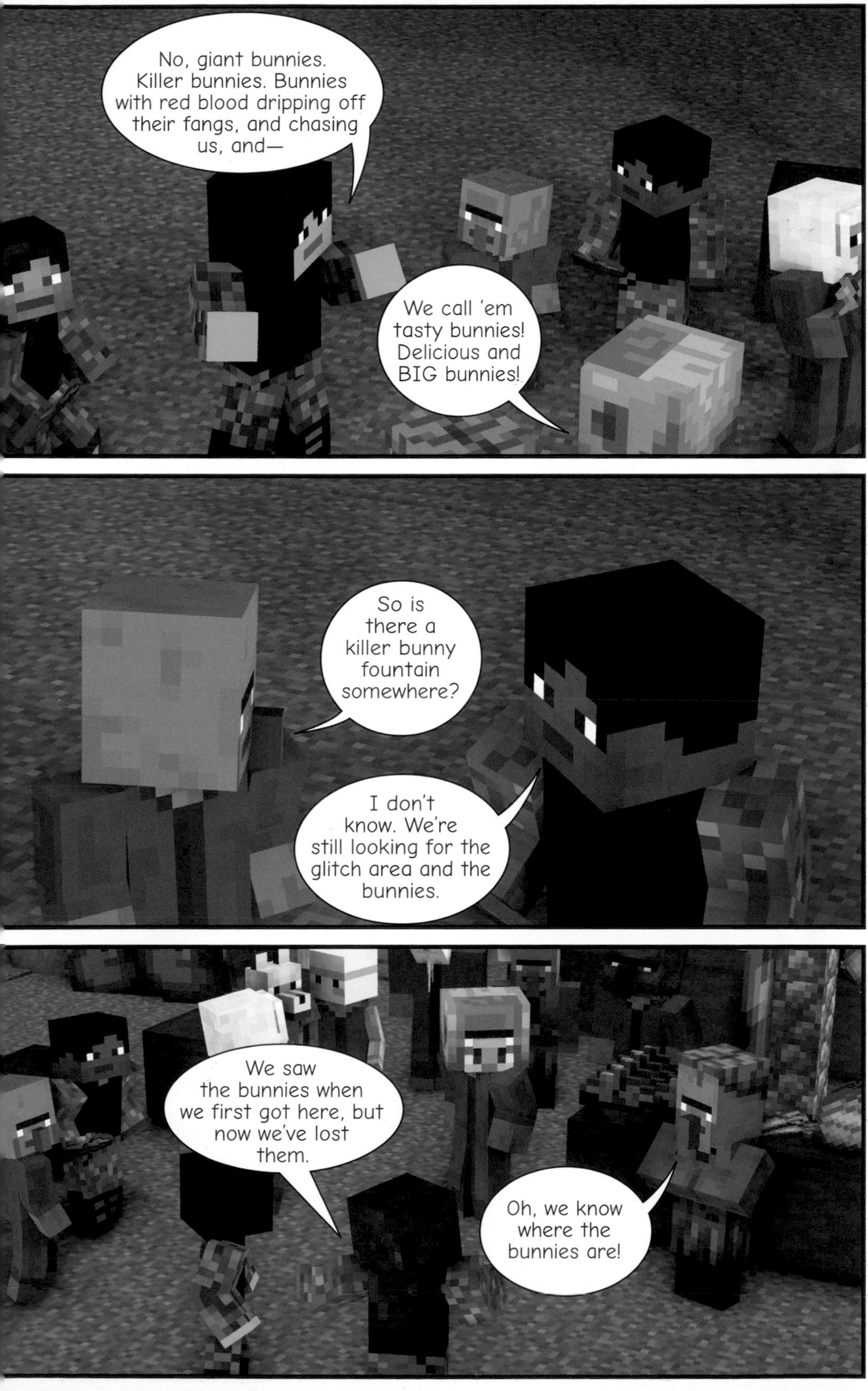
No, giant bunnies. Killer bunnies. Bunnies with red blood dripping off their fangs, and chasing us, and—
We call 'em tasty bunnies! Delicious and BIG bunnies!
So is there a killer bunny fountain somewhere?
I don't know. We're still looking for the glitch area and the bunnies.
We saw the bunnies when we first got here, but now we've lost them.
Oh, we know where the bunnies are!

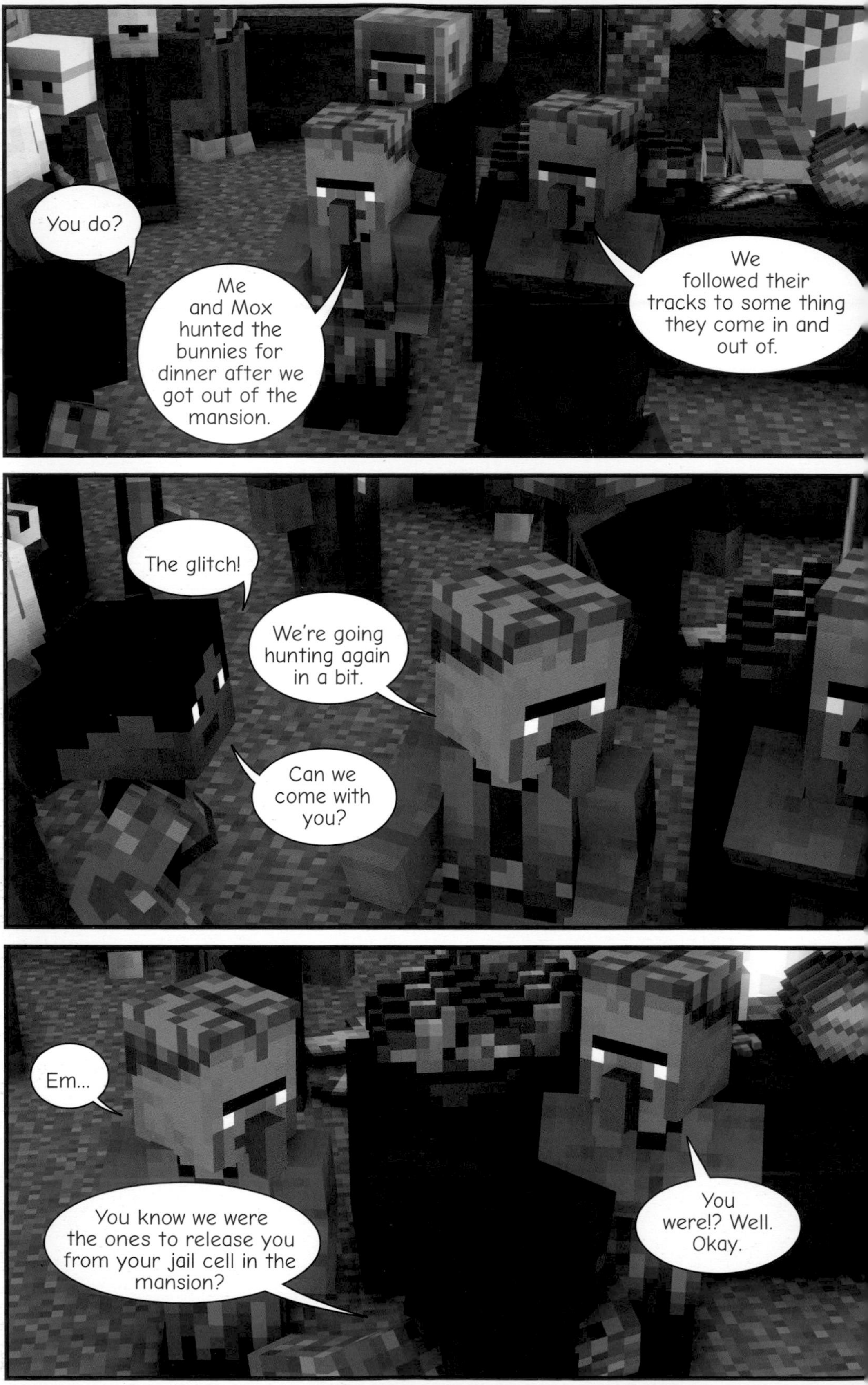
You do?
Me and Mox hunted the bunnies for dinner after we got out of the mansion.
We followed their tracks to some thing they come in and out of.
The glitch!
We're going hunting again in a bit.
Can we come with you?
Em...
You know we were the ones to release you from your jail cell in the mansion?
You were!? Well. Okay.

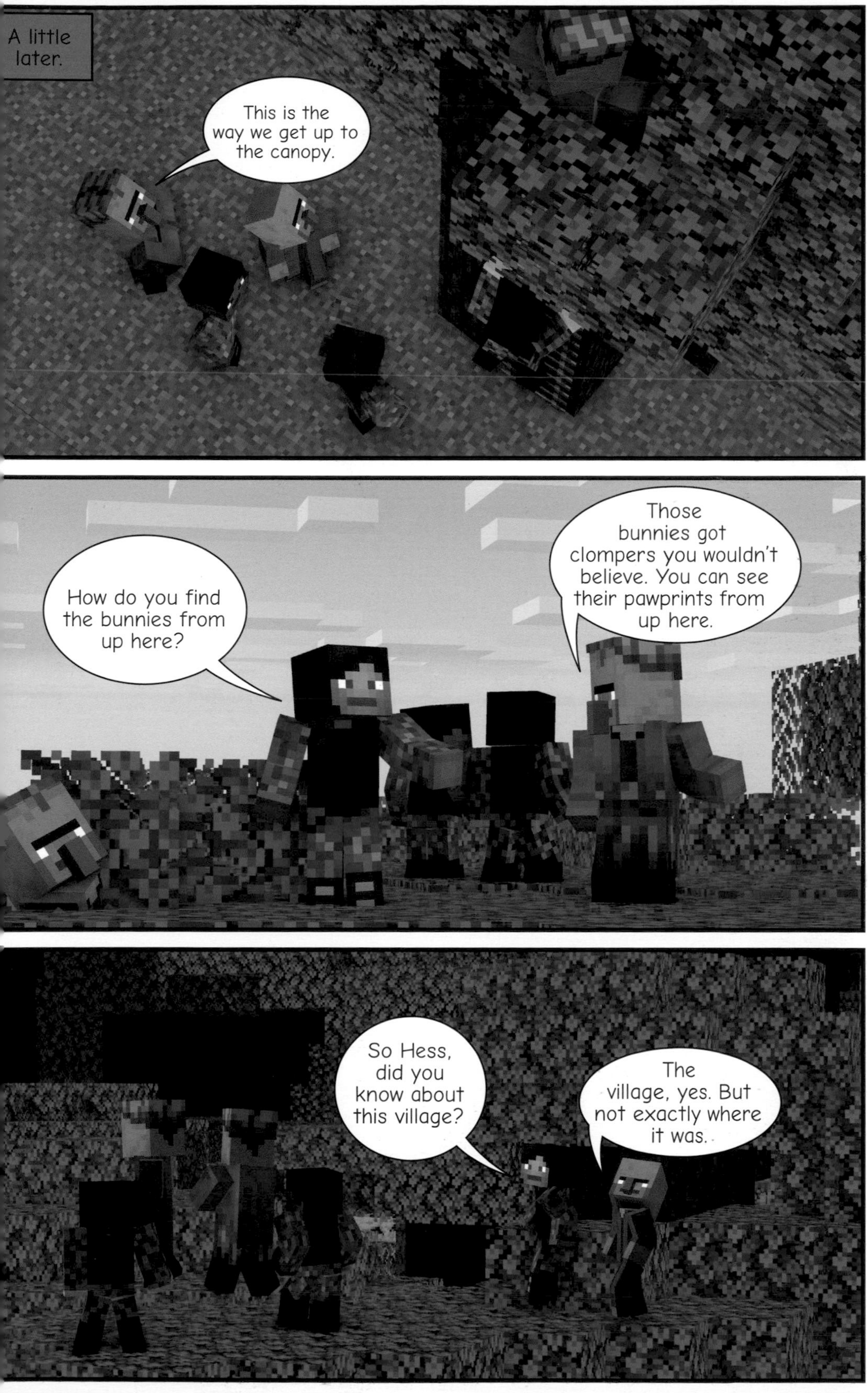
A little later.
This is the way we get up to the canopy.
How do you find the bunnies from up here?
Those bunnies got clompers you wouldn't believe. You can see their pawprints from up here.
So Hess, did you know about this village?
The village, yes. But not exactly where it was.

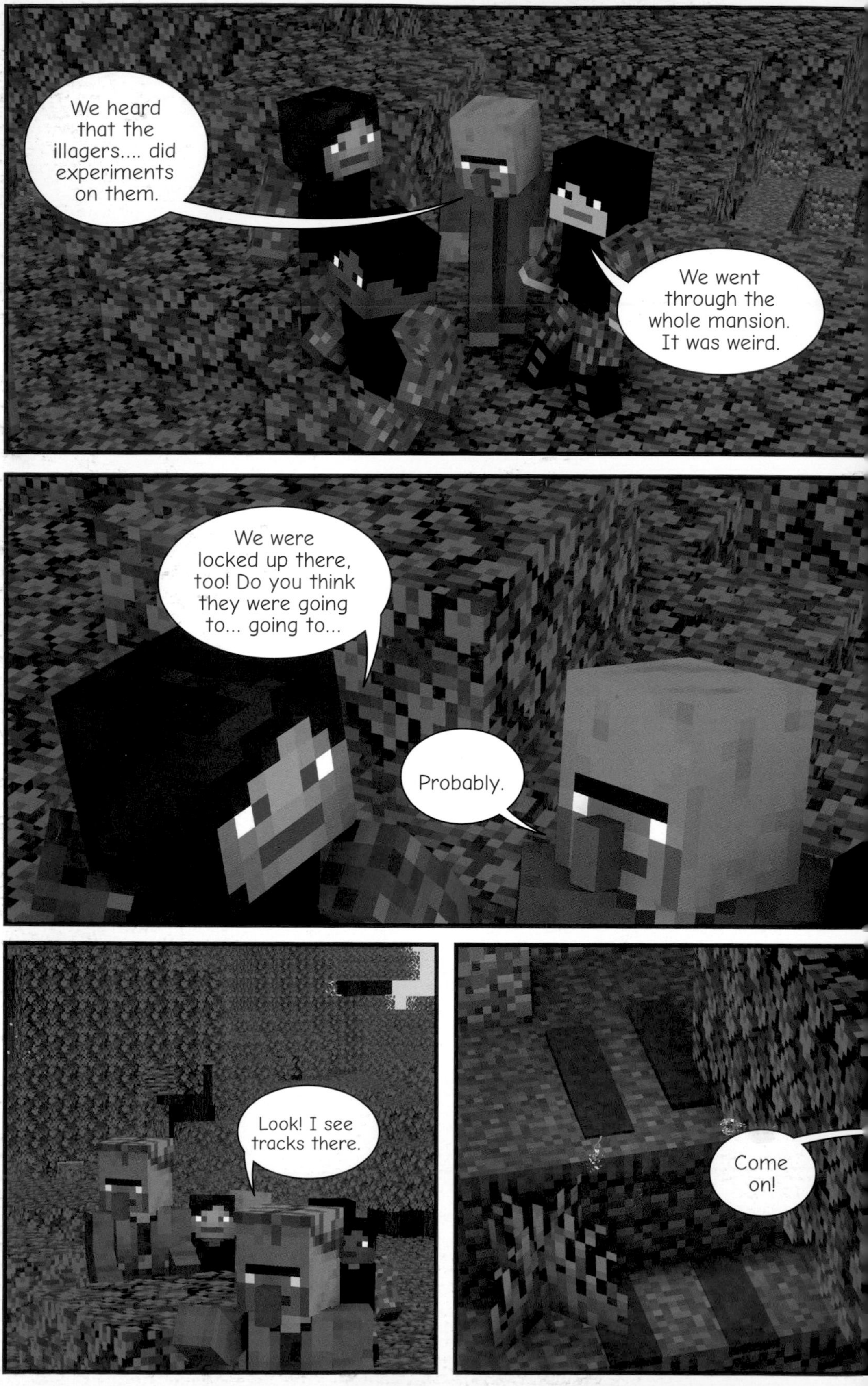
We heard that the illagers.... did experiments on them.
We went through the whole mansion. It was weird.
We were locked up there, too! Do you think they were going to... going to...
Probably.
Look! I see tracks there.
Come on!

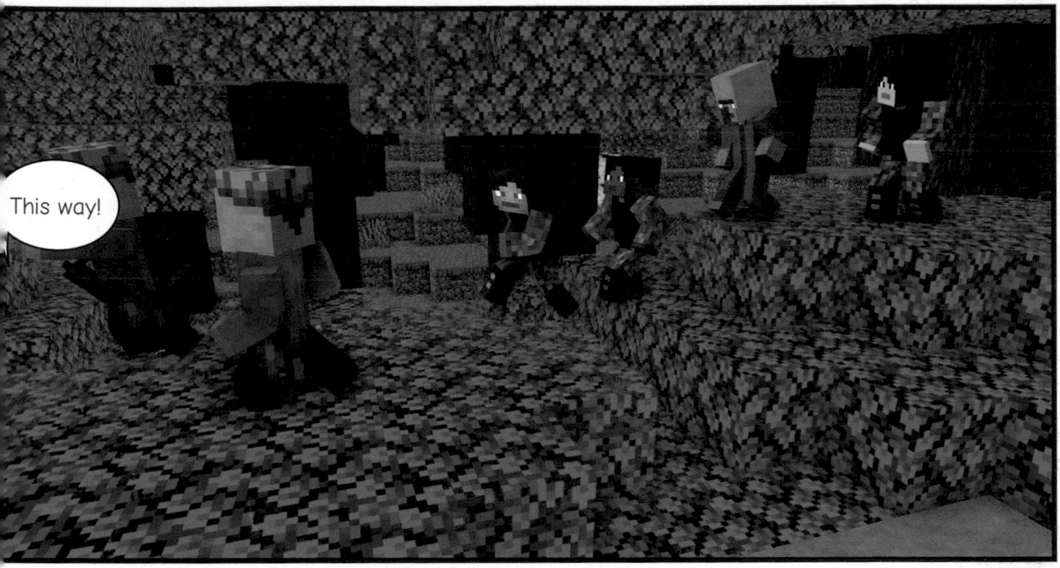
This way!

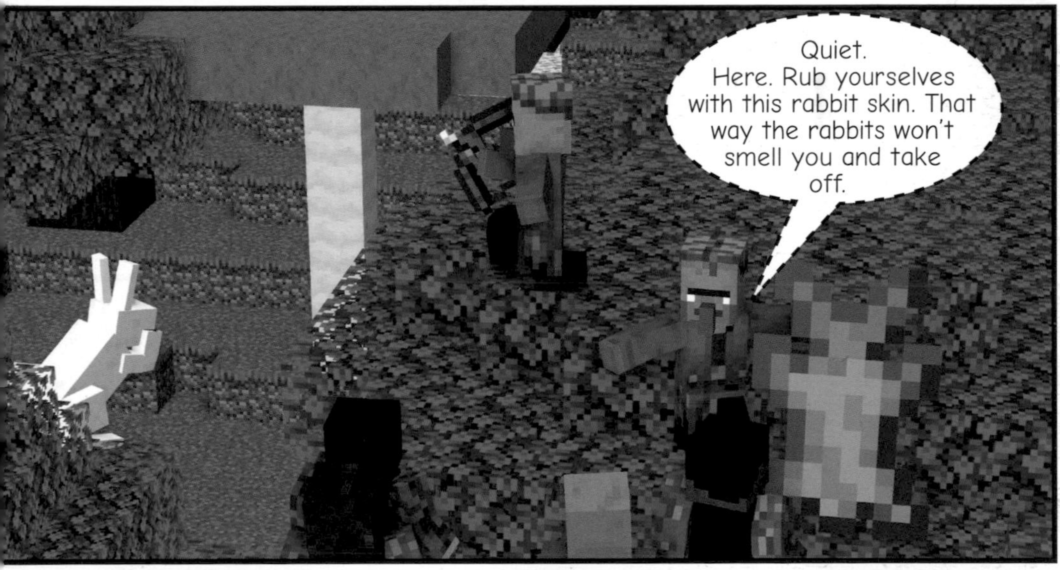
Quiet.
Here. Rub yourselves with this rabbit skin. That way the rabbits won't smell you and take off.

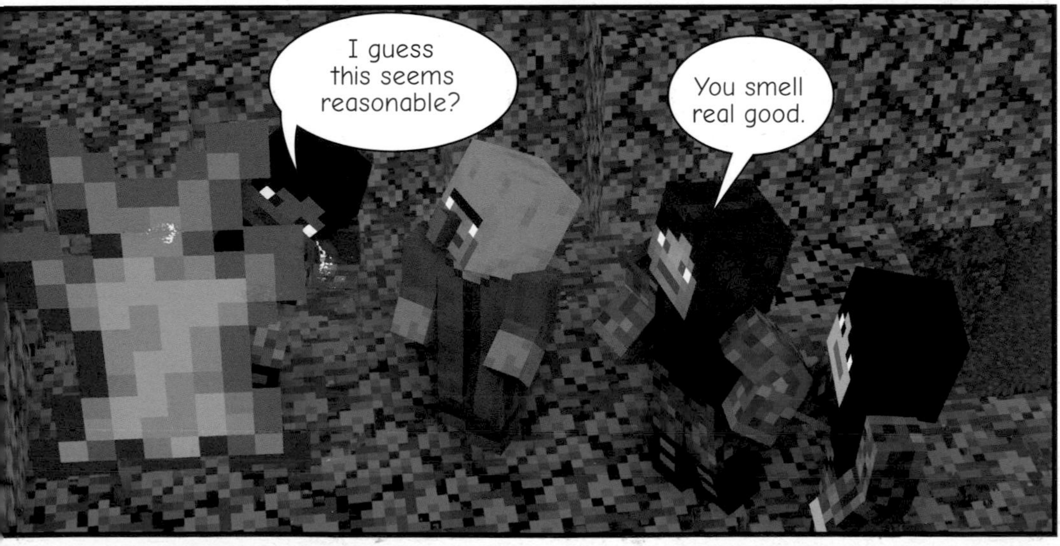
I guess this seems reasonable?
You smell real good.

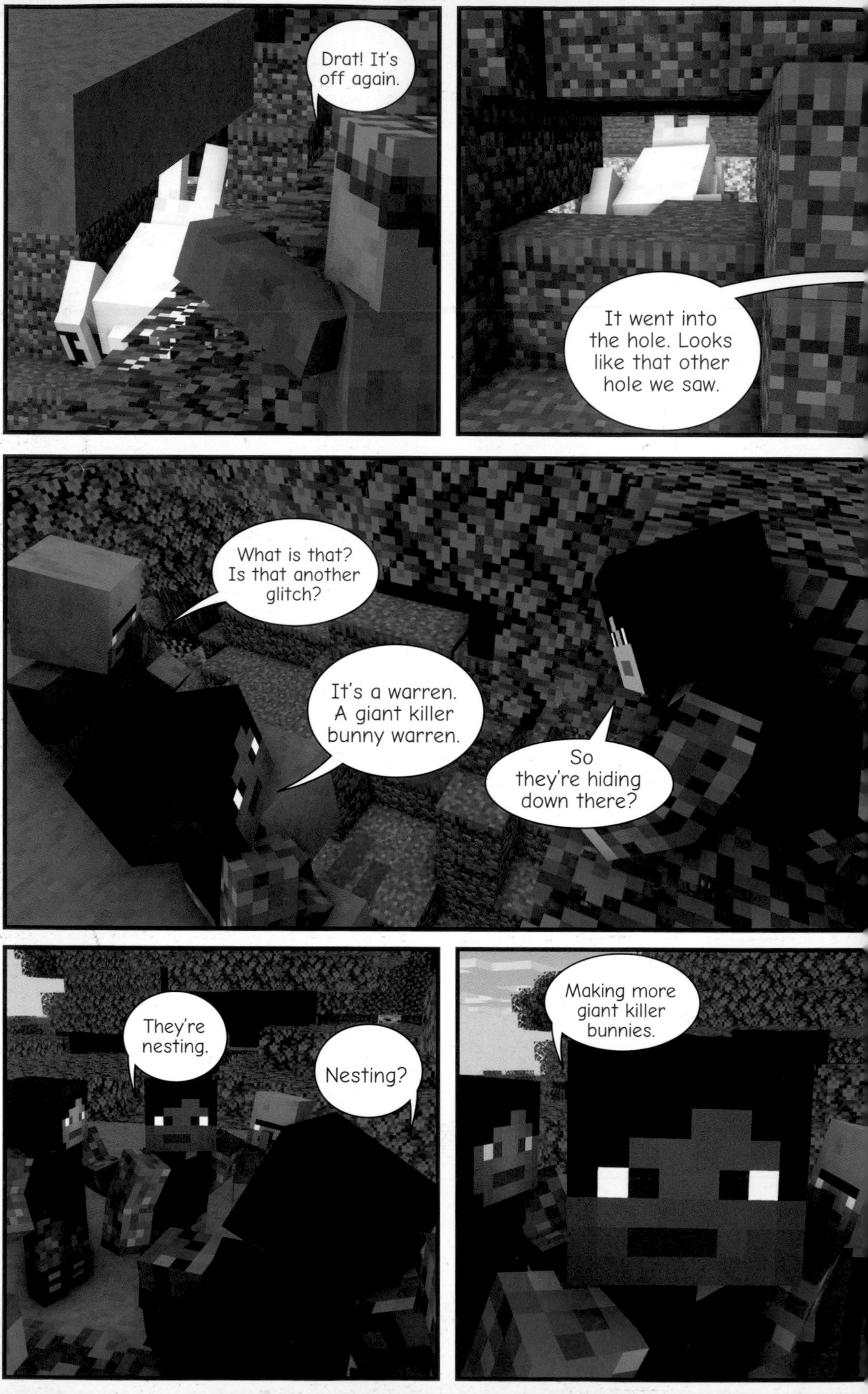
Drat! It's off again.
It went into the hole. Looks like that other hole we saw.
What is that? Is that another glitch?
It's a warren. A giant killer bunny warren.
So they're hiding down there?
They're nesting.
Nesting?
Making more giant killer bunnies.

CHAPTER 10:

WARREN

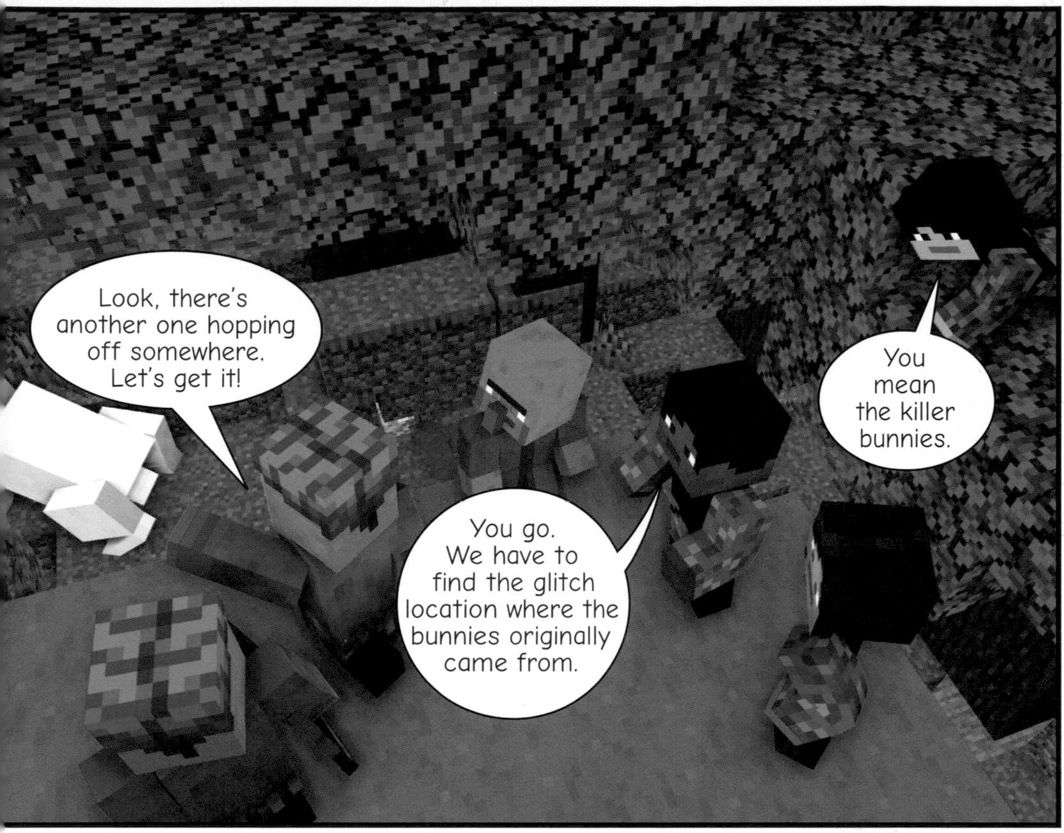
Look, there's another one hopping off somewhere. Let's get it!
You mean the killer bunnies.
You go. We have to find the glitch location where the bunnies originally came from.

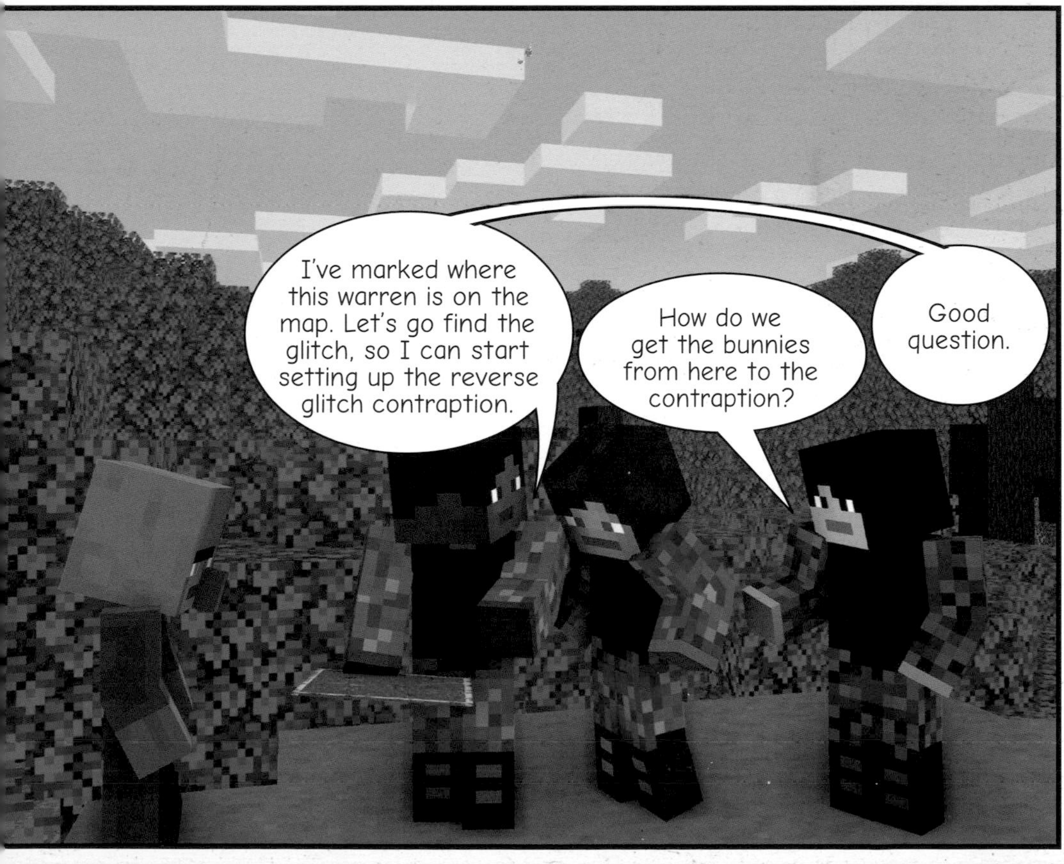
I've marked where this warren is on the map. Let's go find the glitch, so I can start setting up the reverse glitch contraption.
How do we get the bunnies from here to the contraption?
Good question.

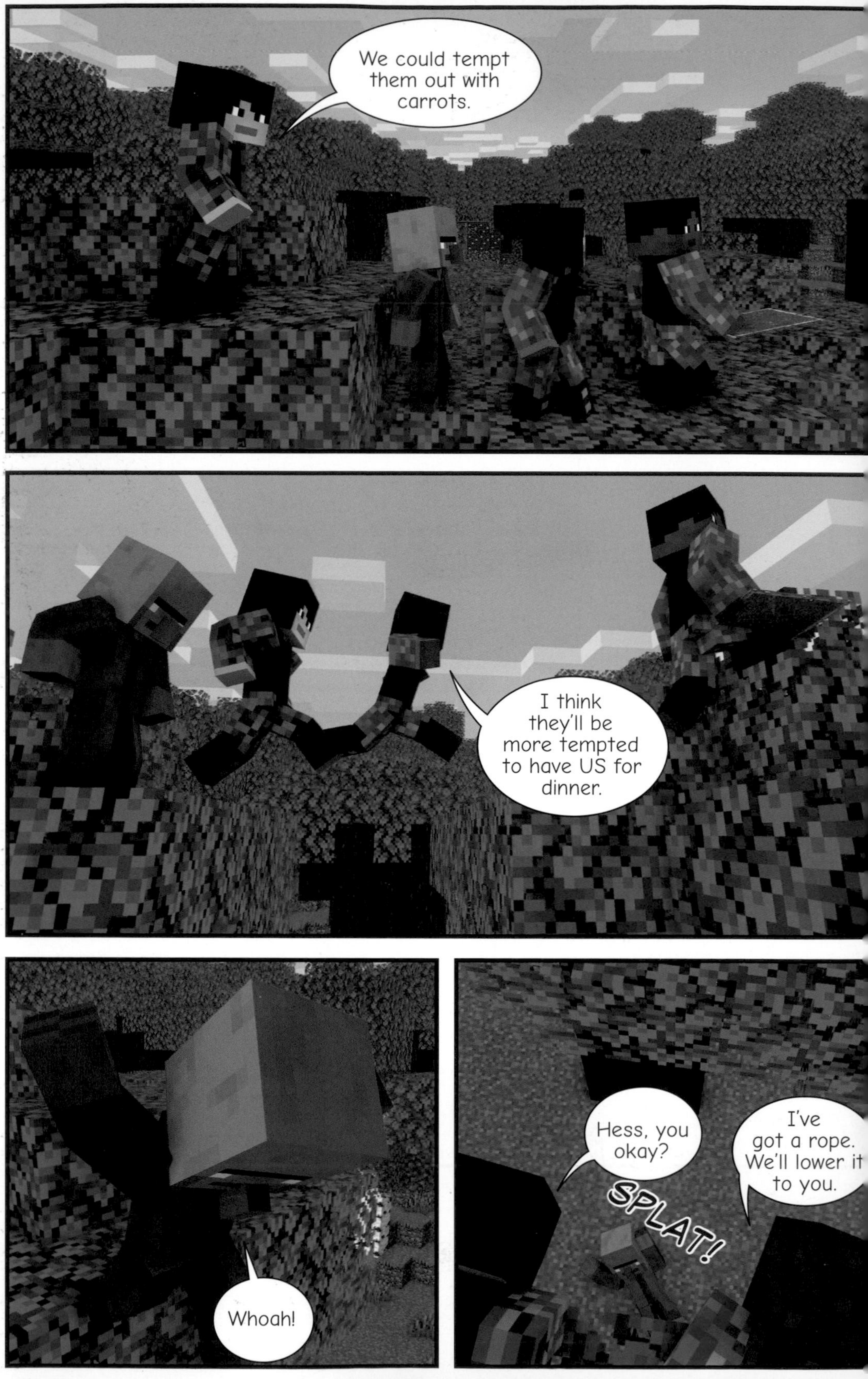
We could tempt them out with carrots.
I think they'll be more tempted to have US for dinner.
Whoah!
Hess, you okay?
SPLAT!
I've got a rope. We'll lower it to you.

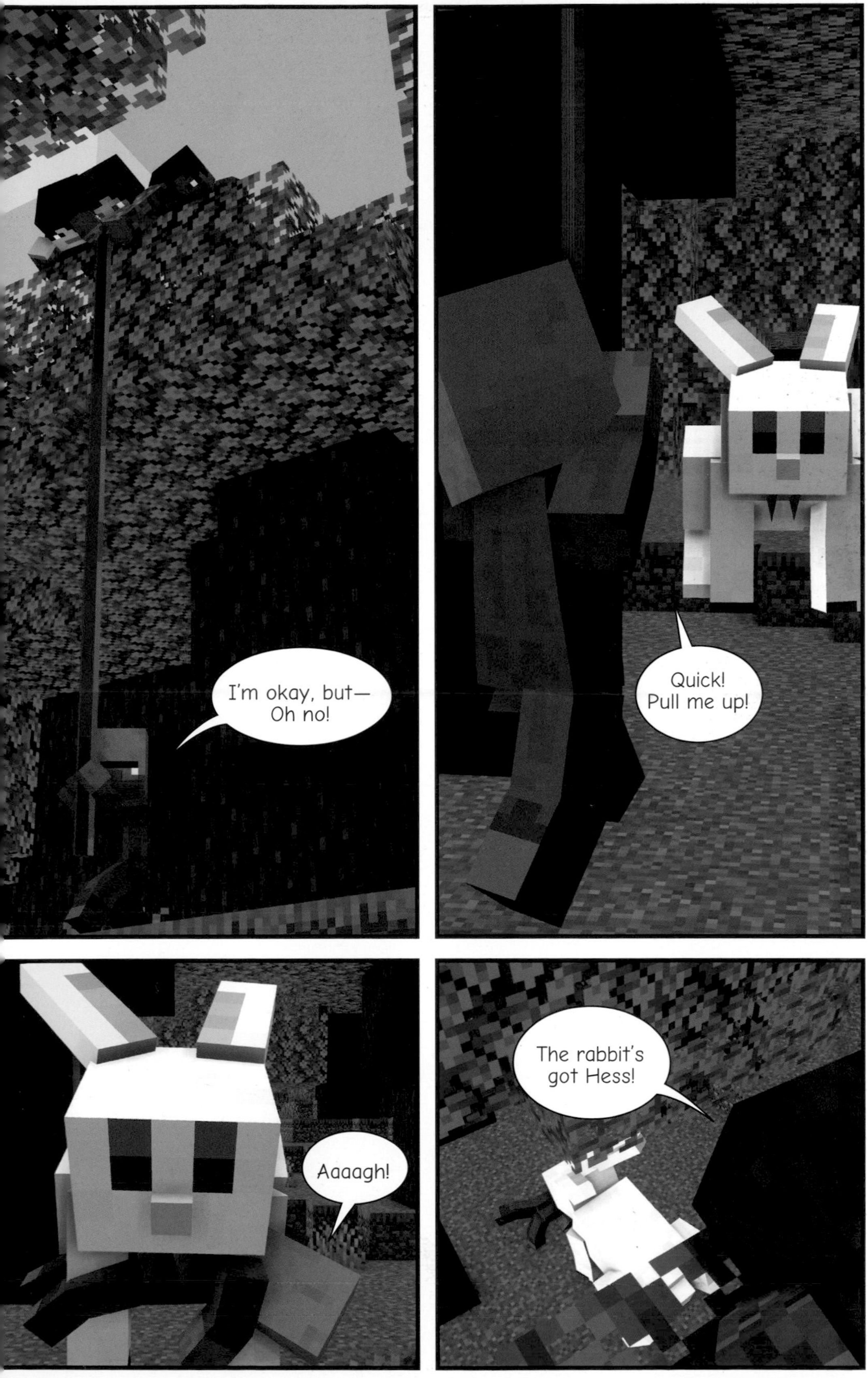
I'm okay, but—
Oh no!
Quick!
Pull me up!
Aaaagh!
The rabbit's
got Hess!

ZING!

BONK!

I hit it, but it's not stopping!

Quick! Let's follow!

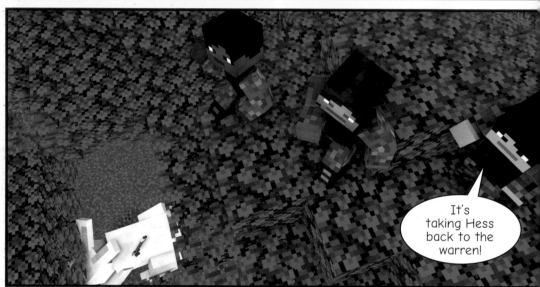

It's taking Hess back to the warren!

We've got to go in.

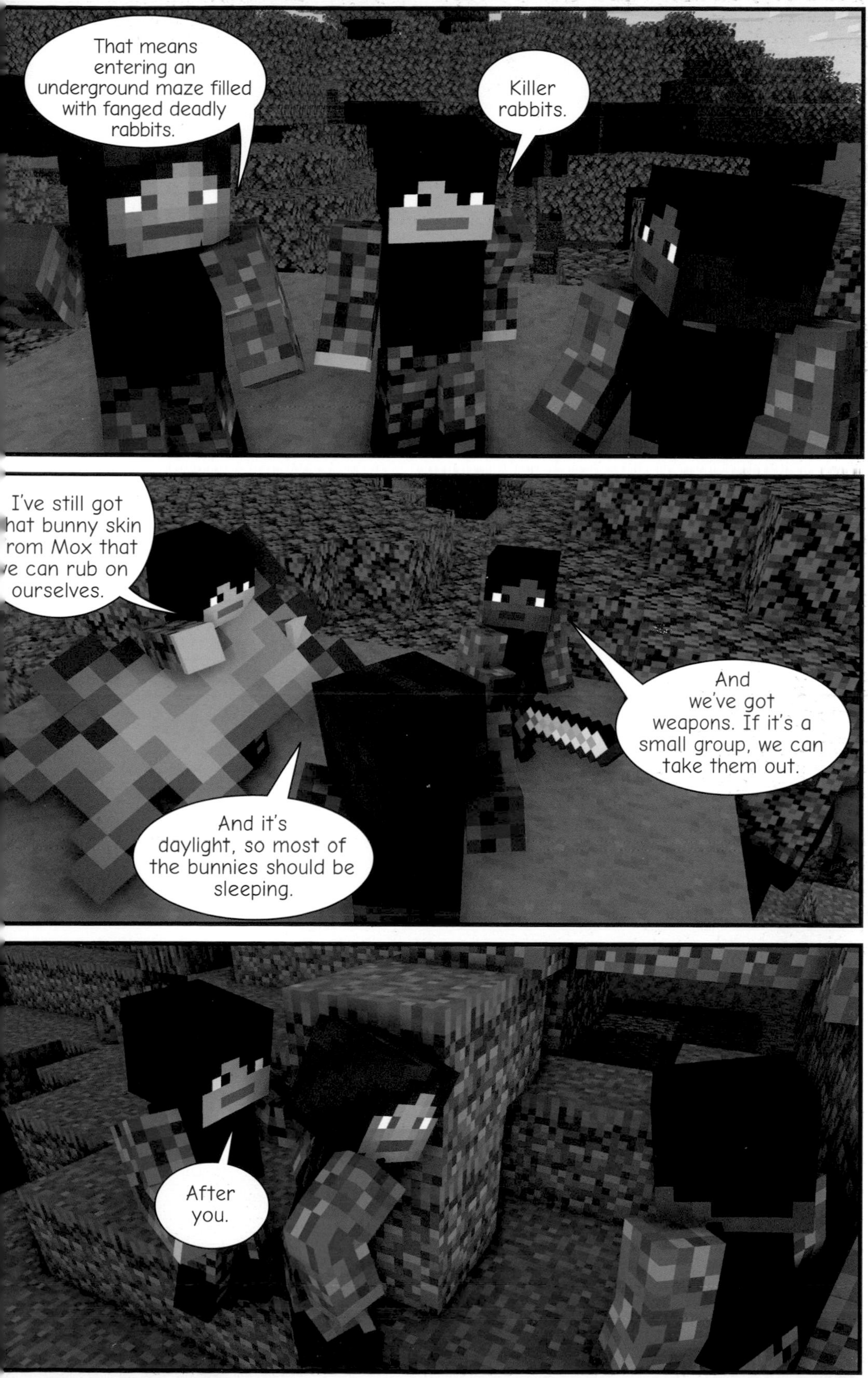
That means entering an underground maze filled with fanged deadly rabbits.
Killer rabbits.
I've still got hat bunny skin rom Mox that e can rub on ourselves.
And we've got weapons. If it's a small group, we can take them out.
And it's daylight, so most of the bunnies should be sleeping.
After you.

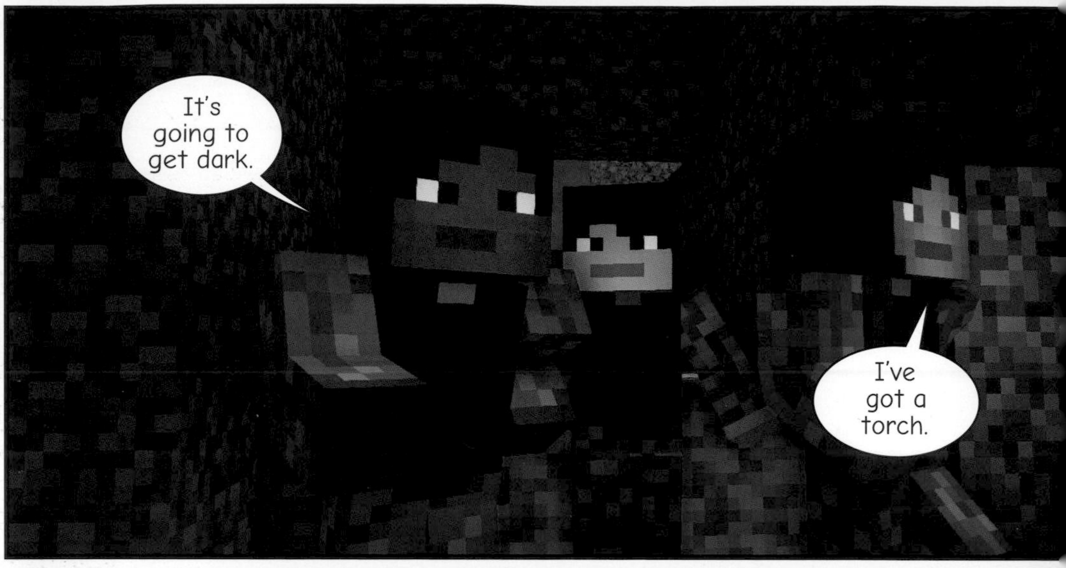
It's going to get dark.
I've got a torch.
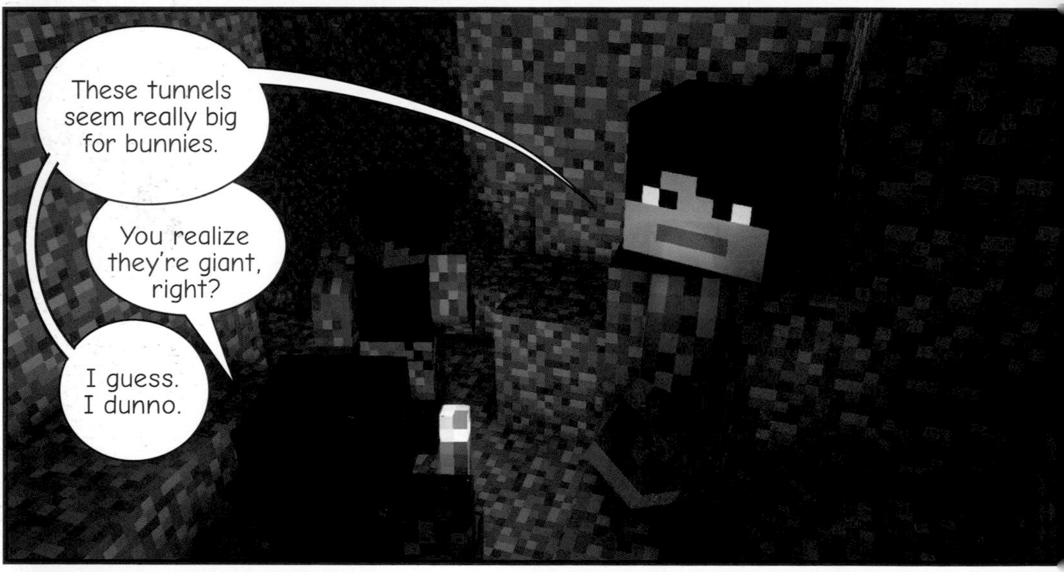
These tunnels seem really big for bunnies.
You realize they're giant, right?
I guess. I dunno.
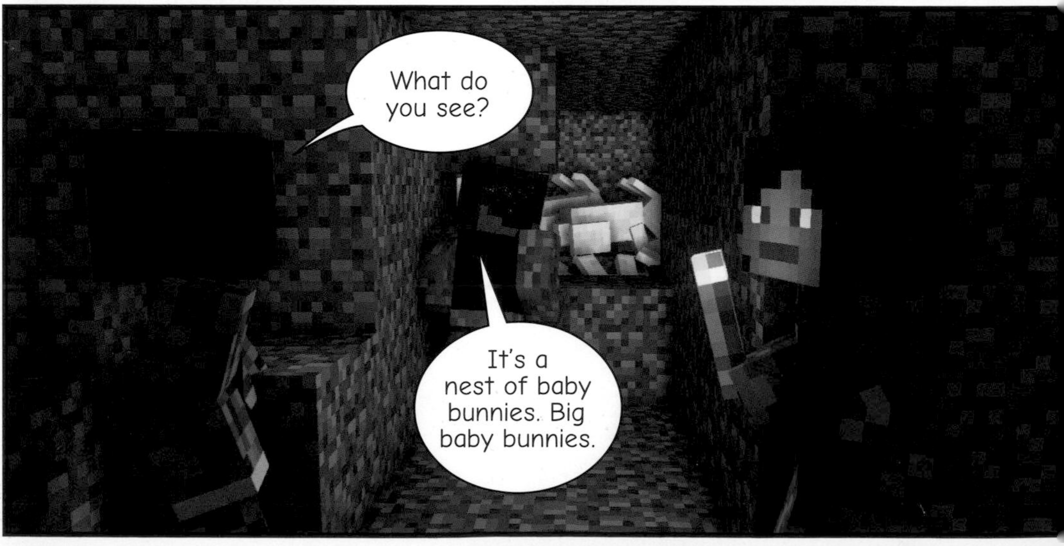
What do you see?
It's a nest of baby bunnies. Big baby bunnies.

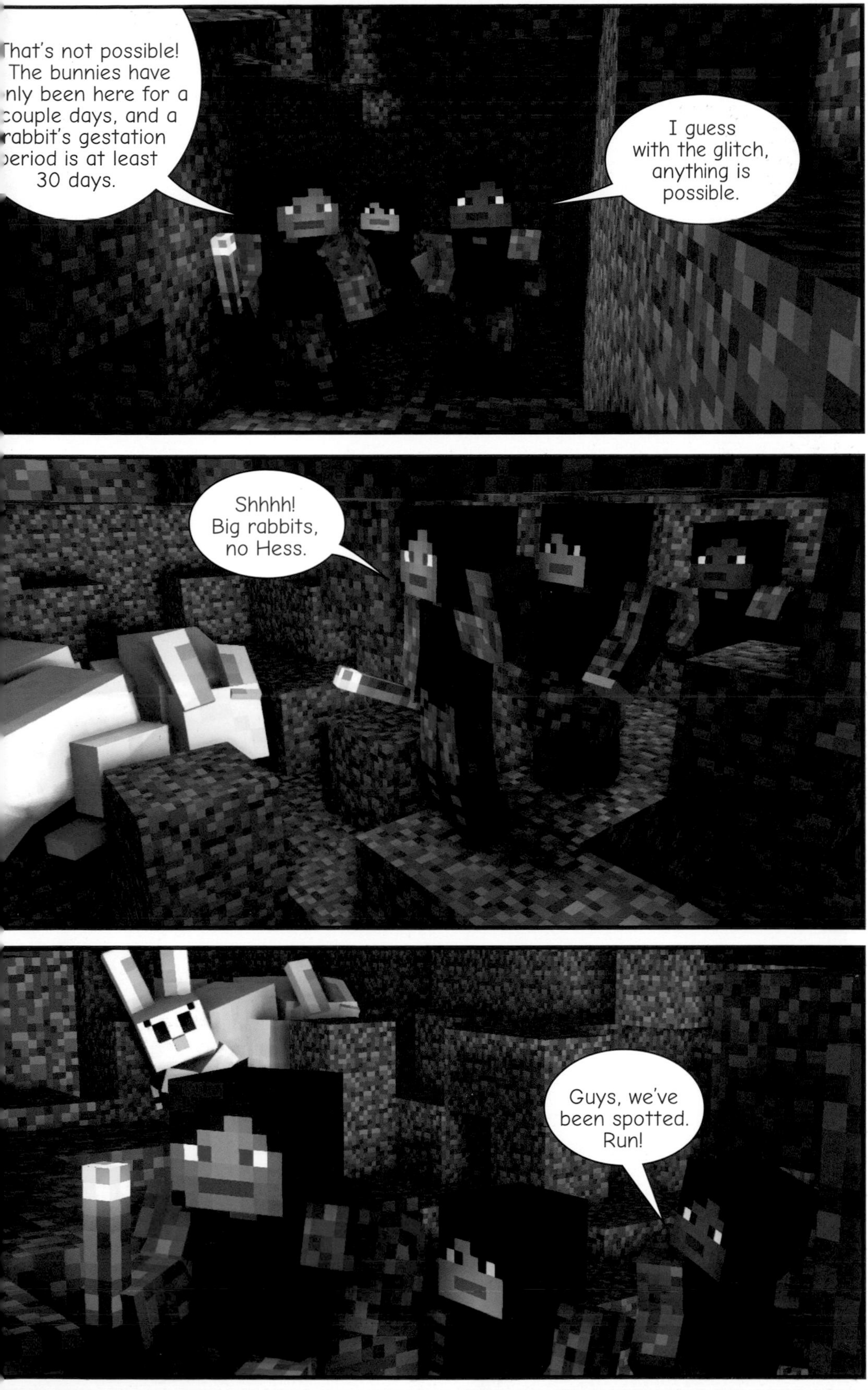
That's not possible! The bunnies have nly been here for a couple days, and a rabbit's gestation eriod is at least 30 days.
I guess with the glitch, anything is possible.
Shhhh! Big rabbits, no Hess.
Guys, we've been spotted. Run!

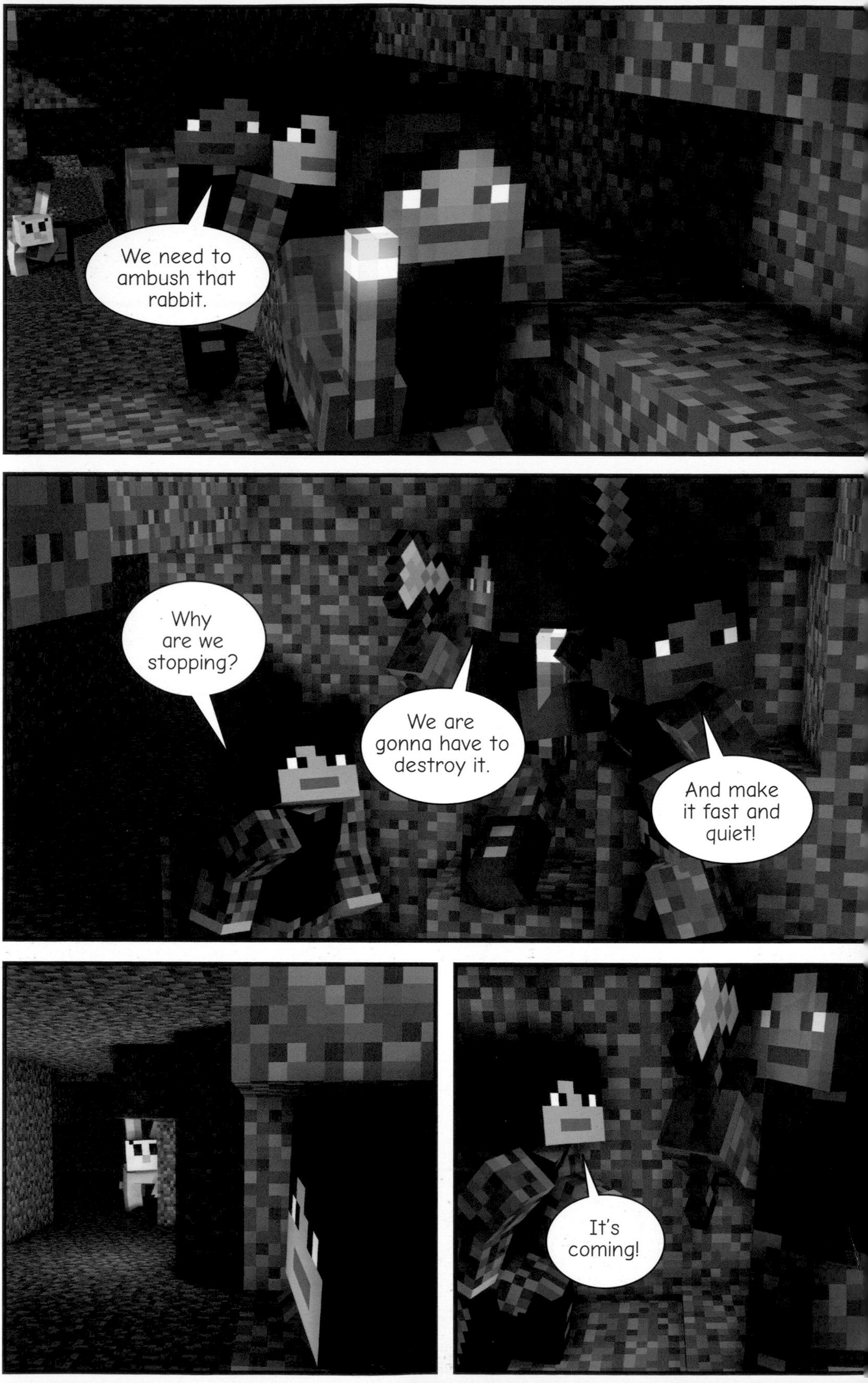
We need to ambush that rabbit.
Why are we stopping?
We are gonna have to destroy it.
And make it fast and quiet!
It's coming!

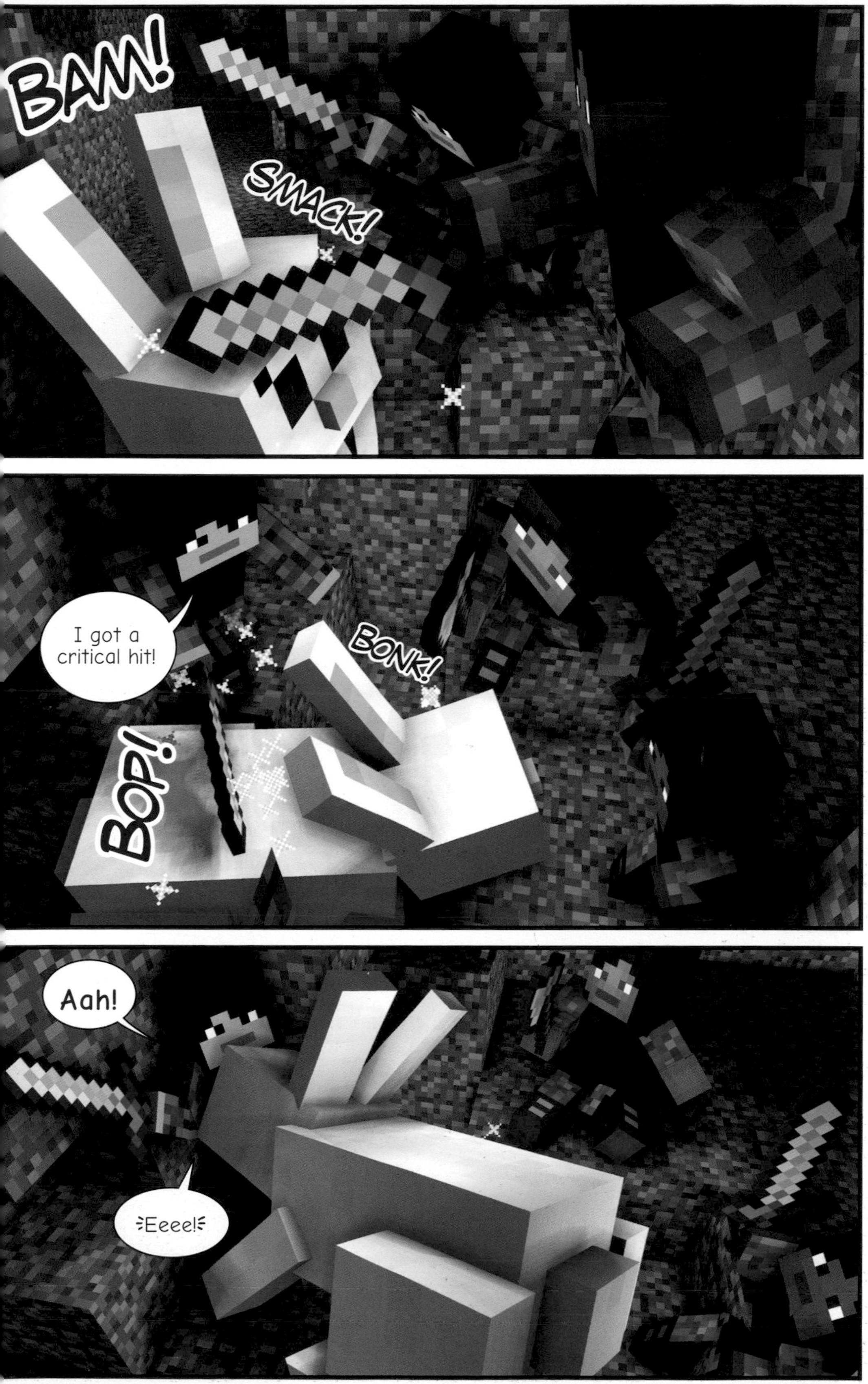
BAM!
SMACK!
I got a critical hit!
BONK!
BOP!
Aah!
Eeee!

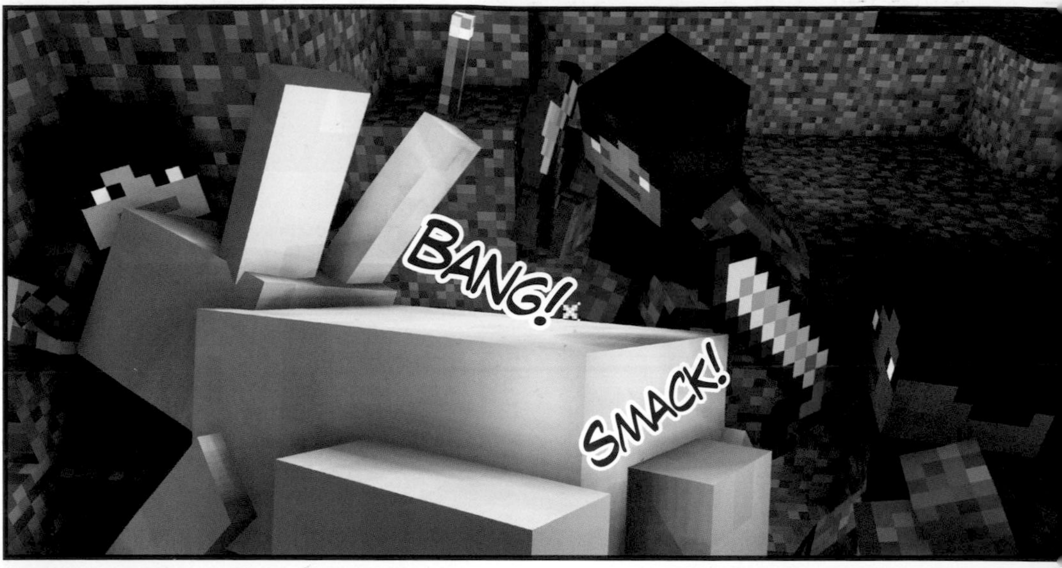
BANG!
SMACK!

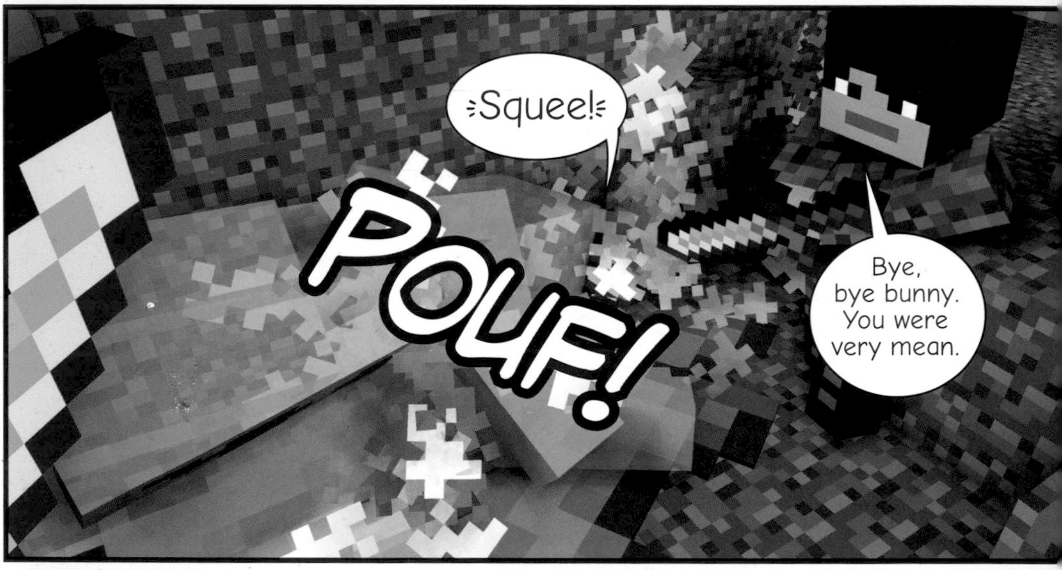
Squee!
POUF!
Bye, bye bunny. You were very mean.

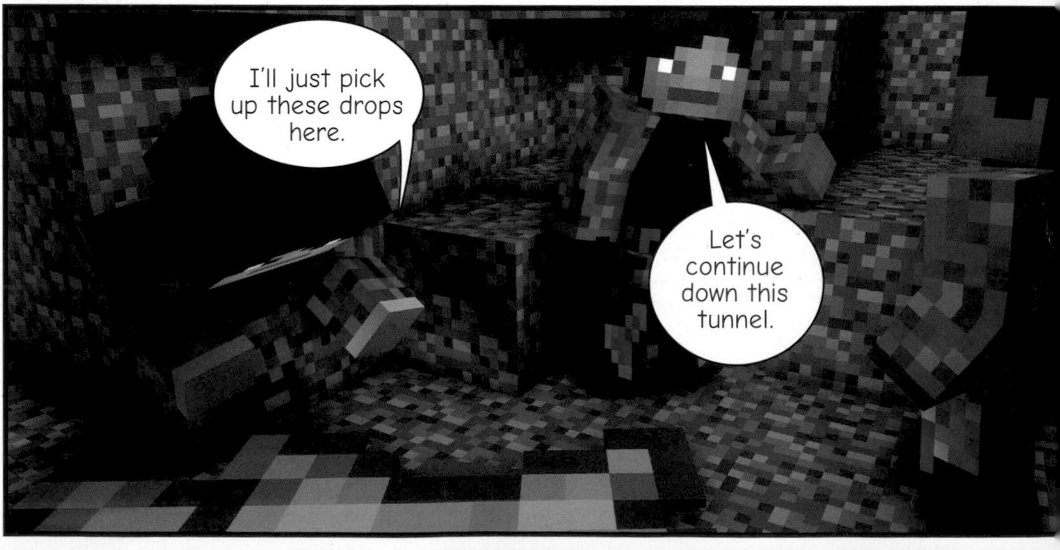
I'll just pick up these drops here.
Let's continue down this tunnel.

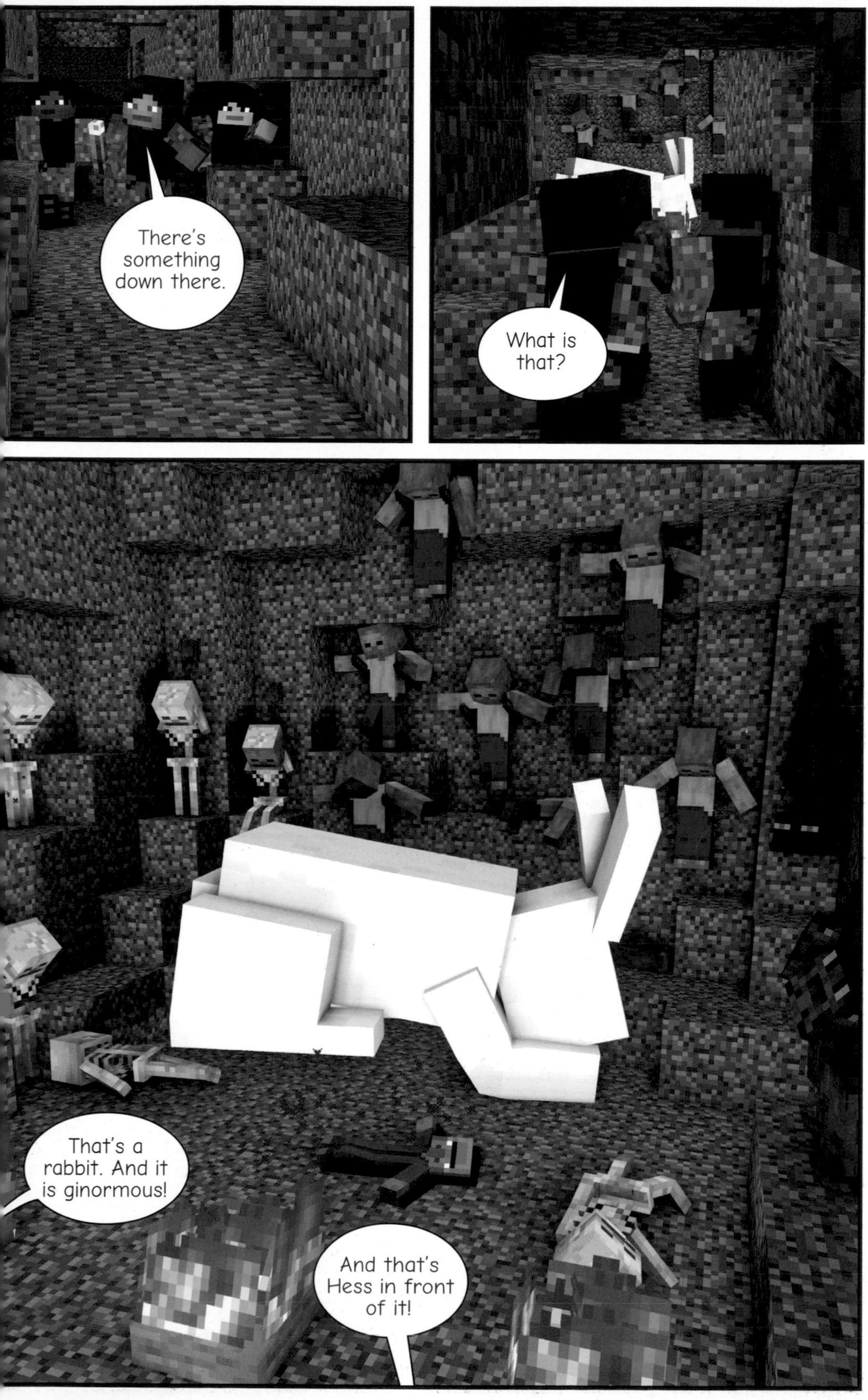
There's something down there.
What is that?
That's a rabbit. And it is ginormous!
And that's Hess in front of it!

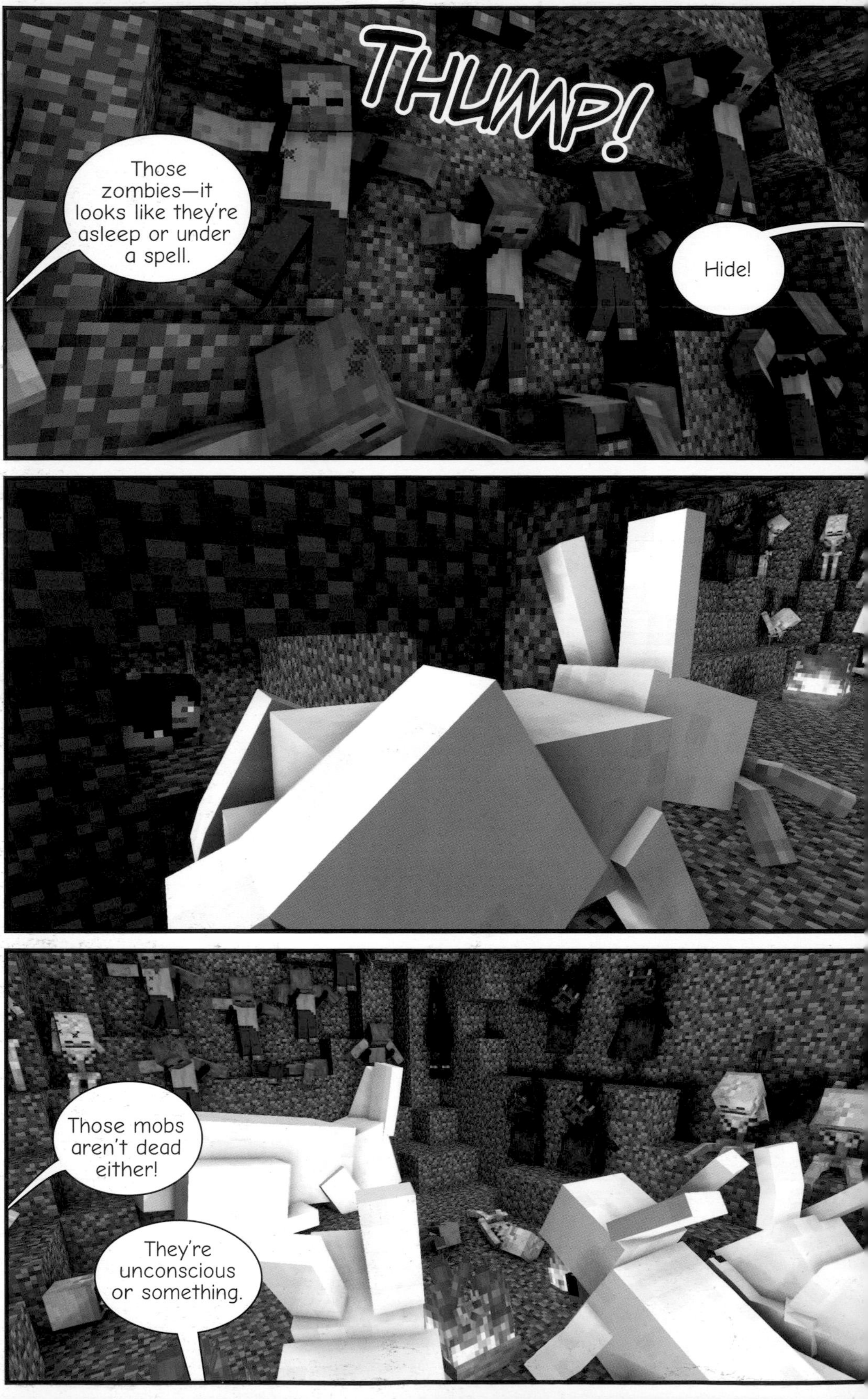
THUMP!
Those zombies—it looks like they're asleep or under a spell.
Hide!
Those mobs aren't dead either!
They're unconscious or something.

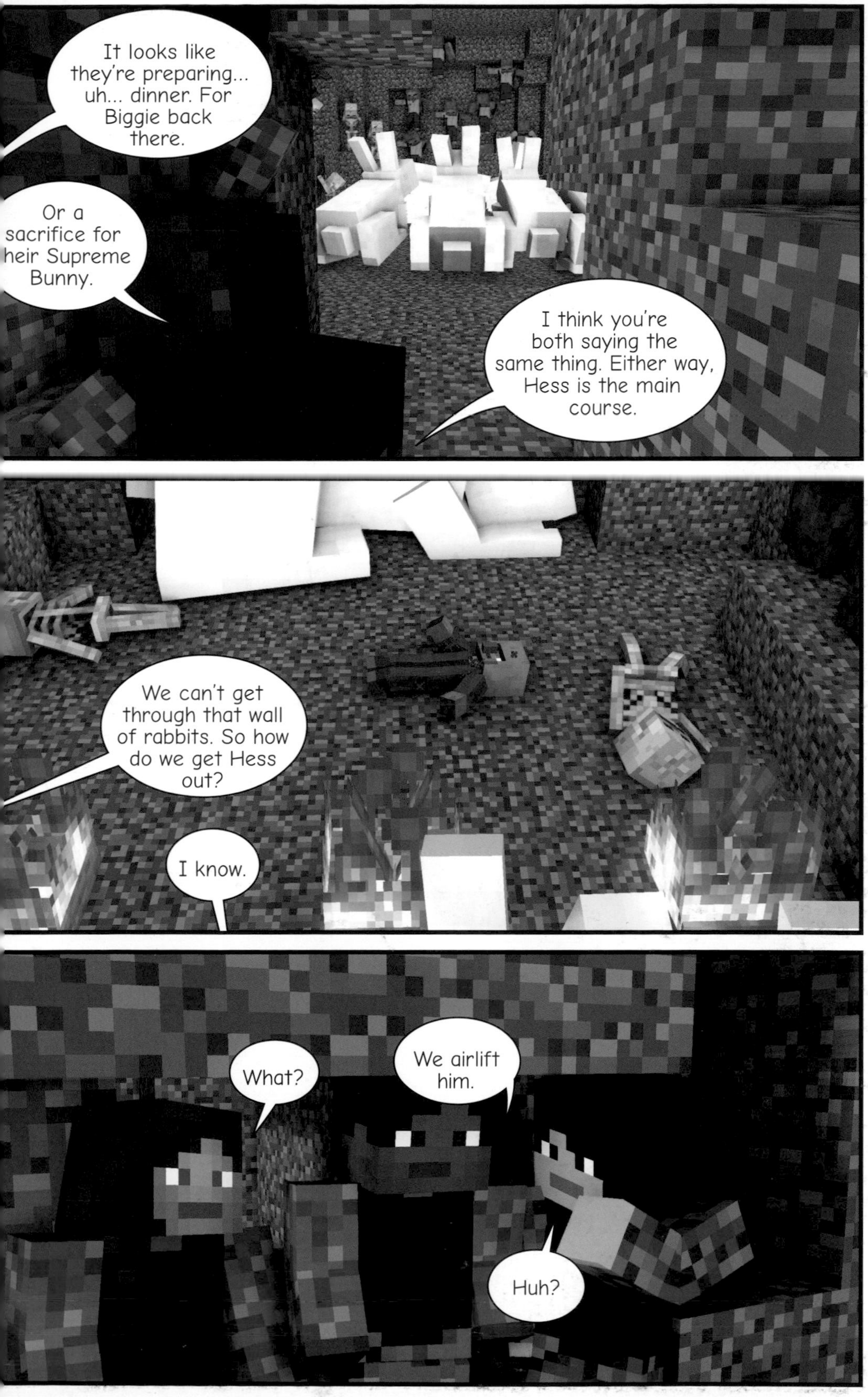
It looks like they're preparing... uh... dinner. For Biggie back there.
Or a sacrifice for heir Supreme Bunny.
I think you're both saying the same thing. Either way, Hess is the main course.
We can't get through that wall of rabbits. So how do we get Hess out?
I know.
What?
We airlift him.
Huh?

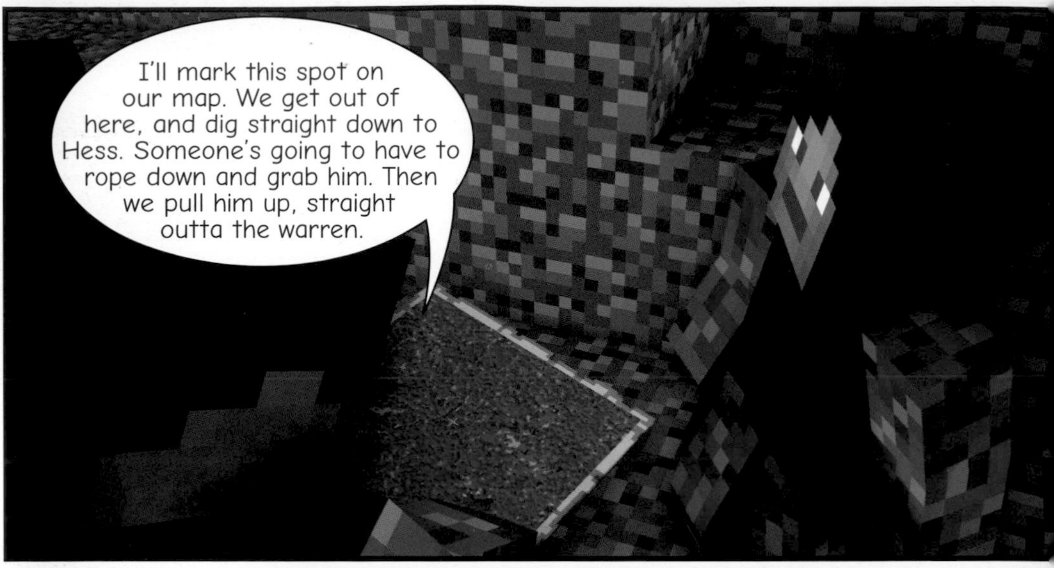
I'll mark this spot on our map. We get out of here, and dig straight down to Hess. Someone's going to have to rope down and grab him. Then we pull him up, straight outta the warren.

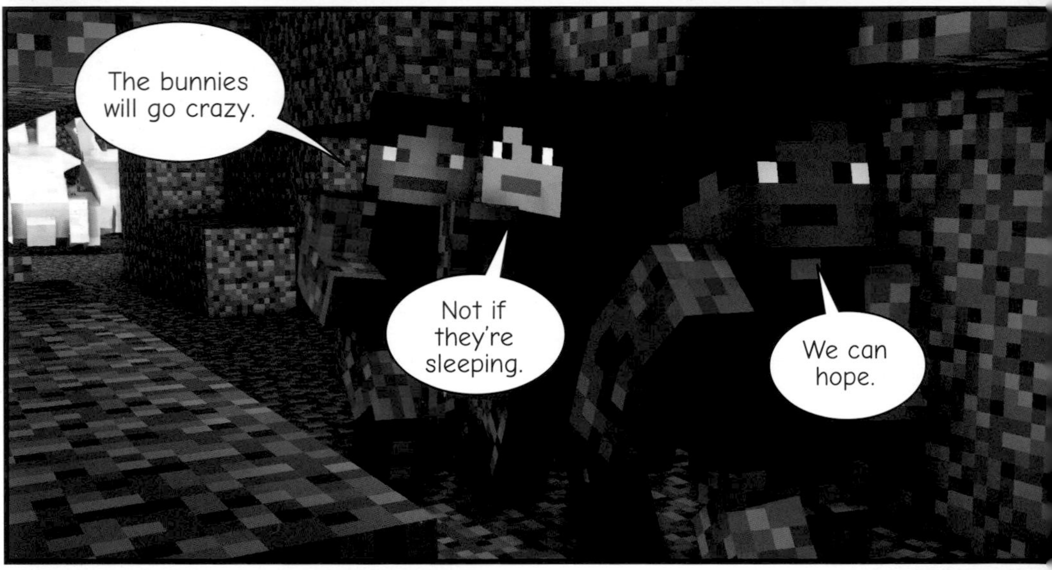
The bunnies will go crazy.
Not if they're sleeping.
We can hope.

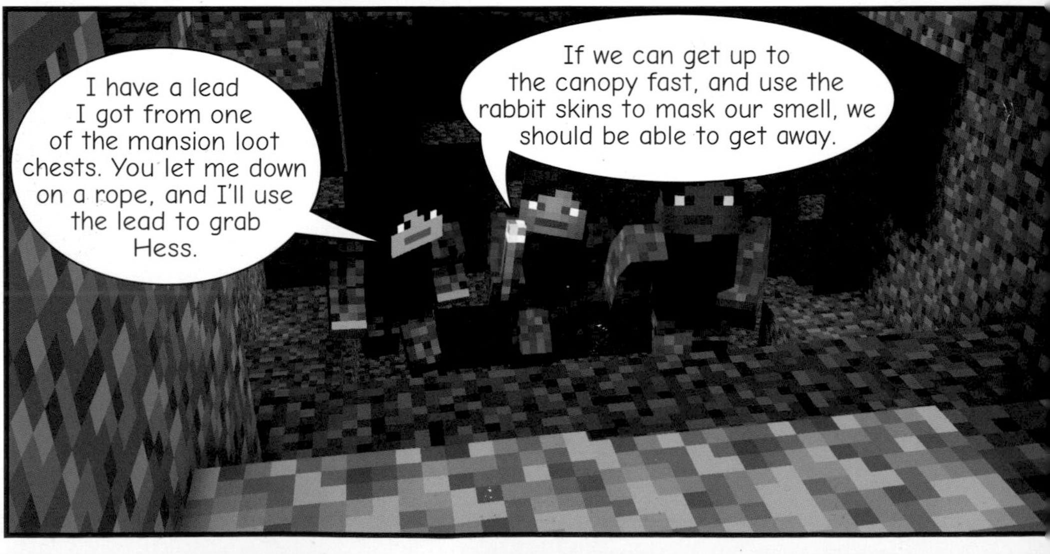
I have a lead I got from one of the mansion loot chests. You let me down on a rope, and I'll use the lead to grab Hess.
If we can get up to the canopy fast, and use the rabbit skins to mask our smell, we should be able to get away.

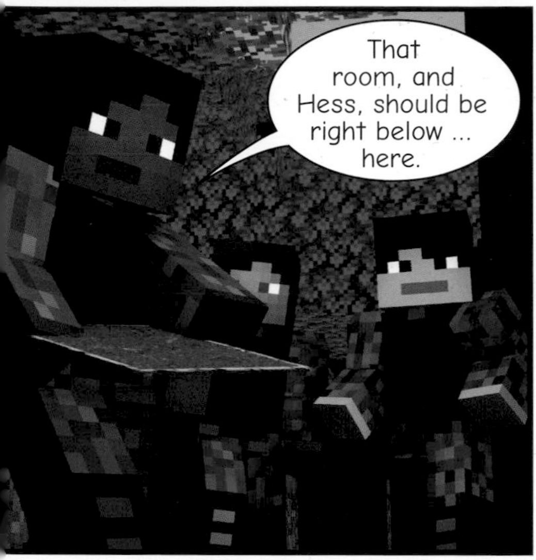
That room, and Hess, should be right below ... here.

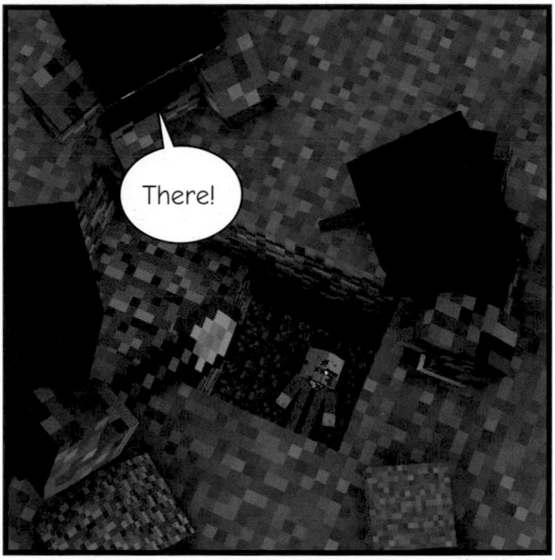
There!

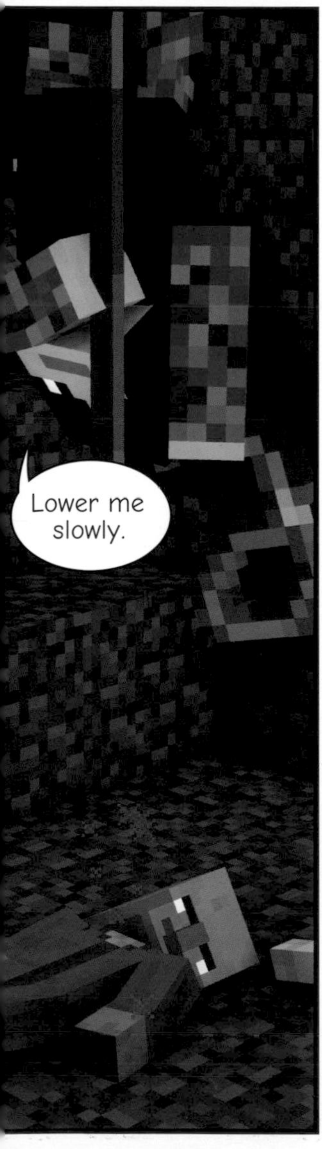
Lower me slowly.

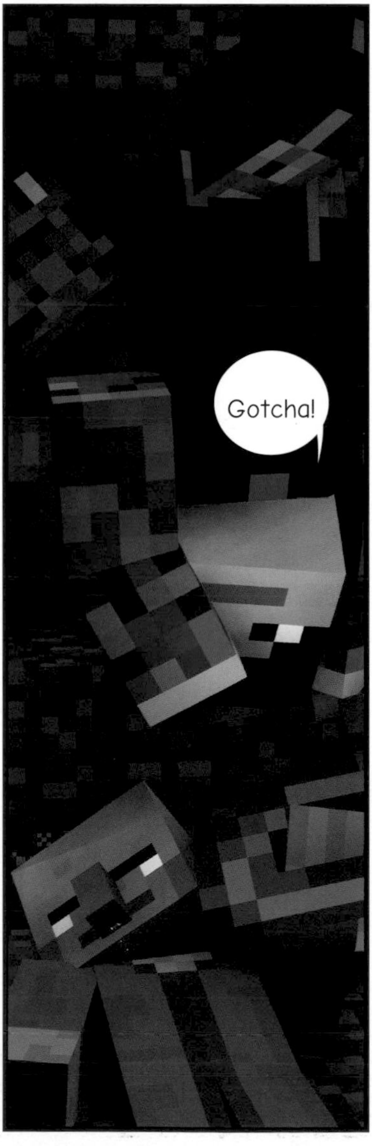
Gotcha!

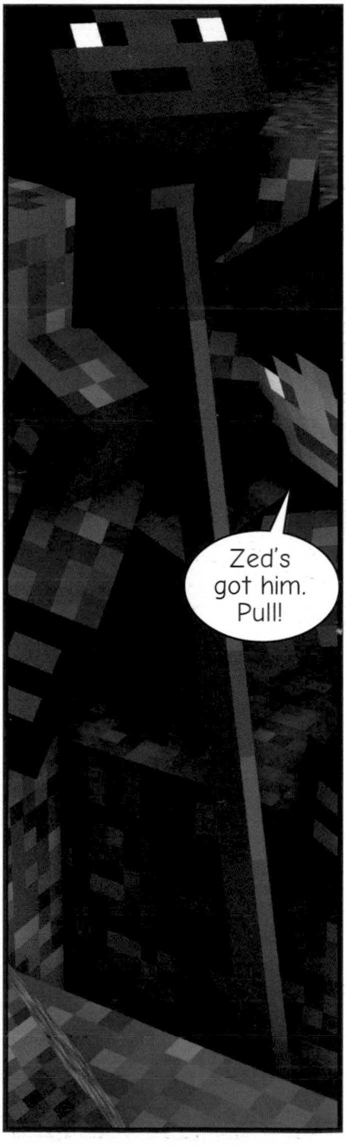
Zed's got him. Pull!

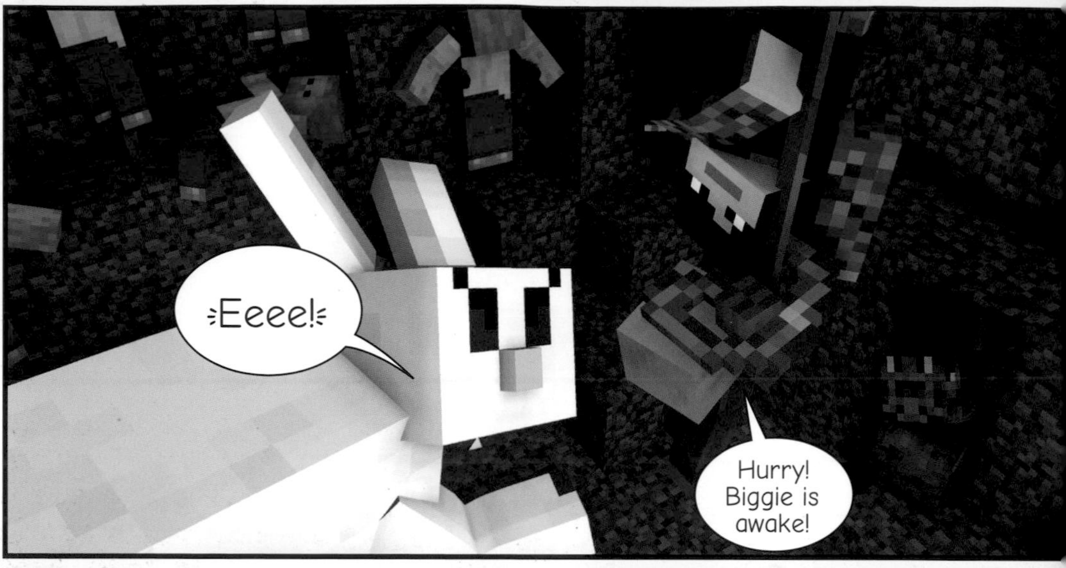
Eeee!
Hurry! Biggie is awake!
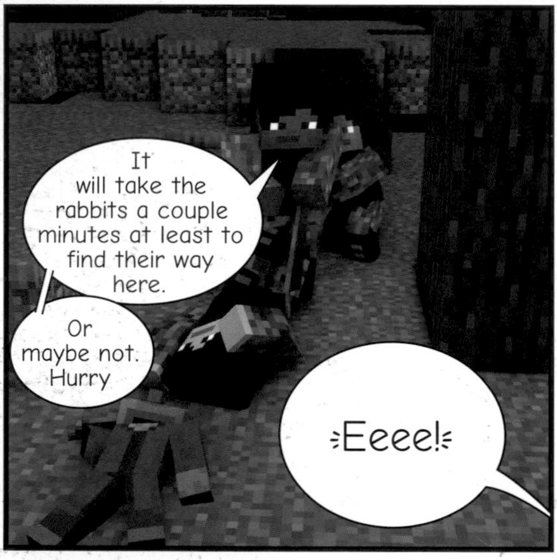
It will take the rabbits a couple minutes at least to find their way here.
Or maybe not. Hurry
Eeee!
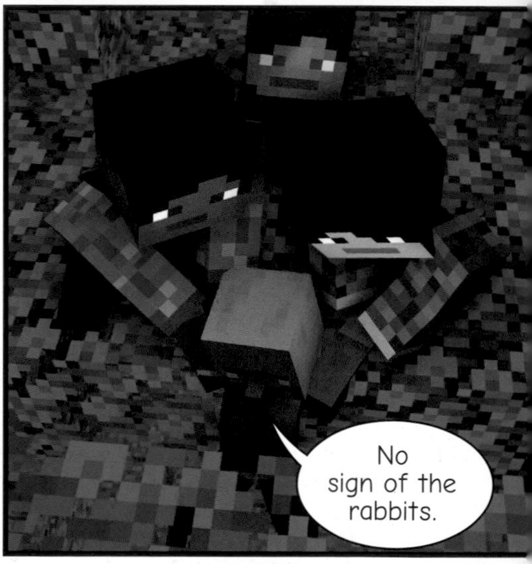
No sign of the rabbits.
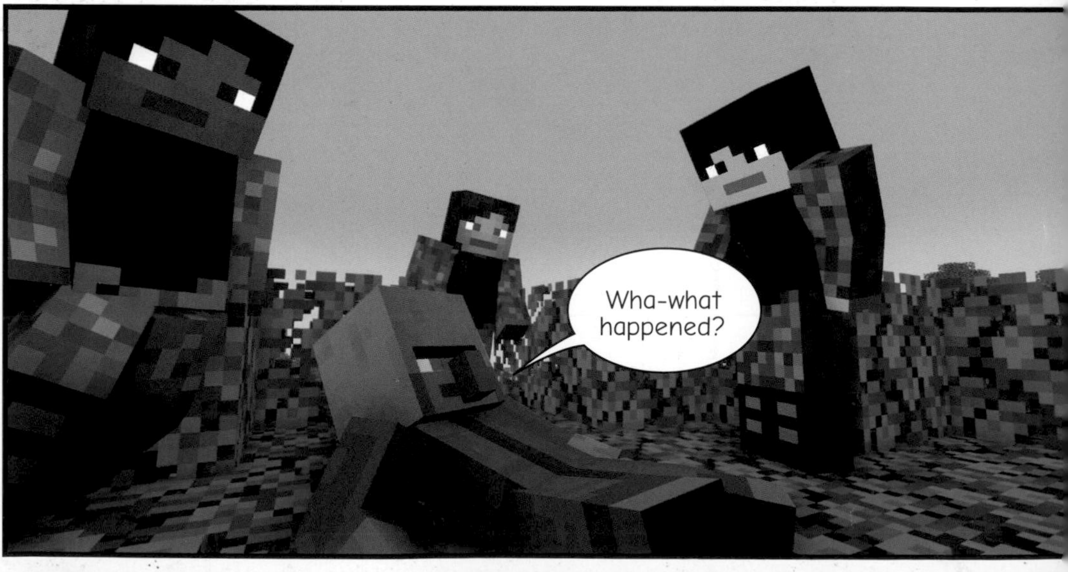
Wha-what happened?

Chapter 11: Extremes

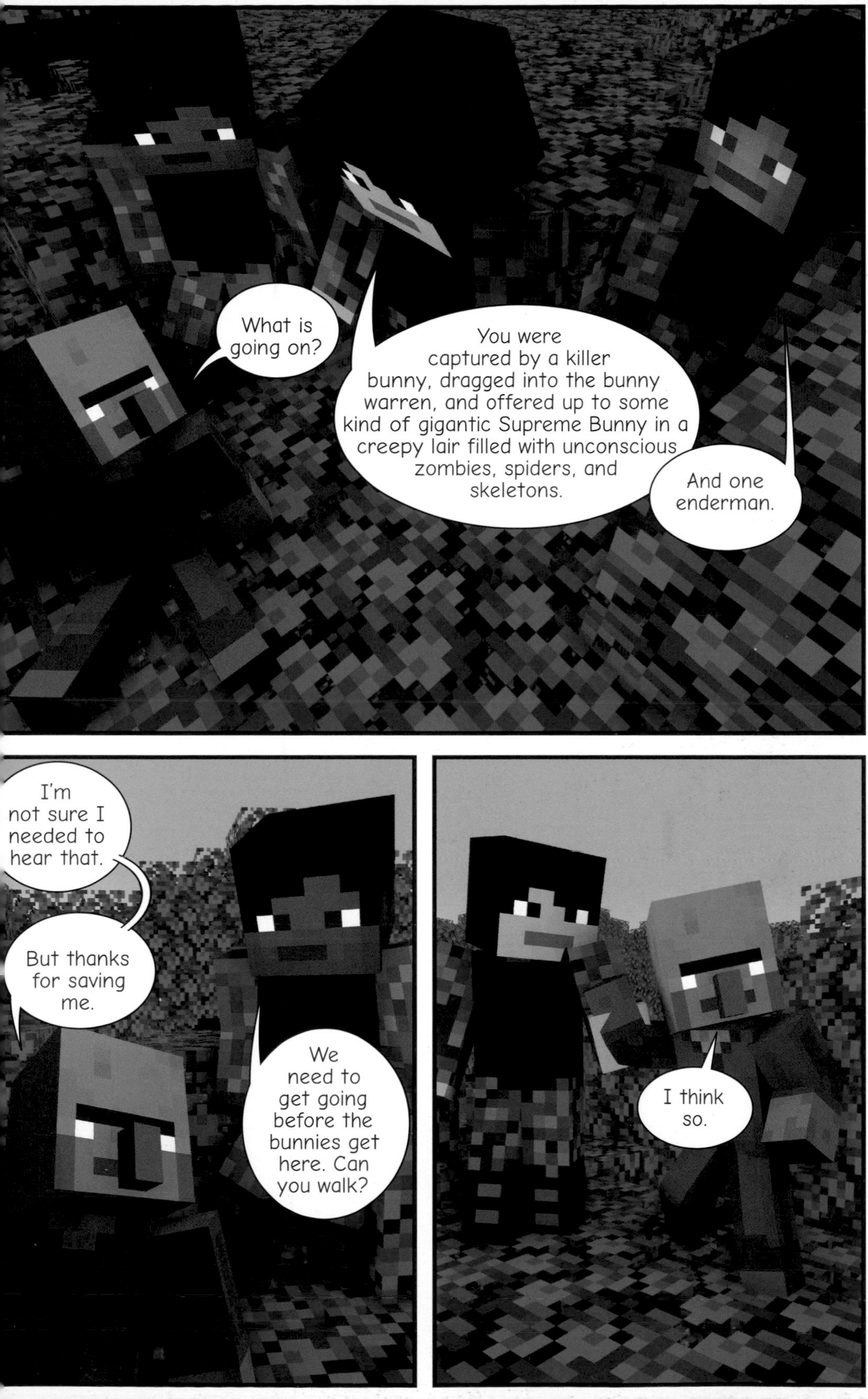
What is going on?
You were captured by a killer bunny, dragged into the bunny warren, and offered up to some kind of gigantic Supreme Bunny in a creepy lair filled with unconscious zombies, spiders, and skeletons.
And one enderman.
I'm not sure I needed to hear that.
But thanks for saving me.
We need to get going before the bunnies get here. Can you walk?
I think so.

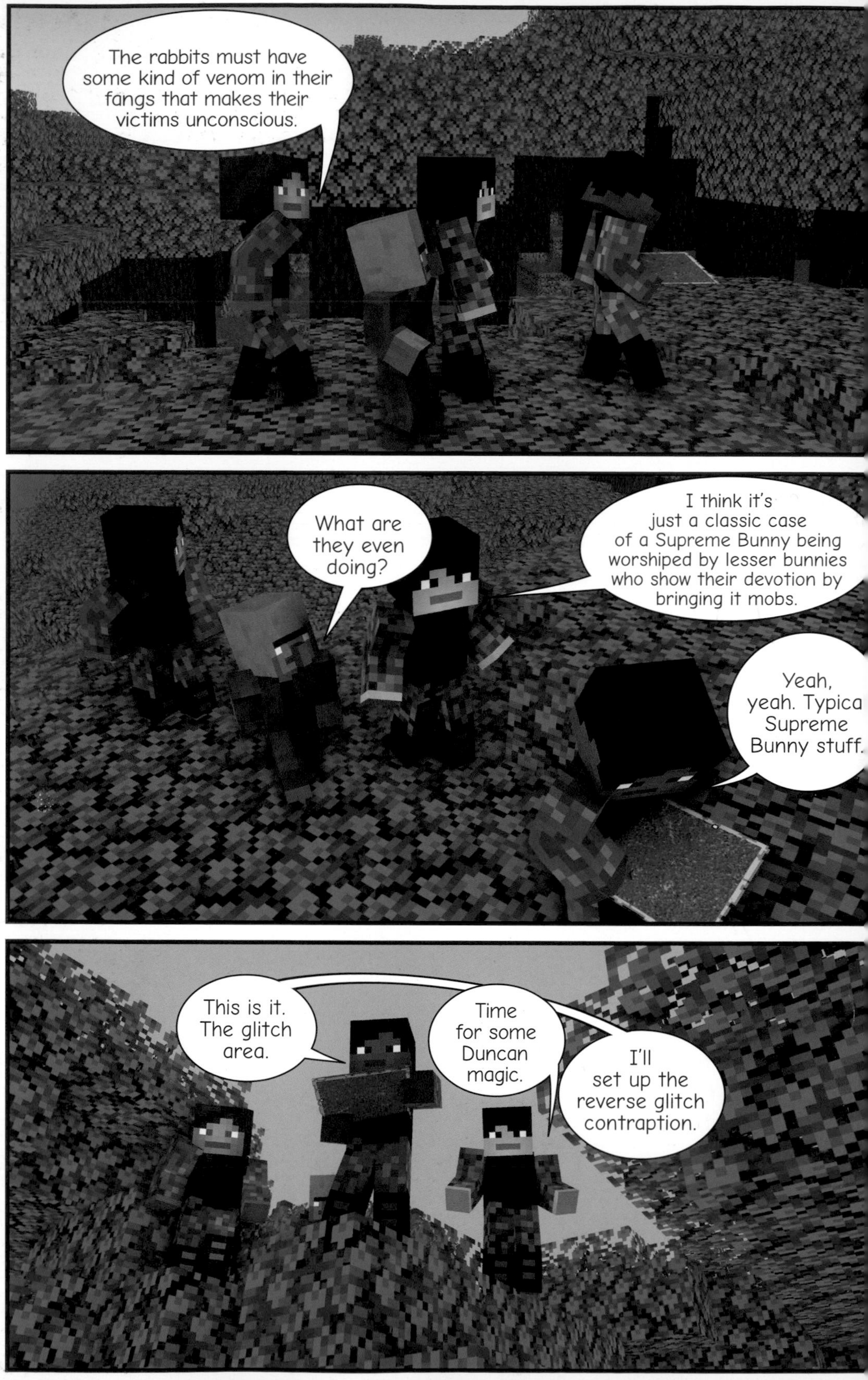

The rabbits must have some kind of venom in their fangs that makes their victims unconscious.
What are they even doing?
I think it's just a classic case of a Supreme Bunny being worshiped by lesser bunnies who show their devotion by bringing it mobs.
Yeah, yeah. Typica Supreme Bunny stuff.
This is it. The glitch area.
Time for some Duncan magic.
I'll set up the reverse glitch contraption.

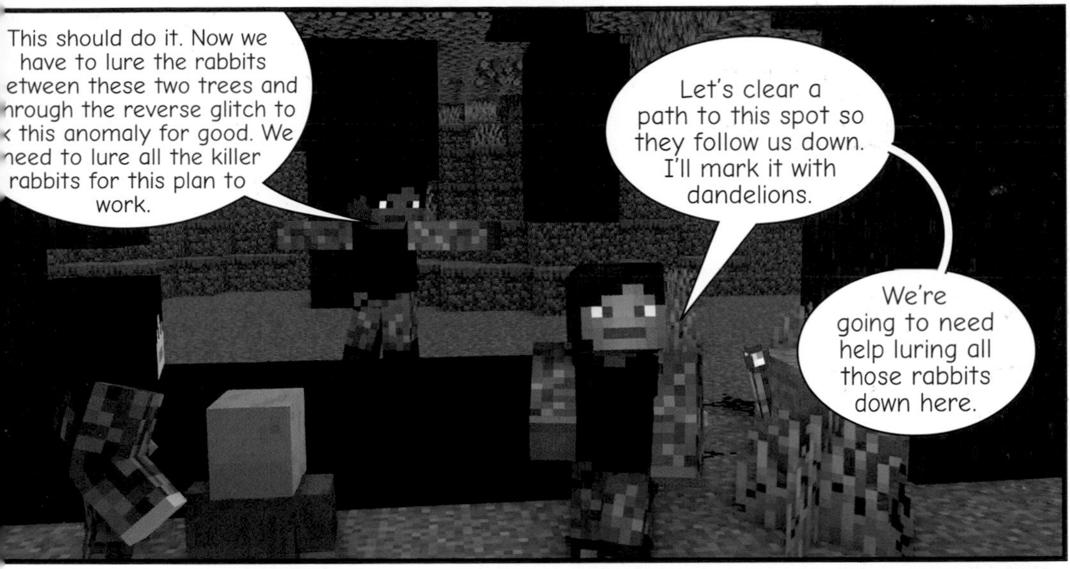
This should do it. Now we have to lure the rabbits etween these two trees and rough the reverse glitch to this anomaly for good. We eed to lure all the killer rabbits for this plan to work.
Let's clear a path to this spot so they follow us down. I'll mark it with dandelions.
We're going to need help luring all those rabbits down here.

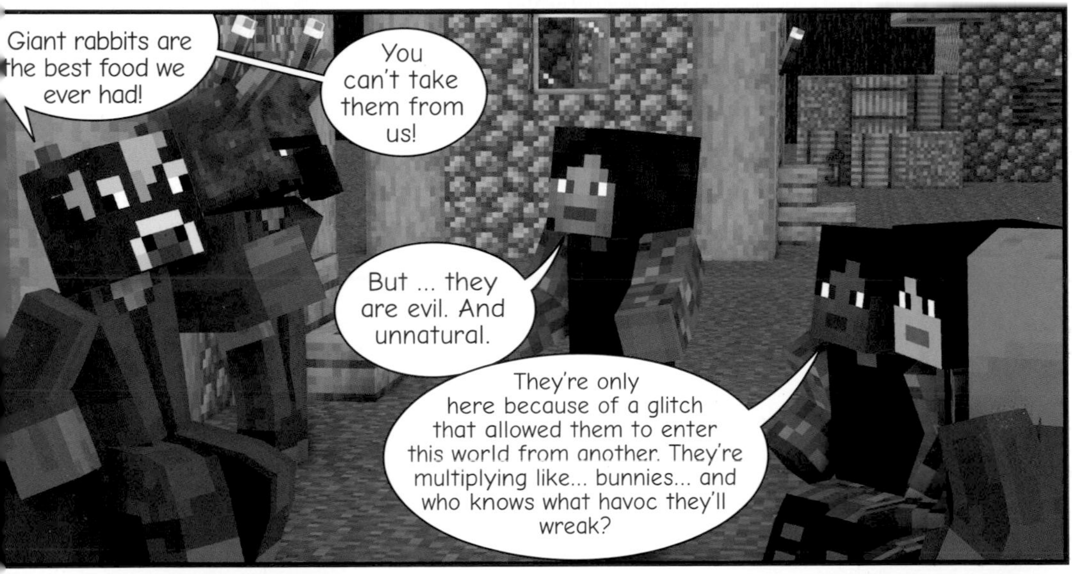
Giant rabbits are the best food we ever had!
You can't take them from us!
But ... they are evil. And unnatural.
They're only here because of a glitch that allowed them to enter this world from another. They're multiplying like... bunnies... and who knows what havoc they'll wreak?

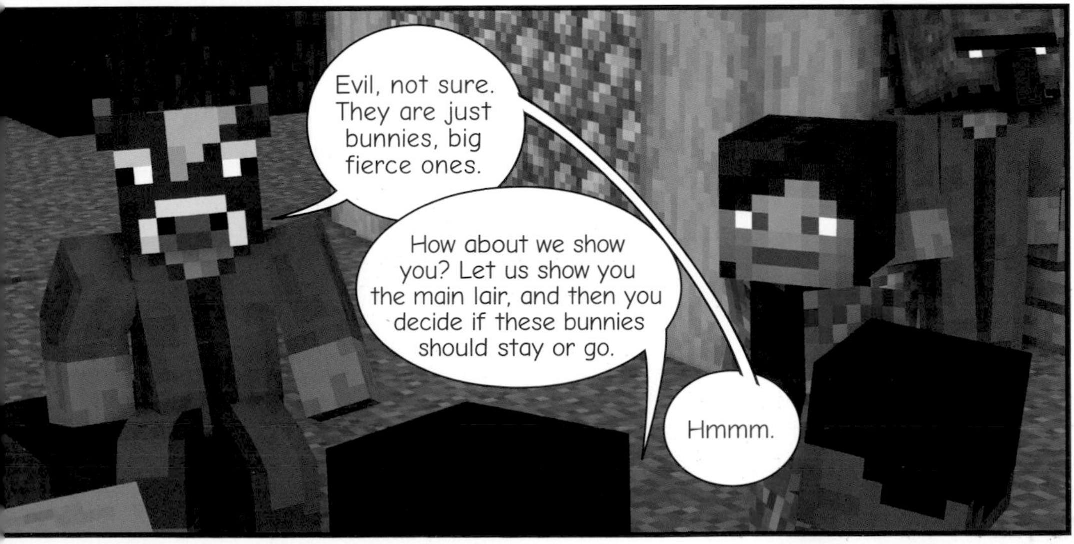
Evil, not sure. They are just bunnies, big fierce ones.
How about we show you? Let us show you the main lair, and then you decide if these bunnies should stay or go.
Hmmm.

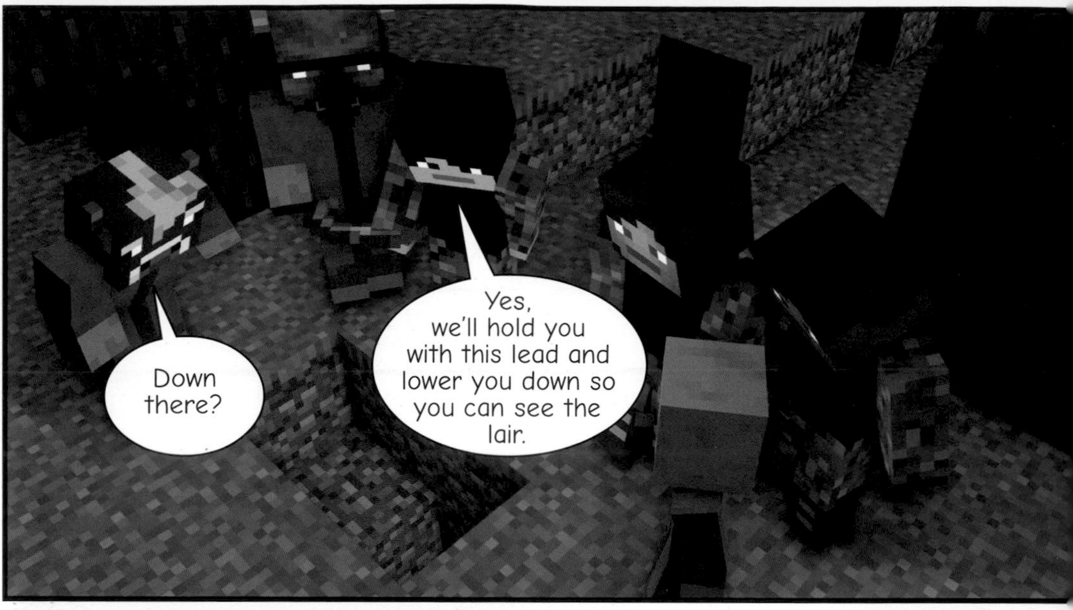
Down there?
Yes, we'll hold you with this lead and lower you down so you can see the lair.

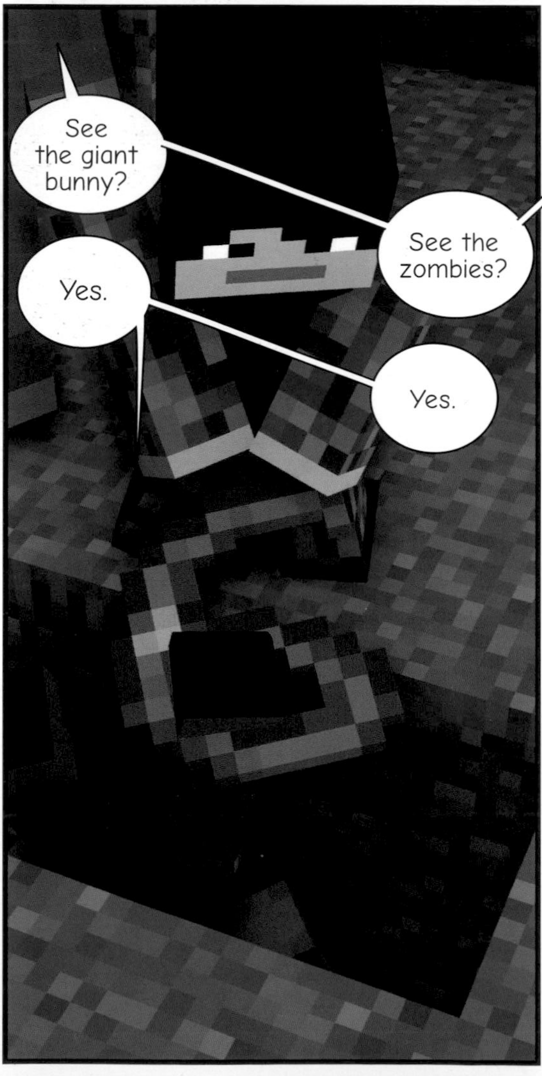
See the giant bunny?
Yes.
See the zombies?
Yes.

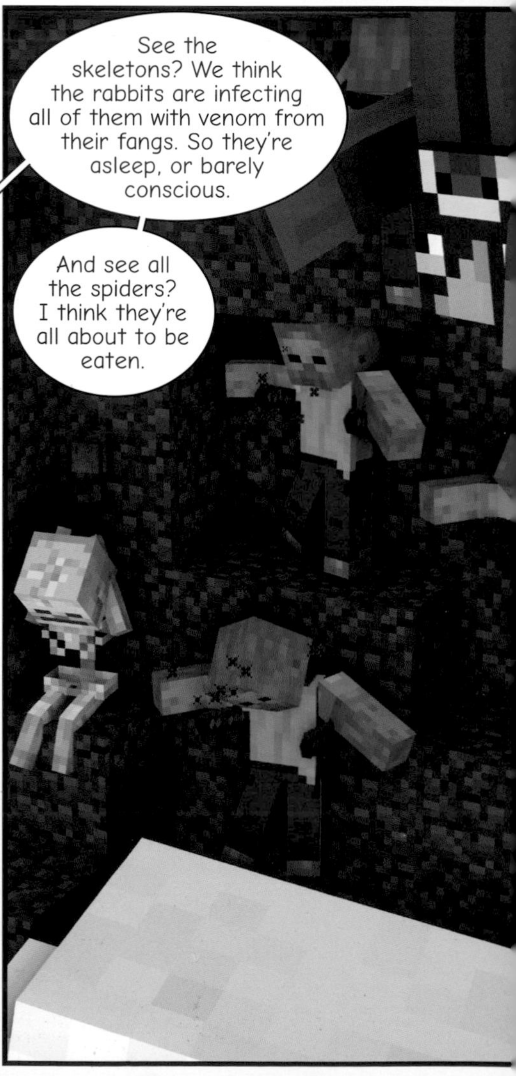
See the skeletons? We think the rabbits are infecting all of them with venom from their fangs. So they're asleep, or barely conscious.
And see all the spiders? I think they're all about to be eaten.

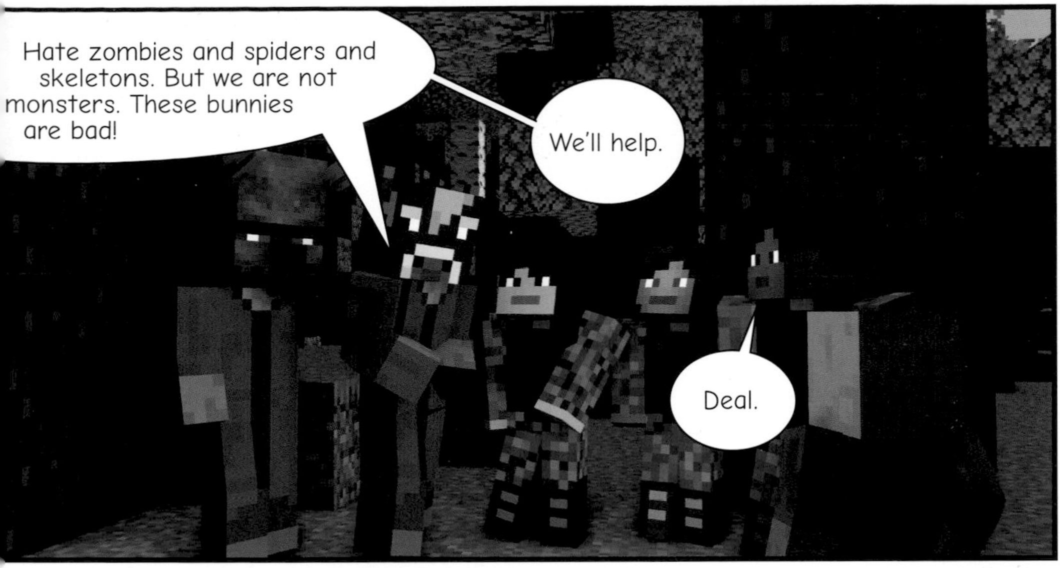
Hate zombies and spiders and skeletons. But we are not monsters. These bunnies are bad!
We'll help.
Deal.

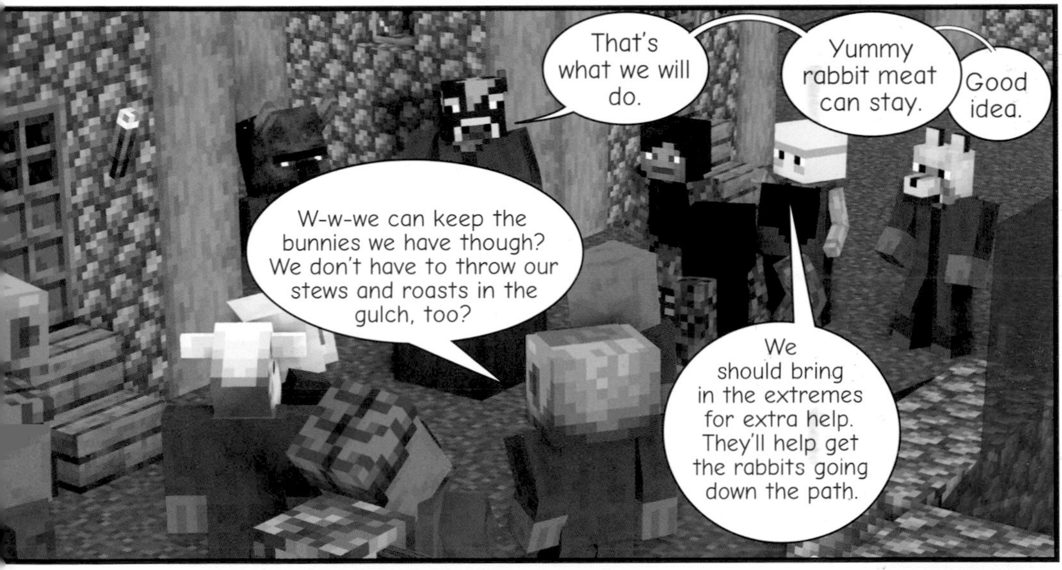
That's what we will do.
Yummy rabbit meat can stay.
Good idea.
W-w-we can keep the bunnies we have though? We don't have to throw our stews and roasts in the gulch, too?
We should bring in the extremes for extra help. They'll help get the rabbits going down the path.

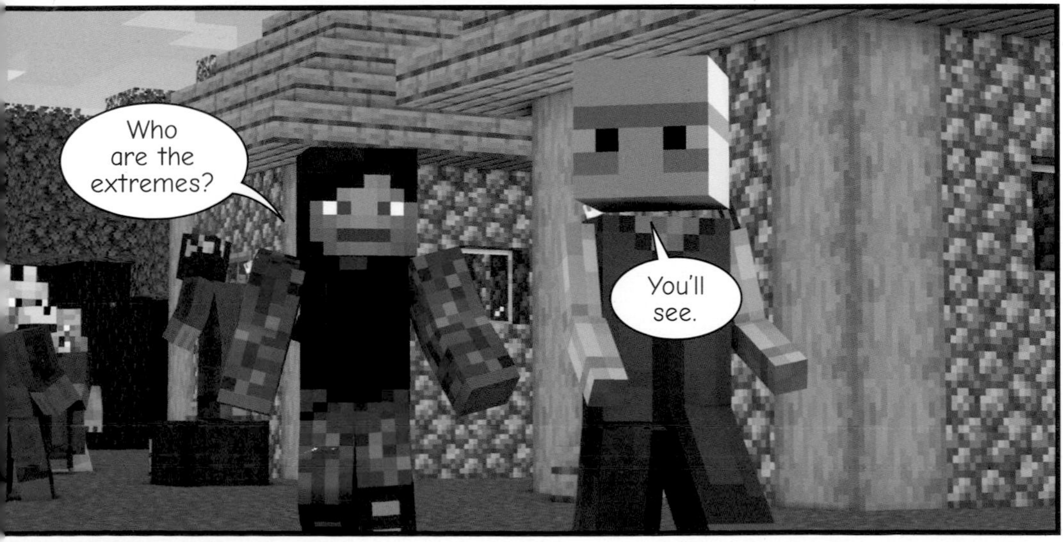
Who are the extremes?
You'll see.

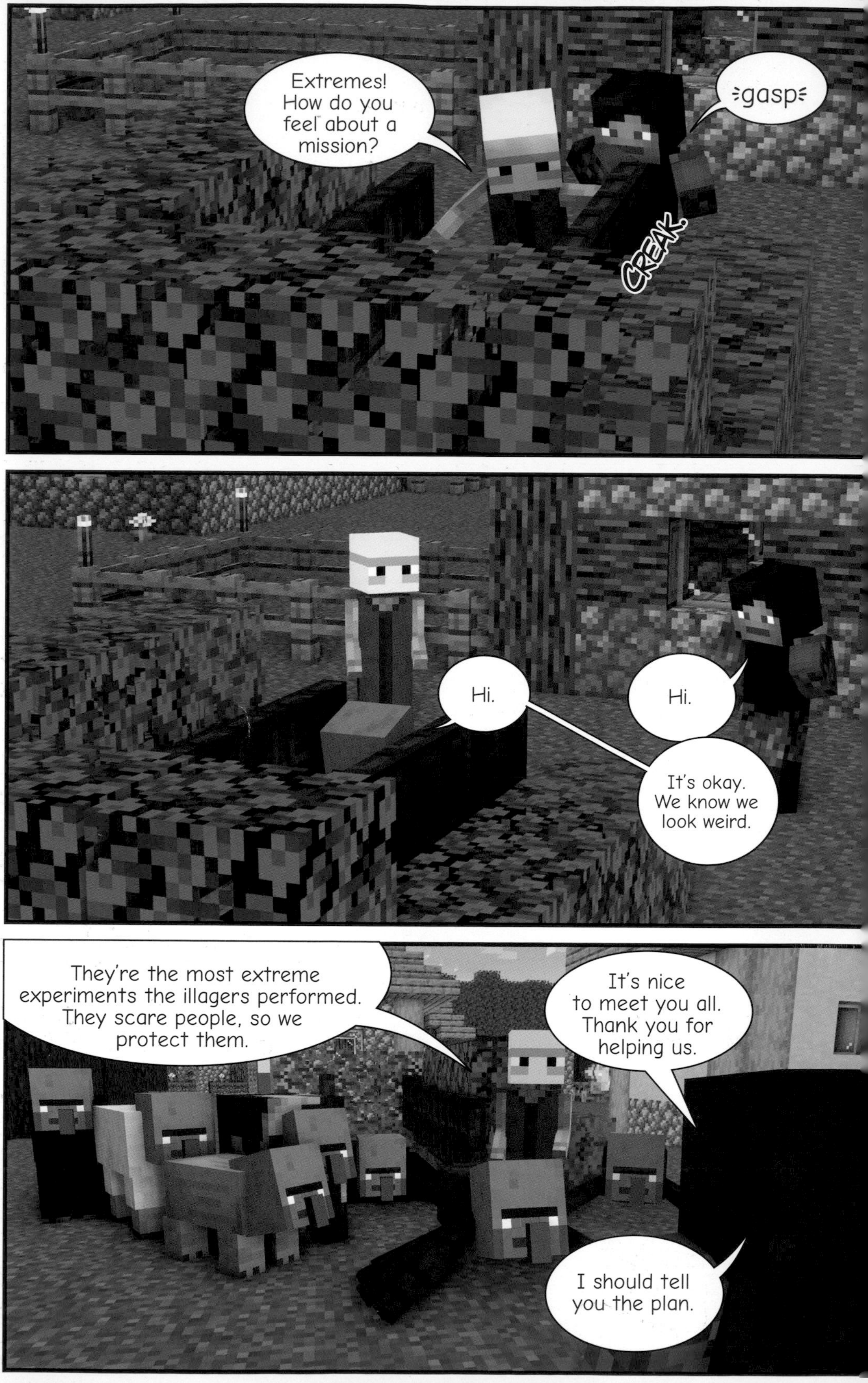
Extremes! How do you feel about a mission?
gasp
CREAK.
Hi.
Hi.
It's okay. We know we look weird.
They're the most extreme experiments the illagers performed. They scare people, so we protect them.
It's nice to meet you all. Thank you for helping us.
I should tell you the plan.

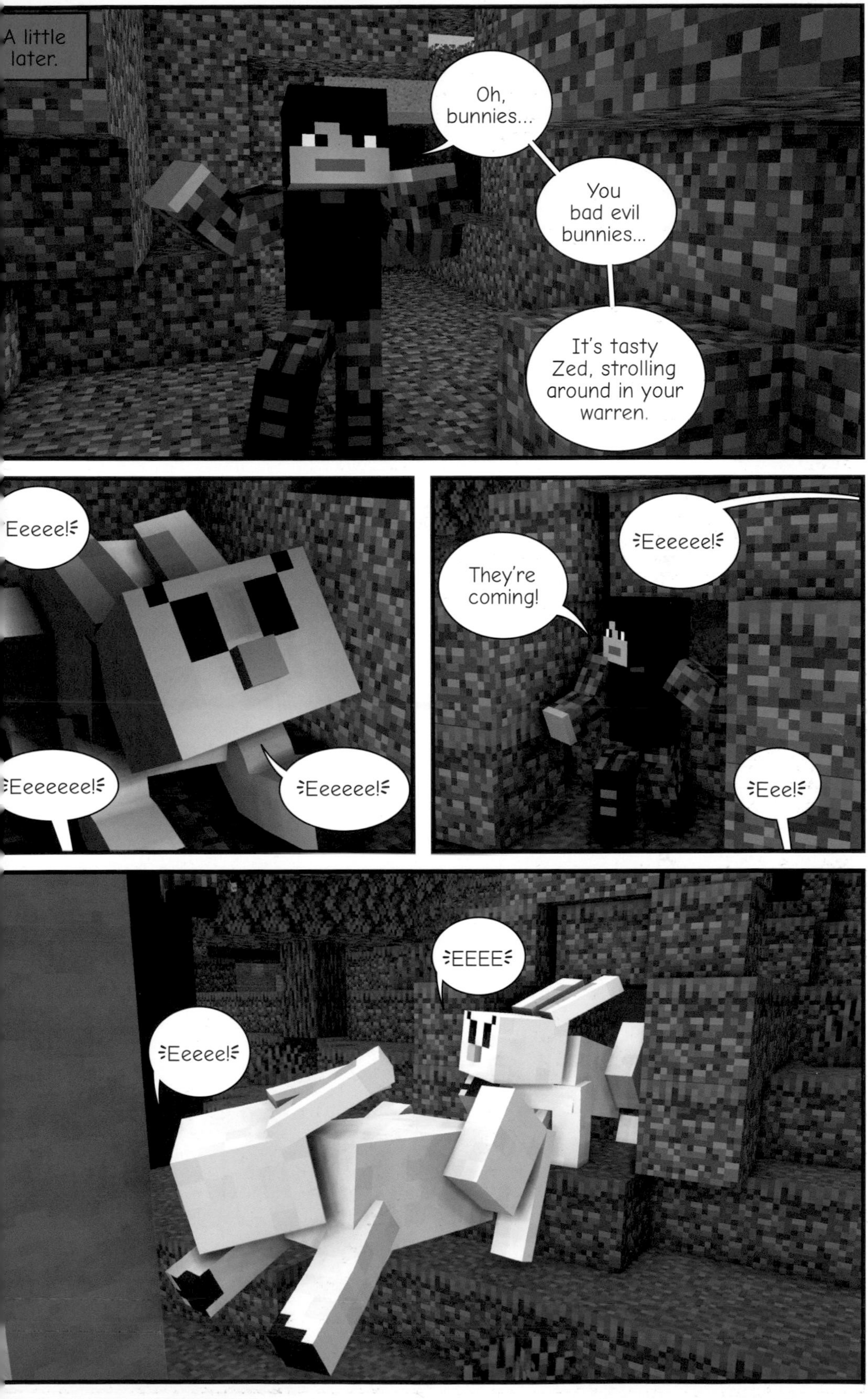

A little later.
Oh, bunnies...
You bad evil bunnies...
It's tasty Zed, strolling around in your warren.
Eeeee!
Eeeeeee!
Eeeeee!
Eeeeee!
They're coming!
Eee!
EEEE
Eeeee!

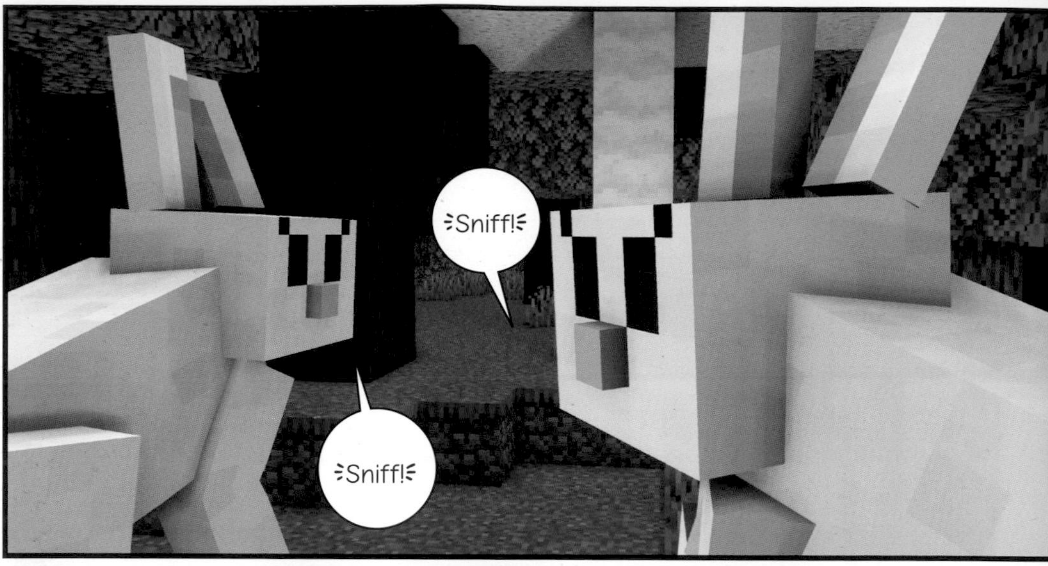
Sniff!
Sniff!

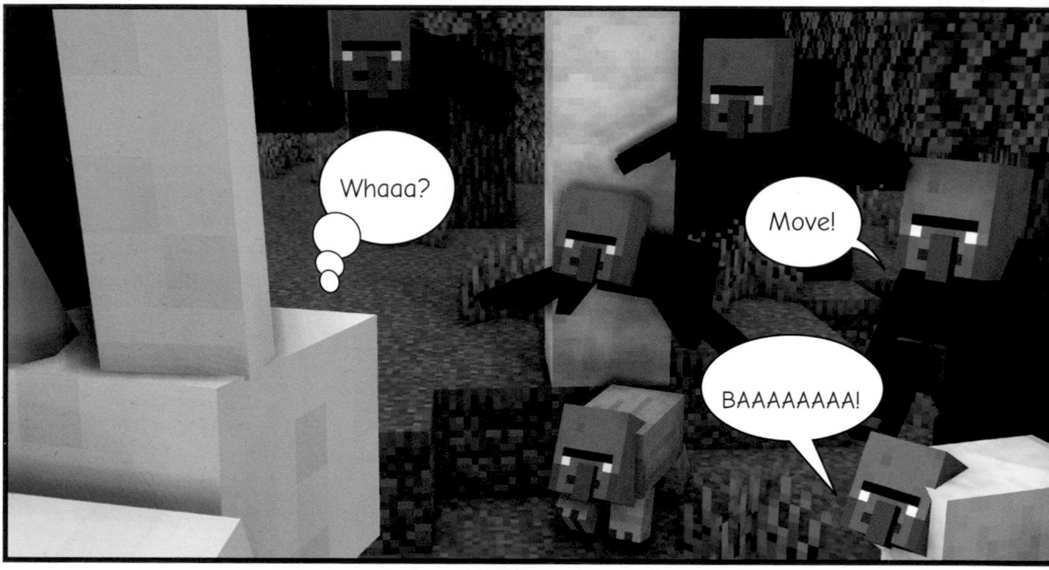
Whaaa?
Move!
BAAAAAAAA!

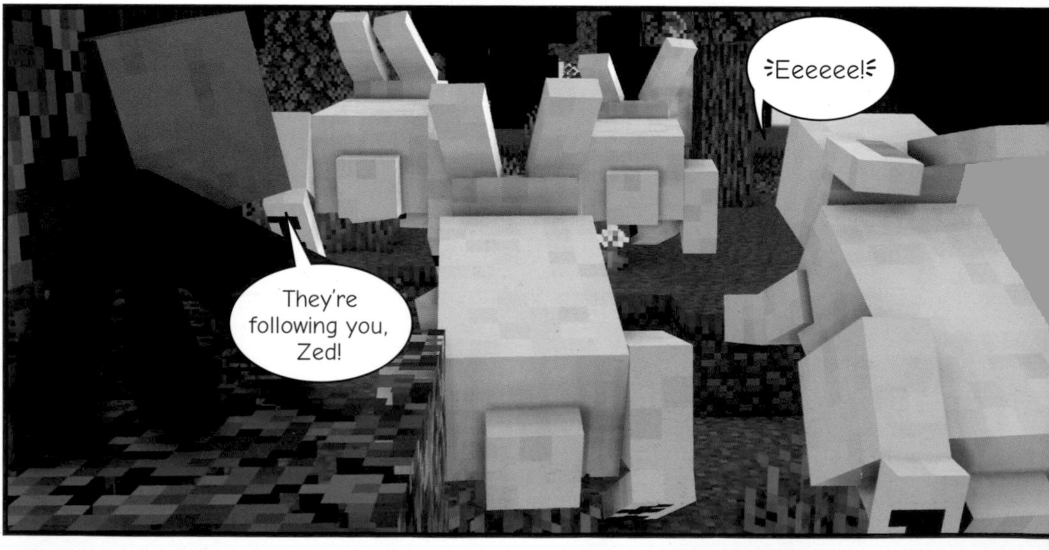
Eeeeee!
They're following you, Zed!

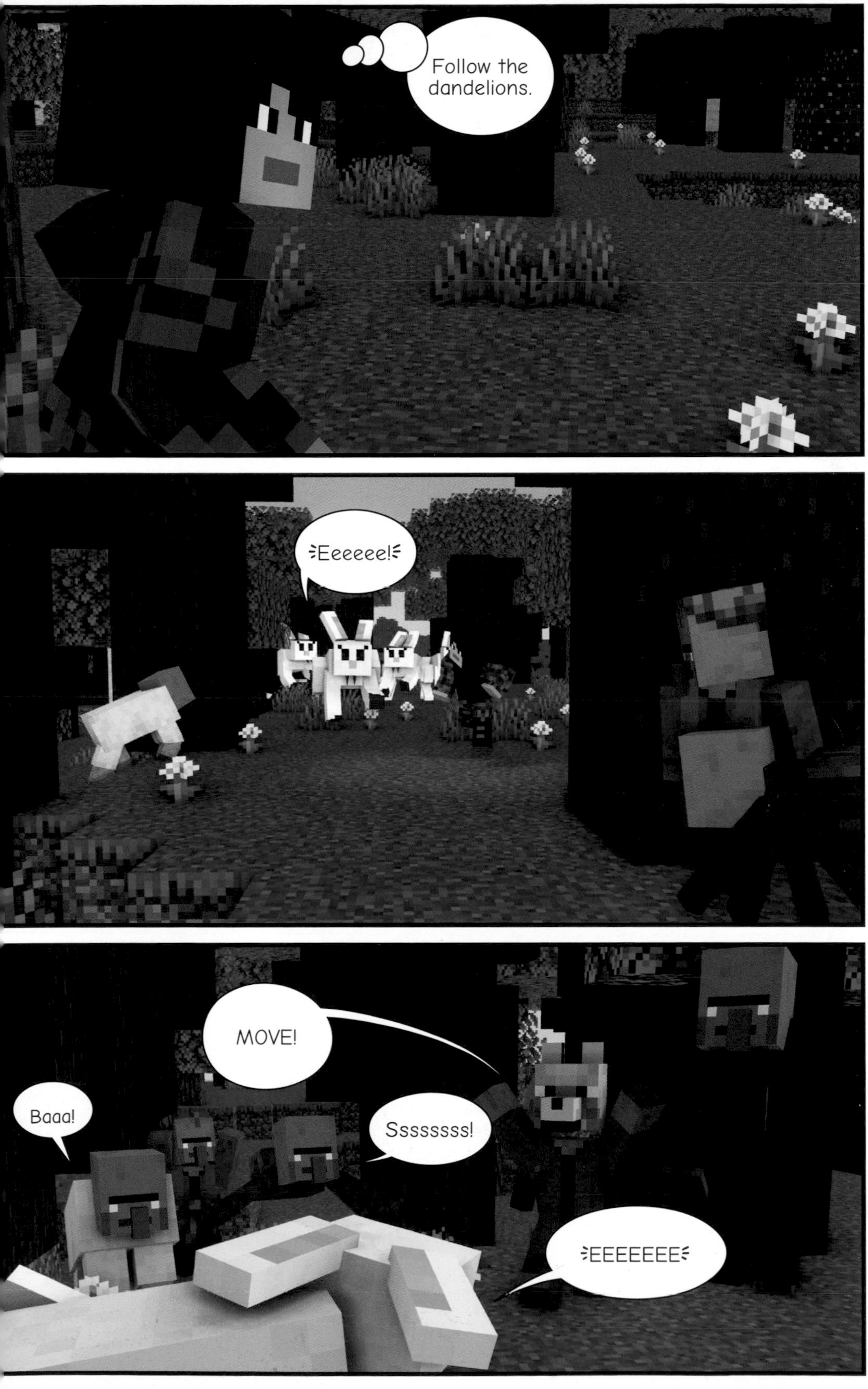
Follow the dandelions.
Eeeeee!
MOVE!
Baaa!
Sssssss!
EEEEEEE

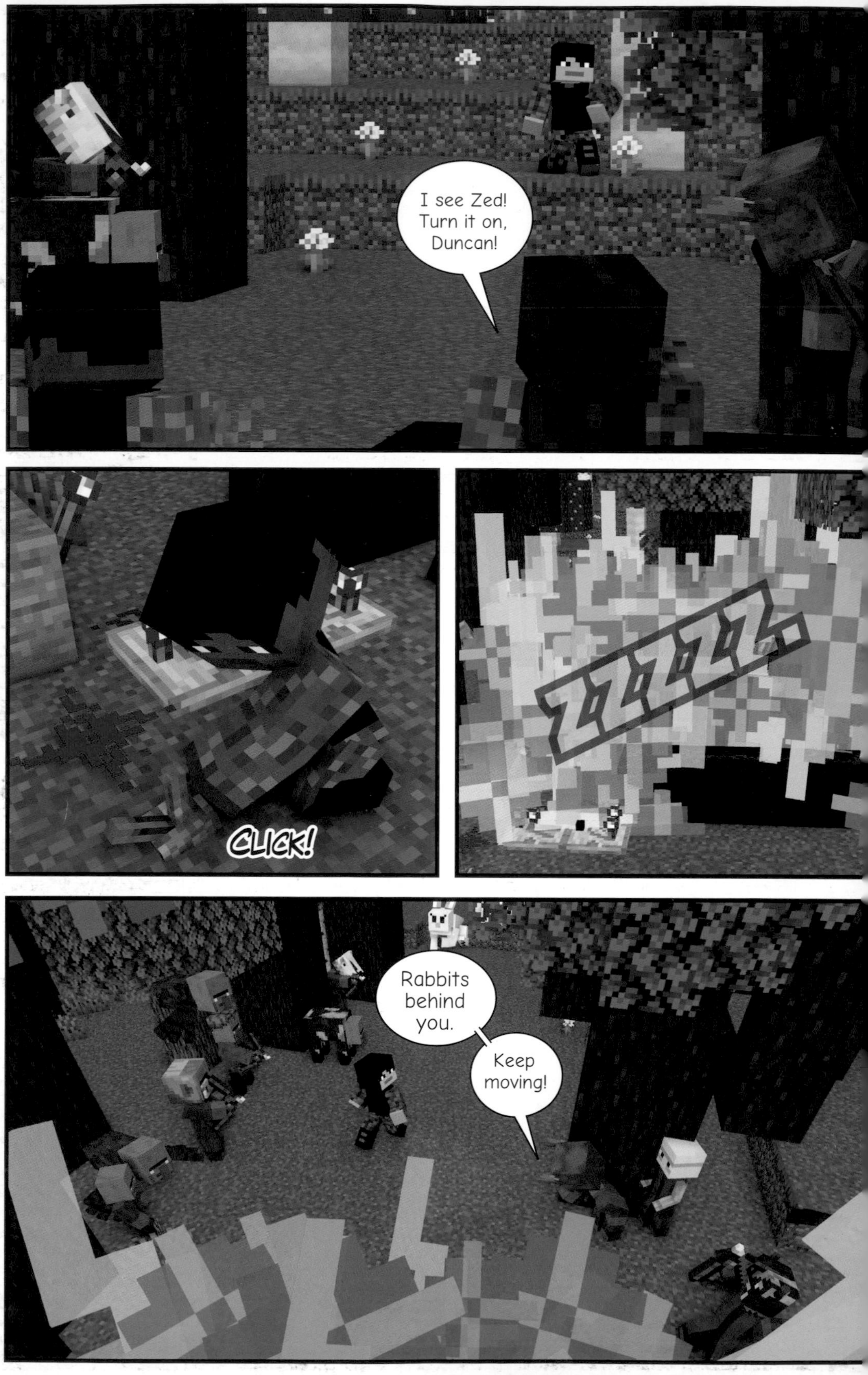

I see Zed! Turn it on, Duncan!
CLICK!
ZZZZZZ.
Rabbits behind you.
Keep moving!

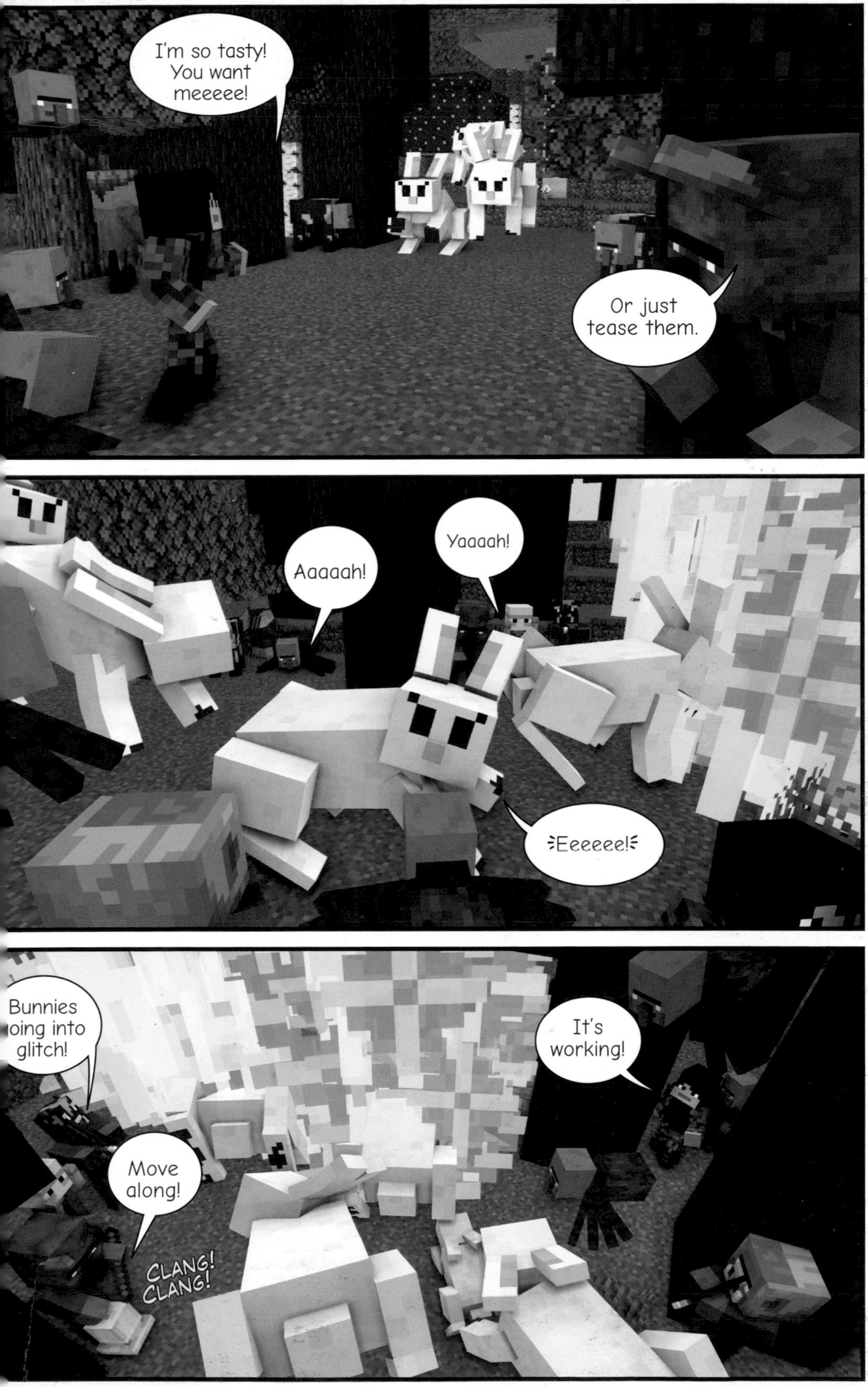
I'm so tasty! You want meeeee!
Or just tease them.
Aaaaah!
Yaaaah!
Eeeeee!
Bunnies oing into glitch!
It's working!
Move along!
CLANG! CLANG!

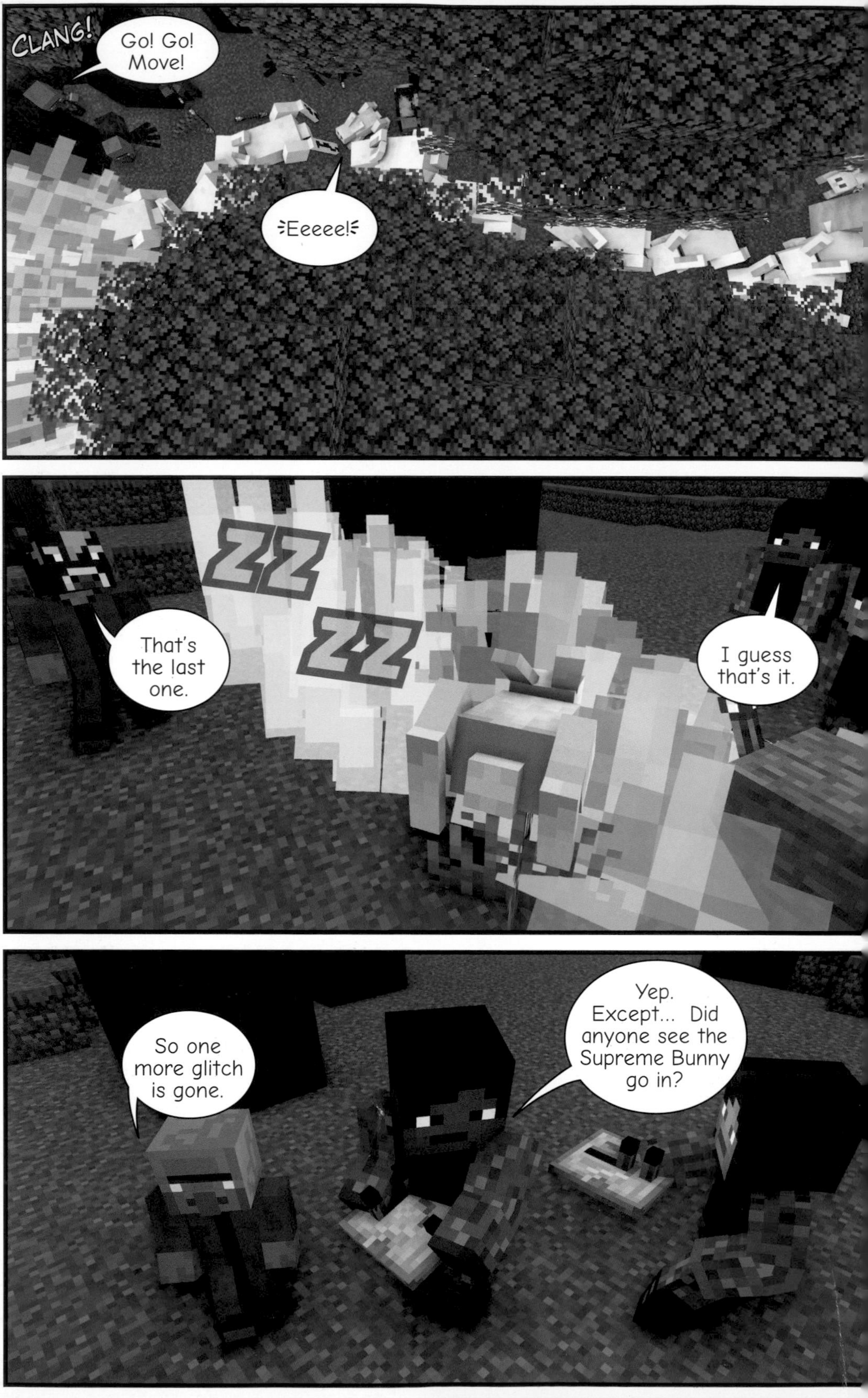
CLANG!
Go! Go! Move!
Eeeee!
ZZ
ZZ
That's the last one.
I guess that's it.
So one more glitch is gone.
Yep. Except... Did anyone see the Supreme Bunny go in?

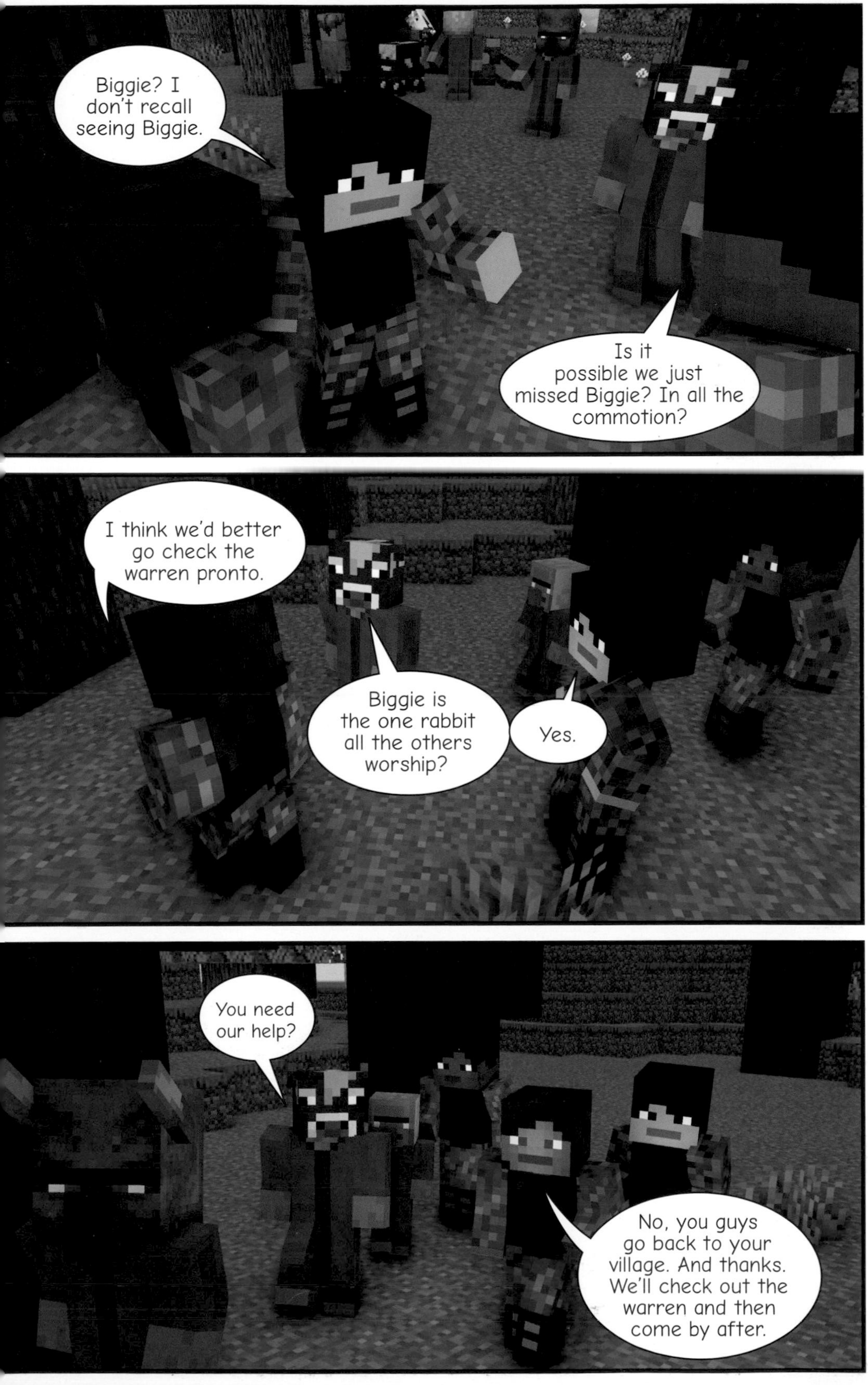
Biggie? I don't recall seeing Biggie.
Is it possible we just missed Biggie? In all the commotion?
I think we'd better go check the warren pronto.
Biggie is the one rabbit all the others worship?
Yes.
You need our help?
No, you guys go back to your village. And thanks. We'll check out the warren and then come by after.

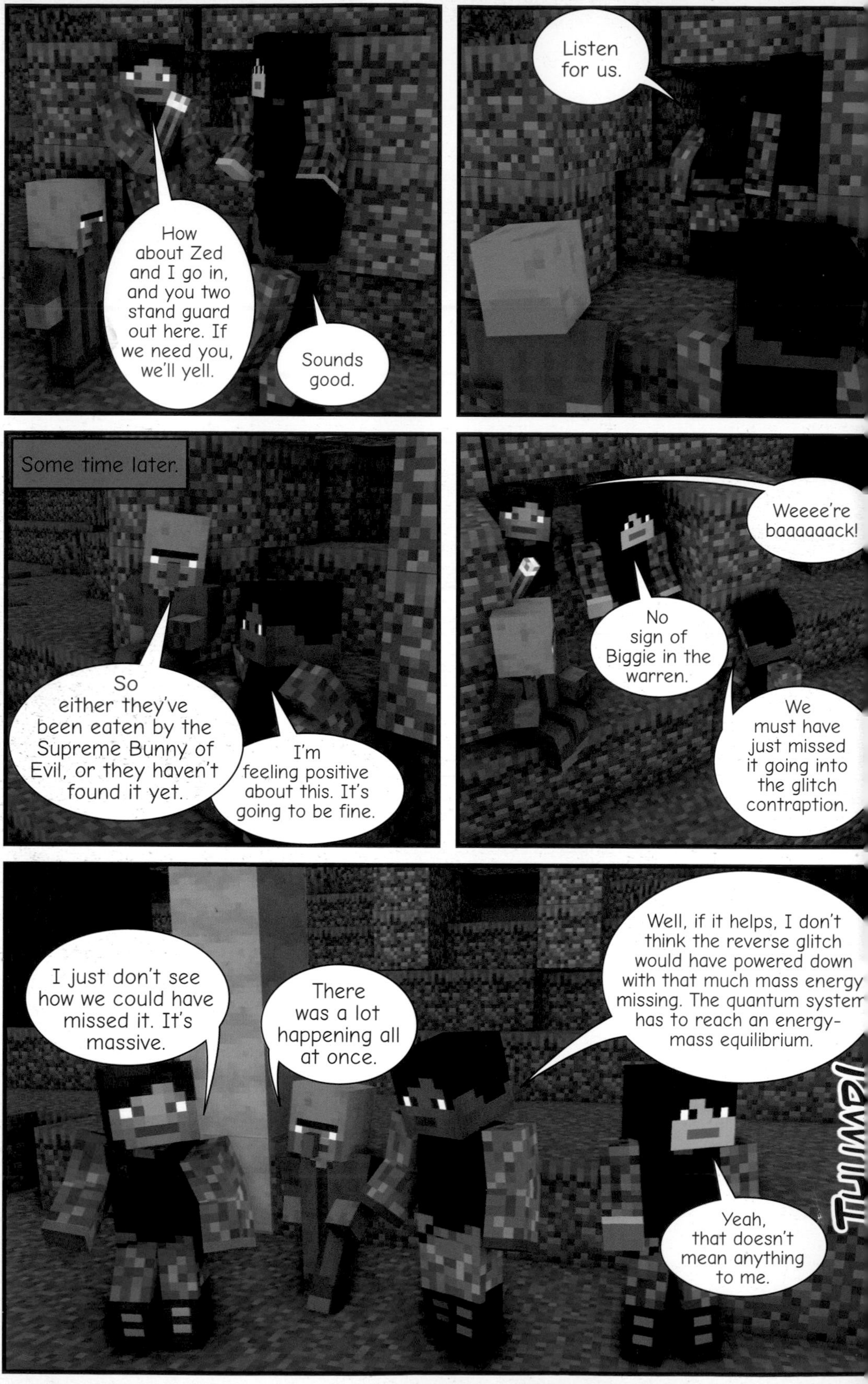
How about Zed and I go in, and you two stand guard out here. If we need you, we'll yell.
Sounds good.
Listen for us.
Some time later.
So either they've been eaten by the Supreme Bunny of Evil, or they haven't found it yet.
I'm feeling positive about this. It's going to be fine.
Weeee're baaaaaack!
No sign of Biggie in the warren.
We must have just missed it going into the glitch contraption.
I just don't see how we could have missed it. It's massive.
There was a lot happening all at once.
Well, if it helps, I don't think the reverse glitch would have powered down with that much mass energy missing. The quantum system has to reach an energy-mass equilibrium.
Yeah, that doesn't mean anything to me.

Chapter 12: Bonfire

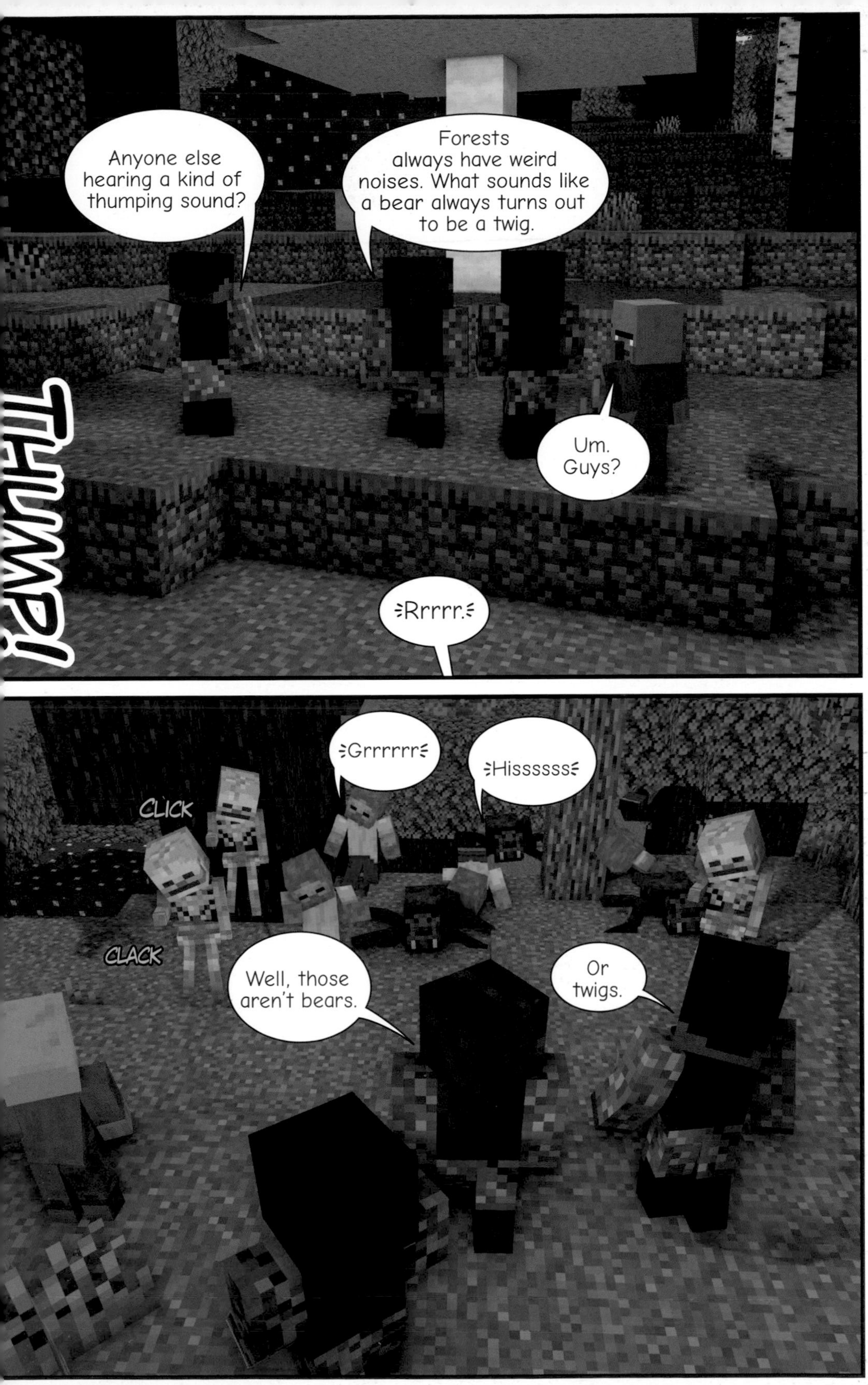

Anyone else hearing a kind of thumping sound?
Forests always have weird noises. What sounds like a bear always turns out to be a twig.
Um. Guys?
THUMP!
Rrrrr.
CLICK
Grrrrrr
Hissssss
CLACK
Well, those aren't bears.
Or twigs.

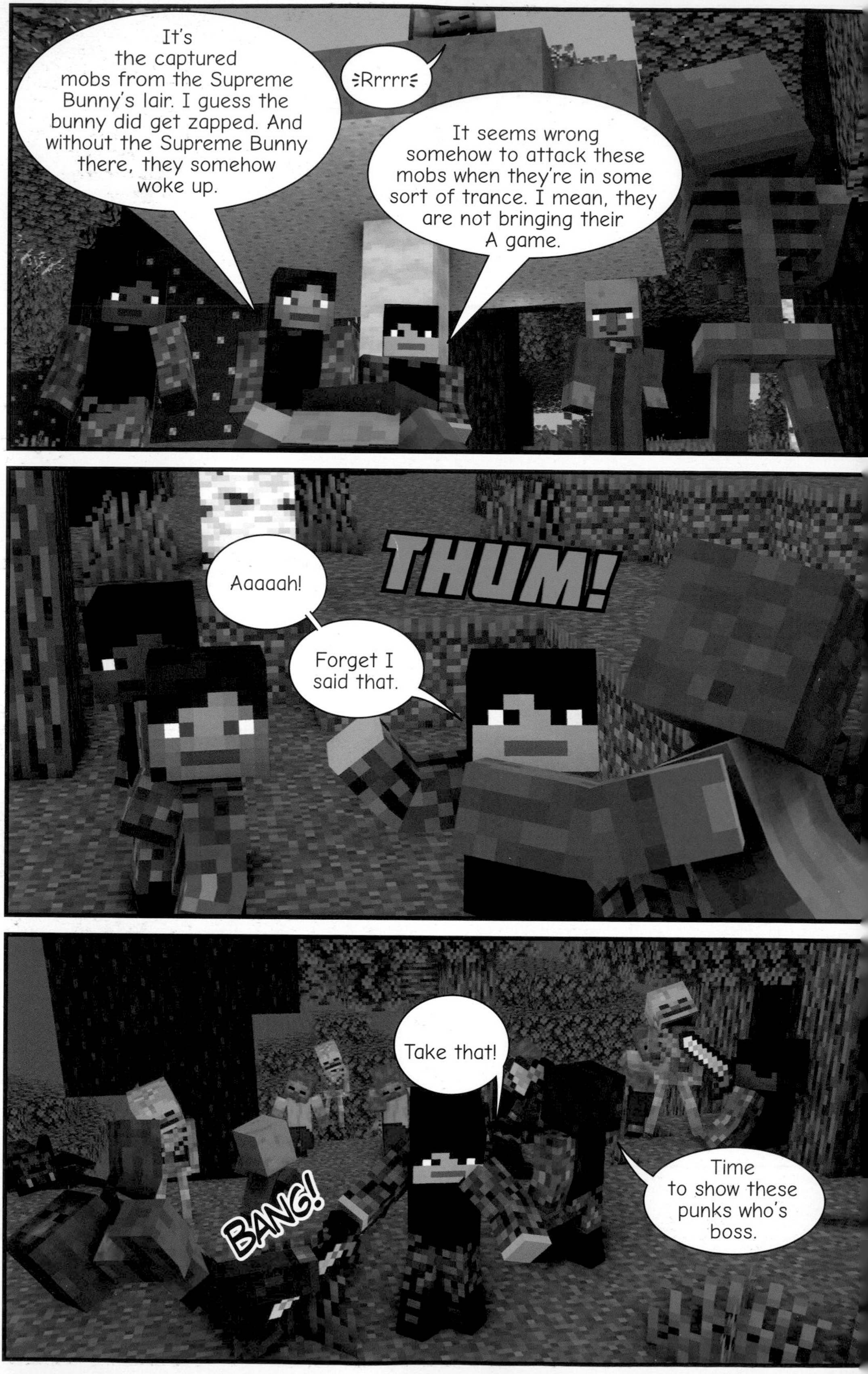
It's the captured mobs from the Supreme Bunny's lair. I guess the bunny did get zapped. And without the Supreme Bunny there, they somehow woke up.
Rrrrr
It seems wrong somehow to attack these mobs when they're in some sort of trance. I mean, they are not bringing their A game.
THUM!
Aaaaah!
Forget I said that.
Take that!
BANG!
Time to show these punks who's boss.

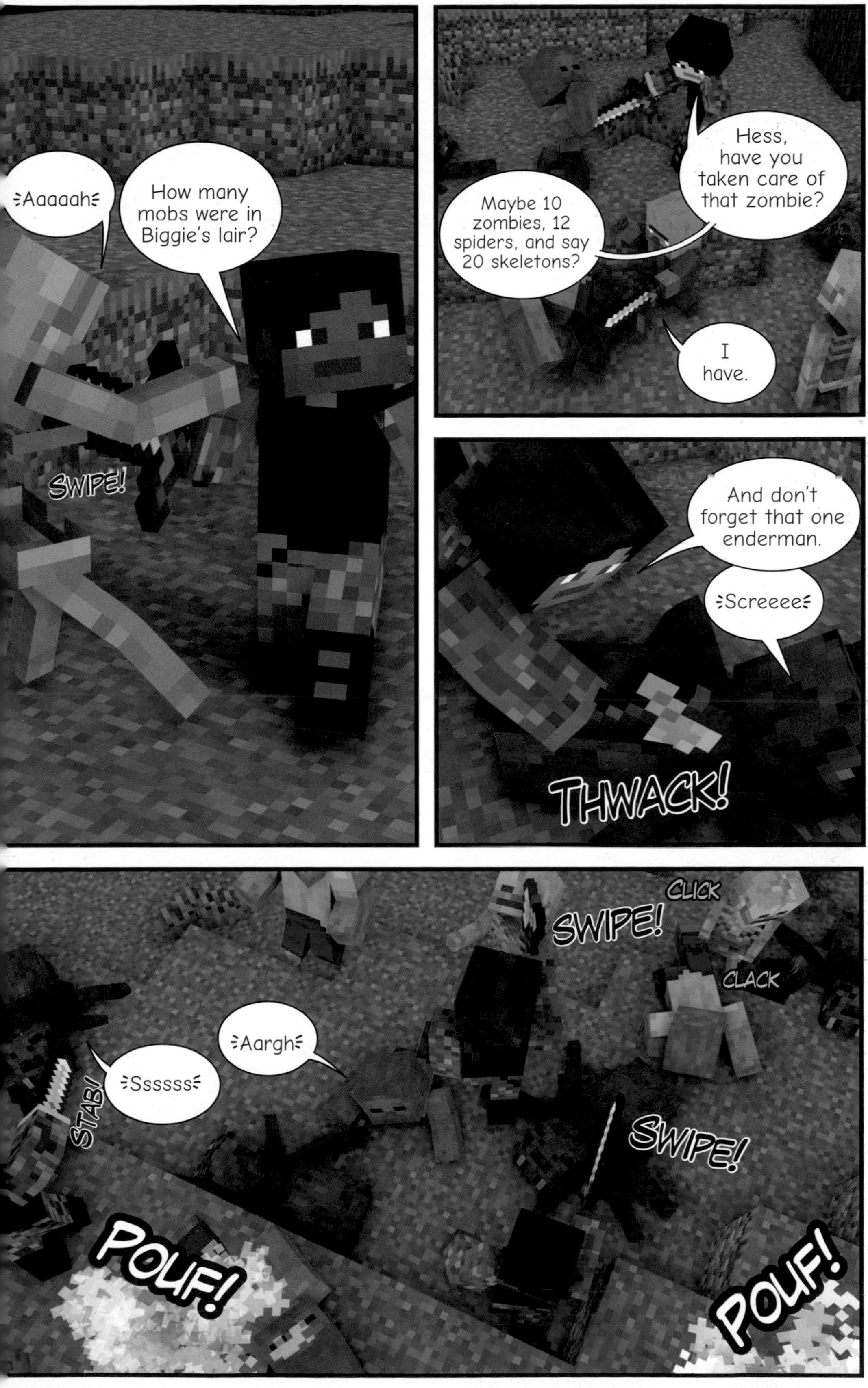

Aaaaah
How many mobs were in Biggie's lair?
SWIPE!
Hess, have you taken care of that zombie?
Maybe 10 zombies, 12 spiders, and say 20 skeletons?
I have.
And don't forget that one enderman.
Screeee
THWACK!
CLICK
SWIPE!
CLACK
Aargh
Ssssss
STAB!
SWIPE!
POUF!
POUF!

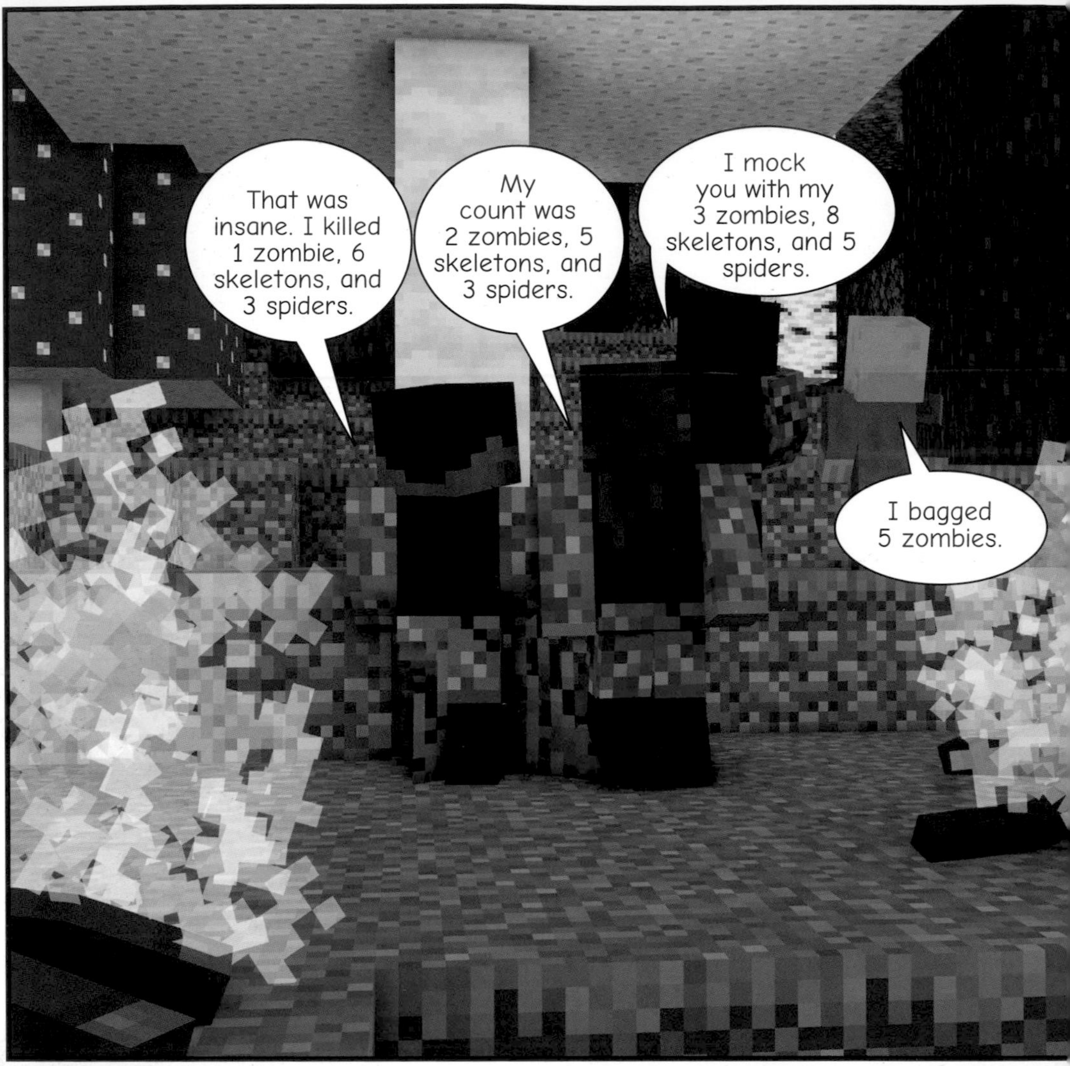
That was insane. I killed 1 zombie, 6 skeletons, and 3 spiders.
My count was 2 zombies, 5 skeletons, and 3 spiders.
I mock you with my 3 zombies, 8 skeletons, and 5 spiders.
I bagged 5 zombies.

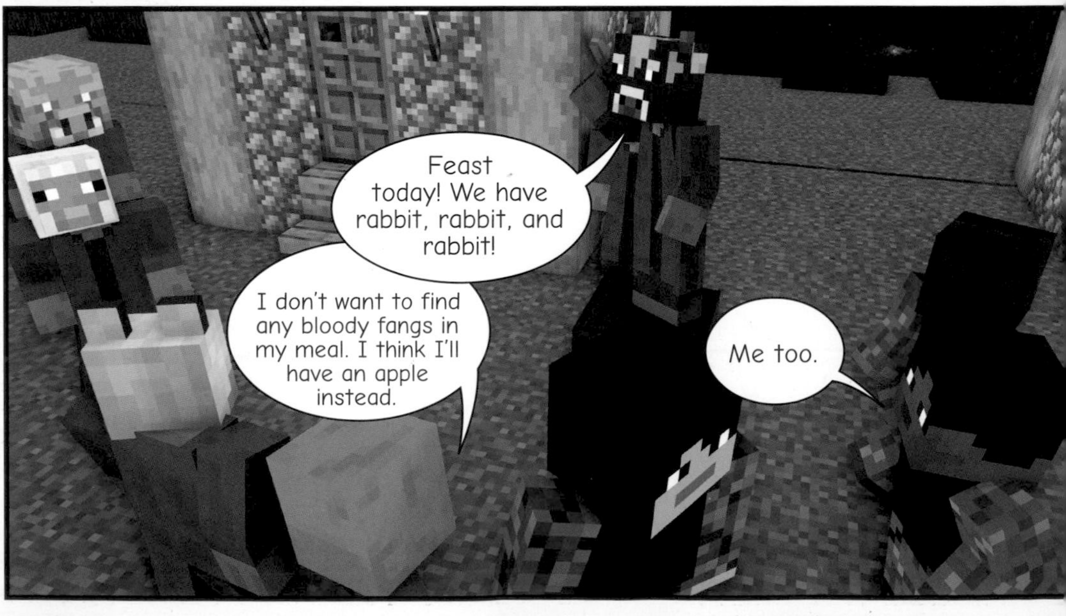
Feast today! We have rabbit, rabbit, and rabbit!
I don't want to find any bloody fangs in my meal. I think I'll have an apple instead.
Me too.

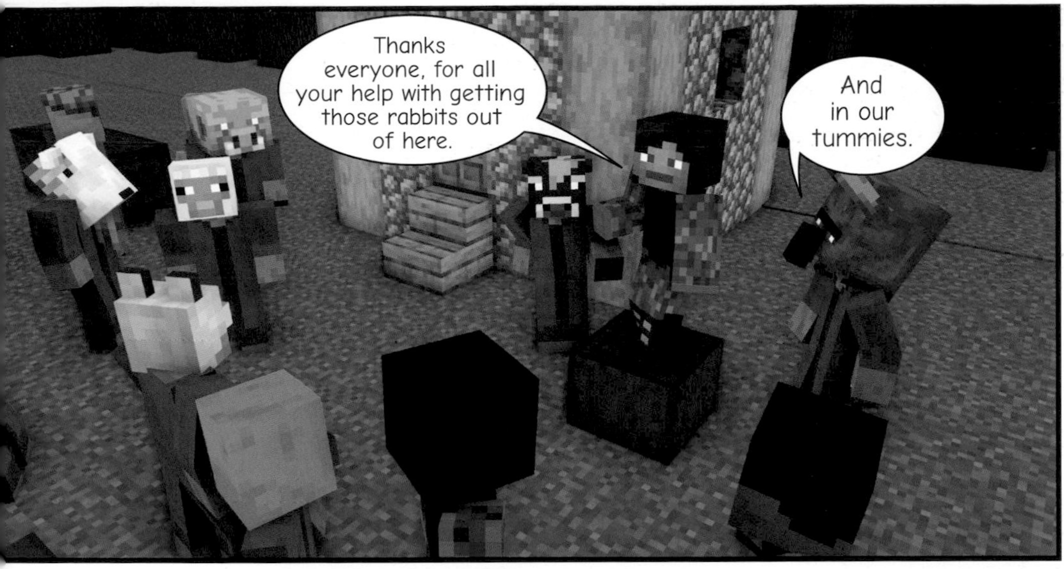
Thanks everyone, for all your help with getting those rabbits out of here.
And in our tummies.

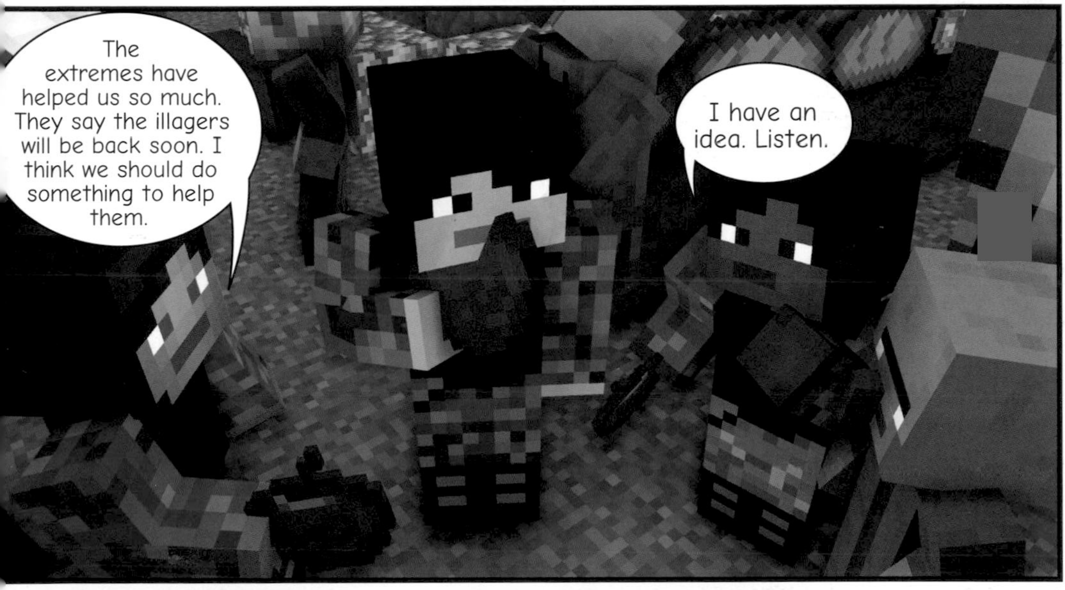
The extremes have helped us so much. They say the illagers will be back soon. I think we should do something to help them.
I have an idea. Listen.

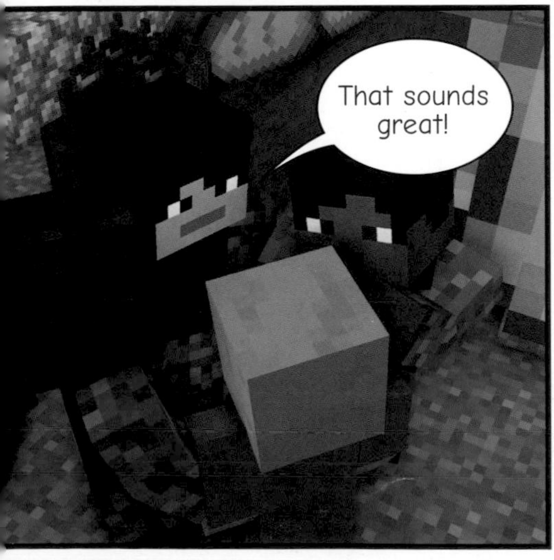
That sounds great!

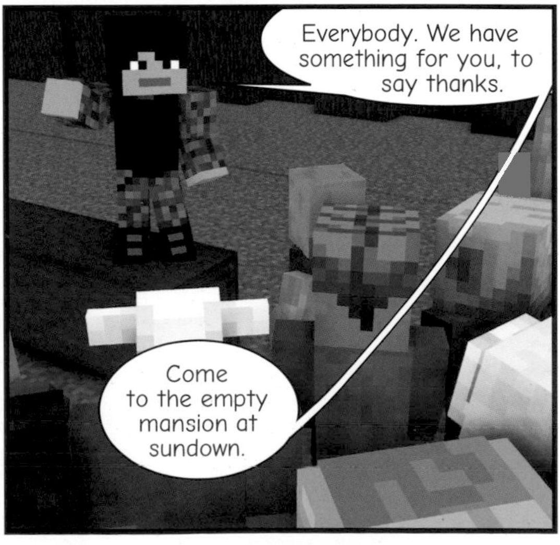
Everybody. We have something for you, to say thanks.
Come to the empty mansion at sundown.

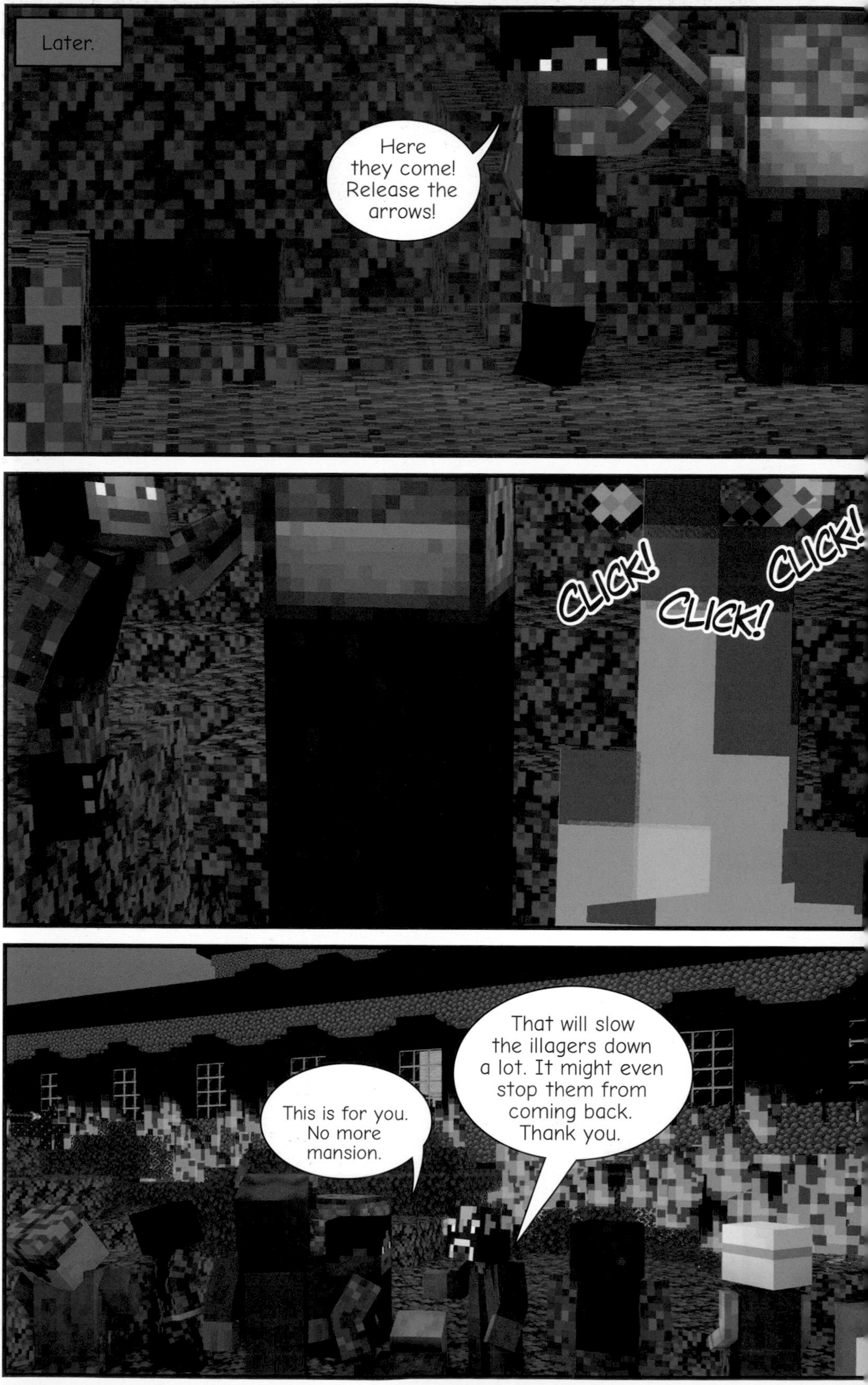
Later.
Here they come! Release the arrows!
CLICK!
CLICK!
CLICK!
This is for you. No more mansion.
That will slow the illagers down a lot. It might even stop them from coming back. Thank you.

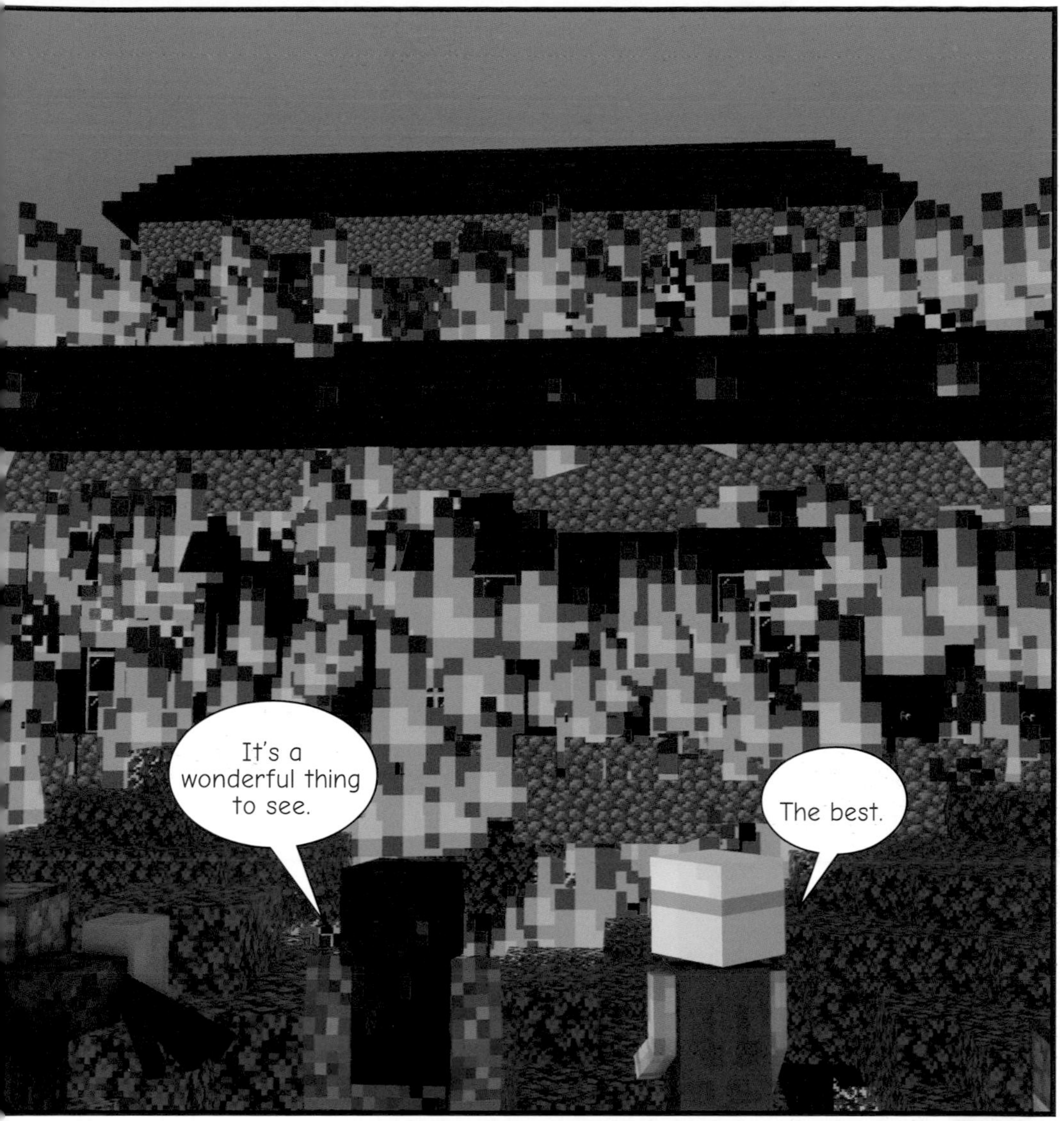
It's a wonderful thing to see.
The best.

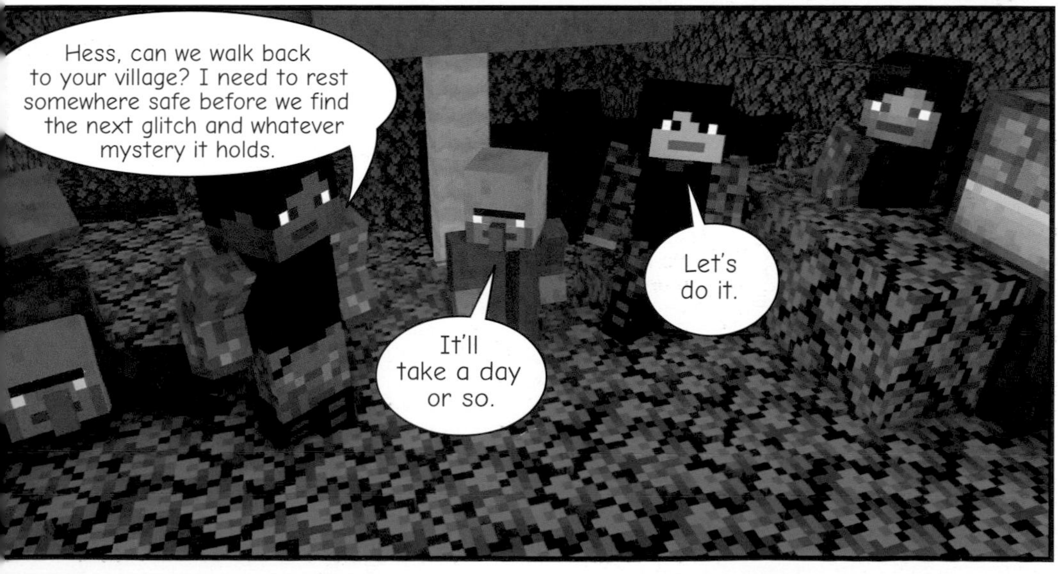
Hess, can we walk back to your village? I need to rest somewhere safe before we find the next glitch and whatever mystery it holds.
It'll take a day or so.
Let's do it.

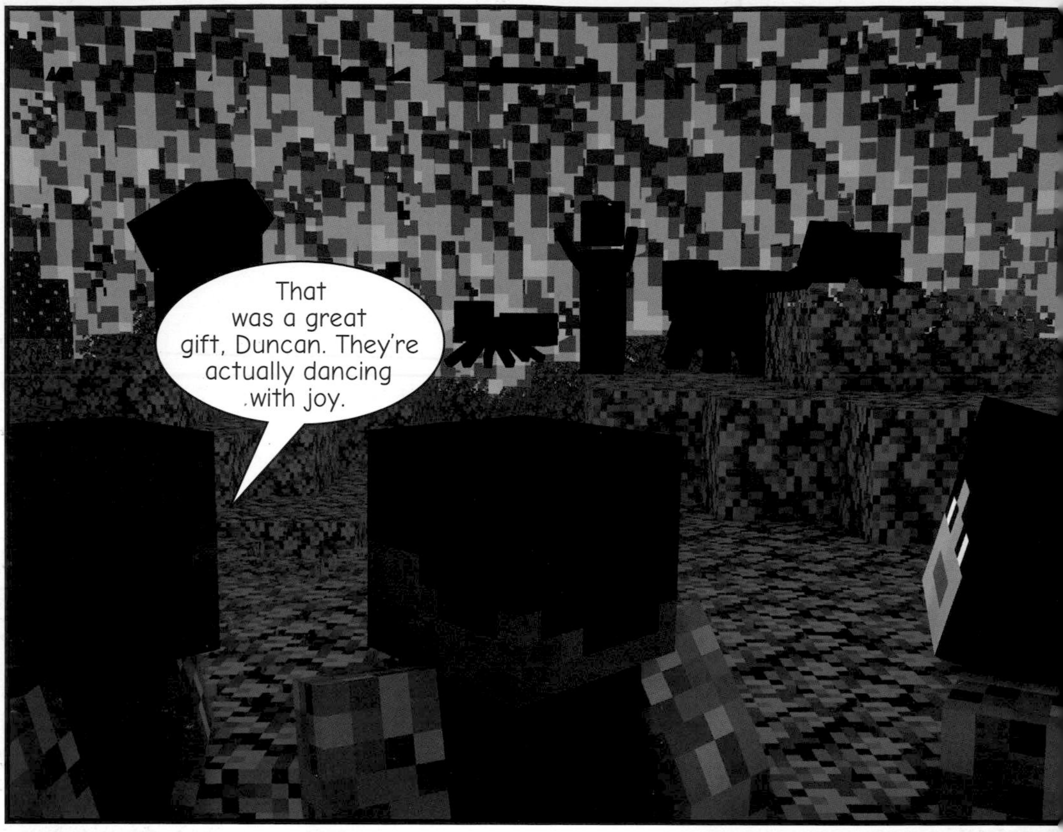
That was a great gift, Duncan. They're actually dancing with joy.

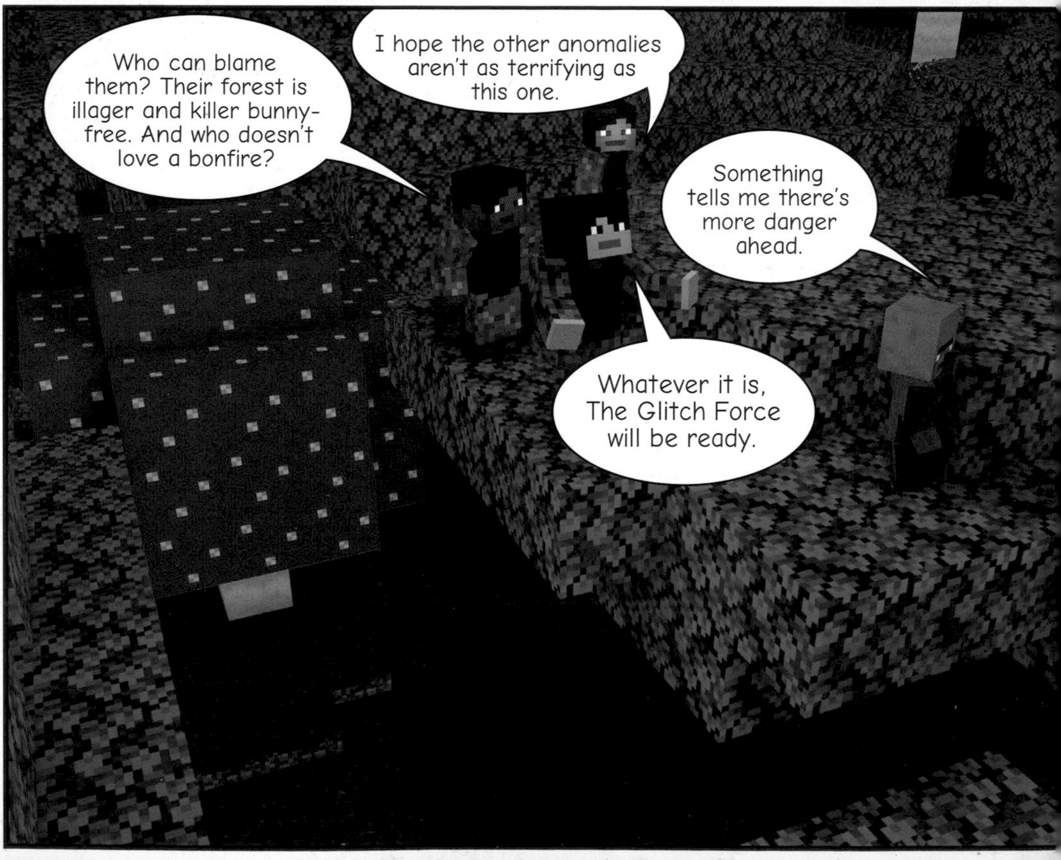
Who can blame them? Their forest is illager and killer bunny-free. And who doesn't love a bonfire?
I hope the other anomalies aren't as terrifying as this one.
Something tells me there's more danger ahead.
Whatever it is, The Glitch Force will be ready.